The Trespass

Scott Hunter was born in Romford, Essex in 1956. He was educated at the now sadly defunct Douai Abbey School in Woolhampton, Berkshire. His writing career was kick-started after he won first prize in the Sunday Express short story competition in 1996. He combines a career in IT with a parallel career as a semi-professional drummer. Where he fits in the writing is anyone's guess. Scott lives in Berkshire with his wife and two youngest children.

The Trespass

Scott Hunter

To Ian —

Best Regards

Scott Hunter

Myrtle Villa Publishing

The Trespass
A Myrtle Villa Book

Originally published in Great Britain by Myrtle Villa Publishing

All rights reserved
Copyright © Scott Hunter, Anno Domini 2009

This book is sold subject to the condition that it shall not, by way of trade or otherwise, be lent, resold, hired out, or otherwise circulated without the publisher's prior consent in any form of binding or cover other than that in which it is published and without a similar condition including this condition being imposed on the subsequent publisher

The moral right of Scott Hunter to be identified as author of this work has been asserted in accordance with Section 77 of the Copyright, Designs and Patents Act 1988

A CIP record for this book is available from the British Library

In this work of fiction, the characters, places and events are either the product of the author's imagination or they are used entirely fictitiously

ISBN 978-0-9561510-0-1

For Claire, Tom and Emily

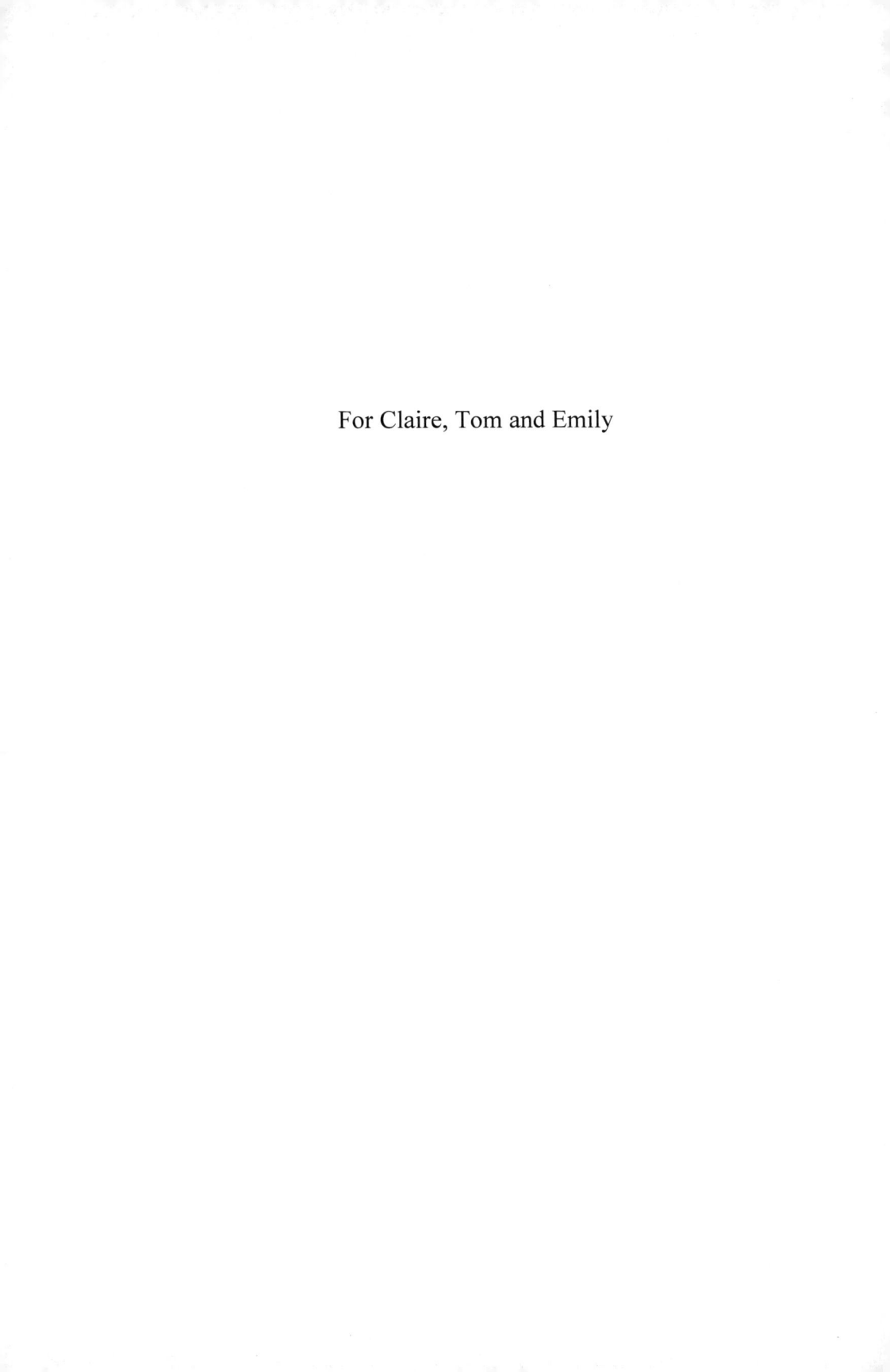

Acknowledgements

My grateful thanks to Hilary Johnson for her sound advice and encouragement. Thanks too to my wife, Katherine, for coping with the vacant stares and various absences of which I am surely guilty during the writing of this novel. Lastly, to my good friend Hugh Thresher, a clap on the back and a pint at The Bell for a swift turnaround of early drafts and encouragement beyond the call of duty.

Original cover photograph:

Krzysztof Dudek

Front cover design:

Jeremy Robinson
www.jeremyrobinsononline.com

'There is a way that seems right to a man, but in the end it leads to death'

King Solomon

Prologue

Smithsonian Institution expedition, March 1920
Location: classified

He placed his hands gently upon the stone, probing and pressing. It would open, given the correct sequence. And he knew the sequence; he'd worked it out. The question was, should he use this knowledge?

"Come on, Theo. Quit stalling."

He felt a prod in his lower back. Theodore swallowed hard. He had no choice. That had always been the case. No choice. *Let posterity remember that, if nothing else.* He turned his attention to the task, fingers moving over the smooth surface. And then a rolling of tumblers, the wall folding away. He heard the American's gasp of surprise and a collective intake of breath from those following. Theodore mopped his brow and squinted into the opening. He'd been expecting wonders, but nothing could have prepared him for this.

Before them was a chamber, empty except for a raised platform upon which rested a large sarcophagus, an object of such beauty he could only stare in awe.

"I said move it, Theo. What are you waiting for?"

Theodore advanced reluctantly, his heartbeat a pounding ostinato against his ribs. Torchlight flickered as they jostled him forward. *No choice. I have no choice.* He stumbled and put a hand out to save himself, grasping the corner of the dais. It was cold to his touch and he pulled his hand away with a gasp. It made him feel – *unholy.*

"Okay, let's get it open."

He was pushed roughly aside, and stepped back in trepidation. *This is wrong. This is not for us to see...*

But the others were heaving at the heavy lid, crowbars grappling for purchase. Slowly it lifted, then fell to the floor with a crash that shook the chamber from top to bottom. Theodore covered his ears and muttered a prayer. *Forgive them. They don't know what they're doing...*

An abrupt silence descended. Heads craned, peering into the sarcophagus. Theodore found himself drawn by a terrible fascination. For a moment he saw nothing, a swirl of colour, then his eyes were brought sharply into focus and he fell back with a cry of astonishment, covering his face in anguish. *It's true. I was right...* With this thought came a renewed conviction. *I can't let them do this – they do not understand...* He felt the weight of the revolver in his pocket, then he was pointing it, the muzzle wavering in his sweat-slicked grip. He heard himself call a warning. A hand reached from behind and grabbed his wrist. The gun exploded towards the chamber roof sending a splinter of rock skittering. He lashed out with a kick but a grip of steel encircled him, pinning his arms. He felt the needle slide into his flesh and he was falling, spinning in slow motion towards the floor. There was no pain but he heard a distant groan; with a shock he realized it was his voice. *I must stop them...* He tried to crawl but bizarre shapes zipped and twirled across his peripheral vision, diving and swooping at him like gulls. He covered his eyes with one hand and groped forward like a blind man in a storm. He felt a boot crunch against his ribs and heard sibilant, chattering laughter. He ignored it all. With his remaining strength he reached out towards the sarcophagus, felt its cool surface under his fingertips and was comforted. As darkness descended he thought he saw angels surrounding the dais, enfolding it with their powerful, protective wings.

Ark

Chapter 1

Simon Dracup's head ached as he walked briskly along the hotel corridor. Surely it couldn't be true? Perhaps his grandfather had invented the whole thing. But why do that? It *had* to be genuine. He tutted with irritation. No point in speculating now – he needed to study the diary in depth before he jumped to any conclusions. The phone was ringing as he swiped the key card over the lock and pushed impatiently into his room. He threw his overcoat onto the bed and made a grab for the beeping instrument.

"Dracup."

A woman's voice said, "Where have you *been?*"

Dracup felt his hackles rising. His ex-wife's directness still rankled. "Give me a moment." He thumbed the phone onto speaker and shrugged off his jacket. The diary was still in his inside pocket. He fished it out and placed it carefully on the bedside cabinet. Unremarkable in appearance, but the contents, if factual, were no less than mind-blowing...

"Are you there?" Yvonne's voice barked through the speaker. "Are you coming on Saturday? What do I tell Natasha?"

"If you'd let me –"

"She has to have continuity. She's only eight years old and it's been difficult enough with –"

"Now listen," he heard himself shouting; Yvonne never failed to light his touchpaper. "I *will* be there at 9 a.m. That's nine in the morning. I will return her at 4 p.m, afternoon, GMT, Okay?"

"There's no need to shout, Simon. I can hear you perfectly well." Yvonne's voice spoke evenly across the miles.

"Tell Natasha I love her. I'll be there." He felt his eyes prickle and bit his lip angrily. "How is she?"

"She's fine. She gets on so well with Malcolm. They're real buddies."

"That's great." He gritted his teeth. "I'm her buddy too. And I'm also her daddy."

"Yes, well. You should have thought of that before –"

There was a soft but clear knock on the door. Dracup swore under his breath. "Just a minute; there's someone at the door."

"Oh, yes?"

The ambiguity in her tone was not lost on him. "For heaven's sake, Yvonne –"

"I'll see you at nine on Saturday then." The line went dead.

The soft tap came again.

"*Yes*. All right. Just a second." Dracup strode to the door and yanked it open. A tall man in a dark suit stood on the threshold. His face was sallow, saddened by drooping eyelids and matching downturn of mouth. In the eyes, however, Dracup discerned a keen intelligence.

"Mr – *Professor* - Dracup?"

"Who wants to know?" Dracup asked, more aggressively than he'd intended.

The visitor smiled thinly. "I hope I'm not interrupting anything? I left my card with reception – James Potzner."

Dracup fished the card out of his trouser pocket. It read:

James Potzner
US Embassy,
Grosvenor Square,
London

"Well. What do you want?" Even as he phrased the question he knew the answer. It was in the buff envelope on the bedside table: the diary.

"If I may –" Potzner took a step forward.

Dracup hesitated. Hold on, he told himself, it might not be anything to do with the diary. Then why this sense of foreboding? Well, if he was right Potzner could at least answer his questions – and he had plenty of those. He stood aside to let the visitor in. "Of course. Be my guest."

Potzner entered the room and walked to the large picture window. The lights of Aberdeen winked in the failing light. "You know, you have a great view here." He admired the scene for a moment, then bent over and flicked a button on the bedside console. The electric blinds folded the view away. "Can't be too careful." Potzner offered a smile and lowered himself smoothly onto the two-seater settee.

Dracup frowned. The diary had been a strange enough addition to his day. And now this stranger settling into his room like an old school friend...

"You don't have something to –?" Potzner made the shape of a glass with his hand.

"Of course. Forgive me. What can I get you?" Dracup fumbled with the cabinet doors under the TV until he found the minibar. "There's coke, white wine, gin." He peered at a label. "Scotch –"

"That's the one."

Dracup poured himself a gin and tonic and sat on the edge of the bed. "So what can I do for you, Mr Potzner?"

"I'll give it to you straight, Mr Dracup. You have something we need." Potzner took a pull at his Scotch.

Dracup's heart skipped. "Need? That's a strong word."

"It's appropriate, Mr Dracup."

"Well, go on, I'm listening."

"You've come to Scotland to hear your aunt's will. The solicitor gave you a diary this afternoon. It belonged to your grandfather, Theodore. Your aunt kept it a secret for many years. She had it placed under lock and key. Until her death." Potzner produced a gold cigarette case and offered it to Dracup.

"No thanks."

"Do you mind?"

"Carry on."

Potzner thumbed his Zippo and inhaled deeply.

Dracup watched him suspiciously. "How do you know what I may or may not be doing in Scotland?"

Potzner sat forward. "Professor; it's my business to *know* things." The American went on. "Your name is Simon Andrew

Dracup. You are forty-five years old. You were brought up in India, but relocated to Berkshire when your father was offered a consultant post at the Royal Berkshire Hospital. You wanted to follow him into medicine but your father dissuaded you. Your first girlfriend was Susan, your best friend's sister. The relationship didn't last because when you visited you didn't know if you were there to see your friend or Susan and neither did they. Boy, that was a bummer. She really loved you.

You got straight As at A level and went to Bristol University to escape home, even though Reading offered a better course in Anthropology. You married Yvonne when you were twenty-eight, although you weren't sure and your friends even less so. Your daughter Natasha was born eight years ago after your wife – sorry, ex-wife – had undergone a prolonged course of fertility treatment. Politically you swing to the left but enjoy a lifestyle that is definitely headed over to the right. Your students respect you and you're known as a reliable guy. Professionally, you're a hot potato. Your special interest is physical anthropology and you've made many field trips to many different countries. Your marriage ended because of the strain produced by successive failures of IVF, but your subsequent and unexpected love affair with one Sara Benham, a student at the University, has kept you on an even keel. You're trying to make a go of it, but your ex and her new man are giving you a hard time. And the other side of the coin is tough too because, irrationally for a man of logic, you blame Sara for taking you away from Natasha, so you're not sure how –"

Dracup had his hand up. "All right. All right." Shaken, he took a long swig from his tumbler. Whoever Potzner was, he had all the facts straight. Detailed facts.

Potzner read his expression. "It's my job, Mr Dracup. Nothing personal."

"Nothing personal? That's my *life*."

Potzner crossed one long leg over the other and flicked ash into the wastepaper bin. "It all goes in the shredder after you give me the diary. You have my word."

Dracup had his doubts but his curiosity was aroused. What else did Potzner know? Why was this so important? He went on the offensive. "So it's genuine?"

Potzner raised an eyebrow.

"What the diary records about Noah's Ark," Dracup continued, "or at least the remains of some ancient vessel – that it was discovered in Turkey in 1920."

"Yeah," the American nodded thoughtfully, "the traditional Biblical location."

Dracup shrugged. "Mount Ararat? Look, I've seen all sorts on the web about possible sites – blurred photos that show boat-shaped anomalies, stories about expeditions that never got off the ground – but my grandfather..." The idea was still preposterous, however he approached it. He frowned. "Theodore was actually *there?*"

Potzner got up and walked to the window. He moved the blind aside for a few seconds, then turned and faced Dracup. "Yeah. He was there."

Dracup levelled his gaze directly at Potzner. "And how did you keep a discovery of this magnitude under lock and key?"

For a split second, Potzner looked uncomfortable. "Before my time, Professor. The Department took care of the details."

"I see." Dracup sipped his drink. A cover-up, then. A big one.

"But the fact is, Professor, your grandfather was part of another expedition – *after* the one that found the Ark. You might say it was inaugurated as a consequence of the success of the first."

Dracup nodded. "Go on."

"I'll tell you as much as I can, Mr Dracup, but in the interest of security – and your own safety –"

"Oh, please, cut the crap."

"Now you're sounding more stateside than I do." Potzner smiled briefly. "Okay. I'll keep it simple. The Ark of Noah contained a number of –" Potzner searched for the right word, "– interesting finds. One in particular created a big stir. It pointed to another location where cargo from the Ark was apparently taken after it grounded. So, the second expedition followed this up six months later and returned with…" Potzner scratched his blue chin with a long forefinger, "… something priceless; something we have kept securely since it was first brought back to the US."

"And my grandfather was part of all this?"

"Oh yeah. Up to his eyeballs. He was a key member of both expos. It was his expertise – and his colleague's – that revealed the second location. He was not only a first-rate geologist but also a gifted historian. Seems that brains run in the family, right Professor? Anyhow, his colleague, guy by the name of Reeves-Churchill, was the archaeologist on both expeditions. We have no record of what happened to him. But as you know, although your grandfather made it back in one piece from both expos he didn't keep too well after his return to the UK."

"That's an understatement. He was committed in 1921, the year after this diary was completed." Dracup had picked up the diary from the bedside table, but quickly put it down again with a silent curse. Brilliant, Dracup. Now he *knows* you've got it.

If Potzner was excited at the sight of the diary, he didn't show it. He reclaimed his former position on the settee and nodded. "Right. It was tough. A brilliant mind wasted – but it wasn't all for nothing. Like I said, they found something extraordinary."

Something in the American's tone sent a cold wave down Dracup's neck. He cleared his throat. "The discovery of the Ark is extraordinary enough, but it might help my understanding if you told me exactly *what* they found in this… other location."

The American shook his head. "I'm not at liberty to say any more about that, Professor."

Dracup leaned back against the headboard and folded his arms. He appeared to have reached the inevitable brick wall. The one that read 'Classified'. "All right. So what do you want from me?"

Potzner hesitated and once again looked uneasy. The cigarette case appeared. "The item I'm referring to has been – mislaid."

"Mislaid?"

"Okay. Stolen."

Dracup exhaled slowly. So that was it; they needed Theodore's record. Some clue, perhaps, to help them find – what? He emptied the dregs of his tonic water into the heavy bathroom tumbler. Another thought occurred to him. "But you knew my aunt had the diary. So why didn't you ask her for it?"

"Our problem has only recently arisen, Professor, otherwise we would have done." Potzner drew on his Winston. "So your little acquisition has come at about the right time for us."

"*Little?* If this is genuine, the implications are – fascinating." That's putting it mildly, Dracup thought. He swigged back his tonic and looked at the American. "So how exactly will the diary help you?"

"I really can't tell you any more, Professor."

Dracup shook his head in exasperation. He wondered how far he could press the American. Potzner hadn't threatened him – yet. He caught Potzner's gaze and held it. "Perhaps I'll keep hold of it for the time being."

Potzner laughed softly. "Mr Dracup – I can't emphasize enough – your cooperation would be a real convenience for us."

"And if I refuse?"

"I'll tell you what." Potzner consigned the second stub expertly to the recesses of the waste bin. "I'll let you sleep on it, okay? Have a read through if you like; hell, I'd do the same myself under the circumstances." Potzner was on his feet and at the door. "I'll look you up in the morning. Perhaps you'll see things in a fresh light."

Dracup got up to see him out. "I'm not parting company with the diary until I know what this is all about."

Potzner shrugged. "Your decision."

Dracup watched him walk down the corridor; a tall man in his late fifties, with a slight limp. Before he entered the lift he called back: "Professor Dracup?"

"Yes?"

"Take care, won't you?" The lift doors opened and Potzner was gone.

Dracup sat quietly for ten minutes before kicking off his shoes and lying back on the king-size bed with a fresh drink. So it *was* true. It had to be if the CIA were after the diary. Dracup had no doubts concerning Potzner's 'Embassy' role. But more fascinating was their stolen item. He picked up his grandfather's diary and began to read. He studied the first entry:

21st Apr '20

First night in situ. Hardly believe we're on board, after all the anticipation. RC is elated. Estimates are that we're in the mid section – 3 fragments theory seems vindicated. The size of it is what thrills me! OT seems spot on re dimensions. It's vast – the decking is clearly visible and quite well preserved

Three fragments? Presumably referring to the condition of the Ark – the way it had broken up over the years. OT? Dracup frowned. Of course – Old Testament. Dracup shook his head in disbelief. Could this vessel really be the Ark of Noah? A dark stain obscured the next two lines. Dracup raised the book to his nose and took a sniff. Impossible to say what had caused it. He picked up at the next legible point in the entry:

RC is concerned re the location of the sarcophagus. Clear indications that it was on board during voyage – the sceptre may hold the answer. I have many reservations.

Sarcophagus? The tone of his grandfather's entry sent a chill down Dracup's spine. He shook his head in puzzlement. Potzner wanted something precious that had been on board Noah's Ark and then taken to another location…

Clear indications that it was on board during voyage

Dracup began to hum quietly. Something they had found on the Ark – some clue – had pointed Theodore to that other location.

the sceptre may hold the answer.

He flipped on a few pages.

27th Apr '20

Never been so cold. Descent halted for the day – driving snow. Tevfik's death has shaken us all. A has not spoken of it, but seems consumed with fear. RC nervous that he'll disappear and leave us. Constantly mutters under his breath. 'Bekci, Bekci' – apparently means 'The Keepers, the keepers'. Some local superstition about the Ark we think. Despite it all I feel frustration above everything else – could only bring one or two finds of interest – the larger finds have to stay of course – have taken some samples from drogues. RC has the curious iron piece – I must say the CF is extraordinary even though I'm no expert! No wonder RC so excited. I just pray we get down safely and can examine all at our leisure.

Tevfik. A Turkish name. Dracup clucked his tongue. That fitted with the Ark's location: Mount Ararat. He read on:

30th. Still in cave. Storm too severe to attempt any further descent. RC is out of his mind with fright. I must hold him together or we'll [here there was a smear across the page] ... eepers, the keepers'. It is unsettling to say the least; there must be a rational explanation. But am compelled to be honest – I saw it too. A was lifted away – not the wind; not a hidden crevasse ... [unclear lettering here].. as taken. Hope to God we are near the track way – not that we'll ever get our bearings in this weather. Food is nearly gone. Resorted to last tin of corned beef this morning. Wait! I hear it again. Something out on the mountainside. RC is muttering in his sleep – he probably hears it too. God preserve us and help us away from here. Tomorrow we must go and face whatever we must face. Whatever happens I shall cling to these treasures. There is much significance in them, I am convinced.

Dracup shivered. What had happened to them on the mountain? Could it be linked to the missing sarcophagus? Was that what Potzner was after? If so, who did the sarcophagus belong to? And why was it so important? Frustratingly the diary appeared to cover only the first expedition. There was no mention of the mysterious second location. He took a gulp of tonic water. At any rate, he knew what to do next. It was what he always told his students: when in doubt, examine available source material. Reluctantly Dracup fished in the bedside cabinet and found the inevitable Gideon's Bible. Clearly it had rarely, if ever, been opened. Dracup flicked the pages and found the book of Genesis. Did it mention burials or death on the Ark? What should he look for? Something valuable; a wide remit.

An hour later and none the wiser he placed the Bible next to the diary, leaned over and clicked a button on his console. The electric blinds hissed open and the lights of Aberdeen invaded the room. He was glad of their company.

Dracup snapped awake. His bedside light was off. Something was wrong. He tried to recall the geography of the room. Which way was he facing? He opened his eyes slowly. The room was filled with moonlight; he could pick out every detail. Somewhere in the bowels of the hotel, a door slammed. The moon went behind a cloud and the quality of light deteriorated. A subtle movement, a paler shadow in the darkness, drew his attention. There. By the opposite bedside table, a tall figure leaning in towards him. Dracup was a big man but he could be agile when the occasion demanded and something told him this was such an occasion. He rolled just as a soft *pop* preceded a thump on his pillow where a second before his head had rested. A pungent, burning smell filled his nostrils, but by this stage Dracup was on the floor and groping frantically for a weapon. His brain raced in panic. Come on, he told himself. Think. That's what you're good at...

His assailant was doing the obvious thing. All he had to do was walk round the foot of the bed and shoot him. Dracup had nowhere to go. They both knew it. And that made Dracup angry. Somewhere in the back of his mind he recognized this as a good thing; anger might give him an edge. He heaved the bedside cabinet in front of him before the next shot came. The round tore into the MDF of the cabinet and a splinter glanced off his forearm. He yelled out and reflexively pushed forward, rewarded by the sound of a soft curse as the cabinet connected with the man's shin. Dracup propelled himself forward in a clumsy rugby tackle, desperately aware of his lack of fitness. He caught the man around the waist but the assassin was strong; he wrenched himself free and aimed a kick at Dracup's head. The blow caught Dracup on the shoulder and threw him back into the corner. The figure lifted its arm again, lining up with Dracup's head. Dracup scrabbled around the floor for something solid. There was nothing. Wait. His hands closed around the cool plastic of the control console. It might do. He clicked the button. Please God let it be the right one...

The electric blinds began their automatic sashay, summoned into life by Dracup's frantic fingers. It was enough. The assassin spun in surprise and Dracup was on him with the full force of his six-foot frame. The impact carried them both to the opposite wall, onto the twisted wrought iron wardrobe handles. The assassin lifted his arm. Dracup remembered his games master's advice: *If you're in a fight and he's bigger than you, a knee in the groin will stand you in good stead*. Dracup brought his knee up between the man's legs. The shot went wide, cracking against the glass of the picture window. The blinds were almost closed. Dracup kicked out wildly, feeling his strength ebbing away. But it was a lucky kick, catching the intruder's arm just under the wrist and knocking it upwards. The bullet passed through the fleshy part of his assailant's chin and continued on its altered trajectory up into his brain. The assassin slipped to the floor, leaving a dark trail against the light wood of the wardrobe, and flopped forward grotesquely onto the carpet.

Dracup remained standing, legs slightly apart, panting like a dog. His arms shook, the tremors quickly spreading to the rest of his body like some fast-acting virus. He sat heavily on the bed. His shoulder throbbed and he felt stickiness on the tips of his enquiring fingers.

Not my blood...

There was an anxious knock at the door. Dracup froze.

Again. "Mr Dracup?"

"Yes?"

"It's the concierge. Is everything all right?"

"I'm fine. I had a dream, that's all." Dracup felt his heart beating wildly.

The footsteps receded. Dracup lay back and listened to his breathing. After a while he retrieved the console and turned on the main light. He looked at the body. A faint mist was rising from the pool forming by the head of the man he had killed. The enormity of the word hit him like a sledgehammer. He swallowed hard and bent down for a closer look.

First thing: it wasn't the American, Potzner. He hadn't expected it to be. But had Potzner sent him? This man was olive-skinned – Mediterranean? No, Middle-Eastern by the look of him. Dracup remembered Potzner's parting words: *Take care.*

Second thing: the diary. He made a quick search under the bed. He realized he was holding his breath just as he caught sight of the little book by the bed leg. He retrieved it and breathed again.

Third thing: the body. He reached for the phone, then checked himself. Would they believe him? His mind conjured an image of the police interview, his reaction as they produced false but compelling evidence fabricated by the CIA, heard his protests overruled by stony-faced Scotland Yard officers...

Dracup stumbled into the bathroom and was violently sick. He retched into the bowl until there was nothing left in his stomach. His legs would barely support him as he splashed cold water on his face and examined his forearm. An angry gash, but not too deep. Could have been a lot worse. He realized he was speaking aloud but his voice seemed distant, as if it belonged to somebody else.

He freshened his mouth with toothpaste and sat on the edge of the bed to consider his next move. Police or no police? He looked at the diary; a small thing, nestled in his shaking hands. He squatted down next to the corpse and made himself examine the pockets. He pulled something out. And froze. He was holding a photograph of Natasha in his hand. She was standing outside her school, lunchbox dangling at her side, backpack askew. Smiling.

Oh God. No.

The telephone shook in his hands. His fingers were jabbing Yvonne's number. He waited. Nothing. *Come on.* The ringtone went on and on. Then he remembered Yvonne's habit of turning down the ring volume at night. *Please. Please pick up.*

Five minutes later he slammed the phone into its cradle. He glanced at the digital clock: 02:25. Dracup took a deep breath and got hold of the corpse's shoulders. The body was heavy. It took him five minutes of heaving and sweating to get it into the bathroom. He closed the door, fished another miniature of Johnnie Walker from the minibar and downed it in one. No police; no time. A handful of tissues took care of the bloodstained furniture. He stuffed his belongings into a suitcase and looked into the corridor. There was no one about. He closed the door behind him and headed for the fire escape.

Chapter 2

The receptionist looked up and smiled coquettishly. "Why, hello again Mr Potzner."

Potzner returned her smile. Hell, she was pretty enough. "Morning. Mr Dracup about?"

Her brow furrowed. "The Professor? Just a moment. I think –" she tapped away at the keyboard. "No, sorry." She looked up and smiled brightly but Potzner's face was a mask. "He checked out, I'm afraid."

"When?"

"Let's see." More tapping. Potzner joined in with his fingers on the counter.

"Sorry to keep you waiting," the receptionist said. "Computer's slow this morning."

Potzner grunted. He'd obviously misread Dracup. Unusual for him.

"He left early, I think," she said. "I can't quite make out – ah – sorry, the records just say 'paid in full' and 'no bar bills outstanding'. I can't tell you any more."

"Okay. Thanks."

"Wait." Her fingernails clicked and stabbed the 'Enter' key conclusively. "'No newspaper collected'. That's it." She shrugged.

"Right." Potzner made his way across the foyer, which was beginning to fill up with senior citizens. When he judged the receptionist's attention fully diverted he slipped up the staircase to the second floor. Pausing outside room 124 he produced a plain card, which he swiped through the entry scanner. The lock clicked. He went in.

The bed was made and the curtains drawn. Everything seemed in order. Room maids had been in already. Bit early though. Then he remembered passing the maid's trolley in the corridor. They hadn't got this far yet. *Someone else has cleaned up.* He turned and something caught his eye. High on the window; something not right. He moved in for a closer look. A small crack radiated outwards from a minute hole at the top left hand corner of the window. Potzner zeroed in with a practised analysis. PB 69P. 9x18mm. Upgraded twelve-round magazine – probably. Silenced; for sure. Mind you – he looked out to the car park where a coach was receiving the exodus from the foyer – that may not have been essential given the average age of the clientele here. He shook his head wearily. *We're all headed that way. Even you, Potzner.* He tried to imagine a pensionable version of himself: cantankerous, hard of hearing, insomniac – Potzner left the room and bounded down the stairs. Surely one of them…

"Excuse me, ma'am," he hit the car park at a brisk trot, drawing alarmed looks from the queue. The old lady stared at him suspiciously. "Yes? Can I help?"

"Ah, yes ma'am. Maybe you can." Potzner cleared his throat. "Did you perhaps hear anything unusual during the night?"

She looked at him indignantly. "Not at all. I slept like a baby. Always do. Now if you'll excuse me." She presented her back.

"Pardon me?" Potzner felt a tap on his shoulder. He turned to see a smartly dressed pensioner wearing a floral dress and matching hat. Her eyes twinkled like pearls in a sea-worn oyster. "I couldn't help overhearing your conversation with that lady." She frowned, knitting her brow with deeper wrinkles. "Very abrupt, don't you think? I sat next to her on the coach all the way from Cardiff. Hardly got a word out of her. This time –" she stretched up to whisper in Potzner's ear but, realizing the impossible logistics of scaling such heights, contented herself with a covert hand over one side of her mouth. "This time I'll be down the other end – you watch me!"

Potzner didn't doubt it. "And did you hear anything unusual at all last night, ma'am? Any noise?"

"Well, as a matter of fact I did. I don't sleep as well as I used to, not at all. There was a lot of thumping and banging. Then I'm sure I heard glass breaking. And then – the strangest thing in the middle of the night – somebody came out of the fire escape and down the back stairs. My room overlooks the stairway, you see. I saw him go into the car park and then he was off. Just like that."

"You say *him*, ma'am – can you be sure it was a man?"

"Oh yes. It was the gentleman I met in the car park yesterday – we'd just arrived, you see. A good looking fellow."

"Dark curly hair, beard."

"That's right!" She glanced around to make sure nobody was eavesdropping. "Has he done something wrong?"

Potzner shook his head. "I don't think so, ma'am. Can you say what time this would have been?"

"It was 2.45 a.m. precisely." The eyes twinkled again. "I had just finished the Times crossword."

Potzner raised an eyebrow. He couldn't do crosswords for Hershey bars. The coach driver had started the engine and only one or two couples remained to board. "You'd better make sure you get a good seat." He inclined his head towards the coach.

She smiled. "I hope I've helped."

Potzner watched her go and felt a wry smile creep across his face. *Boy, I hope my marbles are in the same place as hers when I get to that age.* He rummaged in his pocket for his car keys. Dracup was probably miles away by now so he didn't have any time to lose.

Dracup glanced in his mirror. Every car was a potential tail. He dialled Yvonne's number at ten minute intervals. He phoned the neighbour's house; Mr and Mrs Foster. They were old. And deaf. No one picked up. He slammed his mobile against the steering wheel. Who else? Come on, Dracup. Think. *Charles.* He rang his friend's landline. No response. He called the mobile. Voicemail. Dracup screamed in frustration and drove wildly on.

Heavy rain welcomed him to the Midlands, and by the time he had eased the car onto the M40 it was a driving torrent. He leaned forward and tried to focus through the relentless sheets of spray. Brake lights blinked sporadically in the blackness. He felt himself slide occasionally into a half slumber, shocking himself awake as the car drifted onto the hard shoulder, once even into the other lane. His mind flitted from one thing to the next in rapid, uncontrolled succession. Natasha. Sara, dark hair and deep brown eyes. Potzner: *I'll let you sleep on it, okay?* A dead man. The solicitor's office. *The diary.*

Dracup brought himself back to the M40 with a jerk. What was the time? Nearly eight thirty. *Come on Yvonne. Please.* He thumbed the speed dial again then nearly veered off the road as Yvonne's voice responded after two rings. "Hello?"

"Yvonne. It's Simon."

"Simon. It's a bit early – I've only just –"

"Just listen. Is Natasha all right?"

"What do you mean, is she all right? Why shouldn't she be?"

"Is she all right?"

"She's fine. Well, she was when I last saw her."

Dracup's heart missed a beat. "What do you mean? Where is she?"

"She's at a sleepover. With Maisie. She told you about it last week."

"Right. Call Maisie's mother. Now."

"Simon. You're scaring me. What's going on?"

"Just do it." Dracup saw a police car in his rear view mirror. He checked his speed: ninety-five. Not good. He squeezed the footbrake and held his breath. The police car cruised past in the middle lane.

"Jane's dropping both girls at school this morning. They've probably left by now."

Dracup kept his voice even with an effort. "Call me as soon as you've spoken to her. Without fail. Then get over to the school and bring Natasha home."

"Simon – what –?"

"Just do it, Yvonne. Please." He put the phone on the passenger seat and concentrated on the motorway. He had just entered the Oxford ring road system when his mobile rang. He swallowed hard. Yvonne's voice came over the speaker, the words he had dreaded to hear. Her voice was quiet, almost matter of fact.

Dracup could hear the effects of shock in the evenly spaced syllables. "She's not there Simon. She's not at school."

"Are you sure?" A silly thing to say, he thought. Of course she's sure...

Yvonne spoke again, the words now a series of blurted sobs. "Jane saw them into the playground. Maisie was there for assembly. Natasha wasn't. She's missing."

The young woman pushed a lock of damp hair from her forehead. The sea spray made it thick and unmanageable, coating every fibre with a sticky layer of salt. She looked ahead and saw the bleak shape of the coast through a fine mist of rain. The wind blew the moisture into her face with a sensation like tiny, stinging tendrils. She gave a cluck of exasperation and backtracked across the deck to the cabin. The little one, Natasha, was sitting, half asleep, on the most comfortable seat. The child looked drawn and pale, but she was safe. And that's how Ruth intended to keep her. She would look after her as her own and not even Kadesh would be able to interfere. Not if she had any say in the matter. Although she considered the abduction a harsh judgement, she understood Kadesh's motives and trusted his decisions; they all did. So far he had not let them down. He was sitting next to the pilot, talking in a low voice and glancing occasionally in her direction to check that nothing had altered, that she was in her proper place. How strong he looked. How self-assured, even though he must be hurting inside. She smiled at him, lifted her chin a fraction to acknowledge his attention. How could he think she would leave him? Where would she go, if not with him?

The girl moaned and Ruth bent to stroke her hair. A pretty little thing. Her child would be like that, dark and pretty. The boat bobbed and heaved in the tide swell of approaching land but the girl did not stir again. Now she was fast asleep. They slipped past the harbour and dropped anchor. Ruth waded to the shore, relishing the sensation of sand beneath the bare soles of her feet. The cove was quiet and unspoiled. It reminded her of home and made her long for the heat and the dust and the coolness of the deep, empty spaces. Not long now, not long.

Chapter 3

The door opened as he reached for the bell. Yvonne's tear-smeared face destroyed all remaining hope. A bespectacled man hovered at her shoulder: Malcolm. "What's happened?" Dracup demanded. "Have they found her?"

"Where on earth have you been?" Yvonne blurted. "You'd better explain what's going on."

Dracup was shocked at Yvonne's appearance. He reached for her but the gesture was met by folded arms, a thin, tight mouth.

"Come in, old chap. That's the way." Malcolm extended a white forearm and pointed to the lounge. He pushed his spectacles back to their correct position on the bridge of his long nose and stood awkwardly aside.

"I know my way around. Thanks." Something about Malcolm brought out the worst in Dracup. But he supposed that he would feel the same about anyone stepping into his shoes, living with his wife. *Ex* wife, he reminded himself.

Malcolm responded with forced levity. "Right. Of course. Sorry."

Yvonne's face was pinched with anxiety. "Malcolm. Get some coffee, please."

"Will do."

Dracup stood by the fireplace. He realized this was the first time he had returned to the house since their divorce. The room had been rearranged; a new regime was in place.

Yvonne glared at him. "Well? How did you know she was in danger? If this is anything to do with you, I –" Her fists were clenched.

The suspicion and hostility took him aback. "With *me?* How can –"

Malcolm reappeared. "Milk and sugar?" He waited protectively behind Yvonne, resting a steadying hand on her shoulder.

"Yes. Two – please."

Yvonne blew her nose. "I'm – I'm sorry. Give me a moment."

"Take your time," Dracup said. He softened his voice, hoping to calm her.

The phone rang and Malcolm rushed to pick it up. Yvonne was on her feet. Dracup's heart thudded sickly in his chest. Malcolm nodded then covered the receiver with his hand. "Sorry – work call."

Yvonne slumped back into her chair.

Dracup said, "Go on."

"Nobody saw her after the whistle went for assembly. She was in the playground, then – she just disappeared. I thought you had planned it – I – oh, I don't know what I thought." Yvonne fixed him with an accusing stare. Her eyes were bloodshot, the pupils dilated.

"I would never do anything like that. Give me some credit."

Yvonne looked into her lap where her hands were twisting something around and around: Natasha's hair band. "I know. I'm sorry."

"What about the police?"

"They were here an hour ago."

He knew that. He had waited until the squad cars had departed. "And?"

"They were *hopeless*."

From the next room came the sound of muted conversation as Malcolm dispensed advice to his work colleague. Dracup's mind was in overdrive. Was this Potzner's doing? Why would the CIA organize a kidnap? If indeed Potzner *was* CIA. Was it all linked to the diary?

Yvonne studied his face. "You look awful. What happened in Scotland?" She got out of the chair and came towards him.

He raised both hands defensively. "I don't know. I've had a strange twenty-four hours. It may be connected – I just don't know."

"Well, what are you going to *do?* Do *something. Anything –"* Yvonne was shouting now, pacing the living room. Malcolm reappeared with coffee and an apologetic shrug. He caught and held onto her.

Dracup didn't know where to look. But he knew what he had to do. He was on his feet. "I have to go. If you hear anything, call me."

He needed support. Advice. He needed Sara.

He left.

"Simon – it'll be all right."

He looked into her eyes, searching for truth, wanting to believe her. Would it? How? Sara had no children. She couldn't know how this *felt*.

Sara squeezed his hand. "Look, Simon. She will be found. You have to hold onto that."

The tone of her voice held a conviction that seemed more than a knee-jerk response to grief. But then Sara was a natural optimist and that was the kind of support he needed right now. Dracup cupped her chin. "Yes. I'll try. Thanks."

She reached out and smoothed the frown on his forehead. "I'll help. I'll do everything I can. We'll look at the diary together and we'll find her. But Simon –"

"What?"

Sara looked at him with sympathy. "It may be completely unrelated. You just don't know –"

Dracup was shaking his head. "I *do* know. I found Natasha's photo in the guy's pocket. That makes it related. I mean, for God's sake –" he trailed off abruptly and let his arm drop. "Sorry. I know you don't like me saying that."

Sara laid her cool hand on his cheek. "It's okay. You're stressed. I understand."

The phone rang. Dracup started, then remembered that Yvonne couldn't know the number; the house belonged to one of Sara's University friends.

Sara squeezed his arm. "I'll get it."

He listened to her chatting to her friend. Cats, rent, banality. Outside, the rain teemed relentlessly. Dracup pressed his face up against the window and bunched his hands into fists; he had never felt so helpless.

Sara's hand was on his shoulder. "Come and sit down."

He took a deep breath. He had to concentrate, not panic like one of his students in a first year exam.

"Coffee?"

"Black, please. Thanks."

Sara retreated to the kitchen. He pulled the diary from his jacket pocket and opened it at the first page, trying to push away thoughts of Natasha and what might be happening to her. He made himself focus on Theodore's painstaking lettering. *Find out what it means, Dracup, and you'll find her. Those sketches at the back...*

"That's it?" Sara placed the coffee on the table.

Dracup leaned back on the settee. "Yes."

"It looks very fragile. May I?"

Dracup felt very fragile too. "Go ahead. I'll just use the bathroom if that's okay."

Sara smiled. "Sure."

Dracup presented his face to the bathroom mirror. Lack of sleep had infused his eyes with red streaks and his cheeks had a grey, corpse-like pallor. He found some toothpaste to freshen his mouth, then briefly washed and towelled his face before rejoining Sara in the lounge. He watched as her brow knitted in concentration. She was wearing a white blouse, loosely tied at the waist and exposing an area of brown stomach around the umbilicus, as was the fashion these days. She crossed one long leg over the other and turned the fragile page to a new entry. After several minutes she looked up.

"This diagram – the markings. Aren't they –?"

"Cuneiform. Yes, I'm ninety-nine per cent sure." That much he knew. He also knew an expert would be required to decipher them.

Sara was watching him carefully. "I'll get some more coffee. Rest your eyes for a few minutes. You'll feel better."

"Yes, all right. I'll try." He closed his eyes; as exhaustion overwhelmed him he remembered the first time he had seen that expression, the look that had intrigued and drawn him to Sara at that first lecture. He could picture the scene clearly. He had been outlining the basic concepts of Physical Anthropology…

"…integration of four fundamental concepts is necessary to an appreciation of the nature and importance of physical anthropology: firstly the chemistry of life; secondly evolution as process; thirdly, the interdependence of participants in a global ecosystem; and fourthly, the role of culture in human adaptation…"

And there was Sara. Front row of the theatre, hanging on his every word as he summarized…

"…and so our past and future are necessarily shaped by forces that operate on a scale and time frame outside of our limited human experience. But in spite of this, we are beginning to understand our world and the physical universe beyond it through the window of science…"

And her hand was raised. So pretty.

"Yes – the lady in the front row?"

"Does that mean that anthropologists reject religion on the grounds that superstition is unscientific?"

"Good question. But rejection is too strong a word. Religion has its place, but not as part of a scientific discipline. Let me give you an example. All of us do things every day that fall into the category of superstition. For instance, one could choose – desire – to influence a future event by an appeal to a deity or to some vague concept of an external force – in other words, fall back on religion. Now, the cynic might define superstition as a correlation that is spurious or demonstrably false, but on a cold morning even

the scientifically minded have been known to invoke magic and superstition as they attempt to start their cars."

A ripple of amusement ran through the theatre. Sara's voice again; confident, probing:

"But you said we are shaped by forces that operate on a scale and time frame outside of our limited human experience. If our experience is as limited as you suggest, it would be wrong to sideline religion as unscientific unless it can be scientifically proven to be false."

"I take it you are referring to the concept of the existence of a real deity?"

She had shrugged, a graceful, dismissive movement.

"If deity exists, then by its very nature it would be the ultimate scientist."

After the lecture, they had met for coffee. After a week they had met for lunch...

"Hey."
Dracup jerked awake. Reality hit him like a blow to the head.
"Are you okay?" Sara's face gave away her concern.
"I'm coping." He wasn't. He felt awful. His head was pounding with lack of sleep and excess caffeine. He forced himself to his feet and looked out the window. Evening was drawing in. He should phone Yvonne. As he took out his mobile another thought occurred to him. "Does the TV work?"
"I think so." Sara looked puzzled.
"The news."
"But it won't do you any good to see –"
"I need to know."

Sara switched on the TV. Adverts, then the six o'clock headlines. Dracup watched, waiting for the inevitable. He wondered how he'd react as they summarized the killing. A picture of Natasha appeared on the widescreen. It hit him like a physical blow. Sara's hand was on his arm. A man appeared, a policeman; the caption said: 'DCI Brendan Moran.' He was making the usual statement, the one the police used when there was nothing to report. Dracup heard only a few words: 'Doing all we can', 'every hope of a successful outcome.'

The newscaster handed over to the sports correspondent. Dracup took a deep breath. He hadn't been ready for that, but obviously a child kidnap would be newsworthy – although a murder in Scotland evidently wasn't. Surely the body must have been discovered – unless – unless someone had removed it. He turned to Sara but something about her expression made him hesitate. Surely she believed his story?

"Wait – did you hear something?" Sara held a finger to her lips. "Hey!" She let out an exclamation as the cat sidled into the room and wound itself between her ankles. "Shoo, madam." She pushed the cat away with her leg. "She made me jump. Could you pop her outside, Simon? She'll just be a pain if we let her stay."

"Sure." As he scooped the animal up and made for the back door he wondered if Potzner himself had tidied the hotel room or if he'd delegated the responsibility to some minion. Glancing out of the kitchen window he saw that the sky had cleared and a full moon illuminated the garden. Holding the cat precariously in his left hand he twisted the key and nudged the handle down. As if sensing its fate the cat turned in his arms and made a bid for freedom. He made a successful grab for it, turned and stepped out onto the patio. A man stood in front of him, a dark balaclava obscuring his face. The eyeholes reflected pinpricks of light from the kitchen interior and a duller gleam from something held firmly in his gloved hand. The hand lifted and pointed at Dracup's head.

James Potzner was a thorough man. Not that he prided himself on it; it was in his nature. He had always been the last kid out of school because, he reasoned, if his desk was clear and tidy at the last bell it meant that he had more time in the morning to do what *he* wanted. The other kids got the fallout from the teachers and he got on with the business of – well, whatever business he had to get through that semester. Maybe it was plotting his next fund-raising scheme. Maybe (later in his teens) it was penning a few lines of admiration to his latest object of attraction. He was good with words. He knew that he'd been short-changed a little in the Mr Universe stakes, but he was switched on enough to recognize that the way to a woman's heart – or wherever it was you wanted to gain access to – was not all achieved by how you looked. Women were emotional creatures. You had to switch into that *modus operandi* and address them at their own level. It was a system which had borne fruit on many occasions and it was the same system that had won him his greatest treasure: Abigail Eastwood. Way out of his league, she was already a senior to his self-conscious sophomore status, her father a big shot attorney in Philly. But they had connected in a way Potzner could never have anticipated. She seemed to find something in him that had been lacking in her own life, despite the privileges that undoubtedly came with her background. "*Just an accident of birth, honey, that's all. I'm no different to you.*" But he knew she was. And he had never stopped counting his blessings since the day she had agreed to step out with him.

Potzner shifted his leg with an impatient gesture. He contemplated getting out for a stretch but rejected the impulse in favour of a cigarette. The Zippo flared and he pushed back in the seat, wincing at the familiar ache in his calf. The shell that had removed a significant portion of the muscle had killed the man standing next to him, Corporal Barnes. Nice guy. They had spent the night playing cards and smoking. Trying to forget their fear. He had been scared. *Real* scared. But Barnes had smiled at him: "Ain't nothing to it, Jim. You see 'em comin', you let rip. No way any spook's gonna get past me an' live to chew rice the next mornin'." They laughed and the dawn seemed a long way off. When it came and the shadows receded they saw the ridge again, waiting. The attack began as the sun rose and the world lurched into slowmo, like an old silent movie.

Potzner drew heavily on the Winston. The images were always the same. For years they had replayed in the space created by the constant waiting his job demanded. "No." He spoke aloud and the sound of his voice alarmed him. "*Please* leave me alone." But he knew the scene had to play to its conclusion. He closed his eyes and let it roll. Barnes, next to him, his mouth wide, pointing, encouraging the men to keep pushing on, stepping over the bodies. And then the muffled *thump* alongside, the surprise to find himself on his back. No pain. A glance to the left and the shock of Barnes' sightless eyes staring back, a faint smile on his lips. Then hands on his shoulder, gently lifting him, the vibration of the chopper and the sharp sting of a needle in his arm. It could have been yesterday, but it was *way* back – 9th February, 1969, Chu Pa region; America was out of her depth in the jungles of Vietnam and he was on his way home to Abigail.

They had visited Barnes' widow as soon as his leg would bear his weight again. He could still remember her pale face, the wringing of her slender hands as they sat in the family room of the Kentucky farmhouse he'd heard so much about. They'd promised to keep in touch, but then life moved on. He sometimes wondered about her, if she'd found someone else to fill the emptiness. He hoped so. Life *had* to carry on; those who survived owed it to the dead to live for them. That's what Barnes would have wanted. Handsome, happy-go-lucky Joseph Barnes. His friend. There one moment; gone the next.

Potzner fingered the window button and flicked out his stub. The smoke cleared and he sighed, a deep, soul-weary sigh. Death had always stalked him. It had been his closest companion in 'nam, and an ever-present buddy since he had joined the company. Thing was, it was part of the job. That was fine. He could accept that. But it had no place coming home with him. It had no right to enter *his* front door. But, dear God, it *had*. He could feel its presence, hovering, waiting, biding its time. Abigail knew, of course. The doctor had been direct. They had held hands as the sentence had been pronounced. He was a young guy, the neurologist. Looked a bit like Woody Allen. They had laughed about that afterwards. *Laughed.* Anyway, Woody had a good manner, was sympathetic, pulled no punches. As a straight talker himself, Potzner appreciated that. Three, perhaps five years, at the most. Abigail's hand had tightened on his as they left the hospital and walked out into the sunshine. Traffic crawled past; lunchtime shoppers hurried this way and that, glancing anxiously at their watches. How much time before they had to be back at the office? How much time?

From that point onwards, his and Abigail's time had become dislocated from the rest of the world. The people striding along the sidewalks lived in some parallel universe, where normality smoothed the path ahead. What had they in common? They had sat in silence in the park for a long time, just looking, just being alive. She caught his eye and he remembered thinking, *I have never seen her look so beautiful. I will always remember this moment.* "I'll retire early," he told her. "We'll travel, be with each other." She shook her head. "No Jim, you must carry on. You love your job. I want everything to be normal, as it was before today." She smiled, pressing her finger to his lips to seal the protest. "I *need* it to be that way."

That was three years ago, and the clock was ticking. Should he phone her now? He knew she hated the fuss. Most days were all right. But the bad days... days in a darkened room where her helpless body would be fed with chemicals, nourished through sterilized tubing. Such days came twice, perhaps three times a week now. And he yearned for her, yet could not bear to be there to see her suffering. He would be with her now, had not hope arrived six months ago in a form more unexpected than anything he could have imagined.

Potzner caught a slight movement in the window of the house – *semi-detached,* the Brits called them – and snapped into alert mode. The girl, Sara Benham, drawing the curtain. Looked like the lovers were in for the night. He scanned the sidewalk, their side, then paid special attention to the hedgerow on his left that separated the road from the University grounds. He could just see the grey expanse of water beyond the hedge, the lake that sat between the halls of residence on this, the north side of the campus. He was parked in the driveway of the old gatehouse and had a clear view of the red-bricked houses slightly up the hill on the corner. Dusk was rapidly falling and Potzner's sense of unease increased with the diminishing light. Surely soon? He knew they wouldn't wait long after the bungled attempt at the diary. He patted his coat pocket reflexively, drawing comfort from the contours of the snub-nosed Sig Sauer P229. He was sure he'd need it before the night was out, and that it wouldn't be the last time it would see action on this operation. If he could just wing one of them, just one... then he'd make them talk. Hell, he wouldn't even *need* the diary then.

A few cars swished past the University perimeter, windshield wipers flicking in the worsening drizzle. *Great.* As if it wasn't cold and miserable enough already. He glanced at his watch; 17:15. Check-in time. "Campus one?" His earpiece responded immediately: "*In position.*" Potzner grunted. "Okay, stand by. Two?" A brief pause, then: "*Likewise.*" Satisfied, he settled back and prepared for a long wait. No sweat, though. Waiting was his speciality.

Dracup faced the intruder, heart pounding in his chest. Then he realized he was still holding the struggling cat in his arms. He launched the animal, a black tangle of extended claws, directly at the figure in the balaclava, then ducked and propelled himself back through the kitchen door, colliding with Sara as she entered the kitchen carrying a tray of plates and glasses. One word came out: *Run.* He caught her arm and dragged her through to the lounge into the hallway.

"What...."

"Just *run.*"

Dracup had the front door open and they skidded down the short drive, turning towards the University campus.

"Simon!"

Dracup glanced back. "Save your breath – *and don't run straight.*"

They crossed the road at speed. As they drew level with the gatehouse a parked car flicked on its headlights. Dracup weaved parallel to the vehicle and made for the path by the lake.

"Which way?"

"To the right." Dracup felt the first reaction of his lungs to the unaccustomed strain. His heart thudded and a burning finger moved across his abdomen. The path clung to the lakeside and they pounded down its length, darkness closing around them as the canopy of trees thickened above.

Dracup fumbled for his mobile and punched in a number.

"What are you doing?" Sara gasped as they approached a narrow wooden bridge.

"University security. Come on – this way." His legs were leaden and it was all he could do to spit out a request when the security desk finally picked up.

"There's an armed intruder in the campus – approaching from the North East entrance – crossing the lake..."

"What? Who is this?"

"Dracup – Anthropology."

"Professor Dracup?"

"Yes – get a move on, for heaven's sake."

"Are you sure –"

"Of course I'm – look, just get out here now, would you?"

"On our way, sir. I'll call the police."

"Good idea..."

Dracup pocketed the phone and concentrated on his breathing. He could see the homely lights of the University building ahead.

Sara, slightly ahead, stumbled over a shape on the path. And screamed.

Dracup looked down as he passed the spot. A man was lying across the path, his face illuminated by moonlight. A neat hole had been punched in his forehead and his eyes stared sightlessly up at the stars. The crew cut and suit connected him inevitably with Potzner. "Keep going. Across the grass and head left." He calculated their position and risked a glance behind. A figure emerged from the shadow of the trees by the bridge, stopped momentarily then caught sight of them as they hurried across the open space. Then two others came into view, running towards the bridge. The figure hesitated. Dracup heard a shout. Thank God. Security had taken him seriously.

"Simon! Come on." Sara waited, hands on hips several metres ahead.

He pointed to the buildings. "Go left." If he remembered correctly the Plant Sciences lab lay ahead, close to the Pepper Lane entrance. What he needed was in there – if there was time. He heard more shouting from the direction of the bridge. They turned into the Plant Sciences car park and entered the building by the automatic swing doors. The reception desk was empty – good.

"What are we doing in *here?* We'll be trapped..." Sara caught his sleeve.

"I don't think so," Dracup said. "Security has probably done enough to keep him off our scent for a while. And I need to do this now."

"Do what?"

"Come on." He let Sara tag along as they passed the noticeboard, which was bare save for a large poster advertising Cornwall's Eden Project. A glance through one of the lab windows revealed several white-coated technicians, doubtless absorbed in some green-fingered research project. He pushed into another corridor. It was along here somewhere. The floor reminded Dracup of hospitals; polished and antiseptic. In fact the whole building smelt sanitized, as if scrubbed hourly by an invisible team of cleaners. They came eventually to an office, deserted but for the hum of photocopiers and faxes. Dracup had the diary out and the photocopier lid open.

"You're amazing," Sara said. "I thought you left it at the house."

"I'm not letting it go that easily. Keep an eye on the corridor."

Sara stood at the door while Dracup flicked the diary pages over and pressed the button. The copier whirred. The results were barely legible. "Blast. Where's the contrast button?"

Sara stepped over. "Here. Now try."

After a few minutes Dracup had half the pages copied. Somewhere in the distance the sound of police sirens rose and fell. The paper ran out, and Sara hissed across the room, "Someone coming."

One of the lab technicians peered into the room. "Hullo. Can I help?"

"Just borrowing the copier." Dracup smiled.

"Are you –"

"Dracup – Anthropology. Our machine's on the blink again."

"Of course. Carry on." The technician grinned back.

Sara nodded as the man left the office and walked back along the corridor. As she watched, another man slipped through the double doors at the far end. He was tall and grey haired.

"Simon?"

"What?"

"Someone's coming."

Dracup, intent on his task, waited for the next sheet before responding. When he looked up he saw Potzner halfway down the corridor and closing fast.

"Run." He thrust the papers at Sara, grabbed her hand and bolted out of the office, turning right towards what he hoped was the way to the side entrance – if there *was* a side entrance. Behind him came Potzner's voice: "Dracup...Wait!"

They sprinted the length of the building, and burst out in front of the large greenhouses to the rear of the Plant Sciences lab. Skirting the car park Dracup got his bearings and turned back onto the internal campus road. He shouted to Sara, "This leads onto Pepper Lane." He dog-legged past the security box, stole a glance behind and saw Potzner's elastic frame almost upon her. *Damn.* The man was fast for his age. Sara was mouthing something. He strained to hear what she was saying – her arm was flailing now... a warning? He turned – too late – and saw a car mounting the pavement. He dived to the left but the next second it was on him, catching him a bruising blow on his thigh and lifting him into the air. The world slowed down. He floated towards the ground, twisting his head sideways to avoid contact with the pavement. The dreamlike quality persisted until he landed, shoulder first on the tarmac. A curtain descended. He was vaguely aware of hands in his pockets, probing, pulling. An engine roared, so close it felt like it was in his head.

Then there was blackness.

Chapter 4

Dracup was unsure which part of his body hurt the most: his head or his shoulder. He opened his eyes and squinted in the bright light.

"Simon? Thank goodness..."

Sara's face swam into focus. The curtain twitched and Potzner was at the bedside.

Dracup felt a sudden flare of anger. "I presume you've called the dogs off now you've got what you wanted." The effort of speech made him wince.

Potzner studied the bedside cabinet. There was a Tupperware box containing Dracup's mobile, car keys and wallet. Potzner shook his head. "This wasn't our doing, Mr Dracup. We were trying to protect you."

Sara seemed to be in agreement with the American. Dracup searched her face. She was pale, biting her lip. And then he remembered the body on the campus path. To Potzner he said, "You lost a man."

"Yes." The American's expression remained impassive. Only the jaw worked at a slow tempo, masticating the gum with practised automation.

Dracup leaned back on the pillows. His head throbbed with a slow pulse. So Potzner was on his side; that was little consolation now. The theft of the diary had removed the only tangible link to Natasha.

"Fact is, Mr Dracup," Potzner continued, "it would have been a lot better if you'd just complied with my request and passed the document to me. Safer."

"That's helpful." Dracup's mouth felt thick and there was a residual taste of antiseptic that made him feel nauseous. "You didn't tell me there were other interested parties."

"You handled yourself very well, Professor. But I think it's time to leave the rest to us."

Dracup raised an eyebrow. Even that small action sent splinters of pain across his face. "The rest?" Sara was vehemently nodding her agreement. She moved closer and took Dracup's hand.

"Mr Dracup. I just came to apologize for the inconvenience that's been caused. I wish you the best for a quick recovery – oh, and you needn't concern yourself about the incident in the hotel room. The police know nothing." Potzner turned to leave, one hand on the curtain.

"No. *Wait*." Dracup reached out to grab Potzner but fell back on the pillow at the jarring pain in his shoulder. He heard his voice shouting, "My daughter is missing! You can't just walk away –"

Potzner hesitated; he seemed genuinely surprised. "I'm sorry – I didn't know."

"You're *sorry?*"

A nurse brushed past him into the ward enclosure. "Right," she said brightly. "Calm down please, Mr Dracup. Mobile off inside the hospital." She removed the instrument from Potzner's gloved hand. "You'll disturb the whole ward with all that shouting. Everybody out. I have to change Mr Dracup's dressings." She bustled off, presumably, Dracup thought, to allow his guests a minute or so to make themselves scarce.

Potzner turned to leave. "I'll see you in my office when you're feeling better, Professor. In the meantime I suggest you talk to the police about your daughter. And I wouldn't mention our little chat. Or the diary." The curtains parted and Potzner was gone.

Dracup felt his anger burning. "Now *wait* a minute –." But Sara's hand was on his arm, the nurse poised over him like some starched bird of prey. He listened as the American's uneven footsteps receded along the ward, then turned his attention to the nurse. "I need to get out of here. I'm not ill. There's nothing broken. Is there?" He challenged the nurse with a hostile jutting of his chin.

"You have a little concussion and a bruised hip," the SRN said. "But you'll live. I presume there's someone who can keep an eye on you?" She glanced at Sara. "Well, that's all right then. The doctor will be round shortly. If you behave you'll probably be discharged this evening."

"I'm discharging myself when you've finished the dressings," Dracup told her. She opened her mouth to reply but, seeing his expression, thought better of it and turned her attention to the task in hand.

Potzner's office was a Spartan affair. Dracup slammed the door behind him and pointed a trembling finger at the American. "You'd better start explaining. Right now."

"Do come in, Professor. Take a seat." Potzner waved vaguely in the direction of a chair. His attention was occupied by a set of photographs that lay askew on the surface of his desk. The omnipresent Winston was jammed into the corner of his mouth, although it remained unlit in irritated deference to the 'No Smoking' signs liberally scattered around the building.

"I'll stand if that's all right with you," Dracup said. "Now talk. What do you know about my daughter's abduction?"

Potzner shrugged. "Only what you've told me. I take it there's no news?"

Dracup leaned across the desk. "Is there a connection with the people who stole the diary? If there is, I need to know. For pity's sake, Potzner, there's a child's life at stake here –"

Potzner blew out air. "Actually there's a great deal more at stake, Professor. And yeah, there may well be a connection, but I can't see a motive."

Dracup slammed his fist on the desk. "I don't know where to start looking. Turkey? Europe? America? I had the diary. Now it's gone. I have *nothing*." He slammed both fists down together. The desk shook. He felt an overpowering weakness grip his body, and collapsed into the chair with his head in his hands.

Potzner was unruffled. "I understand your position, Professor. You're overwrought. You deserve a little enlightenment – strictly off the record, of course. I can't tell you much, but you'll recall our conversation in Aberdeen? About the missing artefact?"

"Yes. Go on."

Potzner gave a little grunt. "I guess *artefact* is a misnomer. Firstly the artefact in question wasn't man-made, and secondly it's linked with state-of-the-art research going on back in the US. It *must* be recovered."

"Research into...?"

"Longevity. The human life span."

Dracup nodded. Such research had a counterpart in the UK and he had a few contacts working in the field of gerontology.

The American smiled. "I can guess what you're thinking. No big deal. Everyone's into it, right?"

Dracup nodded impatiently, searching for relevance. "Yes. I was reading recently that our leading research labs have made some progress –"

"Forget it," Potzner interrupted, waving his hand dismissively. "I'm talking breakthrough here. No theories. This is the real McCoy."

"In what sense?"

Potzner regarded the grey outlook from the office window. London was at work, traffic was sparse. The only movements in the street below were initiated by the odd passing taxi and the continually slanting rain. "I'm not a scientific person, Mr Dracup. I'm an outdoors man. Always have been." He carefully replaced the unlit Winston in its packet with an expression of regret. "But I've taken a special interest in this research. It's a subject close to my heart."

Dracup was fighting a losing battle with his patience. He gripped the chair arms tightly and made himself listen. At least Potzner was communicating.

"You'll no doubt be aware, Mr Dracup, that there are *many* theories as to why the body ages as it does," Potzner continued.

"Well, yes. There's cell depletion and damage, DNA affecting chromosome degeneration, toxin intake – alcohol and nicotine being prime culprits –" Dracup waved at the red and white packet on the desk.

Potzner was nodding, ignoring the slight. "I'm not surprised you know a little about this, Professor. But let me tell you, our guys in the white coats have long subscribed to the theory that there is some coded obsolescence built into our DNA structure."

"You mean we are all genetically programmed for the ageing process to kick off at a predetermined time?"

"Exactly. It's as though each of us comes into the world as a machine that is programmed to self-destruct."

"Ah. The ticking of the biological clock. Time to have sex, time to have babies, time to buy a pipe and a pair of slippers. Time to pop off." Dracup shuffled his feet under the desk, fighting the instinct to grab Potzner by the collar and force the truth out of him.

"I'm serious, Professor. When the alarm goes off it sends a signal through our DNA structure to begin the ageing process that ends in death. At that point we become more prone to disease; our bodies lose the elasticity of youth. We take longer to heal. Sometimes, we don't heal at all."

Dracup looked into the American's eyes and wondered what weight of sadness had etched the lines around them. This was personal, no mistaking the signs. A sudden guilt replaced his hostility; he'd trespassed on some deep, emotional property. Strangely it had a calming effect. "All right. I didn't mean to be flippant. Go on."

Potzner's tone became more formal, as if he were quoting from some uncontested results sheet. "Our research reached conclusive status with the most recent experiments performed on the artefact in question."

"Hang on. Isn't it time you told me what the *artefact* actually *is?*"

"Organic tissue. That's all I can say. The codename for the recovery operation is *Red Earth*. It may be easier if I refer to that name in future."

"What kind of organic tissue?"

Potzner hesitated and then said, very slowly, "Tissue that is palaeontologically old."

"And this is what my grandfather discovered on the second expedition?" Dracup frowned, remembering the diary entry: *RC is concerned re the location of the sarcophagus*. A body; moved centuries ago from the Ark; palaeontologically old...

"Your grandfather was a bright cookie, Mr Dracup." Potzner leaned forward. A fresh cigarette was out and tapping on the packet. As if reading his thoughts, the American went on. "As I said before, the *Red Earth* material was originally resident in the Ark. Then it was transported to the location discovered by your grandfather. And so it came to us. For years it waited for technology to mature. That time is now. I have to tell you the possession of this material is critical for further testing and fine-tuning. If the research is allowed to continue uninterrupted the consequence for the human race will be one of inestimable benefit."

"Forgive me if I relegate the human race in general to second place for the time being." Dracup recognized the signs of Potzner's almost religious commitment to his cause and felt his new-found restraint crumbling. "Potzner, I need answers. Who kidnapped my daughter? What has Natasha got to do with *Red Earth*? And *where* do we start looking?"

"*Red Earth* wasn't a straightforward acquisition, Professor. It was the property of a religious sect – for want of a better description – who have been planning its reinstatement, or return if you will, to where it was originally discovered – the place Theodore found. This sect made fools out of us. We assumed the threat was long past." Potzner spoke evenly, as if he were describing the activities of some local charitable committee.

"Reinstatement? But where?" Dracup's heart lurched. At last, a possibility. Could this be where Natasha was being held?

"That, Professor, is the million dollar question. Whoever these people are, they successfully infiltrated one of the most secure organizations in the Western world. You can imagine what level of security we had on this research." Potzner leaned forward again. "Professor Dracup, is there anything you can remember from the diary that we could use? Any detail at all? Take your time."

Dracup closed his eyes and tried to concentrate. "There was a diagram – in the diary – cuneiform script. I only had a brief look at it."

"Brief may be enough..."

Dracup clicked his fingers. "Hang on!" The Plant Sciences lab, the photocopier. "I might still have something…"

Potzner's eyes lit up. "Are you telling me you have some information regarding the contents of the diary?"

"Maybe." Dracup was cursing himself for a fool. How could he have forgotten? He stumbled to his feet. "My girlfriend has it. It's safe."

Potzner pushed back his chair and grabbed his coat. "But *she* may not be, Mr Dracup. She may not be."

Chapter 5

Dracup's worst fears were confirmed when he saw the police cars outside Sara's house. He threw himself out of the car and battered on the front door.

Sara's surprised face met them in response to Dracup's frantic knocking. "Simon – thank goodness you're here – there's been a break-in. They've made such a mess –" She registered Dracup's drawn, anxious expression and took his arm. "It's all right. I'm okay." Then she turned her attention to Potzner. "Hello again. You'd better come in."

He felt Sara's arm guiding him. "Simon, is there any news? This is – trivial – it's just a pain. I don't think anything's missing."

Dracup shook his head and stepped aside to make way for a policeman. "No news. We need to see the diary copies. Can you get them?"

"I'm sure – I know where I put them – oh, you don't think..." Her hand flew to her mouth. "Just a minute. Make yourselves at home." She left them in the front room and after a minute or so Dracup heard her footsteps descending again. Potzner stood by the window, hands in pockets, waiting, analyzing. His eyebrows raised the merest fraction as Sara came back in.

"Gone." Sara spread her arms in a hopeless gesture. "I can't believe it."

"Right." Dracup said. "Wait here."

"Where are you going?"

"Back to the campus. I'll be fifteen minutes. No more."

Potzner's face took on a quizzical expression. "I'll be waiting, Mr Dracup."

Dracup screeched to a halt in the Plant Sciences car park. He ran through the doors, impatiently brushing the large transparencies aside as they swung open. He strode briskly down the corridor past the reception desk, answering the receptionist's unspoken query with a fierce proprietary stare in return. She withered and returned to her paperwork. Dracup found the office and pushed his way past a group of students loitering in the passage. A middle-aged lady in a tweed suit was flicking through the contents of a filing cabinet and tutting lightly to herself. She looked up as Dracup entered and gave him a brief look up and down. Evidently satisfied of his respectability she resumed her task.

Dracup went to the photocopier and slid his hand down the back of the machine. His hands found paper, and he carefully moved the A4 sheets out from their imprisonment between the copier and the wall. At last he had enough paper protruding to make a grab for them. Seven sheets came out. The first was blank and his heart did a little dance of despair. The following sheets bore the familiar marks of his grandfather. He whooped aloud, and the tweed lady looked up in surprise. By then he was gone and running down the corridor. Ten minutes later he was back at Sara's house. The police cars were gone.

Potzner strode out to greet him. "May I?" He took the papers from Dracup and smiled, nodding his head in appreciation. "You're a resourceful fellow, Mr Dracup."

Sara appeared at the door and her eyes widened as she saw the papers. She looked at Dracup with surprise. He returned one of reassurance. *It's okay.*

Sara held the door open. "Simon, how –"

"Just my cautious nature. I set the 'number of copies' counter to two and stashed the second batch behind the copier."

Sara gave him a tense grin. "I'm impressed."

"We'll give you a hand with this first." Dracup indicated the trashed sitting room. For forty-five minutes they cleared and tidied while Potzner made telephone calls from his car. Dracup signalled to him from the window, and Potzner came back in and hung his raincoat over the back of the sofa. His face was sombre and Dracup thought he detected a slight film of water over the American's eyes.

Sara made coffee and eventually they settled around the coffee table while Dracup spread the papers out on the glass surface.

"Are you all right with this, Sara?" Dracup asked. He felt a stab of guilt as he took in Sara's pinched face. Nothing personal had been taken, but it was still a violation. He had suffered a break-in a few years back, and he remembered that the anger had taken a week or so to fade.

Sara managed a weak smile. "Yes. Of course."

He quickly found the sheet he was after: the page featuring what his grandfather had described as a *curious iron* object, with a tantalizing profusion of symbols. "This is significant," he said. "It's an object my grandfather's colleague was excited about – you can read the entries. The script is some kind of cuneiform derivation."

Potzner looked blank. "I'll take your word for it, Professor."

"Why don't we have a look on the internet?" Sara said. "There's bound to be a lot of info about cuneiform."

Dracup nodded. "Right. Go for it."

"I'll shout if I find anything." She sat down at the PC in the corner of the room, leaving Dracup to ponder the contents of the page in front of them.

Potzner pointed to a line of symbols directly beneath the diagram. "This looks a little different to the rest."

Dracup grunted. Potzner was right. A footnote of some sort? There were no lines of connected annotation... The room fell silent save for the tapping of Sara's keyboard. Frustrated, he got up and joined Sara at the computer. "Anything?"

Sara clicked a link on the favourites menu. "There's this. A school website. I don't know how accurate it is – it's for kids really, to translate their names into cuneiform."

"Does it work the other way round?"

"Cuneiform to English? Yep. There's a key symbol chart. It'll be pretty basic though."

"Worth a try. Put this in." He pointed to the line of symbols beneath the diagram. Anything was worth a try. Dracup realized he was holding his breath and let it out in a frustrated rush.

"Okay." Sara's tongue protruded slightly from her mouth as she concentrated on selecting the correct – or closest – symbol from the website's cuneiform chart. "There. Here we go." She completed the selection but Dracup grabbed the mouse.

"I'm not sure that's the same symbol." Dracup pointed to the third letter.

"Hang on – it looks the closest. Let's see what happens." Sara pressed the enter key. In the results box, a sentence appeared:

In time you will find the hole.

A cloud of smoke drifted across the screen. "Great." Potzner said. "Very enlightening."

Dracup felt the hairs on the back of his neck rise. "But the point is made, isn't it? That's *colloquial*, not an inscription from the Ark – it's a message from my grandfather. To the reader. Not to himself."

"Okay, but what does it mean?" The American found a waste bin and flicked ash in its general direction.

"A reference to another compartment on the Ark?" Sara mused. "They originally found the *curious iron* object in a hidden cupboard of some sort."

"Possibly." Dracup wasn't so sure. In some indefinable way the answer felt closer to home. He checked the symbols again. "Hang on a minute. Look – you missed this character altogether."

"Right. Sorry." Sara reselected the symbol and stabbed the enter key.

In time you will find the whole.

"Much better," Potzner observed.

Dracup had had enough. "Damn it, Potzner. A little encouragement wouldn't go amiss." He turned on the American. "Haven't the CIA got *any* record of these expeditions? You must have *something* to go on. Maps, dossiers, anything. You're an intelligence organization, aren't you for God's sake?"

"The archive files were removed, Mr Dracup. There *is* no record."

Dracup turned away in exasperation. Either the organization *had* been negligent in this case, or its adversaries were very clever. Or both. He turned his attention back to the screen, then to the photocopy. There was something incomplete; he'd noticed it before on the original sketch – something about the shape... Then he had it. "Ah. Look." He waved the paper to attract their attention.

Sara and Potzner both looked at the diagram blankly.

"It's not *complete*. Look at how the inscriptions run to the very edge." He pointed excitedly. "And there *is* a border from the extreme left, as you would expect."

Sara squinted at the picture. "You mean if the object was complete, you'd expect an equivalent border on the right hand side."

"Exactly."

Dracup felt his excitement grow. There was significance here, he was sure of it. "And what shape would be produced by adding the mirror image of the object to itself?"

Potzner drew a line in the air. "Right. I'm with you. A cross." He frowned. "Well, leastways that's what it looks like."

"An ornate cross, granted, but you can see the symmetry. It wouldn't look out of place as the headpiece of a –"

Sara whistled softly. "A sceptre, or … a standard? Could be." She chewed her finger. "So we only have half the picture."

Dracup remembered his grandfather's hastily recorded entry – *the sceptre may hold the answer. I have many reservations.* "Yep. This is the object he referred to, I'm positive. Now think about the footnote."

Potzner read aloud. "'In time you will find the whole'. So, your grandfather recognized there was another section – a matching section – to be found." He scratched his blue jowl thoughtfully. "Well, so what? Maybe it was just a reminder – an encouraging entry made for his own benefit?"

"No, no," Dracup said. "Remember my grandfather was a geologist, not an archaeologist. This clearly had *some* interest for him, but he probably sketched it for his colleague, because –"

"Because your grandfather was a talented artist and his colleague, the archaeologist, knew that," Sara finished for him.

"Right. RC – Reeves-Churchill – was the on-site archaeologist. This was for him, I'll bet, by request."

"But why code it in cuneiform?" Sara frowned.

"Maybe they had some inkling that they were dealing with something dangerous, something that shouldn't have been exposed." Dracup was thinking about Theodore, how his mind had gone. And then Potzner's discomfort when he had asked how the Ark discovery had been hushed up...

"All the same," Potzner said, "it doesn't get us any further. To get a clear picture what the inscriptions on the *whole* object actually say, you need both halves."

Sara spoke up. "Well, we have half the script. Surely the first thing is to get an expert review of these inscriptions?"

Potzner nodded. "I'll take care of that."

Dracup was humming. "There *is* one place I can check out. My aunt transferred a number of my grandfather's belongings to her own house. There may be something that'll shed some light – letters, other documents. Who knows?" He walked to the window and looked out onto the street. A mother and toddler were making slow progress along the pavement. An image of Natasha came to his mind, smiling and holding out her arms. "Excuse me," he turned abruptly, his voice catching. "I have to call Yvonne."

"Please do," Potzner said, folding the photocopies carefully and depositing them in his briefcase. "I'm headed back to London. When I've had this analyzed I'll call you."

Dracup went into the hall and took out his mobile. He dialled Yvonne's number. Ten rings later Malcolm answered.

"It's me. Any news?"

"Ah. Simon. Nothing yet, I'm afraid. But the police are being very helpful."

"Right. What have they got?"

"A man and young woman were seen at the school shortly before Natasha went missing."

"And?"

"They're, er, following a line of enquiry."

"Really? So they have nothing. Look, Malcolm, my mobile is always on, day or night, so don't hesitate if anything comes up."

"Yes, of course."

"How's Yvonne?"

"Well, you know. Not so good."

"Tell her – tell her I'm doing all I can."

"Of course. I will. Goodbye."

Dracup joined Potzner and Sara in the lounge. Potzner raised his eyebrows.

"Nothing."

Potzner fixed Dracup with a steady look. "We work together on this, okay? You find out something – you let me know. And vice versa."

"If you assure me that your first interest is my daughter's safe return, I'll share everything I've got."

"Listen, Dracup." Potzner spoke quietly but with an audible edge to his voice. "If you play ball with me I'll help any which way I see fit. If not, you're on your own." Potzner picked up his coat and made as if to leave. "Oh, there's one more thing. I'm leaving you with a little muscle."

Dracup exchanged glances with Sara. A moment later the doorbell rang. Potzner ushered the newcomer into the lounge. Suited, expressionless. Potzner clapped him on the shoulder. "This is Farrell. He's a bright guy. Just do what he says, when he says, and you'll be okay."

"You mean we're stuck with this gorilla?" Sara was indignant. "I can look after myself, thanks."

Farrell's face remained impassive. He was around the thirty mark, with an easy, laid-back manner. He wore a pair of shades pushed up onto his crew cut and a flesh-coloured earpiece in his right ear. Dracup wondered how much he knew about *Red Earth*. He intended to find out soon enough.

Dracup took Sara's arm. "It's probably a good idea." He looked over to Farrell. "No offence."

"None taken," Farrell drawled.

Potzner was rummaging in his briefcase. "I suggest you make the trip to Scotland sooner rather than later. This is a hotline to the London office." He handed Dracup a card. "Check in once a day – without fail. If you don't, like I said before, I'll come looking."

Chapter 6

"There you go – Forest Avenue. Next left." Sara folded the street map and shoved it down into the side pocket.

"Got it." Dracup swung the car into the street and crawled along its length counting the numbers down. He glanced in the mirror. Farrell was scanning the pavements on either side of the street. Next to the agent lay the flotsam of a long journey: empty biscuit packets, juice cartons, chocolate papers.

"There!" Sara pointed.

Dracup found a space, eased the Saab along the high kerb and killed the engine.

"I'll do the neighbourly thing." Sara was out of the car and Farrell followed suit.

"Meet you at the front door. Ah – looks like it's side access," Dracup called over, and walked up the path of the old granite house. The property had been converted into two flats, according to the solicitor, and his aunt had owned the first and second floors. Dracup found the side door and strode briskly past it to the garden gate. He peered over the top. It was overgrown, neglected. His aunt would have been mortified.

"Success." Sara appeared with Farrell in tow. She tossed the key to him and he caught it deftly by its attached piece of string.

Inside, a pile of freesheets and unopened mail greeted them. Dracup picked up the pile and began separating the post from the newspapers. To their left, a staircase led directly up from the tiny hallway. A smell of mothballs permeated the small space.

Sara was flicking the light switch. "Bit gloomy." The bulb remained unlit. "I'm going up."

The landing ran the length of the property and two rooms led off it to the front of the house, while at the far end the kitchen opened out to the right. A further staircase apparently led up to another floor. Sara, hands in jeans pockets, found an armchair in the living room and sat down. "It's very quiet." She shivered and rubbed her hands together. "And damp."

"Darn cold, that's for sure." Farrell was by the curtains, looking out into the street.

"It may be worth lighting the boiler," Dracup said tersely. "Come on. Let's get started. I'll take a look upstairs. You two can do the lounge and kitchen." Dracup ascended the small wooden staircase to the top floor. There was a smell of musty linen, mothballs. On the second floor landing stood a grandfather clock, silent and cobwebbed. He quickly checked the two bedrooms, which revealed nothing but a chest of drawers in the first and a solitary iron bedstead in the second.

He took a deep breath, went back down the narrow staircase, retrieved the pile of letters and began to open each in turn. It seemed a futile exercise, but he knew that he daren't leave anything to chance. The stakes were too high. He rubbed a bead of sweat away from his forehead and, tight-lipped, continued to slit open and discard his aunt's correspondence.

Sara placed a hand gently on his arm. "I'll start in this bureau." She attempted to roll back the lid but it refused to budge. "Blast. Locked."

"One moment, ma'am." Farrell stepped forward and produced a set of keys. A moment later the desk was open.

"Thanks." Sara began sifting through the various pigeonholes of the bureau. Farrell took up his position by the bay window and began a flat, tuneless hum.

Sara drummed on the bureau with her fingers. "You're making me nervous, Farrell. I can't concentrate. Sit down, can't you?"

"I have to keep an eye on things, ma'am." Farrell raised the corners of his mouth slightly and turned back to the window.

Dracup returned his attention to the letters, but his mind refused to cooperate. What if he had been in England? What if Natasha had been at home? What if Yvonne had answered the phone when he had called from the hotel? What if –

"Hey." Sara sat on the arm of his chair. "She'll be all right, Simon. It'll be okay." She squeezed his shoulder and withdrew her hand as Dracup gave a gasp of pain. "Sorry, I forgot."

"It's just bruising." Dracup ran his hand through Sara's hair. She was so beautiful. He wished he could share her optimism. He looked at the pile of letters and rubbed his eyes; a dull, throbbing headache was taking root in his temple. He pushed his chair back and took Sara's hand in his. "I need to maintain focus. Keep occupied."

"Well, there's no shortage of material here. I've never seen so much packed into a bureau." Sara waved a rubber-banded sheaf of papers. "Look at this lot."

"Anything so far?"

"There's some old photos – nothing unusual. It would help if I knew what I was looking for."

"Let's see." Dracup took the bundle and quickly flicked through the photographs. "Yes. This is my grandfather – Theodore." He held the photo up for inspection. The faded image showed a frail-looking man in his early thirties sitting in a chair by a garden pond. A young woman had a hand on his shoulder, smiling bravely for the camera although it was clear that all was not well with the sitting figure. He looked old before his time, hunched and defeated. "That's my aunt standing next to him," Dracup said. "This must have been at the old house – my grandfather's – after he was institutionalized. She used to take him home at weekends. She felt it gave him some dignity. And she was sure that he felt at peace there."

Sara took a long look at the photograph. "She has a kind face – a family trait, obviously." She looked at Dracup and the photograph in turn.

"I don't know about that," Dracup said. "I can be very unpleasant when push comes to shove."

"Usually when you're hungry, I seem to remember," Sara said. "Shall I slip down to the corner shop? And Farrell, make yourself useful –see if you can get a fire going. There must be a few logs in the garden – some coal in the bunker. Something tells me this is going to be a long haul."

Farrell nodded. "Sure. I'll walk you down when you're ready. Leave the fire to me." He left the room and they heard his footsteps on the stairs. The front door opened and closed.

"He's driving me up the wall," Sara said with a grimace. "Our all-American high school baseball star."

Dracup raised his eyebrows. "I think he likes you, though... Anyway, I'm happy to have him around. We're not the only ones interested in Theodore's legacy."

They settled around the small table. Dracup studied the American closely. How much did he know? He swallowed a mouthful of egg and opened with a general question. "Tell me, Farrell; are you up to speed with the 1920 expedition?"

"Yes sir. Mr Potzner has briefed me."

"Surprised that the Ark was found?" Dracup kept his voice conversational and pleasant. Hopefully Farrell would come out with something useful.

Farrell finished his eggs and wiped his mouth with his handkerchief. He looked at Dracup and Sara in turn. "Well, you know, sir; I was brought up in the Southern states. I was right there in Sunday school from way back. I remember the stories we used to hear about Noah and all. I didn't think a lot of it at the time, 'cause, you know, when you're a kid, you kind of believe what the adults are telling you. There's that trust that they're telling you the truth. But when you get a little older, you begin to question it, you know what I mean?" He reached over and popped a can of coke.

Dracup nodded. "I know exactly what you mean."

"And then, I remember one weekend we had this visiting preacher come to our church. He spoke about the Ark and I remember thinking – wow, that's not how I understood it at all before."

"What was different?" Sara asked.

"Well, ma'am, he began by explaining the shape and size of this thing. People have kind of a funny notion that it was a little houseboat with giraffe poking their heads up an' all. But it wasn't like that. Not anyhow."

Dracup's curiosity was aroused, his cutlery idle on the plate.

Sara prodded him with a fork. "Eat. It'll go cold."

He resumed the meal automatically, waved his knife at Farrell. "Go on."

"Yes sir. Well, I used to keep a notebook for all the sermons I heard – we were taught that in Sunday school. I looked it out the other day. The boat wasn't shaped like a boat we would make today. It was a kind of box. The measurements given in the Old Testament, if interpreted as Egyptian cubits, would make the Ark 129 metres long, 21.5 metres wide and 12.9 metres high. This was pretty likely, the preacher said, because Moses – the author of the flood account – was educated in Egypt." Farrell paused and grinned when he saw their faces. "I have a pretty good memory. Particularly for numbers."

He went on, warming to his subject. "Now, if the Sumerian cubit was used, the metric equivalents would approximate 155.2 metres in length, 25.9 metres in width and 15.5 metres in height. Okay, so using the most conservative of these measurements would give the Ark approximately 40,000 cubic metres in gross volume. You remember the Titanic? Well, it's estimated that a vessel with these kind of dimensions would have a displacement nearly equal to the 269 cubic metres of the Titanic."

"Good grief," Dracup said. "That's colossal."

"It sure is," Farrell beamed. "You don't get to hear about that in the kids' story books, huh?"

"No. No, you don't," Dracup replied. Interesting detail; not what he was looking for, but a start anyway. He opened his mouth to ask another question but Farrell was getting into gear all by himself. Dracup let him carry on.

"Now, the account in the Bible says there were two floors in the Ark," Farrell said. "The boat would gain a lot of stability from that design. And it would be internally strengthened."

"So there would have been three decks altogether?" Dracup prompted.

Farrell nodded. "Right. That would yield a total of about 8,900 square metres of space." Farrell nodded his head emphatically. "Plenty of room for a lot of animals."

"I suppose so." And much more, he thought. A sceptre; a sarcophagus...

"That sure is something, sir: your grandfather actually walked on the remains of this vessel." Farrell paused to take a draught of coke. He swallowed with relish and placed the can carefully back on the table. "Now that is awesome."

Sara spoke up. "What baffles me is why no one else has reported any sightings of the Ark. Surely with all the effort that's been made over the last fifty years someone would have succeeded in rediscovering it? It's a *huge* object, you say. How can any serious expedition miss it?"

"Well, ma'am," Farrell replied, "those mountain ranges around Ararat are simply *vast*. And the altitude is a real problem. Weather conditions up there are pretty bad too."

Dracup was thinking about the politics. "And it's in Turkey."

"That's right, sir. The Turkish authorities don't allow research expeditions a lot of leeway."

Dracup thought about two men, bivouacked together, guideless, with the storm raging outside, and something else recorded in his grandfather's precise copybook lettering: *I saw it too. A was lifted away – not the wind.*

"Have you seen the – *Red Earth* material?" Dracup asked. If he could just get Farrell's confidence, put him at ease. "Potzner was telling me about the research project..."

"I've heard a few things, but I'm not security cleared to that level."

"So, what have you heard?"

Farrell looked uncomfortable. "Ah – I don't really have a lot of exposure to –"

Dracup's frustration levels finally burst. "Look Farrell, my daughter has been kidnapped. If there's anything you know that might help, for heaven's sake tell us. You're more clued up than you're letting on, aren't you?" Out of the corner of his eye Dracup noticed Sara watching him anxiously.

"I just have to look out for you, Professor Dracup. That's all. I'm real sorry about your daughter."

Dracup checked himself with an effort. "Yes. Yes, I'm sure you are, Farrell." The American seemed genuine for all the party line stuff. One step at a time, Dracup, don't push it. "Thanks, Farrell," he said. And left it at that.

The fire was blazing as they reassembled in the front room. Dracup went to the pile of letters and picked the next from the heap.

Sara rubbed her hands by the fire. "Nice job, Farrell," Sara said, straight-faced. "You must have been a Boy Scout after all."

Farrell selected a blackened poker from the fire stand and prodded the coals speculatively. "Well, thank you, ma'am." Dracup noticed that he held Sara's gaze until she uncharacteristically looked away. It wasn't hard to spot. He liked her all right.

Dracup shifted in his seat. He read the last letter and threw it on the table. Nothing. He tried to remember what his aunt had been involved in, what contacts she had had within her community. She had been a committed Christian, that much he knew, a regular church attendee. And there was her work for charities. He racked his brains. Which church had she attended? The local one, of course; Forest Avenue Baptist. He glanced at his watch: 5.21. Not too late to call at the manse. He grabbed his coat.

Sara frowned. "Where are you off to?"

"To see the minister. Won't be long."

"To see *who?*"

Farrell reached for his coat.

"No." Dracup told him. "You stay with Sara. I'm only going up the road, and it's still daylight."

Forty minutes later Dracup strode briskly along Forest Avenue, a cream envelope tucked securely in his jacket pocket. His heart was thumping with adrenaline and his face wore a grim smile of triumph. He took the stairs two at a time and found Farrell and Sara at the top, their faces quizzical.

"Listen to this."

Sara and Farrell froze at the excitement in Dracup's voice.

Dracup opened with shaking hands the letter the Reverend Anthony McPhee had produced from his filing cabinet. "It's from the Alexandra Nursing Home, Aberdeen. From the matron."

"But how did –?" Sara's mouth was open.

Dracup shushed her into silence. He read the letter aloud:

Mrs Hunter
c/o Forest Avenue Baptist Church,
Aberdeen

Dear Mrs Hunter,

> *As we haven't heard from you for a while, I thought I'd drop you a wee line to see how you were. We always appreciate Pastor McPhee's visits – and all the wonderful things your church does for the home. Things here are busy as usual – we've had the builders in for quite a time now and the dust makes a terrible mess. But we are looking forward to the finished results and the new lounge extension should be ready by Christmas. We're hoping to hold the carol service there as we'll at last have plenty of room! Now, I must mention that Mr Churchill is asking for you – he won't listen to us when we tell him you'll no doubt pop in soon. He keeps on asking! Well, you know that he does so enjoy your visits and is keeping awfully well considering he'll be 105 in November and is our oldest resident by a long way!*
>
> *Anyway, I mustn't keep you any longer but do accept all our best wishes. Hoping to see you soon.*

Yours sincerely,

Joan Mayfield
Matron

Sara looked blankly at him, searching for significance. Dracup watched their faces for any glimmer of understanding. His words tripped over themselves as he tried to explain. "My aunt – she was a member of the local church – she did a lot of charity work in the nursing homes in the area. There was one in particular that was a favourite. Now I know why."

"Churchill?" Sara's eyes reflected the light Dracup was searching for. He could almost hear the penny drop.

"Yes! Churchill!" Dracup shouted. "*Reeves*-Churchill. Theodore's colleague on the expeditions. He's still alive!"

Chapter 7

The time is now, Ruth told herself. *He will listen.* She hesitated and then heard herself speak, surprised at how calm she sounded. "Forget this Professor Dracup," Ruth told Kadesh. "He cannot harm us."

"He has already harmed us. Harmed *me*."

Ruth pressed on, heedless of the risk she was taking. He was grieving, but she had to know. She had chosen the time carefully. They were resting, breaking their long journey in the anonymity of the French countryside. Kadesh was quiet, thoughtful; pondering his next move. In this mood he was approachable. "It was not the Englishman's doing," she appealed. "It was his father's father. *He* was the one who transgressed."

Kadesh drew himself up to his full height and Ruth shrank before him. He towered above her, though she herself was tall – like all her kind; her ancestry had fashioned her that way.

Kadesh glowered and then seemed to check himself. "The Englishman has taken a life; my brother's life. He must reap the consequences. And the law must be fulfilled."

Ruth changed tack. If she acknowledged his success, then surely he would reconsider. "You have completed your mission. Our treasure will be restored to its rightful place. Surely there is nothing to be gained –"

Kadesh held up his hand in a dismissive gesture. "Gained? There is much to be gained. Justice will be done. And then I will be satisfied."

"What will you do with the girl?" Ruth asked. "She cannot be any use to you."

"We shall see."

"Have compassion on the child, Kadesh. She is innocent."

"No one is innocent in the sight of God." Kadesh motioned to Natasha. She was playing with a doll that he had found for her. Perhaps, Ruth hoped, this was a sign of some latent paternal instinct. They could hear the girl chattering quietly to the doll in her make-believe.

"And when it is finished," Ruth asked, "will you allow him to keep what he has taken?" She held her breath, terrified at her boldness. He knew what she meant; she could see it in his eyes.

"Water will find its own level. Like must cleave to like." He fixed her with his dark, hooded eyes. "It has always been so."

"Yes," Ruth replied, "we must follow the pattern established for us. We must be in His will." She held out her hands in supplication. Was his heart so distracted?

"Do not lecture me, woman." Kadesh turned away, presenting his back. "Leave me. My heart is sorrowful."

"Tarshish was a good man. I – I am sorry." Ruth knew the conversation was over. She made her way back to where Natasha lay, chattering to the dolly. When she saw Ruth approach she looked up, fearful, then relaxed and held the doll up for inspection. "Look, she has a little light inside."

"That's pretty, isn't it? Better not touch her there." Ruth moved the child's fingers away from the tiny pulsing red light just visible beneath the doll's dress and stroked Natasha's dark curls, wondering at a child's capacity to accept the inevitable, to adapt to changing circumstances. If only she could find it in herself to follow the child's example.

Chapter 8

The nursing home was, contrary to Dracup's expectations, set in well-kept grounds in a pleasant suburb of the city. The drive was flanked by a row of stately elms, fading to yellow and red as the chlorophyll lost its potency and little by little relinquished its task of nourishing the leaves; soon the earth would reclaim them and the cycle would begin afresh.

Dracup parked the car and gave Sara a strained smile. He hoped it was the same Churchill and that he was not about to make a fool of himself. Throughout the night he had slept little, tossing and turning, images of Natasha flitting in and out of his exhausted mind. He finally gave up at six and, bleary eyed, decided to tackle the remainder of the desk contents in the front room. At least when he was occupied he felt less vulnerable, less hopeless.

"Will Farrell be all right at the flat?" Sara asked as they crunched their way up the gravel drive.

Dracup knew what she meant. Farrell could take the opportunity to do a little research of his own in their absence. It was clear to Dracup that Potzner's focus was *Red Earth*; Natasha's predicament held little interest for him. And if the CIA were a step ahead and decided to act...He dared not predict what the result would be. Dracup realized that, to Potzner, Natasha was expendable. Compared to his precious research project she was way down the list of priorities. And that meant Dracup needed to guard any information carefully – to work with Potzner until a point had been reached where he had enough to go on without him. Dracup wondered when – if – that point would ever arrive. He took a deep breath and replied. "Yes. I think so. I get the impression he's not fully signed up to the Potzner agenda."

"Me too. Maybe that's a good thing."

"We'll see. Let's hope I'm right about Churchill."

They rang the ancient pull-down bell and were greeted by a cheery-faced woman in uniform. "Good morning! You'll be for Mr Churchill?" They followed her into the reception area where Dracup was immediately struck by the smell, a heady mixture of cabbage, sweat and micturition that floated down the centrally-heated corridors and caused Sara to wrinkle her nose. "It's very warm in here." She gave a small cough and grimaced at Dracup.

"Circulation breaks down as you get older. You feel the cold more," Dracup whispered.

"Just along here," the care assistant told them. "I should warn you that Mr Churchill is a wee bit – wandery. He's a hundred and five, you know, so he's doing amazingly well."

"He certainly is," Dracup agreed. "But I wonder, can you tell me before I meet Mr Churchill – does he have another part to his name? I mean the first part of a double-barrelled name?"

She put a finger to her mouth. "Now, let's see, Oh yes – Reeves. Reeves-Churchill. But we call him by his first name – George."

Dracup's heart missed a beat and he exchanged a glance with Sara. "Thank you."

"We have a church service at ten o'clock for the residents. You're very welcome to join us if you like. Can I get you a coffee?"

"That's very kind," Sara said. "Coffee would be fine. And we'd be delighted to attend the service."

"We would?" Dracup stage-whispered. He couldn't remember the last time he'd been in a church, let alone a service.

"You'll get more out of Churchill if you spend some time with him. Integrate with what he's doing. Believe me, I've dealt with elderly people before." Sara widened her eyes.

Dracup knew that look. It meant: I'm right on this. Just do it, and no arguing.

They were ushered into a long room where between fifteen and twenty residents were sitting in quiet expectation. A few looked up when they entered, but most simply stared into the distance or into their laps. No one was reading or engaged in any activity as far as Dracup could see. The care assistant led them over to the far end of the room where an old man was sitting, or rather propped, in a wheelchair. There was a dark green blanket spread over his knees and a faraway look in his eyes. His hair was white and thin, spread across his head in some cursory third-party attempt at style, while his arthritic hands firmly grasped the arms of the wheelchair as if their owner feared that the chair might tear off unexpectedly on some wild, unbidden ride. The silver head bobbed and smiled. A milky cup of tea lay untouched on the table beside him. The room was even hotter than the reception area and corridors through which they had passed, and the smell in the confined space of the lounge was overpowering. Dracup wondered how they could stand it.

"Two visitors to see you, George." The care assistant bent down to Churchill's level and spoke loudly into his ear. "He won't hear you unless you talk to this side," she told Dracup.

Dracup bent awkwardly, then squatted down on his haunches.

"Wait, I'll get two chairs," the care assistant said. She bustled off to some other room.

Dracup cleared his throat and spoke into the old man's ear. "Mr Churchill? My name is Simon Dracup. You knew my aunt, Mrs Hunter. She used to visit you."

The old man nodded and smiled. Dracup looked at Sara for help. He tried again. "Mrs Jean Hunter. Her father was a friend of yours – Theodore Dracup, my grandfather."

Churchill looked at them blankly. The assistant returned with two chairs. "Give him a wee while. He'll need to get used to you." She smiled and went off to attend to another resident's request. He heard her voice in the background, reassuring and cajoling as she handed out hymn books.

Sara leaned in close. "I'll have a word."

Dracup pushed his chair back. *Why not? This is going nowhere...*

"George. Do you like to sing?" Sara asked the old man.

Dracup raised his eyebrows. But then, to his surprise, Churchill began to sing in a high quavering voice:

"Oh! How I hate to get up in the morning,
Oh! How I'd love to remain in bed…"

Sara smiled and patted Churchill's arm. "Lovely tune, George."

Churchill smiled a toothless smile at Dracup and winked. "We all sang it. In the war, y'know. Ta ta tum, tum tat um. You've got to get up; you've got to get up. You've got to get up this morning!"

The care assistant appeared again. "Sorry to interrupt. This is Joan Mayfield, the matron." Dracup turned to see a trim lady in blue uniform smiling down at the group.

"Mr Dracup. How kind of you to come. Now then, George –" she raised her voice to an appropriate level for Churchill's benefit. "What's all this? We've already got you up this morning." She smiled again and gave Churchill's arm a light squeeze. "He's a lovely old chap. He *will* miss Mrs Hunter's visits." She turned to Dracup. "I'm so sorry about your aunt. It's very good of you to let me know."

"Oh! how I hate to get up in the morning!" Churchill sang.

"Yes, George, we know," the matron laughed softly, "but you should save your voice for the hymns. You'll know them all, I'm sure."

"Very tall, in the hall!" Churchill pronounced.

"I'm sorry – he does fly off on his fancies from time to time," Mrs Mayfield said. "But he's surprisingly lucid when he's in the mood, aren't you, George?"

"Time and again, time and again," Churchill sang in a thin, reedy voice.

Dracup leaned in to ask another question, but Sara motioned him to silence.

"What was that, George?" she asked the old man.

"In time, you'll find it – time in the hole."

Dracup stiffened. Was this just coincidental rambling, or perhaps –?

"Dracup, Dracup." Churchill leaned back in his chair and closed his eyes. "Theodore Dracup –"

Dracup's heart lurched. "That's it, George. My grandfather. Your friend. Theodore." He held his breath but the old man seemed to have gone somewhere else in his mind. He lay back in the wheelchair, smiling, eyelids fluttering. Dracup swallowed and bit his bottom lip in frustration. Sara signalled patience.

"A shame, shame. What they did. Lali, lali. We found it –" Churchill's eyes shot open and he leaned forward. The vacant look on his face had been replaced with one of urgency. "You're a Dracup? Well, yes, you look a bit like him –"

Dracup moved back in alarm. The change in Churchill was disconcerting. "I'm Theodore's grandson, George. But I don't understand what you mean." He looked around but the matron and care assistant had left them to it. Mrs Mayfield was talking to a newcomer, a young man with cropped hair, dressed in black with a starched white collar. The service was about to begin. "I need to know *where*, George – Theodore needs to know," he added desperately. *"Where* did you find it?"

"He's left it for you, he told me. In time you'll find it." Churchill fell back, exhausted.

The care assistant was at Dracup's elbow. "I think he's had enough for the moment. He'll fall asleep during the service, you'll see. Pull your chairs round and you can sit with him."

Dracup heard little of the service. The words of the hymns floated around him, rising and falling in the fragile pitch of tired, worn voices. His mind was racing. There was something left, some residue of experience in Churchill's mind. Somewhere in that frail cranium lay the secrets that could save his daughter. But how to access them? Dracup racked his own brains, playing with keywords that might help the old man remember. He realized that the service had ended only when a portly female care assistant came in with a tea trolley, causing the young minister to conclude his closing prayer with, it seemed to Dracup, irreverent abruptness.

"Tea time all. What'll it be, Doreen?" She began to move around the room taking orders.

Dracup turned to Sara. "You try. You seem to have the touch."

Churchill had his eyes closed again but the muscles in his thin face worked beneath the yellowed, parchment-like skin.

"Come on, George," Sara said, cheerily. "We have to go soon. Tell me about Dracup. About what he wrote in his diary."

"Diary? All the time he wrote. Did some drawing for me."

"That's it, George." Dracup felt a glimmer of hope. "Fascinating drawings. And he wrote in cuneiform. Do you remember?"

"Best that way," Churchill muttered as if to himself. "Can't tell anyone."

"You can tell us, George," Sara replied softly. "Mr Dracup is family."

Churchill looked up and studied Sara intently. Dracup felt as if some spark of recognition had ignited briefly, then been extinguished. "Are you?" Churchill said quietly. "I don't know you. You look like one of *them*."

Dracup's patience was nearing its end. "What does it mean, George? 'In time you will find the whole.' It's very important. A matter of life and death. My daughter – Theodore's great granddaughter –"

Churchill threw back his head and laughed, a harsh cracking sound. Some of the residents turned around and stared in alarm. "Life and death. Yes. From the beginning. And they want to change it." He put a scrawny arm out and grabbed Dracup's wrist. "Be careful. It's not for us to change."

Dracup shook his head in bewilderment. *Great, more riddles. That's all we need.*

"Reverend Burton is leaving now," Mrs Mayfield announced from the centre of the room. "One last hymn before he goes?" She beamed at the assembled ranks. "What's that, Maisie? All things bright and ... yes, number 243 on your hymn sheets."

"This is going nowhere," Dracup said to Sara, who returned a brief, sympathetic smile.

"You're right. It might be worth coming back later. He's too distracted – too much going on." Sara patted Churchill on the shoulder. "Cheerio, old fellow. We'll pop in another time."

Dracup looked back as they made a tactful departure. Churchill was sitting erect in the chair. He grinned as he sang: *"The ripe fruits in the garden, He made them every one..."*

And then Churchill did something strange. He held up his arm and waved it slowly from side to side. The chorus finished and Dracup heard him singing in a high falsetto: *"Tick tock tick tock – in the forest it's seven past seven o'clock."*

"All right, George," the matron said. "Never mind that. Last verse – here we are..."

"He gave us eyes to see them and lips that we might tell..."

Dracup felt a cold thrill run through his body. Churchill grinned back and sang on.

"All things wise and wonderful, The Lord God made them all."

The chorus receded into the background as they found their way along the corridors to the front entrance. Dracup gripped Sara's arm as they exited into the cold, clear air of the car park, their breath leaving white trails behind them.

She looked at him in astonishment. "What? What is it?"

"The clock. Don't you see? That's what he was telling us. *In the forest it's seven past seven o'clock* he sang. Remember Theodore's message? *In time you will find the whole?*" Dracup dragged Sara to the car. "Come on. Quickly. Whatever my grandfather intended to be found, it's in the clock at Forest Avenue."

Chapter 9

"Okay, come on. Let's have it," Potzner yelled, preempting the knock at his office door. Several lab-coated individuals burst into the room, preceded by a slight, bespectacled character Potzner knew as Mike Fish, head of the Forensic Paleontology group.

"Jim. We have a translation for you." Fish removed his glasses and held up a red folder. "But I don't think you're going to thank us for it." He smiled apologetically.

"Try me."

"Right." Fish drew out a sheaf of paper. The other team members shuffled nervously. One of them dropped a biro.

"In your own time…"

Fish glanced up and cleared his throat. "Okay. It's a split message, we think. I mean, we think that around half of the text is missing – there are some connective words that just, well, finish right where they are. Could be that whoever sketched the diagram left out some of the lines. Anyhow, it's definitely cuneiform script, of the style we'd expect to find in or around the Babylonian environs circa 4000 BC."

"And?"

"This is what we've got." He smiled apologetically. "It doesn't make a lot of sense."

"Just spit it out, Fish, will you?" Potzner shoved his chair back and stood up. Fish's colleagues shrank towards the door.

"Right. Here we go. It's very exciting. The use of cuneiform is normally restricted to tablets – writing tablets I mean – and pottery and so on. Soft imprints. It's pretty uncommon having an inscription like this on metalwork. The diarist tells us that the composition of the object is silver, with gold inlay." Fish brushed a stray strand of hair out of his eyes. He was thinning on top and employed a version of the oddly popular comb-over technique, which was, in Potzner's view, the worst form of denial.

"What does it say, Fish?" Potzner spaced the words with a second's pause between each.

"Yeah. Sorry. Right." Fish shuffled his papers. "Okay. Here we go. First line. *From holy resting place to rest upon the water.*"

"Go on."

Fish turned to a colleague who whispered something in response. "Yeah. Well, we're not too sure about this line. We think the name reference is *Noah*, but it may not be. Hard to say. At any rate, it refers to someone about to take an important action. *But Noah, the faithful son...*"

"Action? What action?"

Fish removed his glasses again and polished out an imaginary blemish. "Well, that's the second half of the verse. The one we don't have." He shrugged his thin shoulders.

Potzner grunted. "Next."

"Yeah. This is good. Very clear. *Once more in the earth you will find peace.*"

"If only I could," Potzner said.

One of the technicians grinned, saw Potzner's expression and converted the action to a cough.

"Okay," Fish said. "Two lines to go. *From whence you came.*"

"And –?"

"Nope." Fish smirked. *"Between – between the rivers."*

"I wasn't making a contribution, Fish." Potzner fought his irritation. "Now read it all." He sat on the edge of his desk and snapped his cigarette case open, released a new packet from its cellophane wrapper and began to transfer Marlboros from packet to case.

Fish took a deep breath. "What wouldn't I give to see the real object this guy sketched from. I mean I really have to see the rest of the script to make sense of it all. It's the clearest example –"

"I know. Just read it."

"Okay. Right. Here goes:

> *"From holy resting place to rest upon the water –*
> *But Noah, the faithful son –*
> *Once more in the earth you will find peace –*
> *From whence you came –*
> *Between the rivers –*

"There you go. That's it." Fish nodded conclusively. His assistants smiled and made appreciative noises.

"Anything else?" Potzner asked them. "Any shape, any word, any stroke of the pen, any other diagrams that might help?"

Fish sighed. "I'm afraid not. We don't think anything else cross-refers to this particular diagram. The footnote doesn't really make any sense. It's in a modern idiom. Roughly translated it says –"

"*In time you will find the whole*," Potzner said. "I know."

Fish and his team exchanged surprised glances.

"I don't know why I bother with you guys," Potzner said. "It's kids' stuff."

Dracup inserted his hand carefully into the open door of the grandfather clock. He felt around on either side then slid his hand further up above the door, taking care to avoid contact with the suspended lead weights and pendulum, and was rewarded with the sensation of paper brushing along his searching fingertips.

"Is there something?" Sara asked.

"Yes – I've just got to –" Dracup eased the paper out of its hiding place, "– be careful I don't tear it. It's quite brittle."

"Been there for a while, I guess," Farrell said, chewing thoughtfully on a stick of gum.

"Got it." Dracup removed his hand and inspected his discovery. They all peered at the closely formed writing. "Same as the diary," Sara murmured. "It's him all right."

Dracup felt a familiar weariness creep over him. "Yes, but what on earth does it mean? Come on. Downstairs."

They assembled in the front room and Dracup placed the handwritten note on the table. He rubbed his eyes and gave a sigh of frustration. The note was brief. It said:

L'Chaim Doctor A, and dial a close shave in the nick of time

Dracup found that his mind had gone into a kind of suspended animation. Churchill's revelation had given him a surge of adrenaline and the hope of a quick answer. But the adrenaline had quickly dispersed, leaving him flat and exhausted. His grandfather's strange words danced before him. He looked at his watch, wondering how much progress Potzner had made. Best give the American a few more hours before phoning in – he was confident Potzner would contact him with any news. And he in turn would want an update. "I need a coffee," Dracup told them, and went into the kitchen.

As he waited for the kettle he thought about his aunt. How much had she known about all this? Perhaps she had kept herself in deliberate ignorance. The diary had remained at McPherson & McPherson's offices. She hadn't discovered the message in the clock, placed there by his grandfather probably some time before his committal. It was almost as if his grandfather *knew* what was likely to happen and had been able – rationally able – to leave markers for whoever followed, for whoever *needed* to follow in his footsteps. This was not a legacy of dementia but the premeditated act of a man intent on putting some wrong to rights. There had been something wrong about the second expedition; something had been done that should not have been done. It had not been in Theodore Dracup's power to undo his actions, but he had seen to it that there *would* be a way for someone in the future to do just that; someone to make amends. Someone –

Dracup ran into the lounge. "The salutation is the easy bit."

Sara looked up and frowned. "What?"

"*L'Chaim!* is a Jewish exhortation to good health. It literally means 'To life!' or, as we would say, 'Cheers!' when we raise a glass."

75

"Okay." Her forehead creased again. "But *Doctor A?*"

"Come on – abbreviate *'Doctor'*." Dracup's excitement was rising. "It's not a reference to my profession – he couldn't have known that."

Sara snapped her fingers. "Of course! You drink from a cup; a Dr-a-cup." She blanched. "It's personal... to you."

Dracup nodded. "It seems that way. I was just thinking about Theodore. About what he did. He *meant* me to find this."

"Nice going," Farrell said. "But you ain't home and dry yet."

"Thanks, Farrell." Dracup sank back into the armchair. "Do feel free to make a contribution."

"So," Farrell said. "You got a dial, a shave and a nick. Take each in turn."

"Something on the clock?" Sara suggested, lips pursed in concentration. "You know – a dial. A cog or something like that."

Dracup exhaled deeply. "Maybe. Or a phone?"

"I'd guess not," Farrell said. "We're talking a long time ago. Telephones wouldn't be in common use."

"True. And dial what? There's no number, and even if there were it would be out of date," Sara offered.

"How about the *shave* bit?" Dracup asked them. He looked at Sara expectantly – this was her forte, but her face again wore a puzzled expression. Just when he needed her intellect she was closing down on him. He bit his lip, trying to mask his frustration. They had to make some progress soon before the trail went completely cold.

"*Close* shave," Farrell corrected. "Like something bad just avoided... but the last part – *nick of time* – maybe something really urgent..."

"Yes," Dracup agreed. "It implies precision – the critical moment, the exact instant at which something *has* to take place." Dracup pondered silently for a second or so, then, thinking aloud: "The idea being that a 'nick' is a narrow and precise marker, so if something is 'in the nick' it's *precisely* where it should be."

"Narrow and precise markers. Like the hands of a clock," Farrell said.

Dracup snapped his fingers. "That's it. Yes. Nick *of time*." He was on his feet. "Seven past seven." Dracup banged his forehead with his fist. "What's wrong with me?"

Sara stood in front of him and stroked his cheek. "Simon. You're under strain. It's hardly surprising you're not thinking straight." She kissed him lightly on the lips. "That's what I'm here for, okay?"

Dracup squeezed her hand and forced a smile. "Yes. Thanks. I know."

Farrell was diplomatically looking out of the window. "You goin' to take another look at the timepiece, or what?"

They gathered on the top landing around the clock. "Kind of appropriate, wouldn't you say?" Farrell said, running his fingers up and down the dark mahogany.

"What's that?"

"Your grandfather leaving his messages in a grandfather clock."

"Very astute, Farrell," Dracup said. "But it's the time that's significant. Look." He pointed at the hands, stiffened into their positions by the passing of the years.

"That'd be seven minutes past seven by my reckoning all right," Farrell said.

"Exactly. That's what Churchill was telling us."

"But how do we know the hands haven't moved since your grandfather placed the note in the clock?" Sara asked.

Dracup thought for a moment. "We don't. But there's no indication that this has been working at all in recent times. The only person who would have bothered to do anything with it was my aunt – and she clearly hasn't. Besides, apart from Churchill there's something else that makes me pretty sure that the hands are as Theodore left them."

Sara shook her head. "Sorry. You've lost me now."

"The number seven has great significance in Jewish scripture. And as we appear to be dealing with the legacy of a man who was rescued from a flood by the God of the Jewish scriptures, the use of the number seven is curiously appropriate."

"Sure is," Farrell said. "In the Old Testament seven makes an appearance right away. Creation in seven days, then there's seven days in the week. Also seven graces, seven deadly sins, seven divisions in the Lord's Prayer and seven ages in the life of man. Among the Hebrews every seventh year was sabbatical, and seven times seven years was the jubilee. The three great Jewish feasts lasted seven days, and between the first and second were seven weeks." Farrell paused briefly, then added, "Oh yeah, the Levitical purifications lasted seven days too."

Sara laughed aloud. "I'll take your word for it. Is that it?"

"Let's see." Farrell looked heavenwards as if for inspiration. "Ah, not quite. Naaman was commanded to dip seven times in the river Jordan to be cured of leprosy. The prophet Elijah sent his servant seven times to look out for rain. Ten times seven Israelites went to Egypt, and the exile lasted the same number of years. There were ten times seven elders. And Pharaoh in his dream saw seven years for each of his wives. My favourite story was the fall of Jericho," Farrell smiled fondly at the recollection, "when seven priests with seven trumpets marched round Jericho once every day and then seven times on the seventh day. Then the walls came down."

Dracup looked at Farrell and shook his head slowly. "All right, Farrell, we get the picture. But these sevens mean something a little closer to home." As he uttered the last word, Dracup had a thought. Home. His grandfather's home. It had been sold, but maybe... The clock would have been in situ at the *old* house, not his aunt's, when Theodore had left these clues. *Dial a close shave.* What had been his grandfather's address? 14 St Andrew's *Close.* "I think we're looking at something left at his old address." Dracup felt a surge of excitement. "Sara – you found some old photos in the bureau? I need to see them."

"They were just some old black and whites," Sara said.

"But they were outdoor photos? Of the garden, weren't they?"

"I think so."

Dracup bounded down the stairs into the front room. He seized the pile of photos and papers from the open bureau. Where was the garden shot?

"Hey. Careful – I have a system going here," Sara said, hard on Dracup's heels.

"Don't worry. I'm just after – ah. Here." Dracup held up a photograph and waved it. "This is it. Take a look. What do you see?"

Farrell and Sara peered over his shoulder at the image. "Coupla people. Grass. Trees. House in the background." Farrell clicked his tongue. "Not a lot else."

"Come on. Look again," Dracup said. Surely they would get it. He was right, he knew it. He *had* to be right.

Sara ran a hand through her hair and massaged her neck, yawning. "Simon, I can't see anything. Explain."

"In the middle of the garden." He clapped a hand to his forehead.

"An ornament of some kind," Farrell said.

"Brilliant. What sort of ornament?" Dracup was almost jigging in frustration now. Sara was usually razor sharp. Why couldn't she see it?

"A bird table?"

"Bird table my backside. Come on. Think."

"I give up, Simon. Tell us." Sara flopped onto the sofa and folded her arms.

"It's a *sundial. Dial* a close shave in the nick of time."

Farrell's expression brightened. "Good job, Mr Dracup." The American gave the briefest of grins before a frown reappeared on his forehead. "But what the heck shaving's got to do with it beats me."

Sara's mobile beeped. She reached into her handbag and fished it out.

Dracup frowned in dismay. Surely she wouldn't take the call now? Not now they were getting close...

"Excuse me a sec." Sara left the room.

Shaking his head in dismay, Dracup turned back to the photograph. He was within reach of something at last, something tangible. "Give me a chance, Farrell," Dracup said. "What have we got so far? Two sevens and a sundial."

"Yeah, seven... but seven what?" Farrell took the photo from Dracup and frowned.

Dracup clicked his fingers and paced the room. "We'll just have to go and take a look. Of course the house is no longer in the family; we'll have to pay a clandestine visit." Or could they just knock on the door? Something lay hidden in the garden of Theodore's old house. Near the sundial. Seven *something* from the sundial. He looked out onto the street. The rain was sheeting down; fleeting figures scurried by packaged in mackintoshes and thick scarves, their umbrellas wayward in the northeasterly blast sweeping in from the sea. Hard to think about sundials with a backdrop like this… Dracup ran his finger down the glass, traced the number seven in the condensation, and watched the water gather then ripple down the pane, distorting the outline he had made.

"Cracked it yet?" Sara came in and gave Farrell a smile that said *come on smarty-pants, let's see you get this one.* Dracup knew the expression. It was when Sara had the answer and knew that no one else did.

Farrell read her meaning. "I'm working on it."

Dracup watched Sara slide her mobile into her handbag, but there was something covert about her expression. "Who was that?" he asked her. "Problems?"

Sara's eyes met his then lowered. "Tell you later. It's probably nothing."

"Sure?" Dracup sensed a change in Sara. It clearly wasn't nothing.

"It's fine – don't worry."

"I'm not, I just –"

"Occam." Farrell said.

They both turned to the American and Sara grinned. "Ah ha. Not just a pretty face then."

Dracup racked his brains. Occam. It rang a bell, but a very distant one.

"Occam's razor," Farrell said. "You never heard of that, Mr Dracup?"

Chapter 10

Ruth felt the cool grains beneath her toes and knew at last that she was home. It had been a long journey, the last leg being the most stressful as always. Ruth was nervous in the presence of outsiders, especially when the outsiders in question wore uniform and carried machine pistols. But they were meek under Kadesh's authority, servants to do their bidding in innocence and ignorance, just as he had told her. Her heart had begun to beat faster as the jeep rolled onwards towards the beloved place, a place that had been sullied and empty for so long. But now, all was restored. She felt a profound peace, despite her misgivings about the girl and Kadesh's motives for taking her. She wanted to see, to feel, to worship and rejoice with the others. She felt the girl squeeze her hand and the dark eyes looked up at her in a silent plea for reassurance.

"It's all right, my little one. I'm here. I won't leave you. We must hurry – I have to show you something wonderful."

"I want my mummy," the girl spoke for the first time since the plane had touched down. "When is she coming?"

Ahead of them in the dim glow of the tunnel Ruth could see Kadesh's tall figure walking purposefully onwards. Ruth heard the gentle thrumming of song and knew that they were close to their destination. "Your mummy will be fine," Ruth told her. "She'll be pleased that I'm looking after you."

"But she doesn't know you," the girl said. She stumbled and fell onto one knee. Ruth bent and helped her up.

"It's only a graze. You're all right."

The girl bit her lip and began to cry. "I want to phone her. I don't like it here."

"Look, here's your dolly," Ruth said. She bent down and stroked Natasha's cheek. "Give her a cuddle and you'll feel better."

The girl took the doll and held it close. They walked on, towards the light.

Ruth was sitting quietly in her chamber where she had made a bed for Natasha. The room was furnished with colourful embroideries and wall hangings, many of which dated back to when Ruth was a girl herself. "Do you like them?" she asked Natasha, who was running her hand up and down the silk curtains enclosing Ruth's bed. "I can make some for you as well."

"Am I staying for a long time?" Natasha asked quietly. She flicked the curtains back and forth.

"I don't know, Natasha. It's not my decision. Kadesh will tell you when he is ready."

"I'm scared of him. I don't like him." Natasha sat on the bed, hands clasped together. "This is a funny place. Why do you live here? What were you singing about in that cave?" She toyed with her hair, looking around the chamber with curious eyes.

"Here, let me plait it for you. It'll keep you cool." Ruth sat next to the girl and began to work on the thick, dark tresses, wondering how much to tell her. "You have beautiful hair. I imagine your father is proud of you."

"I don't see my daddy much."

"Oh? Does that make you sad?"

"Sometimes. My mummy has a new boyfriend, though. He's my daddy now."

"Well, that's nice. But your daddy will always be your daddy. I expect he misses you a lot." Ruth's hands worked dexterously, twisting and looping. "Is your daddy a nice man?"

"Yes. But he gets a bit impatient sometimes. Mummy says that's because he's very clever." Natasha brightened. "He said he was going to take me swimming." She turned to Ruth and the confusion showed in her face. "But I don't know when – maybe he came to see me and I wasn't there." Now her face crumpled altogether. "And my mummy doesn't know where I am. I want to see her. *Please.*"

"Oh, Natasha." Ruth held the girl and rubbed her heaving shoulders gently. "I'm so sorry. You weren't meant to be here. I don't know why he –"

"You know." Kadesh was standing at the chamber entrance. "You know very well why."

Ruth felt Natasha jump in fear, and hugged her protectively to her breast. She raised her chin defiantly. "Why prolong this any further? Let the girl go. At least let her speak to her mother."

Kadesh stroked Natasha's hair. "Not until I have what I want."

Ruth felt the girl stiffen in her arms. *But I want you. Can't you see that? Despite everything, I still want you.* She held her head up proudly. "Is that what this is all about? About you, and what *you* want? Since when has that ever been the right way? We are not made for self, Kadesh; we are made to watch and to protect. Nothing else."

Kadesh's eyes blazed in the filtered twilight. "His family perpetrated the evil. His family shall pay."

"But it's not just that, is it, Kadesh? It's *her*. I *know* it's her." Ruth felt her self-control slipping away. She had already said too much, but she couldn't stop. Natasha was trembling, curled up on the bed. Ruth stood between Natasha and the man she loved. "What about me? We were promised to each other." Ruth held up her hand. "What am I to do? Will you cast me off like an old cloak?"

"It is my business to act as I see fit." He caught her arm and held it tightly. "Do not question me again, Ruth." He turned to leave, then paused in the doorway, his lean frame casting a pencil-thin shadow in the pale light. "Come to the central chamber at sunset. There is a disciplinary matter to attend to." In a moment Kadesh was gone, leaving the faintest trace of incense hanging in the still air of the chamber.

Ruth let her breath out in a half sob, taking comfort from the child's warm body. She had been taken from despair to elation and back in the space of an afternoon; the resultant confusion of feelings left her with nothing but a growing sense of emptiness and dread. "My sweet, my sweet," she muttered, rocking Natasha slowly back and forth. "What will become of us? What will become of us both?"

That night, Ruth dreamt the dreams of a child. Her mother cradled her, whispered words of love. They moved silently through the familiar passages but their path ahead was strewn with flowers and the scents were those of high summer and celebration. Her mother smiled and set her down. A great gathering rose up to welcome them into the central chamber and her heart gave a small lurch when she saw him waiting. How handsome he looked, dressed in robes of white with his dark hair tied loosely back against the brown skin of his neck. She was a woman now, her steps assured and confident. She joined her love at the centre of the chamber and felt her mother's blessing settle upon them like a gentle rain. The assembled ranks opened their mouths in silent song and she felt the thrill of destiny running through her veins. She turned to look into his eyes, but he was gone. The girl, Natasha, stood before her, her face unsmiling, accusing. A voice in her head spoke clearly: *Why are you letting him do this? Look at me; I am only eight years old...*

Ruth woke with a start. She heard the sounds of gentle breathing from the bed of down and silk she had fashioned for Natasha, and her feet carried her automatically to where the girl lay. As she looked at the girl's sleeping face the images of her dream fell away from her like fragments of translucent glass. She returned to her bed and found it cold and comfortless, eventually drifting into a half slumber as the first sounds of prayer issued forth along the tunnels and pathways of her home. High above the dawn sun sent probing fingers of light across the ancient sand, highlighting the criss-crossing of vapour trails in an otherwise unbroken sky.

Chapter 11

"Occam's razor?" I know it – I've heard that somewhere..." Dracup tugged at his beard with irritation. "It's a methodology, isn't it? The best way to approach a problem?"

"Correct," Sara said. "Agreed, Farrell?"

"You're right. It's a logical principle," Farrell nodded. "Basically it goes something like this – 'don't make more assumptions than the minimum needed.'"

"In other words, you 'shave off' any concepts or variables that are not needed to explain or get to the bottom of what you're trying to figure out," Sara said.

"Good." Dracup looked at Farrell. "So come on then. Apply that to two sevens and a sundial."

"Well, how about 'find the angle on the sundial for seven and take seven paces in that direction.'"

Sara gestured in a *comme ci, comme ça* fashion. "Could be."

"And then what?" Dracup shrugged. "Dig a hole?" It seemed simplistic, but then that was the point Occam had tried to get over with his 'razor'. Dracup rubbed his eyes wearily.

"Depends where the seven paces takes you, I guess," Farrell offered. 'If it's diggable, dig there. Just hope it ain't concrete."

Dracup sighed. He was just going to have to find out by trial and error. "Right. That's settled then. Tonight we do some midnight excavating."

"Simon?" Sara said quietly. "Can we have a word?"

"Yes. Of course."

"In private."

"Oh." He looked at Farrell apologetically. "Excuse us a moment."

The American waved a dismissive hand. "No problem. Just pretend I'm not here."

In the kitchen, Sara leaned on the draining board and folded her arms. "Simon, I'm really sorry. I have to go back south. Something's come up. It's nothing awful – don't look at me like that."

Dracup's first reaction was cautious relief. "Anything I can do?"

Sara laughed softly. "You've enough on your plate without my problems as well. Don't look so crestfallen." She moved towards him and put her arms around his waist. "It's just some domestic bother. I'll sort it out, but I have to deal with it straight away."

"Want to tell me about it?"

She tilted her head to one side and sighed. "Compared to your problems it's nothing. Maria wants me to vet the new girl before she signs up."

"Your new flatmate?" He knew she'd had issues with her landlady before – the Spanish owner of her rented house. Still, this was a bit sudden. He gave her a tight smile. "When do you need to leave?"

"Asap really. If you drop me at the airport I can be back home tonight."

"That urgent?"

She shrugged. "I'm really sorry. You know what Maria's like. She wants to see me first thing tomorrow." She tapped him lightly on the nose. "But keep me in touch – I can still use my brain in transit."

Dracup felt a strange foreboding. "Right. Sure. I'll call the airport."

Two hours later Dracup returned to Forest Avenue with a heavy heart. She had held him tightly in the departure lounge; her lips had spoken the expected words – "See you soon" – but Dracup worried that her eyes had said something else.

Potzner was thinking about his wife, enduring her post-lunchtime chemo. He wanted to call; to tell her that their dreams had come true, that he had the answer to her condition. *Here, just take this, my darling – our guys have come up with something to regenerate your damaged cells; the cancer cells will be destroyed and re-*

placed. And your new cells will be better than before. Stronger. Longer lasting. You've never seen anything like this. Trust me. Everything's going to be fine. We're going to live forever, you and me. Imagine that! We're going to live forever.

He rubbed his eyes and stretched back in his chair. The afternoon had sped past like a runaway automobile. And had ended a write-off. How did he feel? Disappointed. Despairing. *Desperate?* The phone rang. He sighed deeply and snatched the buzzing receiver from its cradle.

"Yeah? Oh, Mr Dracup. How's it going?" Potzner listened carefully. "Yep. Right. Okay, that sounds very promising. I kind of had a feeling that old Theodore had a trick or two up his sleeve. How's Farrell shaping up?" Potzner gave a sardonic grin as he listened to Dracup's reply. Farrell had an IQ of 158 and had scored the top results in his training year – in fact his had been the highest mark obtained in the Department's rigorous logic and numeracy tests since 1969. All packaged up in a baseball star's physique. Even Potzner thought he was too good to be true.

"He does what? Yeah, I know. But then he'll come out with something that'll blow you away – what's that? Sevens?" Potzner gave a short laugh. "Yeah, just like that."

Potzner's PC beeped as a new email arrived. He glanced at it briefly. It was from Art Keegan, head of Molecular Biology. He knew what it would say; he'd been expecting it. He opened his drawer and extracted his A4 notepad. "Well, Mr Dracup, I wish I had some encouraging news from this end, but the fact is I don't. What I do have is a translation of the cuneiform verses from the diagram. You want to hear them?" Potzner smiled wryly. "Yeah, I know. They don't make a lot of sense on their own. Here they are, for what it's worth:

> *"From holy resting place to rest upon the water –*
> *But Noah, the faithful son –*
> *Once more in the earth you will find peace –*
> *From whence you came –*
> *Between the rivers –'*

"That's all we've got so far." He paused, listening to the precise enunciation of the Englishman's voice. "Okay. Well, tread carefully – I don't need the police after you on top of everything else. Farrell will take care of any problems." Potzner wondered briefly whether he should share the flickering electronic information with Dracup, then quickly decided against it. There was nothing to be gained from confirming that the Department's hopes were resting on the conundrums of a deceased, mentally unstable geologist and his grandson's determination to find a missing daughter. Potzner hoped the daughter was still alive, but had his doubts. He didn't share that thought with Dracup either. He signed off and stared at the screen.

Hi Jim –

Project: RED EARTH – Status: Highly sensitive

As requested, here is an update on exactly where we are with the research – or rather, where we got to before the 'problem'. I'll try and keep this as simple as possible. You'll be aware that the study of chromosomes and cell regeneration/division has been central to this research program, particularly with regard to telometric longevity and length.

Telomeres, as I've outlined before, are effectively the 'tip' of any given chromosome, and we became convinced that the composition and length of these tips was the key to understanding the ageing process with its associated links to health in old age and the human life span. Now, a cell's normal life is around 50 divisions, and tests on a cross-section of human subjects have shown that cells that have stopped dividing have <u>much</u> shorter telomeres.

Telomeres become shorter with time because unlike the rest of a chromosome, they don't replicate during cell division. The shortening of these tips acts like a sort of clock, which ultimately causes the cell to slow down and stop working. There has been some experimentation with an enzyme called telomerase that slows the erosion of these telomeres – and lab experiments with this enzyme have met with some success, although I wouldn't personally consider these to be spectacular. What it did tell us – or what we understood from the results of these experiments – is that we were on the right research track.

The right track. Potzner ran a hand through his greying crew cut. So close. So near to a breakthrough. How could it have happened? Just as he was coming to terms with the possibility of salvation, just as he had begun to dare to hope... His fists bunched and he read on.

Then came the Red Earth material – well, you remember how we found the telometric loop anomalies – it proved the point. These were super telomeres like we'd never seen before in any subject. There appeared to be no degeneration or shortening of telometric strands despite the obvious age of the material. I can now say conclusively that the age of the subject was in excess of 500 years – possibly older – at the time of death. Death was caused not by 'normal' cell senescence but by something else. What that is right now I can't say – I'd need more tissue samples to reach a conclusion as the original material is breaking down rapidly, which is no surprise given that we had to perform an invasive operation just to get through the resin block. Incidentally, we are still unsure of the composition of this outer coating – whatever it is, it's not something we've seen before and its preservative qualities are nothing less than astonishing. Nevertheless, the small sample we retained also seems to be degenerating too fast for us to save.

In summary, Jim, I'm real sorry – I know what this means to you, believe me, but I can't proceed without fresh material derived from the source.

Do let me know if you need any more information at this stage.

Kind rgds

Art Keegan,

Head Dept. Molec. Biology
Mob: 07720 8732567

Potzner looked at the solitary photograph on his desk. It was a fun shot, taken before Abigail had become housebound. They were in an amusement arcade and Abi had just won the jackpot. Some passing trucker had offered to take their photo to mark the occasion. She looked so... so carefree. So happy. He picked up the frame and etched a kiss onto her celluloid cheek, then placed the photograph carefully back in its usual position. *Everything's going to be fine. We're going to live forever, you and me, babe. Imagine that! We're going to live forever...*

He held his head in his hands and wept.

Dracup peered cautiously over the low wall. It didn't give him much cover, but at least the sky was moonless and the expanse of the garden lay in comforting shadow. He stepped forward gingerly into the open. Immediately he felt exposed and foolish. What was he doing in a stranger's garden in the middle of the night? And yet, it was not an unfamiliar landscape. He had been here long ago, in another life. How old had he been? Eight or nine? A pang of grief stabbed home. Natasha's age. The thought gave him a fresh focus, and he peered into the darkness, searching for the marker he prayed was still in position. The sundial. If it had gone, leaving no reference point... No! There was something, a broken contour on the flatness of the grass.

He edged carefully up the lawn, keeping to the borders and fearful that some hidden security light would flood the garden and leave him stranded in its glare like a fly in a spider's web. Dracup risked a glance to where Farrell stood guard at the gate. It was hard to pick the agent out, but then Dracup discerned a movement against the whitewash of the house. A second later a torch flashed once. All okay. They had simply walked up the drive, Dracup conscious of the weight of the shovel in his hand, Farrell striding ahead confidently. Business as usual for him.

The house was in darkness, with only a single light showing upstairs, candle-like behind the small window – probably the bathroom. The place was comfortably asleep. *And so it should be,* Dracup thought. *It's 3.30 in the morning.* He held his breath as he moved slowly forward towards the object. He realized he was grinding his teeth, as he used to in his parents' home when he wanted to creep down the old staircase without alerting the grown-ups to his presence; he imagined the noise of his teeth rubbing together would obscure any noise issuing from his own movements. Dracup shook his head. *Nuts. You've always been a bit nuts.* Now the stillness had a volume all of its own which seemed more unsettling.

Something rustled in the hedgerow and he dropped to his haunches, crouching low. He waited thirty seconds. Nothing jumped out at him. No lights flicked on. *Keep moving.* He took a breath and went forward again. Sara would be home by now, fast asleep in her own bed. *Or maybe not. Maybe she's somewhere else altogether.* He shook his head, unable to sustain the thought. He felt diminished without her, as if some central process inside him had been shut down.

Enough. Concentrate. He reached the object and squatted next to it, running his hands over the stone column. Relief washed through him. The sundial still presided over the garden, a solid connection between now and the past. He traced the Roman numerals. Five, six, *seven.* Dracup looked to see the direction of the angle created by the *VII*. He measured seven reasonable paces from the dial and found himself by the herbaceous border. With some misgivings and considerable sympathy for the owners he began to dig. The noise jarred his senses, and he worked the shovel as cautiously as he could into the stiff earth, keeping one eye nervously on the Farrell corner of the property.

After a few minutes he had succeeded only in creating a superficial hole, no more than a hand's breadth into the stubborn soil. He bit his lip in frustration. He couldn't even be sure he was digging in the right place. Dracup retraced his steps to the sundial and measured out another seven paces. It brought him to the same spot. With a sigh of resignation he resumed the laborious task of softening the earth with the edge of the spade. Sweat ran down his back as he worked, and soon his shirt was soaked through. To add to his discomfort it began to rain, lightly at first but then more persistently. Dracup cursed as he toiled away until he realized the rain was beginning to work for him, rather than against him. The more soil he exposed, the more effective the softening rain became.

Thirty minutes later he was standing at the side of a muddy pit several feet deep. Panting, he stood back to assess his handiwork. He heard the thrum of an engine accelerating past the house. Somewhere out towards the city a siren's wail rose and fell. Dracup returned to his work, probing with the spade into the thick mud. Farrell remained out of sight. Dracup hoped he was awake, then realized he had never actually seen the American sleep; he seemed to be on perpetual alert.

The spade hit an unyielding portion of his hole, returning a hollow sound that made Dracup jump in surprise. He threw the spade aside and got down on his hands and knees, scrabbling to clear the detritus away from whatever he had uncovered.

Five minutes later he had exposed the rectangular shape of what appeared to be the lid of a metallic container. Several minutes' more effort and he had cleared space enough to get his hands under the container and free it from its bed of earth. It was heavier than he expected for its size, but eventually he gained enough purchase to lift it out and set it down carefully beside its former resting place. Dracup sat, exhausted on the damp grass, feeling the rain trickle down his mud-spattered face. He was about to signal Farrell to give him a hand when some intuition made him change his mind.

The box opened easily, and Dracup shone his pencil torch into its depths. Within lay the object from Theodore's sketch. Elated, Dracup pulled the perished covering aside. Beside it, also wrapped in what appeared to be some kind of waterproof cloth, was a smaller square parcel. Dracup stole a furtive look towards the house. He flashed the torch in a prearranged signal. For a moment there was nothing, then Farrell's torch pierced the darkness. Good.

He had time. Dracup uncovered the smaller parcel and extracted the contents.

He peered at it, running the beam across its surface. It was a wax writing tablet, similar to those he had seen in museums and on boyhood excursions to Roman villas, but clearly modern because it was inscribed with that familiar hand he knew belonged to Theodore. But now was not the time for a lengthy perusal. He re-wrapped the tablet and placed it carefully in his coat pocket, then quickly replaced the lid and signalled to Farrell for assistance. As he waited for the agent he marvelled at Theodore's provision; he was gaining a healthy respect for his grandfather. What better way to preserve a buried message than to inscribe it on wax? Theodore had been neither fool nor lunatic, but something had happened to him, something destabilizing. Dracup watched Farrell's noiseless approach. He patted his pocket protectively. Whatever Theodore had intended to communicate, Dracup wasn't prepared to share it with Potzner's team. Not yet.

Chapter 12

They were assembled in the great chamber. Ruth held Natasha's hand and waited for Kadesh to make his entrance. She was nervous. He had mentioned a matter of discipline, but it was not the usual practice of the *Korumak Tanri* to air such things in public. Over and over her mind was repeating like a mantra: *It is not our way. It has never been our way.* The chanting began, quietly at first, like a gentle wave breaking on a distant shore, then louder, growing in volume until the whole chamber was filled with the resonance of song and subtle drum beat. Ruth felt her heart pounding and joined in with the familiar words.

She looked at Natasha. Her eyes were closed and she was swaying gently with the lilting rhythm. Her growing attachment to the girl gave her new concerns, concerns that overrode even the unwelcome forebodings she had experienced since their arrival. It should be a time of rejoicing, but the unsettled atmosphere was distracting. She couldn't remember a time when she had felt so exposed, so *unprotected*. Furthermore, the directness with which she had spoken to Kadesh frightened her. She hadn't believed herself capable of such boldness. But she knew the truth. She hesitated in her recital of the ancient verses and bowed her head low, allowing the knowledge to run free in her mind. *It will never be. He does not want me. He wants someone else.*

She raised her head before anyone noticed her distraction and caught Jassim's eye. He smiled at her reassuringly. At least she had her brother to offer some measure of sympathy. But he was a man, and as such could not enter into discussions of intimacy, of passion, of longing. And, like everyone else, he was under Kadesh's authority.

She felt a tug on her sleeve and found Natasha's face looking up at her. "I'm thirsty."

"We have to wait, 'Tash. Kadesh will speak with us soon."

"Don't call me that. Only my mummy and daddy call me that."

Ruth bent and whispered, "What would you like me to call you?"

"I don't know. Just Natasha."

"All right. But we must be quiet now." Ruth pointed. A procession had entered the chamber. She recognized most of the male acolytes, led as usual by Kadesh. There was one dressed in red, the traditional colour of celebration, walking beside him. She stood on tiptoe to identify him. It was Ibrahim, her cousin. She knew of his long absence, of his training under Kadesh's guidance. Next to Mukannishum, he was the favoured son. She pursed her lips and wondered at the purpose of the assembly. *A matter of discipline.*

The cortège had reached the centre of the chamber. Kadesh held up his arms. Silence fell immediately, and his commanding voice rang out. "Our legacy has been returned to us and it is right and proper to celebrate. For decades our plans have been laid; our people have been sent forth to integrate and befriend, to work alongside and to learn; to listen and to emulate. To become as one with our offenders. It has been a long journey – a journey fraught with many obstacles and setbacks. But we have overcome by our patience, by our commitment and by our obedience to Him who is eternal. And your praises *are* heard by the most high God. It is He who commands us, not I. It is He who is judge, not I. It is He who watches over us to see that we have not fallen into halfheartedness or worldliness. We must remain set apart, a holy people. He alone has guided our hands and has brought us to this moment of triumph."

The chamber erupted into applause. Ruth felt the words warming her soul. She forgot her misgivings and clapped her hands wildly to the beat of the acolytes. *Our legacy has returned. That is all that matters. I must put my feelings aside for the good of the community. It is right and proper.*

Kadesh's raised hand signalled quiet. "Our brother Ibrahim has also returned. His mission was important to us." Kadesh placed a hand on the young man's shoulder. Ibrahim was shorter, of stocky build, dark eyes alert behind low brows. He seemed at ease, relaxed and confident, continually glancing around the assembly, smiling as he recognized a familiar face. Kadesh's voice went on. "The outsiders who invaded our sanctuary and committed the great act of sacrilege have received justice – not by our hand directly, but from those whom they served. But *they* will not stop until they have found our sanctuary and destroyed it. For they always destroy that which they cannot understand. That which is *different*." Kadesh shook his head emphatically and a murmur of assent rumbled around the hall.

"However, the time of fulfilment is almost upon us. Prophecy will become reality. The world will know the power of God, and we will know his favour!"

Applause broke out again as his words sank in. Ruth's heart was beating with excitement. The fulfilment? Surely not, that she should be so privileged to live in these days –

Kadesh's voice escalated in volume, cutting into her amazement. "For that reason, we must be thorough in everything we do. We must apply rigour. If we slacken we shall fall. Failure will not be tolerated."

"What is he saying?" Natasha whispered to Ruth. Ruth placed a finger over her lips. "Hush. We must not interrupt."

Kadesh's voice filled the space. "Yes, Ibrahim has achieved a *measure* of success. The transgressor's diary is now in our possession. In it are pictures, records of the blasphemous and evil violation of the great boat."

The silence in the chamber was now absolute. All eyes and ears were attentive to the leader. Ruth was fascinated. She had heard of the outsiders' expedition to Noah's great ship – and had longed to see it herself, because of what it had carried. Sometimes she dreamed of the solitary vessel, afloat upon a dead world with nothing but sea and sky surrounding it. In her mind she wandered amongst the animals, feeding them, caring for them, chatting with Noah's sons and their wives. Shem, Ham and Japheth were her friends. She had known them in her visions for as long as she could remember. She made a mental note to describe them to Natasha.

"The boat was raided," Kadesh was saying. "Many treasures were removed, including parts of the sacred staff of Noah. These were deciphered and our home was found, for the inscriptions tell of Ham's journey into the dark land and how his people settled there. They revealed where the *Korumak* had settled. *Here*, where God has placed us away from prying Western eyes. Then the greatest violation of all took place."

Murmurs of anger now reverberated through the chamber. Kadesh raised a hand and silence fell abruptly. He paused, then continued in a low, hoarse whisper. "While the diary remained in Western hands the threat to our security was *always* present. *Always*."

At this point Kadesh looked to Ibrahim who, for the first time, Ruth observed, began to look puzzled. She wondered herself at Kadesh's intent. The diary had been secured, so all was well. *Or was it?*

"Ibrahim has returned to us," Kadesh repeated. "And his return will serve as an illustration for our benefit. He is going to teach us an important lesson."

Ruth turned and looked nervously behind her to see if she could make a swift exit. Something was very wrong. She could sense it. She reached for Natasha's hand and began to back away. The girl shot her a questioning look as the drums began again in a low, insistent rhythm. Ruth was pushing through the packed chamber now, regretting her decision to secure a position near the front. People jostled them disapprovingly as they passed, one woman even grabbing Ruth's clothing to hinder her progress. She prayed that Kadesh would not notice the disruption.

"We are *not* secure," he continued, his voice carrying authoritatively even to the far corners of the chamber, "because the diary was *copied* before our brother recovered it." The last words were spoken in a whisper of judgement. Ruth's heart was beating a tattoo in her chest; the hand that held tightly onto Natasha's was slick with sweat. She was almost pulling the girl along behind her.

"Ibrahim will learn that we cannot tolerate mistakes."

Ruth found the exit passage as the assembly's confused mutterings gained in volume so that Kadesh was forced to raise his voice above the hubbub. Ruth stopped and turned, fixed to the spot in horrified fascination. She saw a glint of metal raised high, heard a moan escape from the crowd in a corporate exhalation of surprise and fear. She pulled Natasha into the tunnel's protective shadow as Ibrahim's screams rang out above the din in a high shriek of despair.

Natasha gave a little cry of pleasure and stepped forward to the water's edge. "Careful now. It's slippery." Ruth steadied the child with her outstretched arm as she scrambled over the mossy stones. Water cascaded down the rock face from the opening high above into a wide, foaming pool, from where it began its final, secretive journey to join the great river. Natasha's delighted eyes danced from the pool to the waterfall and back again. "I like it here!"

"Yes, but it's dangerous too – wait – don't step on that." Ruth grabbed the girl's arm again.

"Ow. You're hurting."

"Yes, but look." Ruth pointed to the far edge of the pool where, masked by the spray, a dark void opened up as the rocky shelf dropped away.

"Ugh. A hole."

"Yes, and you don't want to go down there. It's very deep."

"Have *you* been down there?"

"I have not. It probably goes down a long way. No one goes in there."

"Really? It might be fun."

"We *never* go into an unknown chamber. Now come – we're here to get water, remember?" Ruth bent and dipped her jar into the stream. "Like this. Go on, you try."

Ruth watched Natasha filling her jar. Two days had passed since the public execution, and the atmosphere had changed from celebratory to fearful at a single stroke. Now the writing was on the wall. Kadesh's headship had turned from inspirational to dictatorial. And yet no one had crossed him. No one dared. Ruth's fear for her child hostage grew with each passing hour. She lived for the moment, expecting at any time to hear the footfall at her door that would reveal Kadesh's intentions for her charge. To make matters worse the girl asked questions constantly, questions that had no answers. Why? When? What next?

Mad thoughts chased through Ruth's dreams. She would take the girl and escape. They would leave in the early hours and find a hiding place. Perhaps they would be picked up by the Americans, or the British. By anyone who would protect them from Kadesh. There were vehicles hidden above, she knew. She would make enquiries, find a way to take one and drive into the wilderness. She would hand herself over to insurgents, to anyone except *him*. Perhaps they would even make it to the city, board a plane, fly away to – anywhere. America, perhaps. They would start a new life under assumed names. And, and – Ruth covered her eyes with her hand. It was all impossible. She could never leave him. Not while there was hope. His feelings could change. Perhaps he was distracted, confused, preoccupied by his responsibility. He could love her, surely. And with her gentle spirit, she could change him. He would see how wrong he had been. There would be forgiveness – not without repentance, of course. But he would see. She would be his saviour. He would rule them justly, with her steadying hand on his shoulder, guiding, supporting.

"What's the matter?" Natasha held up her jar. "Look. It's full. I can hardly lift it."

"I'll carry it." Ruth took the jar and let Natasha dip her toes into the water.

"It's freezing!"

"It comes from the mountains – underground all the way. It sees no sunlight until it joins the river."

"Can we go to the river? Is it beautiful?"

"Yes, very beautiful." She smiled at the child's unsullied enthusiasm. "But it is a long way and very dangerous. We cannot come and go as we please."

"What else can we do? I don't expect I'll be here long, will I? I want to see everything."

A male voice spoke. "Has she seen the paintings? She would enjoy those."

Ruth turned to see her brother, Jassim, watching them calmly. His head was uncovered and he wore a long, loose-fitting dishdash with colourful, embroidered cuffs. His beard was short and oil gleamed slickly in his hair.

"Hello brother. Natasha is enjoying the waterfall. She wanted to help me carry the water."

"It's all right. I'm not checking up on you." Jassim smiled and sat informally on a boulder. He threw a pebble into the stream, making it skip across the surface. Ruth relaxed and sat next to him.

"Can I try?" Natasha scooped a handful of stones and began throwing them into the water.

"Not like that. Look." Jassim repeated his trick and guided Natasha's next effort with his own hand. The pebble skipped obligingly across and rattled against the rock face on the far side of the stream. Natasha laughed delightedly.

"So you're Natasha," Jassim said. "I've heard a lot about you."

"She's a good girl," Ruth said. "No trouble."

"I'm sure." Jassim smiled and chucked the girl under her chin. "Very pretty, too."

Natasha giggled. "That's what my dad says."

Jassim nodded seriously. "Well, he's quite right. He is obviously a discerning man."

"What does that mean?"

"It means he can recognize what is beautiful, what is ugly and what is good; what is right and wrong," Ruth said.

Jassim looked away, avoided her eyes. "Yes, that's it." He bent and drew a line on the soft ground, parting the pebbles with his fingers. "Tell me, Natasha, what would your father do if he lost something? Would he look everywhere for it until he found it, or would he become frustrated and decide to do something else instead?"

"Frustrated means angry and annoyed at not being able to do something," Ruth said.

"I know that," Natasha said indignantly.

"See – she is a bright girl," Jassim said.

Natasha chewed her thumb thoughtfully. "He would keep looking until he found it. Once he pulled the carpets up in the lounge to look for his cufflinks. Mummy was very cross. She said he was stubborn and he wouldn't find them there."

"And did he?"

"Yes – and he found Mummy's necklace too, so she wasn't cross any more. She said he was single-minded. And they laughed a lot." Natasha bit her lip. "I remember because they didn't used to do that much."

Jassim nodded attentively. "Adults sometimes behave in ways that are hard to understand. But there is usually a reason. When you are older you will know what I mean. Now then –" he stood up and clapped his hands. "Would you like to see some paintings?"

"Yes. All right."

"You don't sound very sure," Ruth chided. "These are no ordinary paintings."

"They are very old." Jassim frowned. "Some say even older than me."

Natasha giggled, and Ruth forced a smile for the child's sake.

"Come, child," Jassim said. "I will show you." To Ruth he said, "You can collect these later. Leave them where they are." He waved at the water jars. "No –one is going to touch them. We're all friends here."

Ruth raised her eyebrows, but Jassim met her gaze and held it. His eyes said, *Nothing has changed. We just carry on as before.* She sighed, took Natasha's hand and together they followed Jassim's tall figure as he threaded his way confidently along the ancient passageways of their home.

Chapter 13

Dracup pulled into Forest Avenue and eased the car alongside number 185. His back ached and he wanted to inspect the wax tablet. Not with Farrell around, though. Farrell said, "Douse the lights and get down."

"What?"

"Do it, now."

Dracup complied. He half slid onto the floor and compressed his body under the steering column. He knew better than to question Farrell. Someone was onto them. He heard an engine purr alongside, a car door close softly. Dracup held his breath and thanked God that the street lights cast his own vehicle in shadow.

"Keep still," Farrell hissed.

Footsteps alongside. A hesitation. Then receding up the path to his aunt's flat.

Dracup eased his head up. He caught a glimpse of a tall figure silhouetted against the light woodwork of the gate. *Very* tall.

Farrell nudged him again. "Get *down*, Professor."

He'd left the light on in the hallway. That was good. Whoever it was thought they were inside.

"On my say so, start her up and get going," Farrell told him.

"Which direction?"

"Forward would be good."

How many? Dracup wondered. One in the garden, one maybe in the other car. He thought quickly. "Where's their car?"

"Directly in front," Farrell said. "So keep out of sight."

The agent raised his head a fraction. "Another one coming out. Get ready."

Dracup tensed his body. His heart was doing a drum solo.

"On three. One. Two. *Three.*"

Dracup was in the seat, hand fumbling for the ignition. Farrell reached over and flicked the lights on. The engine roared. Dracup pumped the accelerator and the car hurtled forward. He caught a glimpse of a young man in the headlights, bearded, dark skinned, hands thrown up to protect his eyes. Then they were past him and careering down the road.

Farrell was fiddling with something. Dracup looked over and moistened his lips. He saw the magazine, the neat clip of bullets as Farrell loaded the automatic and turned around in his seat. "Okay. Next right."

Dracup hauled the wheel, glanced in his mirror. "Where to?"

"I'll tell you in a while. Just drive."

The wheel was slick with sweat. Dracup drove on.

They turned into a nondescript street on the other side of Aberdeen. There was nothing to distinguish one house from the next. A line of terraces. Anonymous.

"Nice place you have here, Farrell," Dracup said as the agent turned the key and the tatty door swung open.

"It's safe. No, not the hall lights." Farrell held up his hand. "Kitchen's in there."

Dracup laid his wrapped bundle carefully on the kitchen table and sat down. He noticed his hands were trembling. A yellowed cottage clock tacked to the wall told him it was 5.14, but sleep was the last thing on his mind. He unravelled the cloth, exposing the base metal underneath. The smooth locking groove ran the length of the broader upright, confirmation that another, matching piece existed. Dracup ran his fingers over the mottled surface. It was exquisite in design and pattern, true to his grandfather's sketch and more; an artist, however talented, could not hope to capture the intricacy and beauty of the object lying before him. He wondered if modern technology could replicate such workmanship.

As if echoing his own thoughts Farrell let out a soft whistle. "She sure is a beauty." He placed his automatic on the table. "Not surprising they want to get hold of it."

Dracup shifted uncomfortably in his seat. "You're sure they didn't follow us?"

"Sure as I can be." The agent shrugged.

Dracup wasn't convinced by Farrell's casual attitude. He'd feel safer if they kept moving. "Aren't you going to keep an eye on the front?"

"Relax, Prof. We'll get moving shortly. Meantime, you'd best clean yourself up. You don't want to attract any unwelcome attention if we're pulled over."

Dracup looked at his hands. They were thick with dried mud. "The police, you mean? Yes, all right. In a moment." He picked up the object in one hand and hefted it. It *had* to provide the answers he needed. "Look at the engraving – I've never seen anything like it."

"Uh huh. But does it get us any further?"

Dracup felt the weight in his pocket with a slight flux of conscience. He sighed heavily. "It will. It *has* to."

"How about coffee?"

"Farrell, I could get to like you."

The American gave Dracup a puzzled look.

"Sorry. British humour."

Farrell grunted. Dracup slipped off his coat and made for the bathroom, locking the door behind him. His mobile buzzed in his pocket. He pulled out the vibrating instrument and checked the number. Yvonne.

Dracup sat wearily on the toilet and thumbed the answer button. "Hi."

"Simon? I – I'm sorry. I know it's the middle of the night."

"No problem. I was awake anyway."

"I can't sleep. I – I just need someone to talk to."

"Malcolm?"

"Out like a light. He's very busy at work, you know –"

"I know."

"Simon? Where are you? The police have been round again. They've been asking questions about –" Yvonne hesitated.

"What?"

"About you. They want to know where you are. They think –"

Dracup groaned. "I know what they think. They've no leads, so I'm their chief suspect." There was a moment's silence, then:

"Yes."

"Great."

"So?"

"So what?"

"So where *are* you, Simon?"

Dracup let out his breath in a long sigh. "In Aberdeen."

"Scotland? But you've only just –"

"I know. Something came up. I think it may be significant."

A brief pause, then: "Simon, do you know where she is?"

"Not yet. But I'm getting closer."

Dracup heard Yvonne catch her breath. He imagined her standing downstairs in the dim light of the standard lamp, Malcolm unconscious upstairs. When she spoke again her voice was even. He wondered what inner strength sustained her when all she could do was wait. And hope.

"Simon. Do you think she's all right?"

"Yes. Yes, I do. I think she'll be fine. She's as tough as old boots." He gave a short laugh and regretted its hollow sound.

"You don't think she's – I mean –"

"No. I don't." He reached inside his coat pocket and drew out the wax tablet. It was about the size of an envelope. "Listen. I'm sure I know *what's* happened. I'm almost sure *why*. The question I'm working on is *where*."

"It's to do with your aunt, isn't it? Her will."

"Yes. Look, I'm coming back down to Reading tomorrow. I'll keep you in touch, okay? Everything will be fine."

"Are you going to talk to the police?"

"I suspect I'll have no choice in the matter. I don't want them to think I'm running away."

"Can't you tell them what you've found? Then they can investigate, you know. They have procedures –"

"Not for this they don't. Listen, I'm not acting alone. I have help already. The police will just mess things up, complicate everything. It's complicated enough as it is, believe me."

"You okay, Mr Dracup?" Farrell's voice floated through the keyhole.

Dracup covered the phone with his hand. "Fine. On the phone."

"Okay. No problem. Coffee's on the table."

"Who was that?" The tone of Yvonne's voice shifted to one of suspicion.

"A guy I'm working with."

"Who is he? Not a policeman?"

"Sort of. CIA."

Another pause as she took the information in. Then: "Oh God, Simon. What is this? What have you got us into?"

Dracup took a deep breath. "I'll tell you more tomorrow. You should get some sleep," he added gently.

There was a moment's silence across the airwaves. He could imagine her smoothing her hair back from her forehead the way she did when she was anxious about something. "Yes. I suppose I should. And you should too."

"I'll call you tomorrow. Sleep well."

Again the silence. Then, "You too – and Simon?"

"Yes?"

"Bring her home, won't you? Just bring her home."

The line went dead. Dracup sat for a few minutes, listening to the sound of his own breathing. Then he picked up the tablet and began to read.

Sceptre/Staff of Noah – prob. pt crest? B ref. Staff of A? **A** *section alpha…*
Exp. 1920 Smithsn. Retrieved from remains lge aq. vessel. Corresp. Ark of Noah. Ararat, Turkey.
Inscr. – cuneiform, refers cargo of ship in cun. vrse.[Part only]
Projectns. Repr. 3 sons Noah –

Shem, Ham, Japheth
Hamitic/Sth, Semitic M. East/Israel, Japheth/Eur.
Loc. Remaining part staff, trad. Ethiop.
Ityopp'is – Cush – sn of Ham – fnded Axum.
Match. crest. Lal., Ω section 1921, TD,GRC. Left in situ.
Formed basis of expo. 1922 C of Tr.
K. zig. – 7 by 7

Dracup's heart beat faster as he scanned the tight, indented script. *Left in situ.* He replaced the tablet in his pocket and pulled the chain. An image of George Reeves-Churchill came into his head. Perhaps the old man hadn't been raving after all – what was it he had said? *A shame, shame. What they did. Lali, Lali.* Was this a reference to somewhere in Ethiopia? *Match. crest. Lal., 1921.* He remembered Potzner's voice on the phone, the incomplete translation:

From whence you came –
Between the rivers –

Dracup ran a basin full of water and washed the mud off his face, then ran the nailbrush across his fingertips. *Keep going, Dracup, you're one step closer.* He peeled off his wet shirt and lobbed it into the sink. What he needed was a bath and a change of clothes. No time for that. A strip wash would have to do for now.

He exited the bathroom to find Farrell on his haunches, eyes at table height, scrutinising the crest and muttering sounds of admiration. "I'd sure love to know what all this means, Prof – there's a lot more detail than on the sketch."

Dracup looked again at the object he had disinterred. There in the top left hand corner was a clear indentation, set apart from the cuneiform:

A

Alpha. The beginning .He picked up his coffee and took a long swig. "We'll let your boss take a look," Dracup said. He waved his empty mug at Farrell. "Better have another of these. We're heading south."

Dracup turned the key and simultaneously fished out the free sheet protruding from his letter box. He turned to consign it to the depths of the wheelie bin. A thin, wiry man in a fawn coat stood at the bottom of the steps. He looked familiar.

"Professor Simon Dracup?"

"Yes?"

The man advanced up the steps and waved a wallet at him. Dracup had it before he saw the pass details: the DCI from the TV news report.

"DCI Moran – Thames Valley. Can I have a word?"

Dracup opened the door and stood to one side. "Be my guest."

"Thanks."

Dracup followed Moran into the flat. It felt cold, unlived in. He found the boiler and turned the heating on. Moran was standing in the centre of the room checking it out, ceiling to floor. He reminded Dracup of a ferret.

"Can I offer you a drink?"

"Tea, thanks. If you're making."

Dracup grabbed two mugs from the cupboard and watched the policeman from the corner of his eye.

"Nice place. Church, was it?"

"Yes. Methodist, I believe."

"They're all closing down these days, aren't they? World's moving on," Moran said. "Still, nice conversion. Kept the old stained glass, I see."

"Yes. It brings an unusual light into the room."

"Been away?"

"I've been in Scotland. My aunt died recently and I've had a number of issues to attend to regarding her will."

"You haven't contacted us about your daughter."

"I was hoping to hear something from you."

"You don't seem that concerned."

Dracup turned, kettle in hand. "Of course I'm damned well concerned. My wife has given you all the details."

"Your ex-wife."

"Yes. My ex-wife. I spoke to her earlier today and she'd heard nothing from you people at all."

"We're making enquiries, Mr Dracup."

"Well you can forget *this* enquiry. It's a dead end."

Moran strolled to the window and looked up at it admiringly. "Do you get on with your ex, Mr Dracup? Any problems regarding access arrangements for your daughter?"

"We get on all right. And no, no problems to speak of."

"To speak of?"

Dracup handed Moran the tea. "Look, there are obviously frictions. She has a new man. He finds the whole thing difficult. We've had our run-ins about access, but nothing to get excited about."

"Thanks." Moran sipped his tea. "What about the new man? Stable sort, is he?"

Dracup snorted. "IT nerd. He hasn't the imagination to be unstable."

Moran laughed. "I see."

Dracup shrugged. "I can't be expected to get on with someone who's taken my place, can I? Who reckons he knows what's best for Natasha?"

"I understand. I just wondered if you'd formed an impression, that's all."

Dracup sighed. "He's a hard-working guy. Jewish background, I'd guess. He's all right. I just haven't taken to him, I suppose. I can't really say why."

Moran nodded and scribbled in his notebook.

"So. Have you made any progress?" Dracup folded his arms and assessed the policeman. He imagined the incident room in the town centre. A noticeboard, heavy with pins. Photographs of Natasha, Yvonne, Malcolm, himself. A semicircle of earnest faces listening to the briefing. *It's a marital. Ex-husband's a boffin up at the Uni; wife's got an occasional live-in. Check 'em all out. I'll take Dracup.*

Moran sighed. "We have reason to believe that a couple – a young couple – abducted Natasha. No clear witnesses. Just a part-time cleaner who reckons they were foreign – if it was them."

"That's it?"

"Could be illegals. We've no confirmed sightings at any airports or ports."

"You think they'll try to leave the country?" Dracup splashed tea on his wrist and swore.

"It's a possibility. I'd get some water on that sharpish."

Dracup ran his wrist under the tap. "No confirmed sightings, you said. How about unconfirmed?"

Moran gave an appreciative nod. "I was told you were on the ball." He looked for a suitable place to park his teacup, settling on the windowsill. "French coastguard chased a suspicious fishing boat near Calais. They couldn't get to it in time, but they did see two adults and a child disembark. The child had long curly hair. Dark. Female."

Dracup's heart did the cardiac equivalent of a back flip. It must be her. She was alive. "When was this?"

"Three days ago. Gendarmes drew a blank on further sightings."

Dracup grabbed the policeman's lapels. "You have to find her. You've got to get after them. I want – I –" He was suddenly aware that he was shaking Moran from side to side. He stepped back, hands over his face. "I'm sorry. I –"

Moran straightened his tie. "That's all right, Professor. I understand."

Dracup moistened his lips. His hands were trembling. With an effort he said, "Do you think it was her?"

Moran shrugged. "Could be something; could be nothing. I have an Interpol contact. She's getting back to me. When I hear, you'll hear." He approached Dracup directly and looked at him inquisitively. "I understand that you were attacked in the University grounds recently. What was all that about?"

Dracup shrugged. "Just an opportunist – I caught him trying to break into a friend's house."

"But you ran away. Why was that? If he was just a burglar –"

"He seemed violent. I thought it best to get my friend to safety."

"Uni security reckons he was armed. There were shots fired."

"I don't remember – I had an accident shortly after – it was careless. I wasn't thinking."

"According to the security guard at the Pepper Lane entrance, the car drove straight at you."

Dracup ran his hands through his hair then opened his arms in a gesture of appeal. "I really can't remember much about it. A break-in – he thought we had money, probably – maybe he had an accomplice –"

"Sounds very organised for a common or garden burglary."

Dracup shrugged. His explanation sounded weak. For a brief moment he contemplated telling Moran the truth. But the police and the CIA? The truth would provoke a parade of red tape, misunderstanding, conflict of interest –

"Anyone try to contact you? Make any demands?"

"No." Dracup shook his head. If only they had – it would be a link, it would be *something* –

"What about your friend?"

Dracup felt his hackles rise. "What about her?"

"How long have you known her?"

"About nine months or so. We met at the University. She's a mature student."

"I know. Smart girl too, by all accounts."

"Yes. She is." Dracup felt tiredness ambush him in its usual underhand way. He suddenly felt bone weary. *Does everybody know everything about me?* He walked behind the kitchen bar and put the mugs in the sink with a clatter.

"We wanted a word with her as well – just to be on the safe side."

"With Sara? Why on earth? She's nothing –"

"That's what we thought, but we haven't been able to get hold of her either. Thought she must be with you."

Dracup couldn't think straight anymore. "Well, she was. I mean, she had to come back for some emergency. Something to do with her landlady – wretched woman's a pain. Hang on – I'll give her a call." He wiped his hands on the tea towel.

"I wouldn't bother – there's no one there."

Dracup stopped in mid-wipe. "What do you mean?"

"What I said. We've been round there this morning. The house is empty. No one home."

"Well, she's probably at a friend's – she has a friend up by the University – she cat-sits for her occasionally. That's where we –"

"Mr Dracup, when I mean there's no one there, I mean the house is empty bar the furniture. No personal possessions. Nothing. It's bare."

Dracup grabbed his mobile and punched in the familiar sequence. Three pips. *This number has not been recognised.* He looked at Moran in bewilderment, hoping the DCI could impart some further explanation. "I don't understand."

Moran gave him a sympathetic smile. "Looks like you've been had, Professor. Don't feel too bad about it. Happens to us all."

Dracup made for the door, but Moran caught his arm. "One more thing, Professor. Don't leave the country, will you? I might need another word."

Dracup shook him off angrily and unhooked his keys from the niche by the front door. "You have my number."

Moran called after him. "If you hear from your friend I want to know about it."

Dracup arrived at Sara's front door. He rang the bell. Nothing. He tried to remember anything she had said in Scotland, some hint that she was in trouble, or… the thought jarred his brain like a runaway truck… perhaps *they* had followed her at the airport, and then... His imagination rampaged out of control. He cupped his hands around his face and squinted into the front room. There was no sign of life. No coffee cups left half finished on the table. No magazines scattered untidily by the sofa. No flowers graced the sideboard. She always had flowers. He dialled the landline. He dialled the mobile again. Nothing. He walked down the lane to the campus, past the spot where the agent had lain white-faced in the moonlight, skull perforated by the killer's bullet. One of Potzner's. Another disappearing body. They were good at clearing up behind them – the CIA and *them,* whoever *they* were.

He stood on the bridge. The lake lay beneath him, scudding clouds reflected on its glassy surface. He leaned on the rail for support. First Natasha, now Sara. He chewed his thumb, checked his mobile again. No new messages. He remembered Potzner's promise to call when he had an update on the Aberdeen find. They must have made *some* progress. And why had Farrell left him to his own devices? Then he twigged. *They've got what they need. I'm no longer useful. Worse. I'm expendable.*

Dracup kicked his way through piles of leaves, remonstrating with himself. Who could he trust now? What if Potzner sidelined him and cut to the chase? What would happen to Natasha? And Sara? They were just footnotes in the American's agenda. But maybe he had an advantage – as long as nothing else pointed Potzner in the same direction – the wax tablet's mention of Ethiopia. It was down to him to make the most of it. Dracup stretched his legs to a brisk pace. He needed to find out more. And quickly.

The hard disk grunted and rattled as Dracup typed two words into the search engine: *Ethiopia* space *Lal*. He scanned the results: 'A journey to visit the astonishing religious centres of Ethiopia', 'Lal Hotel', 'Lalibela, Ethiopia'. Dracup chose the third, and sat back to peruse the site:

> *'They say it's the 8th wonder of the world, the monastic settlement of Lalibela, perched upon a natural 2,600-metre rock terrace surrounded on all sides by rugged and forbidding mountains in the northern extreme of the modern province of Wollo.'*

Dracup felt his heart rate increase. Something felt right about this. He read on:

> '– the passing centuries have reduced Lalibela to a village. From the road below, it remains little more than invisible against a horizon dominated by the 4,200-metre peak of Mount Abuna Joseph. Even close-up it seems wholly unremarkable, but legend has it that God told King Lalibela to build a series of churches. The churches are said to have been built with great speed because angels continued the work at night. Many scoff at such apocryphal folklore.'

Me for one, Dracup thought. But he still felt an intangible excitement as he scanned the website's summary.

> 'The Lalibela churches, however, silence the most cynical pedants. These towering edifices were hewn out of the solid, red volcanic rock on which they stand. In consequence, they seem to be of superhuman creation – in scale, in workmanship and in concept. Close examination is required to appreciate the full extent of the achievement because, like all mysteries, much effort has been made to cloak their nature. Some lie almost completely hidden in deep trenches, while others stand in open quarried caves. A complex and bewildering labyrinth of tunnels and narrow passageways with offset crypts, grottoes and galleries connects them all – a cool, lichen-enshrouded, subterranean world, shaded and damp, silent but for the faint echoes of distant footfalls as priests and deacons go about their timeless business.'

Dracup clicked on the 'photographs' link. The first jpg, captioned 'Bet Giorgis', was a church lying in a deep trench and fashioned in the shape of a cross. Theodore had buried the half-sceptre from the Ark deep in the earth. Lalibela in miniature in a Scottish garden. It felt like the right connection; his gut feeling told him the missing section was hidden in Lalibela. If he could find it and translate the cuneiform... The incomplete stanzas ran through his mind:

> *'From whence you came –*
> *Between the rivers –'*

But which rivers? His mobile vibrated briefly in his trouser pocket and he started in alarm, fishing for the instrument with shaking hands. He read the text message. *"Simon. I'm so sorry. Don't try to find me. S."* Dracup selected the call register icon. Number withheld. He threw the phone down and pushed his chair back. He strode to the window and beat his fists on the stained glass. So she hadn't been kidnapped. The policeman was right; he'd been taken for a fool. Moran's cold teacup sat on the sill. Dracup picked it up and flung it at the wall, where it exploded into fine fragments that flew skittering across the floor. Was anyone on his side? He looked for something else to destroy and, finding nothing, turned his anger against the sofa, punching and kicking the thick cushions until exhaustion quietened his whirling limbs.

Some time later he picked up the phone. He dialled a number and waited a few rings. A cultured voice at the other end answered curtly, "Sturrock."
"Hello Charles. Simon here. Listen. I need a favour."

Chapter 14

Ruth had visited the Cave of Treasures many times but still felt a sense of childish wonder as they entered its vaults. She stole a glance at Natasha and smiled, knowing how the girl would react. There was an atmosphere in this place, something intangible, almost sacred. But that was unsurprising, given its history. Ruth shivered. She could feel the presence of her ancestors, those faithful carriers of the ancient torch whose feet had trodden this same path. Countless generations protecting, overseeing, watching, waiting.

"Mind your step," Jassim warned. "It's a little uneven."

"Where are the paintings?" Natasha craned her neck, struggling to pick out any shape from the rock walls, some contour that suggested premeditated design.

"You'll see. Just follow and be careful," Ruth told her.

The roof began to stretch away as they rounded a sharp corner, moving into a wider, danker space. Something flicked down from the heights and fluttered around their heads. Natasha let out a cry of surprise and ducked.

Ruth pulled her close and tucked the girl's head into her bosom, shielding her. "It's all right – just bats. They'll go away in a moment."

Jassim led them on, using his fly swat to swipe at the diving creatures. "No harm; they're just curious – like you."

Natasha gave another exclamation and wiped her mouth. "My fingers – they're all salty."

"It's where you touched the rock – the walls are composed of much salt," Jassim said. "After the flood the rivers moved. They left behind these tunnels we are walking through."

Ruth's gaze traversed the sheer walls to their right where the first of the tombs was visible, cut from the rock like a toothless mouth. Soon, as their eyes became accustomed to the reduced light, others became visible above and below. Every opening was delimited by a frieze of worked stone, each scored by the mason's artful markings; they were pictures of another age, repositories of ancient lives lived in obedience to their fathers. Ruth watched Natasha. The girl was silent, taking it all in.

"Are there dead people in there?" she asked in a whisper.

"They are our forefathers – they have served in past ages and have gone to their rest. There is nothing to fear from them."

"It's creepy."

"Now look over there." Jassim pointed ahead to where the wall curved gently, sweeping back on itself to form a wide U-shaped bend. Natasha craned her neck. "No, higher. See where the shadow lies across the last opening. Look to the left."

Ruth heard Natasha give a little gasp. Now it was clear. The rock face of the extended crescent was covered in drawings of such intricacy that the images appeared to have a life of their own. There were many scenes: sprawling gardens populated with lush vegetation and exotic plants; a king and queen seated on two thrones of startling artistry, bejewelled and clothed in the bright, opulent garments of royalty; a city of evident prosperity under siege from an army of strange, winged creatures; a map of the heavens, each constellation glowing with an eerie blue brightness. But the most striking of all was the centrepiece: a huge, barge-like ship afloat on an empty sea. It was set in a circular frame, each segment of which represented some interior detail of the vessel. And such detail! Ruth had lost herself here on many occasions, slipping away from her brothers and sisters, finding herself guided inevitably to this spot.

"What do you think?" Jassim asked Natasha. "Do you know what this is?"

"It's Noah. Noah and the Ark," Natasha said slowly, but Ruth noticed that her eyes never left the paintings and that she was gently humming to herself, caught up in the spectacle.

They watched in silence for a long time. Ruth knew that the longer you looked, the more the paintings seemed to take on a life of their own, until you could feel the wind in your face, the swell of the great ship beneath you, the smell of the warm animal dung floating up from the huge decks beneath. The effect was hypnotic.

"Noah was our father," Jassim said quietly. "His family were the only survivors of the world before the flood. A world that God judged."

Ruth found a projection of stone, worn smooth by centuries of spectators, and settled herself on it. She motioned to Natasha. "Come."

The girl came meekly and sat beside her, Jassim's voice an aural backdrop to the picture show unfolding before them. Ruth put her arm around Natasha's shoulders and closed her eyes, stepping into the familiar story as if into the presence of a much-loved friend.

"Noah was a wise man, walking closely with God – and for this reason he was shunned by the people," Jassim said. "The world was corrupt, degraded. It deserved judgement. But God remembered Noah. He warned Noah of what was to come and commanded him to build a boat, the like of which had never been seen before. His family came with him – they were aboard when God shut the door and let the waters collapse upon the Earth." Jassim paused, moved by the recollection. "From the old world Noah had gathered many things onto the boat, many sacred things that had been revered from far off times. They were not to perish, but to be preserved until the end times, until the world would again face judgement." Jassim turned to Ruth. "We are part of that."

"You are Noah's children," Natasha murmured.

"All the peoples of the world are Noah's children, Natasha," Ruth said. "A testament to God's mercy. But we are pure, set apart for God."

"We are the *Korumak Tanri*," Jassim said quietly.

Natasha whispered in Ruth's ear. "What does it mean?"

"We are those who do his will. We are the keepers of the sacred things. His caretakers," Ruth replied. "It is our destiny. Until the fulfillment of prophecy." She looked at Jassim.

Her brother nodded slowly. "Yes. The time is upon us. The father has come home. Now his sceptre must also return."

"What's a sceptre?" Natasha looked away from the wall for a moment, a frown creasing her unmarked forehead.

Ruth looked at Jassim. She had never seen her brother's face more serious. More *awestruck*.

"It is a symbol of power. Of authority." Jassim spoke solemnly, his eyes fixed on the paintings.

"Like a king," Ruth whispered to Natasha.

"Like a king," Jassim agreed. "The king's sceptre will return; the awaited sign that the end of the ages is near."

After a while Jassim called them away. Ruth felt she was rising reluctantly into consciousness from a particularly pleasant dream, the characters and scenery flowing into one another like colours in a child's painting. Her footsteps were light as they picked their way back along the labyrinthine walkways; she felt cleansed by the experience, spiritually recharged.

When they reached the stream, Ruth found her water jar and allowed Natasha to sit and dip her toes. She watched the child skim a stone, languidly, carelessly, as if her thoughts were elsewhere, exercising her new skill with an indifferent movement of her wrist. Ruth knew what she was thinking. The paintings always had that effect. Even now she felt soporific, sluggish; there was the usual reluctance to return her mental faculties to the present.

Jassim took her arm. "Ruth." His eyes fixed on hers. There was something in his tone. At once she was alert.

"What? What is it?"

Jassim took her hands in his own and held them. It was a gesture of sympathy which, combined with his expression, implied a degree of helplessness, an inability to change something in her favour. "Ruth. Your sister –" He paused briefly then took a decisive breath. "Sara is coming home."

Chapter 15

Dracup parked the car outside his old house. He had passed another sleepless night, haunted not only by Natasha's but now by Sara's disappearance. He had tried to push thoughts of her aside – he needed the thinking space more than anything else – but his emotions refused to be tamed. He pulled himself together with an effort. This wasn't going to be easy. He checked his appearance in the mirror and wished he hadn't. It would have to do.

"Hello." Dracup gave it his best shot, stretching his facial muscles into something he hoped resembled a confident smile.

"Hi." Yvonne studied his expression briefly. "You'd better come in."

Dracup stepped into the hall. Strange how a once familiar place could change. It didn't smell the same. Houses adopted the smell of their occupants but his contribution was long gone, superseded by whatever equivalent Malcolm's sweat glands were programmed to generate. And there was something else missing; the smell of a child. Toys, paints, Mr Foamy bath bubbles. Yet he could feel Natasha's presence. Her reading folder lay on the telephone table. A teddy bear sat on the window ledge in silent witness to the household's youngest member. He accepted Yvonne's offer of a seat, strangely formal, and watched her arrange herself equally formally in the armchair as if about to embark on a conversation with her financial consultant. She had lost weight and the strain was showing around her eyes, where dark circles had appeared, a foretaste of a future where such marks would be a permanent feature.

He opted for a conciliatory starting point. "How's Malcolm?"

"Fine. Busy as usual."

"Has he been able to take any time off?"

Yvonne studied the flower arrangement on the side table. "A little – but the client needs him on site, you know."

"I think you need someone on site too."

She smiled weakly. "I'm all right."

He shook his head. "You're not." He hated seeing her looking so crushed. "Look, I can't tell you much, but I can tell you enough to keep you going. Enough to help."

"Fire away. I'm listening."

And she did, stopping him occasionally for clarification, asking him about Sara, which she understandably found difficult, soliciting his opinion about the French sighting. He covered everything apart from Sara's sudden disappearance, found himself at the end of his update and waited for her reaction.

"And you're going to *Africa* – against police orders."

"I have to. I really believe that I can find her."

Yvonne rubbed her temple with a surprisingly steady hand. "I can't believe this. It's like a TV drama."

"I know how you feel."

"Natasha's alive. I know she is."

"So do I." He saw the first signs of emotion, a betraying tear angrily wiped away.

Yvonne took a deep breath. "Sorry. What do they want, Simon? They haven't asked you for anything. It's not blackmail – I don't understand."

"I think they want to punish me."

"For Theodore? For stealing... whatever it was he stole?"

"Yes. Potzner will do anything to get this thing back. It's critical for the CIA. That's why I don't want him along – he'll go in like Bush and Iraq. His priorities are different."

"I just hope you know what you're doing. What am I supposed to tell that weasel of an inspector? That you've gone chasing after some archaeological trinket like England's answer to Indiana Jones?"

Dracup dug into his coat pocket. "Look. This is Theodore's summary – an explanation of what I found in Aberdeen. It clearly indicates Lalibela as the location of the missing part of the crest –

the headpiece of Noah's sceptre. The section I found is marked *Alpha*, and the African section –" he passed the tablet to Yvonne for inspection, "– according to Theodore, is marked *Omega*. If I can find it, all I need to do is record the cuneiform and we'll have the whole stanza. And it will tell us where she's been taken. I'm convinced."

"And then what? You just walk in and collect her?" Yvonne held the tablet gingerly, as if afraid to touch it.

Dracup bit his lip. "Something like that, yes."

There was a long silence, then, "Simon –" Yvonne hesitated, frowning.

"What?"

"I'm sorry about the way things have been – between us. I never meant to cause you any difficulties – it's just, I don't know. Things have changed."

Dracup nodded. "Inevitably. We've both moved on. We did the right thing."

"Did we? Or did we lose sight of what we had?"

"Probably. We were under permanent stress."

"Self-imposed."

"Yes, but we both had our minds set on what we wanted."

"But it's not wrong, is it, to want a family?"

"No, of course not. But everything has its price."

"It's so unfair. Some people have it so easy. They pop them out like peas. They never think about it. They don't realise how hard it is for some –"

"Life's not fair, is it?" Dracup spoke softly. "But we did something right, didn't we? Something went right for us in the end."

"But not now – now that –" Yvonne had reached the end of her emotional resources. The sobs came, wracking and desperate; the sound of a mother whose child has been taken away.

Dracup swallowed, teetering on the edge himself. He sat on the arm of her chair and put a steadying hand on her shoulder, but even this small intimacy felt unnatural. She was not his property any more. Not his to comfort. The shock of touching her, even a slight physical contact, made him realise how far apart they had grown.

Her sobs reduced in volume, just the shoulders moving involuntarily. "I'll be all right. I'm sorry."

"Don't apologise. You'll feel better for it." He moved away towards the fireplace. A photograph of Yvonne, Malcolm and Natasha nestled amongst the bric-a-brac of the mantelpiece. They looked happy, sitting together on some summer beach, eating ice creams. Natasha had a blob of ice cream on her nose and Yvonne was pointing to it, laughing. Dracup felt a sudden surge of anger and possessiveness. He wondered who had taken the photograph. Just a passer-by? Or one of their close circle of friends from which he was, of course, excluded?

Yvonne finished blowing her nose. "You'll never get out of the country. Moran will be watching you."

"He won't be watching in the right place," Dracup said. "If he asks, tell him I'll be back. I'm not running."

"*I* know that."

"It's the only thing to do. You have to trust me."

Yvonne looked at him carefully. "You know, Simon, I do. I really think I do."

A confirmed bachelor and familiar figure around the University, the archaeologist Charles Sturrock lived in a comfortable set of rooms in the original gatehouse building. He was a man of slight physique with a pair of finely-balanced spectacles perched on a permanently knitted brow. The overall effect was one of studious detachment from the world, but the man was an enthusiasm powerhouse when it came to pet subjects and hobbies. This had its pros and cons, as Dracup knew from past experience. Once the chocks of restraint had been kicked away there was no stopping Charles; it was a question of carefully managing the direction of the conversation, steering it onto a more relevant and productive flight path.

Sturrock's study was the physical representation of his mental processes and the antithesis of Dracup's ordered domain. Papers littered the desk, bits and pieces of rock, an old skull, a set of ritual daggers from Nepal, reference books acting as elevated resting places for several days' intake of coffee. The walls of the room were covered with charts, pictures, noticeboards festooned with yellowed scraps of paper and long-forgotten reminders. Dracup couldn't fathom how Sturrock could spend his days in such energetic turmoil yet still achieve consistently spectacular results from his students. But the answer was simple. Sturrock's enthusiasm was infectious. He grabbed life with both hands and wrung every shred of enjoyment out of it. A happy by-product of this enthusiasm was that it always cheered Dracup enormously to spend time in the archaeologist's company. Whatever Dracup's mood at the outset, he always took his leave with a foolish smile plastered across his face. Not today though, Dracup thought as the housekeeper showed him in. Not *ever* unless he got this right.

Sturrock looked up from his collection of ephemera and smiled broadly. "Simon! Splendid! Come in! Ready for that trouncing yet? I played a scorcher the other day – won it with a lob to die for. You're in serious trouble this term, laddie."

"I think the big match will have to wait for a bit, Charles." Dracup, fearing a major digression, let his expression bring Sturrock's concentration into focus.

"Serious, eh? Righto, what's all this about a trip to France, then? Got some floozy tucked away? Bet she's not as cracking as that corker you've been escorting recently."

Dracup sighed. "No, nothing like that, Charles. Listen, I'd better give you a rundown on the situation. It's not good."

Sturrock was a good listener. When Dracup had finished he let out a low whistle. "Well I'll be damned. I can't believe it. And this girlie of yours – she just vanished?"

Dracup nodded. "Yes. Her house is empty."

"Her disappearance could be nothing to do with Natasha's, of course." Sturrock removed his glasses and began polishing them with a grubby tissue.

"That's what I'm hoping. I can't believe she knew something and kept it from me."

"Funny creatures, women," Sturrock observed. "Never got the hang of them, personally." He put his glasses back on and tossed the tissue back onto the desk. "But she could have been under threat herself."

"You think?"

"Why not? Perhaps she was tasked to keep an eye on you – to make sure that the diary found its way back to base."

Dracup's eyes widened. "Oh come on, Charles. Do I look that gullible?"

Charles looked at him over his glasses.

"All right. I suppose it's possible," Dracup conceded wearily. But *back to base?* You make her sound like a member of a terrorist cell. And we haven't a clue where *base* is."

"No. But you've made a reasonable deduction, Simon. The wax tablet summary does appear to suggest a link with Lalibela. So I rather suspect I know what this favour is going to be." Sturrock raised his eyebrows theatrically.

"You're the only pilot I know. Otherwise I wouldn't risk it."

"A vote of confidence, as expected. Makes a chap feel good."

Dracup sighed. "Look, Charles, if I can get across the Channel I reckon I'll be on for an international flight without getting picked up. If I try from Heathrow, odds are that Moran will nab me. Is it possible, or am I clutching at straws?"

"Of course it's possible. I just need to make the arrangements with White Waltham and book it up. Only proviso is that the other syndicate chaps haven't made a reservation." Sturrock absently scratched his head with a pencil. "Come to think of it, two of them are abroad on business, so we should be all right."

"Charles, I'd really appreciate it."

"Then consider it done!" Sturrock leaned forward. "Simon, I'd love to take a look at this metalwork. Any chance?"

Dracup shook his head. "Not for the moment. I had to let the CIA take it away for analysis. But I have photocopies. That'll keep you happy for a bit."

"Love to. You never know, I may be able to shed a bit of light." Sturrock rubbed his hands together in anticipation, then fixed Dracup with an expression of barely concealed excitement. "Have you considered the implications of all this?"

"Implications?"

"Yes. That the Ark exists."

Dracup sighed. "I went through this with Sara. So 'The Ark' – or at least a large, ancient, vessel – exists. There *was* a flood. Someone had the good sense to build a boat and get his family on board. Period."

"Oh come on, Simon – even you can't be that blinkered. Look, the book of Genesis contains a lot more than Noah's story. But at any rate the diary kicks out the old tradition that Moses borrowed the flood story from the epic of Gilgamesh when he wrote Genesis."

"Possibly. But then I've always thought the Gilgamesh epic had all sorts of flaws – particularly in the design of the vessel."

Sturrock chortled. "That's right. The boat was cube-shaped according to Babylonian records – not a particularly seaworthy design, whereas the Biblical Ark of Noah –" Sturrock jumped up and fished a book from his teetering shelves. "Here we are. Noah's Ark had the proportions of a true ship. The ratio given in Genesis 6:15 can't be faulted: 300 by 50 by 30 cubits. Perfect for its purpose."

"Well, the majority of primitive societies have a flood story, Charles. The Bible record is one of many."

"I'm aware of that, dear boy. And the reason is that the flood was a reality. China, India, South America, Greece, Africa – they all have their own version of the same event. But the essentials are the same: a global flood; and out of the Earth's population, one family saved. The Chinese in particular consider the head of this family – chap called 'Fuhi' – to be the father of their race."

"Wait a minute. Who said anything about a *global* flood?"

Sturrock fixed Dracup with a challenging look. "Really, Simon. I'll have to put your diminished cranial functionality down to stress – quite understandable."

"What are you talking about, Charles?"

"It's quite simple. If the flood was merely a local catastrophe, then why go to the trouble of building a huge boat like the Ark? It took years to build, you know." Sturrock flicked through the pages of the Old Testament searching for a reference.

Dracup held up a hand in surrender. "Okay, okay. I'm with you. So Fuhi, Noah, whoever, could have just migrated to a higher altitude – found a convenient mountain to hole up on until the flood waters subsided."

"Precisely."

Dracup was silent for a moment, drumming his fingers on the chair arm. "I can accept a catastrophe – a serious one, maybe. And the Ark's existence looks to be beyond doubt. But the rest – I don't know. There's a great deal of fanciful stuff in Genesis I just can't go along with."

"Dear me. What is it with this fear of Biblical veracity? I'm not trying to convert you, Simon."

Dracup grunted. "No. I know. It's just that I've formed my opinions and it'll take a lot to change my mind."

"You evolutionists are all the same."

"Don't get me started, Charles. This isn't the time."

"Well, you've got me going now. Take the sedimentary rock strata – any geologist worth his salt will tell you they show clear signs of having been laid down quickly, *not* over a period of millions of years. It points to a global catastrophe – and the fossil record supports the geological evidence too. It simply screams 'global flood!'" Charles shook his head up and down like a terrier worrying at a ball, waiting for Dracup's response. When none came he shook his head again and sat back. "Put your preconceptions behind you, Si – all is not as it seems."

Dracup shut his eyes and groaned. The ongoing debate. Many an evening had been spent like this; argument and counter argument. Surprisingly, they'd never come to blows. "Listen Charles, if you want to help you could start by thinking about a sceptre. *Noah's* sceptre, maybe. Ever heard of such a thing?"

Sturrock frowned. "Nothing springs to mind, old boy – but that's not to say it won't, given the right stimulation. I'll mull it over. Now, Professor D. – you'd better tell me where you want to go. Paris? Lyons? Or maybe –"

"I can get a direct flight from Toulouse to Addis."

"Addis? I know a chap in Addis – he might be able to help." Sturrock fumbled in a drawer. "Here we are – used to teach here a while back. Don't think you ever met him? Couldn't resist the call of the wild. You'll see what I mean if you meet him." Sturrock adjusted the position of his glasses and read the business card he had retrieved from the depths. "Daniel Carey – The Fountain Language School, Addis Ababa." He handed Dracup the card. "Bit zany – but a good sort. New Zealander – knows the Ethiopian ropes, if you see what I mean. I imagine he can point you in the right direction – to Lalibela and so on. I'll wire ahead and let him know you're coming."

Dracup took the card. "Thanks, Charles. I need all the help I can get."

Sturrock smiled with satisfaction. "Good. Toulouse it is, then. Give me a couple of hours to sort it out, and I'll call you this evening."

"Charles, you're a good friend."

"Did you ever doubt me?"

Dracup threw his coat on the sofa and went to his desk. He shivered; the apartment was freezing. He fired up his laptop, found the Lalibela URL from the favourites menu and scrolled through the selection of photographs. What would he find? Where would he begin his search? There was nothing recorded on Theodore's abbreviated time capsule to suggest an exact location for the missing part of the crest. Why hadn't the old man been more specific? The phone rang.

"Dracup."

"Mr Dracup – I was expecting a call. Everything okay?"

Dracup had prepared himself for this conversation. Potzner sounded concerned rather than annoyed. That was the balance to be maintained.

"Fine. Any progress from your end?"

"I'm still waiting on our guys. Mike Fish is pretty good but not the fastest thing on two legs."

"Time's pressing."

There was a short silence. "Yeah. I know."

"I had a visit from the police."

"Right. That was inevitable. Tell them anything?"

"No. As you said, no point." Dracup could almost see Potzner leaning back from the desk, Winston in mouth, finger flicking at the Zippo.

"I'm going to send Farrell back to you, just to keep things safe."

Dracup clenched his fist. "It's okay. I'm fine."

"It's your lady friend we need to keep an eye on. Farrell tells me she went home on her own."

"Yes. Some domestic crisis."

"She okay now?"

"Yes."

Dracup heard the silence this time; an active, analytical silence.

"All the same. I'm sending him down. He should be with you by – say ten o'clock?"

"If you insist." Dracup cursed under his breath and looked at his watch. Under two hours. He had to make himself scarce. He scanned Yellow Pages for a hotel list. Five minutes later he was on the road.

Potzner looked across the desk at Farrell.

The agent returned the look. "Well?"

"He's holding out. He knows something."

"You sure?"

"I can always tell. Are you sure there was nothing else in that box?"

"Sure as I can be."

"And you were there when he opened it?"

"Pretty much."

Potzner shook his head. "That's not what I expect from you, Farrell."

The agent chewed his gum sheepishly. "I was watching the house. He called me over when he found it."

"Or when he wanted you to *think* he found it, you mean. I'm betting he had time to hide whatever it was he didn't want you to see. It would only have taken a few seconds."

"Must have been pretty small then, whatever it was, 'cause we carried the box out of there together."

"Coat pocket, Farrell. Did you check it back at the Aberdeen flat?"

"Well, not as such. We got back from the dig, hit up the safe house; he was in the bathroom. Then he got a call from his ex."

"So he was in the john *with* his coat?"

Farrell smiled awkwardly. "Yeah. I suppose."

Potzner leaned forward. "Suppose *nothing*, Farrell. Get your ass down that M4 *now*."

Farrell was out of the door in seconds.

Chapter 16

Dracup checked in, left his suitcase in his room and headed back to reception. He had to get out. Do something. He went outside to the Thameside promenade where a group of students were manhandling their boats from water to boathouse. He headed up the riverside towpath. Now he was walking alone, his feet crunching a solitary beat on the gravel.

His attention was drawn by a movement on the towpath. He saw it again. A tall shape moving quickly – no, running – up the path. Just a jogger? Dracup studied the figure; and then knew it was coming for him. He thought quickly. Which way? If he continued along the towpath he would be moving away from the nearest public place into the empty water meadows that stretched up to Mapledurham lock. He began to jog across the meadow towards the main road. The road led to a narrow bridge, then continued onto the Oxford Road. He glanced behind. The gap was closing. He drove his legs harder. Traffic was sparse as Dracup hit the pavement and veered right towards the bridge. He reached the traffic lights with lungs heaving and looked back. The runner burst onto the road, turning towards him. Now Dracup could see his features more clearly. He was unusually tall, wearing patched jeans and a black open-necked shirt. His head was partly obscured by a multi-coloured bandana – the object that had caught Dracup's attention on the towpath. The face was dark, partially bearded with a long, hooked nose curving down toward the upper lip. Dracup entered the darkness beneath the bridge at a brisk trot. The Oxford Road T-junction lay mockingly distant. Dracup took a deep breath and went for it. He heard the sound of trainers slapping on damp paving, made a half turn but lost his footing, tripped over something on the ground and crashed to the pavement in a tangle of metal and limbs.

Dracup gritted his teeth at the pain and hauled the bicycle upright. He pushed away and pedalled hard along the terraced street, turning right into the Oxford Road. A bus was disgorging passengers on the other side. If the timing was right... Dracup threw the bike down and ran into the traffic. He made it across. There was one passenger ahead in the queue, fumbling for money. The runner appeared, looked right and left. Dracup searched his pockets desperately for change.

"Where to, mate?" the driver asked him with bored indifference. Dracup found two coins in his pocket. The bandana man was crossing the road, a slalom virtuoso between taxis and cars. "Anywhere." Dracup thrust the money into the machine. The doors hissed. The bus shook as a fist banged the rear end. Some of the passengers muttered in alarm. The bus moved away; slowly, too slowly. Dracup saw him at the door, eyes like coals, but he was slipping back now, losing the race against the horsepower of the Reading Transport bus. "Sorry mate," the bus driver shouted, "you won't get me to stop like that." He looked at Dracup and laughed, a friendly, easy sound.

"You'll have to get off at Purley," the driver told him. "I'll give you a shout, all right?"

"Yes. All right." When the bus had pushed on half a mile or so he fished in his pocket for his mobile. He dialled a number.

"Charles? Look, I'm in a spot of bother. Can you pick me up? I'm sorry to – you have? That's excellent." He listened to Charles describing the agenda for tomorrow's flight. He'd been lucky. Their slot was booked for 10 a.m. "Where? Hang on." Dracup peered out of the window. "Purley – Oxford Road – on the way to Pangbourne, you know? Twenty minutes? Make it fifteen and hopefully I'll still be here. I'll explain when I see you. Thanks, Charles. Bye."

Dracup fell back into his seat. Traffic was moving swiftly and he thanked whatever life-preserving force was looking out for him that this wasn't happening in rush hour. The bus rumbled on.

He disembarked at Purley and waited an anxious five minutes until eventually Charles pulled smoothly alongside.

Charles leaned out of the window and grinned. "Hop in, old boy."

Dracup eased his aching body into the front seat of Sturrock's Citroën. Bach was playing softly on the stereo and Charles as usual seemed on top form.

"This is all very exciting, Si. What's the scam?"

"Someone tried to kill me."

Sturrock's face assumed a concerned expression. "Well, in the light of what you told me earlier, I'm hardly surprised. But are you absolutely sure? You've been under a lot of stress –"

"I saw his eyes, Charles..." Dracup realized that Charles intended to retrace the bus route back into town. "I'd rather go in the other direction if that's all right with you. He may still be on the Oxford Road – or heading this way." Dracup recalled the impact of the fist, how it had shaken the bus.

"No problem – we'll go via the motorway." Sturrock U-turned the Citroën and headed out through Purley Beeches to Pangbourne.

Dracup shifted uncomfortably in his seat, massaged his leg.

"Are you hurt?" Sturrock shot him an enquiring look.

"It's nothing. Fell over a bicycle."

"Trouble with you, Simon, is you're not fit. Got to keep the joints active when you get to our age." Sturrock turned briefly to gauge Dracup's reaction.

"Charles, I'm not in the mood."

Sturrock's face fell. "Sorry. Why don't you tell me what happened?"

Dracup almost laughed at Sturrock's deflated expression. He felt as if he'd just reprimanded a precocious schoolboy. He leaned back on the headrest and closed his eyes. "I didn't mean to bark, Charles. My nerves are a bit frayed."

Sturrock stole another glance at Dracup. "Quite understandable. Stiff drink and an early night in order, I'd say. You can have a shakedown on the sofa."

Dracup grunted. "No luxury spared, eh?"

Dracup held up finger and thumb in response to Sturrock's refill enquiry, and resisted the urge to down the shot in one. Charles had a fire burning in the hearth and a reflective glint in his eye as he replaced the brandy on the mantelpiece and stood with his back to the flames, rubbing his hands in anticipation of conversation. But Dracup was exhausted. He no longer felt confident about his deductions, nor his African plan. In the homely surroundings of Charles' digs it all seemed preposterous, a desperate shot in the dark.

"Any better?" Sturrock prompted. "Bit of colour coming back, I'd say."

"I'm knackered, Charles. I can't think straight. It all seems – quite mad to me."

"You didn't sound mad earlier on. And you have the evidence."

"Had. Potzner and co have it now."

"You said you had a copy –"

Dracup looked at Sturrock's earnest face. His eyes shone like an excited child's.

"Of the sketch? Yes, I have a copy."

"May I see it?"

Dracup reached into his jacket pocket and produced the set of folded A4 sheets.

Sturrock spread them out on the table and adjusted his glasses. "Hm. There's something about this that rings a distant bell. But I'm damned if I can think what it is." Sturrock sat back and perused his wall-to-wall bookshelves. "Sceptre of Noah you say, sceptre of Noah..." He tutted and scanned along the dusty shelves with a long forefinger. "Nope. Can't think where I've seen that reference."

"I've never heard of it," Dracup frowned. "Staff of Moses, maybe."

"Yes, yes. Quite. Let's have those stanzas – the translation I mean."

"On that sheet." Dracup leaned over and slid the paper across the table.

"Now then." Sturrock squinted.

> *"From holy resting place to rest upon the water –*
> *But Noah, the faithful son –*
> *Once more in the earth you will find peace –*
> *From whence you came –*
> *Between the rivers – "*

"Right. Well, the first line implies something that was in one place – for a long time, I'd say. And obviously venerated." Sturrock peered at the verse. "And whatever it was, it went on the Ark. *To rest upon the water.* Yes?"

"Yes. I suppose so." Dracup felt his eyes beginning to close. He rubbed them and blinked.

"And when the Ark grounded, *Once more in the earth you will find peace*, and particularly *From whence you came*, both imply a return to the original location."

"Possibly. I have a problem with that, though."

"Namely?"

"You global flood people would accept that the antediluvian and the post-flood world were – are – very different?"

"Yes."

"With a considerably altered ecosystem and geological foundation?"

"Highly probably. But that's not to say *all* areas were altered beyond recognition. Depending on the geology of the location *pre* flood, when the waters eventually receded there may have been little or no change to solid formation land masses, rock strata, whatever."

"Charles, it's not my area of expertise."

"Nor mine, but I've read some interesting papers on the subject. Bottom line is, if something had been secreted below ground, provided the geology was sound enough it may still be there today." Sturrock's expression changed.

"What?"

"You look absolutely knackered, Si. Early start tomorrow. White Waltham for eight thirty. You need to get some sleep."

Dracup let out a groan.

"Problem?"

"Yes. I've left my suitcase at the hotel."

"Ah. I'll pick it up if you like."

"And risk getting your head blown off? I don't think so. I have my passport, fortunately." Dracup patted his pocket. "The clothes are just an inconvenience."

Sturrock downed his brandy in one. "Right. Perhaps I can lend you some essentials."

Dracup smiled. "Charles, you're a good man."

Sturrock shook his head. "Just helping an old buddy." He replaced his glass on the table with a deepening frown. "Simon – are you going to be all right?"

Dracup was glad he'd chosen Charles as a confidant; the archaeologist's concern was almost comical. He shook his head. "Charles, I have absolutely no idea if I'm going to be all right."

Sturrock fixed Dracup with a mock serious expression. "I have every confidence." He raised his glass, which he had subtly contrived to refill. "My dear chap. Here's to Africa."

It was a bright, sunny morning. White Waltham's windsock ruffled gently in a cool westerly breeze as Dracup was led reluctantly onto the grass where several aircraft were sitting expectantly, like seagulls waiting for tourists to arrive with ice creams and sandwiches. He watched suspiciously as Sturrock gestured towards the smallest aircraft, which looked to Dracup rather like a grown-up version of the boyhood models he had painstakingly constructed in his bedroom.

"You've got to be kidding."

"What do you mean? She's a beaut. Perfectly airworthy."

"But we can't both fit in there." Dracup examined the cockpit with a growing sense of alarm.

"Of course we can. It's only a short flight. You'll get used to it in no time."

Dracup carried that thought through the pre-flight preparations. Sturrock chattered excitedly about oil pressure, crosswinds and fuel checks. Dracup's hands were cold and clammy. He attempted a kind of self-deluding detachment, as if he wasn't really about to climb into an aerial coffin. Forty-five minutes later Sturrock opened the throttle and they rumbled across the grass to the take-off position. When the ground fell away beneath them, leaving Dracup's stomach with it, he was beginning to wish he'd risked Moran's vigilance and gone for the Heathrow option after all.

Africa

Chapter 17

"You lost him?" Potzner listened incredulously. "How hard is it to find a University Professor in his home town?"

"I never actually found him, sir. He wasn't *at* home." Farrell's voice crackled defensively.

"And you checked the girlfriend's?"

"Yessir. Place is empty. She's AWOL."

"Think they're together?"

Farrell clicked his tongue. "Hard to say."

"He's onto something." Potzner jammed the receiver under his chin, grabbed his coat and stuffed his cigarettes into a pocket. "And he doesn't trust us. Stay where you are – I'm on my way."

An hour and ten later they were outside Dracup's flat. His car was parked in its allocated space. Potzner checked it out. A couple of CDs lay on the passenger seat; a few books in the back. Nothing unusual. Farrell took the front steps two at a time and waited at the door. He signalled to Potzner, whose sixth sense was already vibrating like a tuning fork. The door was ajar, a minute crack of darkness. Potzner joined Farrell at the top of the steps, listened briefly at the latch then nodded to Farrell's unspoken question. He began the time-honoured countdown. On the count of *two* his P-229 was nestled comfortably in his right hand. *Three.* Farrell's foot hit the door hard and they spun into the room, crouching, one on either side of the front door.

Potzner's first impression was that some basketball player was rifling through Dracup's possessions. Absurdly his mind replayed a Harlem Globetrotters point – it had been a great match, and some piece of entertainment when the centre dummied then spun the ball into the basket with the wonderful leisurely disdain for the opposition that had made the 'Trotters a global phenomenon. He remembered it well – even down to the burger he'd eaten that night. Must have been '79 or '80? Abigail had been with him, and had turned to share the enjoyment of the moment. Her eyes were wide with pleasure; there was a small ketchup stain on her chin and he loved her for it. All this fast-forwarded through Potzner's mind as he levelled the handgun and his lips framed a warning.

The intruder straightened up. The guy was over two metres, surely – his head would've scraped the ceiling in a normal apartment. Maybe it was the bandana that added to the impression of extraordinary height. He was holding something – Dracup's laptop – unplugging the snaking connection from the wall socket.

Freeze. Farrell's order came loud and clear. The man hesitated, sizing them up. Potzner was confident. There was nowhere to go; they had the exit covered. "I said get your hands *up*." Potzner began to move forward, creeping across the polished floor like a ballet dancer on rice paper. And then the man did something odd. He smiled. Potzner felt rather than heard Farrell just behind and to his right, supporting, watching. Then the warning: *"Sir!"* But Potzner had seen it too, a smooth, unhurried movement from the large hands in which two small cylinders had appeared. They detached themselves and rolled gently along the parquet towards them, bumping in an irregular pattern as the asymmetrical shapes found their rhythm on the slippery surface.

His immediate thought was *No way... not this time.* He'd been on the receiving end of this kind of welcome before – on a standard patrol, even before the hell of Chu Pa. A quiet morning, ten buddies together, talking about home, girls, movies. No Charlie around – they were told the area had been cleared. And then the sudden shock, the air filled with rifle fire; three of his friends falling red-shirted to the jungle floor. Then came the lethal canisters of explosive, some airborne, some clanking along the path, the sudden dull thump of ignition, cries of surprise rather than pain on either side. And himself, somehow, unscathed in their midst. Still alive, the only one that by some quirk of physics or geometry had avoided the whirling metal and was doomed to face the accusing stares of the boys back at camp. *So you made it? Too bad about*

Chuck, and Rich, and Al. They had clapped him on the back, left him to his guilt.

Farrell articulated all this in one word: "*Grenade!*"

Potzner threw himself at the nearest cover – the sofa – and found Farrell just ahead of him. The rolling death passed them by and rebounded off the skirting board by the bathroom. Then the sofa was driven back on a cushion of warm air, pinning Potzner to the ground. His eyes were filled with stinging smoke and a loud, whistling shriek invaded his ears just as the second grenade exploded. He felt the patter of shrapnel on the leather of the sofa's backrest, and something hit his shoe with a sharp report. It felt like he'd been stamped on by a horse. He yelled and drew his legs in, waiting for another packet of explosive to come rolling along. Potzner clutched his pistol and made himself as small as he could. He had no intention of dying under a sofa. A few moments later when his instincts told him the danger had passed he broke cover and surveyed the scene with practiced thoroughness. They were alone in the apartment.

"He's out," he called to Farrell. But Farrell was already moving through the smoke towards the gaping hole in the wall that had previously supported Dracup's front door. The apartment was a chaos of brick fragments and mortar; flame licked lazily up the blackened woodwork of the bathroom doorframe, exposing vulnerable electrics beneath stricken plaster.

Coughing and hacking they burst into the air. Dracup's car was moving. Potzner clipped off a couple of shots, but Farrell laid a restraining arm on his shoulder. "Forget it. He's out of here." A small crowd had begun to gather, their shocked expressions accusatory and fearful. How should they engage with these two strangers who appeared to be responsible for what had just occurred? Questions began to fly from the crowd, some of concern, some openly hostile. "You all right?" "What's your game, mate?"

Potzner waved them away with his pistol, as if swatting a swarm of irritating flies. Farrell moved amongst them. "It's all over, folks. Nothing to see." He flapped his open wallet at them.

"Police business. Now move on. Move on." He turned to Potzner. "You okay, sir?"

Potzner made a quick examination. His right foot squelched in its shoe; there was no pain. That would come later. He sat on what remained of the doorstep and inspected the damage. A jagged tear criss-crossed his leather upper. His fingers probed the gash and came away red. He cursed under his breath, then a little louder for the benefit of one woman who remained staring, mouth open, with shopping spilling from a supermarket carrier onto the rubble-strewn pavement. That hit the button. She fled, trailing her bargains behind her.

"I'm fine, Farrell. Just hunky-D."

"He was packing some serious kit, sir." Farrell helped Potzner struggle upright. "Kinda caught me out there."

"Yeah. I guess that about covers it." Potzner winced as he tested his full weight on the foot. Damnation. He'd need to get it seen to.

"Shall I call a paramedic, sir?"

"An ambulance, Farrell, an ambulance. This is England, not LA."

"Right. An ambulance."

"No. I do not want an ambulance. Just get a fix on that car, and get after Dracup. He can't be far away. And get me to ER – I'll direct you to the hospital."

Farrell allowed himself a small grin. "Sir, I believe the Brits call it 'Casualty'."

Three hours later Potzner emerged from the hospital. He'd been lucky. Superficial damage only; five stitches, no broken bones. Hurt like hell though. He popped one of the prescribed pills and called a minicab. He watched the passing trade in broken humanity, raw materials for some junior doctor. Potzner hated hospitals; he'd spent enough time in their sterile embrace, heard the whispered conversations, the fearful encouragements, the bravery of the terminally ill. He was glad when the cab arrived. Sitting in the back he checked the time. *Time to be an encourager yourself, Jim.* He tapped the shortcut key and waited.

"Hello?"

She sounded okay. He knew the signs. Today was a good day. "Hi. It's me."

"Well, hi yourself. How's it going?"

"Had a little trouble earlier but I'm better now."

"Want to tell me about it?"

Potzner flexed his toes and regretted the movement. He suppressed an exclamation. "Honey, you know the rules." He tried to inject a light-heartedness into his voice but she was too perceptive, knew him too well.

"You're hurt, aren't you, Jim?"

"It's nothing. Just a scratch."

Her voice was warm with concern. "Jim. You shouldn't be doing this stuff any more. It's time to let the youngsters take the risks. Are you really okay?"

"Yeah. Really. It's just a cut on my foot. You can hardly see it. But what about you? You sound pretty good." He bit his lip. *Keep it up, Jim boy.*

"Well, you know. Some days up, some down. Today is good so far. I've done some housework. Mary's in later so she can finish up."

"That's great. But you've gotta take it steady. Conserve your energy, right? Your body needs all its energy for healing."

There was a small sound, almost a sigh on the other end. "Jim. We both know there's no healing. Only the time we've been given."

"I'm not letting that time go, babe. I'm working on it, believe me. I'm on the case. Soon we'll be able to –"

"Hush, Jim. Just tell me when you're coming home. I miss you."

He gritted his teeth. "I miss you too."

"Jim – I – I want us to be together – you know – while – while we can." Her voice faltered a little.

He took a deep breath. "I know." Potzner cleared his throat. "I just need a little longer. I have to fix something for our guys, then they'll be on the case for us. They know how important it is."

"Just come home soon."

"I will. You bet."

The signal broke up; his phone gave three short beeps. Disconnected. He put it back in his pocket. That's how it would be at the end, he knew. One last word, a last thought. Then disconnection.

Chapter 18

By the time they began their descent Dracup was past caring. He had experienced every conceivable discomfort, ranging from airsickness to paralysing terror. Closing his eyes brought little relief. He knew only a thin Perspex bubble separated him from several thousand feet of nothing. Sturrock was babbling stuff about vectors and altitude, giving the impression of thoroughly enjoying himself. Dracup risked a quick look out of his window just as Sturrock banked. Dracup groaned and closed his eyes again. He hoped he could hold out a little longer; he'd run out of brown bags.

Twenty minutes later Dracup's feet were in contact with French soil, and the object of his misery was parked securely in a hanger reserved for light aircraft. His legs were rubber as they walked to the exit. Sturrock clapped him on the back. "Wasn't so bad, eh? Bit blustery over the Channel, though – still, soon cleared up. Listen, while you've been retching I've been thinking. I have an idea about that stanza – I've seen a reference in a late apocryphal tome – twelfth or thirteenth century, I recall. Have you heard of 'The Book of the Bee' or 'The Cave of Treasures'?"

Dracup shook his head. His mouth felt gritty, acidic. "*B* what? No. Why?"

"Well, I don't think Theodore's sceptre, or staff if you will, was originally Noah's at all." Sturrock smiled cryptically.

Dracup fought a new wave of nausea. "Charles, I need a while to restore my faculties –"

Sturrock laughed and punched him playfully on the arm. "Understood, understood. Well, listen, I tell you what: if I find anything useful, I'll drop you a line. Have you still got your hotmail account?"

"I think so – I haven't used it for a while."

"Right, splendid. I'll pop something in the old electro-post if I think it's worthwhile." He wagged a finger at Dracup. "Don't forget to check."

Dracup smiled weakly. He was going to miss Charles. "Thanks. I won't – *if* I can get online in Addis."

Sturrock groaned theatrically. "Simon, you can get online from *anywhere* these days." A French official appeared, gesticulating with a clipboard. "*Ah, oui m'sieur, nous allons vite* – come on, Si, buck up. We've got to check in at security." Sturrock rubbed his hands gleefully. "Quick toddle around duty-free then back over the water in time for supper. Can't be bad, eh?"

The airliner was half empty. Dracup chose a window seat, closed his eyes and tried to piece together everything he had discovered. He remembered the conversation in Potzner's office: *"I'm talking breakthrough here. No theories. This is the real McCoy."* The American had spoken of longevity research, a critical program utilizing some material that was quite irreplaceable. *The artefact* – no, *organic tissue*. Stolen – reclaimed rather – by its original owners. People who held a century-spanning resentment of his family line; a covert, intelligent, persistent organization who had targeted himself and his family for some act of sacrilege committed by his grandfather. Dracup smiled bitterly. *The sins of the fathers.* Not for the first time, he wished they had taken him. He would be a willing substitute for his child. Let them do whatever they wished to him. Just let Natasha go. Natasha. *My baby.*

He remembered his child when she was small. He wondered at her uniqueness, so like her mother and father yet very much an individual. She was headstrong, like him. She was focused, like her mother. Had they taught her enough to survive a crisis? Did she have the required skills to emerge from her ordeal unscathed? Her survival depended on a combination of both instinctive and accumulated resources. And on his deductions, his actions.

Dracup looked out of his window and for the first time wondered if he would ever see his daughter again. The thought was terrifying. He racked his brains. Organic tissue, stolen. Noah's sceptre. *Alpha. Alpha* and *Omega*. The aeroplane droned on, passing out of French airspace into the open skies above the Mediterranean. Stewards moved up and down the aisle, smiling and attentive. He smiled back automatically, ate the proffered plastic food, read the in-flight magazine from cover to cover. There was a photograph, a young girl modelling executive yachts. She looked a little like Sara. Sara, the girl who had come into his life and saved his sanity; the girl who seemed to him like an Egyptian queen. The girl who had rekindled love in his bruised and battered heart; the girl he thought was his, however unlikely it had seemed. He couldn't believe she'd had anything to do with Natasha's abduction. No, that wasn't true; he didn't *want* to believe it. But without her, he had nothing left. Dracup replaced the magazine in its elastic folder and reached for his earphones, listened to the piped classical music. He felt nothing but emptiness. After a while he slept.

Chapter 19

Sara took a deep breath before entering the chamber. She was tired from the journey, tired of the deceit and racked with guilt over what she had had to do. Her dreams were of Dracup; his drawn, anxious face, his helplessness. She had been recalled and the only sensible course of action had been compliance. Could she have resisted? Could she have turned back when her two worlds hung in the balance? Pointless thoughts. It was done. She had stepped across the boundary and tasted the forbidden fruit. She had loved and deceived in the same breath. And Kadesh knew. She could see it in his eyes. He knew. And her fate had become an internal struggle for him because he loved her. And so her life hung by the most slender of threads. She bit her lip, took another breath. Then she pulled the curtains aside.

A woman stood in the centre of the chamber, silent, expectant. She extended an arm but remained where she was, as if reluctant to make contact. She spoke softly, a breath of recognition. "Sara."

"Ruth." Sara moved slowly forward. "How are you, sister?" Her eyes scanned the chamber for the girl, but Ruth was alone.

The women embraced. Ruth's body was taut, defensive.

"Well enough."

"And where is your charge?" Sara asked brightly. "I expected to find her with you."

Ruth looked away. "Natasha is with Jassim. He is teaching her."

Sara nodded. "I see. And is she well?"

Ruth's expression hardened. "*I* am looking after her."

"Sister –" Sara held out her hand, but Ruth moved away, sat before her mirror and began brushing her hair with short, bristling sweeps.

Sara stood by her. "You are angry with me." She sighed. "Let me talk to you. Please." She placed her hand on Ruth's shoulder, feeling the muscles stiffen at her touch.

"Not angry." Ruth put the brush down and stared at her reflection. "Look at me, Sara. I am old. My time is passing."

"Oh, Ruth." Sara put her arms around her sister's neck. She felt her tears hot against the warm flesh. "It's not too late. You are beautiful. There will be others –"

Ruth spun around and stood up, eyes blazing. "There can be no others. There is only one. And he doesn't want me. He wants *you*."

Sara stepped back, alarmed at her sister's transformation. "Ruth –"

"No. Listen to me. You are young. You have someone. You should stay with *him*, make him your own, then perhaps I have a chance." Her eyes blazed.

"But you know I have been called. I can't refuse –"

"You did what you wanted. You had no remorse then. Why do you come now to torment me?"

Sara held out her arms. "Ruth, please – I – I'm frightened of Kadesh. I don't know what he'll do. I'm frightened for Natasha. For you and me. I can't help how things are – I never encouraged him, I promise you."

Ruth gave a hollow laugh. "You *should* fear him. He is changing. We all fear him." She put out her hand and touched her reflection, stroking the glass. "But only I – only I *love* him."

Sara went to the small bed in the corner. She picked up a dress, a pretty shade of purple. A flower motif was embroidered delicately on the pocket. "And what will he do with the girl? There is no reason for her to be here."

"I am taking care of her." Ruth's voice quavered slightly. "She is my responsibility." Ruth took the dress from Sara and began to fold the discarded clothes and place them in a drawer. "She belongs to me."

Sara felt a chill in her stomach, a cold dread. She said, as gently as she could, "Ruth. She belongs to her father and mother. They grieve for her."

Ruth spun and her hand lashed out, connecting with Sara's cheek. Sara reeled back in surprise, caught her foot on a corner table and fell heavily onto the floor. She lay there, disbelieving, looking up at Ruth.

"She is mine now." Ruth nodded emphatically. "Mine." She stabbed her finger into her breast. "She has been given to *me*. Remember that."

Sara fled along the passages of her childhood. She headed for her special place, the place she'd always sought out when she wanted solitude. The stream met and accompanied her to the waterfall and she entered the dark, foreboding gash in the cavern bed she called the funnel, half falling, half stumbling down the twenty or so stepped projections until she reached the low-ceilinged gallery. A soft phosphorescence lit the void; the stream was a distant whisper of sound, comforting her. She cried for a while, then as the tears subsided she forced herself to think.

She had to get Natasha away. It was the least she could do for Simon. Now that she had torn herself away from him she found it easier to assess her feelings. All the while she had known their time together was like water escaping through her fingers. Kadesh was always in her mind's eye, watching, waiting, expectant. *Wait for the diary. You are the safeguard. If it falls to you, you must bring it home. We will be watching.* If. She had played her part with alacrity, never expecting to be called upon. He was attractive, certainly, but she could keep a distance, couldn't she? But then it all changed. And Simon was no longer the subject; he had become the lover. Sara held her head in her hands. She had lost him anyway, and he had lost more. She must act before Kadesh came to a decision. If the security of the *Korumak* was at stake he would show mercy to neither lover nor enemy. She remembered Ruth in her chamber, wild-eyed: *We all fear him.*

Her brother had related Ibrahim's fate. *It is not the same here, Sara. You are in danger.* Jassim had smiled grimly. *It may be that we are all in danger. I will speak with Kadesh. Perhaps he will listen.* Sara lay flat on the smooth bed of stone. She felt cool air venting from the funnel, soothing her spirit, breathing courage into her veins. She heard the soft sigh of the wind passing down the length of the gallery and hugged her knees, a delicate shiver running down her spine. She had never ventured beyond the gallery, not even as a childhood dare; it was considered a haunted place, a place to be shunned. But here... here in the familiar quietness she was safe.

Sara lay still, staring at the arches, the gently glowing strata above her. She felt her ancestors' presence, and with the feeling came a crushing weight of responsibility. Who was she to place her needs above those of the *Korumak*? Her life was of little consequence, a drop in the millennia. But her knowledge might yet prove advantageous to her people. The CIA man, Potzner, was dangerous. With Simon's help he would find the caverns, and there would be an end to it all. Simon would not rest until he found Natasha; he was smart. It was only a matter of time. Together they were a powerful partnership, but she knew that Simon mistrusted Potzner. So she needed a lever, something to exploit Simon's intuitive reservations and split them apart. Then she could concentrate on returning Natasha to Simon whilst Potzner scrambled around in the dark.

The archives, the pre-CIA records were in Kadesh's possession. They were damning; case histories of the drugs which had been used to control and finally destroy the minds of those participating in the Twenties expeditions. She knew what Theodore Dracup had experienced on Ararat: dreadful, terrifying hallucinations, the effects of the chemicals injected as they slept at the instigation of the US government. Her people had watched and observed. The Americans had wanted at first to control the minds of the expedition members but then later, when the implications of what they had found became clear, to impose a permanent amnesia – the discoveries were too significant, too contentious to be made public. Dracup's grandfather had had his life erased like an unwanted recording. Simon had the right to know. And once in possession of that knowledge he would drop Potzner like a brick.

Sara bent and picked up a handful of stones, threw them one by one into the blackness of the gallery. She bit her lip. Kadesh would never agree to the release of such information. She would have to obtain it herself. And the final step would be the hardest: to gain Ruth's confidence and free the child.

Sara took a deep breath. To do this she had to be prepared. She must go to the one they protected. She must see for herself. And having seen, she would be strengthened. Sara stood up and began to climb the funnel, back to her people.

A handful of the faithful were gathered for their evening vigil. Sara joined them, bowing cordially to those she recognized. The holy chamber was suffused with a deep emerald light. One by one they were shepherded forward to lean into the deep-cut circle of brilliance. The slow, ritualistic approach tested her patience; the need to experience the truth had become an imperative. Her life up to this point had been marked by expectancy, a looking forward to what would inevitably be revealed. Now the reality was before her. She felt a coolness invade her nostrils, a faint smell of some preservative chemical.

Then the mist cleared and she saw. A small gasp of astonishment escaped from her mouth and she fell to her knees. She felt a prayer tumble, unbidden, unrehearsed from her trembling lips. Her hands came together and her head bowed in acknowledgment. He had walked with God and now he rested in the bosom of his people. Sara lifted her head and the attendant acolyte returned her smile, nodding slowly. He knew, he understood. For decades they had lived without purpose, only hope and patience sustaining them. Now the wait was over.

Chapter 20

"No dice." Farrell replaced the receiver. "No one of that description has passed through any major UK airport."

Potzner wasn't surprised. "Well, he must have got out somehow. How about the wife?"

"She's not giving anything away. I don't reckon he filled her in. Either that or she's a damn good actress."

"Maybe, maybe," Potzner grunted. "What about the car?" He shifted his legs under the desk and grimaced as his injured foot caught the pedestal.

Farrell shook his head. "It was found two blocks away from Dracup's apartment. Empty."

"Terrific." Potzner picked up the phone. "Get Fish on, would you?" He arranged his legs across the desk, taking care to place right over left. Farrell wandered to the glass wall, gazed out onto the busy office thoroughfare.

Fish's high voice announced itself in Potzner's ear.

"I need an update, Fish. Preferably a good one." Potzner listened impatiently. He had learned to dissect Fish's offerings, weeding out the scientific gobbledegook from the pertinent information. "Yeah, yeah. And?" Fish rambled on. "What's that? Say again –" Potzner covered the mouthpiece and called over to Farrell. "He has a theory about the purpose of the cross." Then into the phone: "Yeah, go on. I'm listening." As Fish spoke, Potzner reflexively began the task of associating new information with what he currently understood. "So it's a staff headpiece, a sceptre of some sort. Marked with cuneiform script and a large A indentation, possibly the Greek letter Alpha. Yeah, I know Greek wasn't around that far back. No, I can't explain it either. It's partially complete, uh huh. The rest is most likely on the missing half.

Right. Traces of wood splinter within the bottom join, hence the sceptre theory. Carbon dated – 5–10000 BC. Okay. That figures."

Fish's voice was rising with excitement. "You've commissioned an artist's impression of the whole thing? Very nice, Fish, but we need results, not airy-fairy art exhibitions. What about the additional markings? Shem, Ham, Japheth, represented on each arm of the cross. Okay, so? Noah, yeah. That was expected. What's that? Something on the *Ham* extension? Africa? Right, traditionally that's where Ham's descendants migrated. Yeah, Fish, I know it's a big place. Okay, so let me see if I understand this correctly. The two separate parts that form the headpiece of this sceptre, staff, whatever, are deliberately designed to be separated – ritually separated? All right, maybe – one is left on the Ark, as we know, the other you theorize was taken to Africa somewhere – as a marker, a pointer, one to the other. So the African half will point to the Ark half and vice versa? Right. Reason being to preserve and protect the whereabouts of *another* location, to provide a clue, a kind of map, yes? It's what Theodore Dracup found, some link with Africa, and what? He discovered the missing piece and put two and two together. Then came the second expo to *X*, which led us to our acquisition. Too many blanks, Fish. Keep at it and call me with anything new, okay?"

"Sounds like he's getting there," Farrell said.

"Not fast enough." Potzner rubbed his eyes. For a moment his vision was filled with dancing black specks. High in his temple a vein throbbed with a heavy pulse. "Dracup's ahead of the game, somehow. What have we got? Missing subject, missing girlfriend..." Potzner tapped the desktop. "Bandana man?"

Farrell shook his head. "Not a trace."

"Have we checked Dracup's cell phone tariff?"

Farrell nodded. "I made the request this morning. Network's sending it through asap."

"Give me their number. I want it faxed. Now."

Smoke was emanating from the blasted entrance of Dracup's flat. The firemen had done their work efficiently and a few of them still moved among the hoses and paraphernalia, packing away and tidying up with the efficiency of an army unit. Chief Inspector Brendan Moran looked on approvingly. Nice to see some order in the midst of chaos. He flashed his ID and approached the chief fire officer. "All right to have a look around?"

The fireman wiped sweat away from his forehead. His face was covered in soot and grime. "I suppose. There's no structural damage as far as we can see - it's a right mess, though. We've turned the electrics off at the mains. You'll need a torch – the windows are black. Hey! Careful with that!" He barked out an order to a subordinate. Turning back to Moran he said, "No naked flames either. Gas is off, but you never know."

Moran nodded and went in. The sofa was upended in a corner of the room and fragments of furniture were scattered across the floor. Moran moved amongst the debris, his feet crunching on the littered parquet. The kitchen area had escaped most of the blast, probably due to the screening effect of the utilities wall. He looked over. Ah, perhaps not. The sink had been blown out of the other side and a makeshift bung prevented water escaping from the exposed pipe.

He retraced his steps to the lounge area. The sofa was studded with what appeared to be shrapnel. He reached into his pocket and produced a penknife, winkled out a shard of metal. *Grenade? Surely not.* This was the Thames Valley, not Seventies Northern Ireland. He went back outside and found a neighbour. Five minutes later he was satisfied. Americans. And one Middle Eastern guy, got away in Dracup's car. This was beginning to stink. Moran smiled to himself, quietly pleased. A routine tug-of-love child abduction this was not. This had CIA written all over it. Question now was, where would he find them? Which part of Dracup's life would they take as their next lead? Wife, girlfriend, colleagues? Wherever they popped up next, he'd make sure he was there. This was his jurisdiction and no one was going to trample all over it without his say-so.

Charles Sturrock was busy. Since returning from France his friend's predicament had taken centre stage. His subconscious had been churning away, worrying at the missing connection, looping and retrying his memory like some dogged computer program. It was on the return flight that all the pieces had finally come together; two thousand feet above the ground his brain seemed to achieve maximum efficiency. Perhaps it was the oxygen.

He remembered the apocryphal 'Cave of Treasures' manuscript he had read many years ago. *Me`ârath Gazzê*, a Syriac manuscript dating back to 306 AD. Many scholars had rejected the manuscript as a mere collection of 'idle stories' and 'vain fables', but Sturrock had never been that convinced. As with all the apocrypha there was some truth to be found amongst the many embellishments and fanciful additions – if you were careful with your interpretation. They were not canonical texts and so were not authoritative in the way that the New or Old Testament manuscripts clearly were. Sturrock was very sure of his ground with the latter texts – and for good reason: he was in learned company. The council of Nicaea had recognized apostolic writing for what it was, and the gospels had been continually treated as such from their first appearance – in a sense the council had only confirmed what was already understood and accepted as authentic. Far from reinventing Christianity at Nicaea, the Emperor Constantine's signature had merely rubber stamped the gospels, thus facilitating their global acceptance.

But you digress, Charles. Sturrock shook his head and allowed himself a little smile. *Or do you?* He poured himself a diluted refill and thought about the apocrypha. Now these writings had to be handled very differently. The centuries had produced many religious writings claiming veracity, but Sturrock understood that scholars down the ages had taken great care to expose fraudulent and misleading texts. He sipped his brandy and contemplated *Me`ârath Gazzê, The Cave of Treasures.* Was the author's intention to deceive? He thought not. More likely the opposite: to highlight the wonder of it all. Sturrock grunted. He spent many solitary hours in his study and found vocalizing his conclusions helpful.

The carriage clock on the crowded mantelpiece struck ten. No matter; the night was young. Charles gazed at the ceiling and ordered his thoughts. So: a wonder book indeed, the purpose of which was to reinforce Christian doctrine and introduce detail of a secondary nature – necessarily excluded from the canonical scriptures. Nevertheless, caution was Sturrock's watchword. As he had begun his investigation he reminded himself that much of this particular apocrypha was founded on nothing more substantial than good old-fashioned myth and legend, but he also reminded himself that remnants of truth lay scattered within if you knew where to look. Willis Rudge was the scholar in question here and Sturrock could only agree with his summary:

> *'The 'Cave of Treasures' possesses an apocryphal character certainly, but the support which its contents give to the Christian Faith, and the light which the historical portions shed on early Christian History, entitle it to a very high position among the apocryphal Books of the Old and the New Testament.'*

Sturrock typed in a new search string and waited. He read for several minutes, but hesitated before scrolling to the next paragraph. In that moment he had guessed the truth. He reached for his brandy with shaking hands. *My God, Simon. My God...* He took a long pull, set his glass down with trembling fingers and pasted the text into a new email message. As his conclusions tumbled onto the screen he prayed that his friend would check his email account. He reread the message and clicked on the address book icon. *Disley, Donnington, Dracup.* The doorbell rang.

"Just a minute." Sturrock replaced the brandy bottle on the mantelpiece, muttering and shaking his head. If there was one thing he couldn't stand it was interruptions. Some student after a stay of execution for a late assignment, probably. Why had he let the housekeeper go early? Perhaps he *should* have moved off campus as he had originally intended.

He unchained the bolt and swung the door open. His mouth opened in surprise. He turned and stumbled back into the hall. The computer was a long way off. He wouldn't make it. Sturrock let out a yell as he felt hands catch at his clothing. He shrugged off his jacket and fell forward, lunging for the keyboard. Something cold entered his back, a probing metallic sharpness. And then came the pain, savage, permeating. He twisted in his agony and looked into the face of his attacker. The eyes were dark, relentless. Sturrock's vision began to fade; an overwhelming blackness was descending. He focused on the row of control keys and stabbed a finger out, feeling for the small, concave button: F9. *Send/Receive.*

The first thing Moran noticed was the smell. He knew it before he stepped over the threshold. A thick, cloying scent that pervaded the entire house. He stepped gingerly into the hall, one hand on the door frame. The lock was intact – no sign of forced entry. Nice old building, good solid stone. Moran had made this his first port of call, deferring a visit to Yvonne Dracup in favour of the Professor's oldest friend, Charles Sturrock. Eccentric, but brilliant. Internationally famous for his archaeological aptitude, but probably better known around the campus for his odd predilections. Moran smiled grimly. He had seen Sturrock on the box only a few weeks ago, some time slip series about Roman Britain.

The door to the study was slightly ajar. Moran approached and listened. All quiet. He pushed the door a fraction and the smell hit him full on. He found a handkerchief in his pocket and advanced purposefully once he saw the body. You couldn't miss it.

Charles Sturrock lay across the desk, his throat a gaping hole through which blood still oozed thickly onto the green leatherette surface. The eyes were open, shocked. Moran winced, leaned forward and closed them. Always the worst bit, the eyes. Another wound caught his attention: a neat perforation in the corpse's back, ringed with dried blood. A two-pronged attack, then; a knife in the back, another across the throat. Moran's nose twitched. There was something else. Spirit. He lifted the archaeologist's arm. Glass fragments were embedded in Sturrock's flesh, the tumbler crushed by the weight of the corpse's body.

The computer had been given similar attention; its guts had been ripped out. The flat screen stared blankly at him. Moran poked around in the drawers. A couple of floppies – did people still use these things? He slipped them into his jacket. All sorts of sundry items fell under his gloved fingertips. Moran ejected them without ceremony. He hated an untidy mind, brilliant or otherwise. Sheaves of papers came out and were consigned to the floor. Magazines came next. Moran picked up the first and groaned aloud. Its title was artistically shaped into the outline of a jet fighter. 'Flying Magazine.'

He clapped a hand to his head. *Moran, you're slowing down.* Using his handkerchief he picked up the phone. Two rings. Come on. They answered. "This is Moran. Get me an ambulance and a squad car." He told them the address. "And get me Sergeant Phelps." He tapped his foot until Phelps came on. "Phelps – I want you to check all local airfields in the south east – Blackbushe, White Waltham, Old Sarum, whatever. I want to know who went where over the last few days, especially one Professor Charles Sturrock."

Moran listened to his Sergeant's reaction and curled his lip. "Yes, Phelps. Dracup's friend was a blasted pilot. Yes, I did say 'was'."

Moran watched Forensic pick their way through the contents of Sturrock's flat, dusting, picking, bagging. The body had been taken away and he felt the usual relief. Now it was just a crime scene, not a morgue. He went outside and found his Sergeant, a lugubrious-looking officer in his late thirties; a plodder, but more often than not that's what you needed. Who said police work was glamorous?

Phelps strolled over. His eyebrows reminded Moran of the forward and backslash keys on a computer keyboard. It gave the man a sad, put-upon look, as if he carried the world's weight on his thin, raincoated shoulders. "Any joy, Guv?"

"Not so far. Messy killing. Looks like he put up a fight – for a small bloke. You?"

Phelps shook his head. "Nope. Closest neighbour is down the road and round the corner. Didn't hear a thing – well, they wouldn't have."

Moran sat on the low ornamental wall of the unkempt front garden. "The hard disk is gone," he told Phelps. He produced a brown bundle from his coat pocket and unwrapped a sandwich. Food stimulated his thinking. "But I've retrieved a couple of floppies. Can you take a look?" He handed Phelps the disks. "Oh, and find out which ISP he was signed up to? They can give us access to his email account – with any luck we might hear from our little flown bird."

The Sergeant headed off to his car and Moran took a bite of the sandwich. Cheese and pickle; not his favourite but it would do. He chewed thoughtfully, enjoying the tang of the pickle alongside the waxy texture of the cheddar. Through the front door he caught the occasional snap of blue as the Forensic officers worked methodically from room to room. When they were finished he would spend time in there alone, soaking up the atmosphere, allowing any missed evidence the opportunity to present itself. It was the little things, always the little things that turned a case from mystery to revelation. What was it his old guv'nor had said? He could see him now; grey Yorkshire eyes creasing with the enjoyment of communicating a lifetime's experience to a promising pupil – the next generation. 'Moran, my lad, remember this if you don't remember anything else: every case is like a *large* door swinging on a very *small* hinge. The detail, boy, get down to the detail.' It could be a splinter of wood, the merest speck of paint that made sense of the strangest conundrum.

Moran took another bite of his sandwich and looked up. Two men were advancing along the narrow pavement towards him. Not Uni types. The first – tall, middle-aged – wore a long grey coat and covered the distance with measured strides. Perhaps a slight limp. The second, a younger man in a charcoal suit, walked a pace or two behind, eyes scanning the gardens and campus hedgerows as they walked. Professionals. American professionals. Well, at least he wouldn't have to go looking. The CIA had come to play, and on his patch too.

"Morning." The older man spoke. "I believe we have a mutual interest here. James Potzner, US Embassy." He extended his hand.

Moran placed his sandwich carefully on the wall. "DCI Moran. Thames Valley. This is a crime scene, gentlemen. If you know anything about what happened, I'd like to hear it."

Potzner squared his shoulders. "We have a US security issue here, Inspector. If it's all the same to you we'll take the lead on this one. I can get clearance, no problem. If you could let me have the name of your superior –"

"Actually, it's not all the same to me," Moran interrupted. "This is a police matter. A crime has been committed, and as far as I'm concerned it's in the hands of the Thames Valley Police. Our normal procedures apply." Moran spoke evenly. He'd met Potzner's type before; a big man, using his presence to intimidate. Used to getting results.

The younger man in the suit spoke. He wore his hair slicked back, like Michael Douglas. "This goes a lot deeper than you'd be comfortable with, Inspector. If you'd allow us to explain, I'm sure you'll have no problem with it. I –"

"My apologies," Potzner interrupted. "This is Farrell, one of my senior operatives. He's absolutely right. If we could have ten minutes of your time we can give you an overview of our situation."

Moran stuck his chin out. "I don't think I've made myself clear. I'm conducting a murder enquiry here. Your security situation will have to be taken up and attended to at a higher level. Until I hear otherwise I'm not handing anything to anyone, nor am I wasting time on subordinate matters that don't concern me. What I *would* like to know is what you were doing at Professor Simon Dracup's flat yesterday, and specifically what part you played in the explosion that followed." Moran folded his arms. It was a punt, but the description fitted. And he was in the mood for a fight.

"Murder enquiry? We'd assumed a break-in." Potzner looked genuinely shaken. He took a step towards the gatehouse porch.

Moran stepped in front, blocking the way. "This is police business, Mr Potzner. Unless you have anything useful to tell me I suggest you obtain a letter of authority to involve yourself in this case. I'd also like an answer to my last question. Perhaps you and your colleague would like to accompany my Sergeant down to the station and we can get to the bottom of it?"

Phelps had sidled up to the group and was hovering, hands in pockets, observing.

"The hell I will, Inspector." Potzner glared. "Okay, if that's the way you want it. I'll be back. Very soon."

"Have a nice day, gentlemen." Moran raised a hand in farewell. He watched Potzner and Farrell retrace their steps along the perimeter of the campus. To Phelps he said, "Get onto the Chief Constable, Phelps. Tell him to expect a call. I'll fill him in when I get back."

Phelps nodded and made his way back to the squad car. He exchanged a few words with a uniformed officer, who nodded vigorously and started the engine. The car departed, siren ululating, into the distance. Moran found his place on the wall and unscrewed the lid of his Thermos. He reckoned on a day or two's grace before Uncle Sam got the all-clear to muscle in. He sipped his coffee with satisfaction. Something big was going down and, for once, Brendan Moran was in the right place at the right time.

Chapter 21

The hotel foyer was cool in contrast to the baking street outside. A large rotating fan swished soundlessly above but Dracup still felt a trickle of perspiration run down his collar. He took another sip of iced water and replaced the glass carefully on the brass tabletop.

"So what brings you to Addis, Prof?" Dan Carey grinned. His main feature was a wide, roguish smile, enhanced by a long vertical scar that ran from one side of his mouth to the corner of his right eye. It gave him a rakish, dashing look. He was a wiry, tough-looking man in his mid to late thirties.

"It's a long story," Dracup replied. Where could he begin? Better to stick to a simple explanation. "I'm interested in Lalibela and its religious background. I want to spend a few days gathering information, taking photographs."

Carey nodded. "Research project, is it? Charles seemed pretty excited."

"Of a kind," Dracup agreed. He felt uneasy at his economy of truth; there was something about Carey that invited openness.

"Well, I've been to Lali a couple of times and I can tell you this much – you won't get a lot out of the priests and holy men. Their lips are sealed, especially to Westerners. Start asking too many questions and they clam up like old maids with their dentures stuck together."

Dracup forced a laugh. "I'll be persuasive."

"You'll need to be."

"And you're okay with tomorrow morning?" Dracup fought to mask his agitation. Tomorrow wasn't soon enough. *Now* wasn't soon enough.

Carey shook his head. "It's not a problem. I've been wanting a weekend off for a while – the school's been busy. I need to get out of town, rough it a bit." He laughed. "It's in my nature. I'm a bit of a nomad. I'll pick you up first thing and we'll head off."

"How long will it take?"

Carey shrugged. "Couple of days – the roads are pretty bad. We'll stop off at Dessie and maybe Weldiya – that'll be an experience for you." There was a glint in the Kiwi's eye. He knocked back his drink and stood up. "Right now you'll have to excuse me, Prof – I have to get to a meeting. Someone's got to cover for me while I'm away."

"Of course. See you in the morning, then." Dracup watched Carey walk away, reassured that he'd found an ally. He drained his drink and headed back to his room to re-examine Theodore's tablet. He traced the inscriptions with his thumbnail. Ω *section 1921, TD, GRC. Left in situ.* Theodore had been successful; he had seen *Omega* with his own eyes. But would Lalibela give up its secrets so easily to his grandson?

"You wait," Carey grinned. "Thirty minutes and the word'll be out. We'll have company all right."

Dracup frowned and shuffled closer to the fire. The drive had been a careering, pothole-avoiding rally all the way from Addis. Much of the driving had been off-road, an inconvenience that Carey seemed to find enjoyable. Dracup shifted his weight. His backside was a painful pad of bruising. They were parked several hundred metres from the road – apparently in the middle of nowhere. "There's nothing around here," he replied. "Company from where?"

Carey looked over Dracup's shoulder and laughed. "How about there?"

Dracup turned to follow Carey's pointing finger and saw to his amazement a line of young Ethiopians approaching the campfire. They were singing, a low rhythmic melody, and smiling. They showed no fear of the two men.

"Told you," Carey said. "They know when strangers are about."

The group of newcomers settled themselves by the fire, chattering among themselves. They grinned at Dracup and his Kiwi companion, pointing to the tents and the jeep. One of the youngest, a girl of about fifteen or sixteen, produced some substance from her bag and threw it on the fire. A sweet smell wafted over the gathering. Dracup recognised it. "Eucalyptus." He smiled and touched his nose. The girl grinned and said something to her companion, a boy of about the same age. They laughed and began singing again, clapping and slapping their thighs in time to the music. The moon shone brilliantly in a clear sky, illuminating the youthful faces of the visitors as they celebrated the simple joy of being alive.

It was a mesmerising moment, and as Dracup drifted off to sleep later that evening he carried the scene with him into his dreams. In the campfire circle of his imagination Natasha was beside him, her voice joining the others in song. The song was heartbreakingly beautiful; he could hardly bear to listen. The fire burned slowly down and the voices hushed into reverential silence. They stepped forward, bending to look into what appeared to be a deep trench filled with colours – a bowl of reflected light.

Dracup wanted to see and stepped forward but Natasha gripped his arm, shaking her head. *We can't, Daddy. It's not for us.* There was another, a tall figure by the light. Natasha shrank from it, clinging to his arm. The figure stepped forward, beckoning. *She is mine.* Dracup opened his mouth to protest but his tongue was impotent, glued to the roof of his mouth. Natasha let go of his arm and took a faltering step towards the light. *No – NO.*

Dracup woke with a start; he sat up, disoriented. It was freezing cold but sweat was running freely down his back. He crawled forward, opened the tent flap and went out into the night. The campfire had burned low, its embers glowing like fireflies, but there was no sign of the children, just a faint trace of perfumed bark in the air. He walked a few paces from the tent and relieved himself. The moon hung in the sky like a yellow orb, the distant mountains silhouetted against a backdrop of ochre. He raised his head to the stars, far-off pinpricks of blue, the dust lanes of Andromeda a distant smear of matter. For a long time he looked into the cosmos. And strangely, he found a prayer on his lips: *Oh God, if you are there, please help me. I can't do this on my own. Help me find her. Just help me find her.*

Carey rose with alarming cheerfulness at first light. Dracup heard the Kiwi whistling, a tuneless parody of the children's harmonies from the night before. The tent flap parted and a steaming mug of coffee presented itself. "G'day Prof – good sleep?"

Dracup groaned. His bones were ice. "I didn't realise the nights would be so cold."

Carey laughed. "Too right. We can get a few more blankets in Dessie this afternoon if you like – they've got a general store."

Dracup eased his battered body into the chill dawn. A few scattered clouds drifted in the metallic blue of the new day. A faint drone from the north announced the presence of an aircraft, a speck in the huge canopy above. Like the flying machine, he felt very small in this huge country, diminished by its timelessness.

"Another coffee?" Carey offered the pot. "Warm you up for the journey."

Dracup shivered and held out his mug.

They drove on in the ever-increasing heat of the day. Dracup looked up and winced at the brightness. Another aeroplane was heading in the same direction but parallel to the road, slowly pulling ahead. Dracup squinted at the small machine. He turned to Carey. "Seems to be a popular flight path."

"Oh yeah," Carey replied, shouting above the noise. "There's a small airstrip at Lali – you can hire a two-seater in Addis. A lot of people do that – it's a little quicker to get there." He grinned. "I prefer this way, though. You feel part of the country."

Dracup's rear end had felt enough of the country by now, but he knew what the Kiwi meant. His thoughts strayed to the one subject he wanted to avoid: Sara. His anger, which had made it easy to exclude her from his thoughts, had slowly been replaced by the emptiness of loss. He thought of the last night in Aberdeen, remembered her expression of concern at the airport. How could he have been so wrong? Charles had theorised about her involvement in the diary episode, perhaps even Natasha's abduction. He still couldn't believe it. There were too many missing pieces to make a judgement. Perhaps Lalibela would change all that. The jeep clattered on, Carey spinning the wheel every so often to avoid a pothole. "How long to Weldiya?" he shouted in the Kiwi's ear.

"A few hours. We'll stop and rest up for the night, get something to eat – they do a good milkado there too." Carey let go of the wheel with one hand and gave Dracup the thumbs up.

"Milk what?"

"Milkado." Carey gave a wide grin. "Legacy from the I-ties – it's similar to a latte. Milky coffee, but a little stronger. Good stuff. Almost worth a visit on its own."

The route became progressively hillier as they climbed higher into the mountains. The sheer beauty of it took Dracup's breath away. "What's our altitude?" he asked.

"About three thousand metres I reckon. Look at this." Carey honked his horn as they eased past a group of cyclists. "Crazy bastards." He waved as they overtook the leaders. "Not the easiest way to travel." He grinned. "They do a lot of bike tours up this way." Dracup looked back at the bikers' slow, sweaty progress. The front cyclist waved then pointed. All the bikes stopped at his signal and dismounted. Dracup half turned in his seat but was nearly flung out of the vehicle when the jeep veered sharply to the side of the road. He heard Carey let out a yell of surprise as he saw the oncoming silhouette of an aeroplane. It tacked lower on its trajectory and headed straight for them.

"What the h... get down!" Carey jerked the jeep back onto the tarmac and slammed on the brakes. The plane skimmed overhead, engine screaming, banked steeply and swept back towards them. Carey gunned the engine, heading off the road towards the hillside where the steep incline offered some protection. The machine came lower and lower and then lower still, causing the cyclists to throw themselves flat on the tarmac as it passed a few metres over their heads.

Carey's foot crashed down on the brakes a second time. "Out!" Dracup yelled and threw himself under the jeep. The earth erupted around them as a chattering line of bullets ripped along the driver's side, clanging against the metal like a team of manic steel band drummers.

Carey appeared next to him. "Friends of yours?" he shouted.

Dracup curled himself tightly by the front wheel and listened for the throb of the aeroplane's engine. Would it make another pass? The noise receded. He stuck his head into the open and checked the sky. The plane was a retreating smudge, becoming smaller with each passing second. Half a minute later it had disappeared altogether. Carey rolled out from under the vehicle and brushed himself down. "What was all that about?" He looked at Dracup suspiciously. "Something to do with your 'research project'?"

Dracup wiped sweat from his forehead and nodded. "I'm sorry. I didn't intend to drag you into all this."

Carey shrugged. "No worries." He scanned the open skies. "Looks like they've gone for now."

"They'll be back." Dracup sat heavily in the passenger seat and took a swig from his water bottle while Carey conducted an inspection of the vehicle.

"They missed the tyres – that's a miracle." Carey climbed back in. "And the petrol tank. You're a lucky old jalopy." He patted the dashboard affectionately.

Behind them the cyclists were picking themselves up and pointing to the two men in the jeep. Dracup sensed a confrontation looming. "Better be off before we have a steward's enquiry."

Carey glanced back. "No damage? Well, I guess you're right – no need to hang about. Hold tight." He let the clutch out. For a few kilometres they both nervously surveyed the empty sky.

"Well that's a first for me. I'm normally treated pretty well by the locals." Carey grinned and shook his head ruefully. "For a moment I thought we'd carked it good and proper back there."

"They weren't locals," Dracup said. "Not by any stretch." He would have to come clean. Perhaps it was just as well that Carey had all the facts. He took a deep breath and clapped the Kiwi on the shoulder. "Dan, I owe you an explanation."

"So, what's the plan, Prof?" Carey asked matter-of-factly. "You might find a reception committee at Lalibela – then what? If that plane's anything to go by, someone doesn't want you poking around."

Dracup smiled grimly. As they had checked into Weldiya's Lal hotel he had scrutinised every face – waiter, guest or otherwise – for signs of bad intent. It had taken a couple of hours and a few beers to put his worries to rest. Carey seemed unperturbed, as if he were used to being shot up on a standard 'weekender', as he liked to call their trip. Dracup wished he could adopt some of the Kiwi attitude himself – Carey had accepted his story with no more surprise than if Dracup had been recounting a successful fishing trip. Maybe it would rub off.

"I'll tread carefully."

"You'd better. The aim is to get hold of the missing piece of this sceptre, right? The *Omega* section?"

"Yes. But I've no intention of removing it – not that I'll have the option anyway, judging from what you've told me about the custodians of Lalibela's treasures. I just need to get some clear photos of the cuneiform inscriptions. That's it – Charles can do the rest." You'd better, Charles, Dracup thought. You'd better.

Carey was silent for a moment, digesting this information. He inclined his head in a swift gesture of assent. "You're the boss. We'll check into the New Jerusalem. The view is something else."

Dracup raised his eyebrows. "The what?"

"The New Jerusalem. Best guesthouse in Lali. Trust me." Again came the lopsided Kiwi grin. "The whole of Lalibela is structured on the belief that it represents a kind of New Jerusalem – the churches all fit into different aspects of that concept. They're a pretty amazing sight."

"I know. I had a look on the web. The tradition is fascinating, the way it links back to King Solomon and the Queen of Sheba."

Carey looked reflective. "Yeah – the original Ark of the Covenant is supposed to be in a church back up north at Axum – brought here by Solomon himself. Almost makes you believe there's something in it all. Well let me tell you, Lali has a kind of feel about it – tranquillity. It's a strange place all right. It's kind of hard to explain – you've got to experience it yourself. All I can say is that if there are any secrets to be found, Lali's the place to find 'em." He took his hand off the gear shift and rubbed his chin thoughtfully. "I reckon you're headed in the right direction, mate, I really do."

Lalibela was smaller and busier than Dracup expected. They drove past a motley collection of ramshackle houses, peaked huts and tin-roofed buildings, Carey skilfully picking his way through the busy streets clogged with wood-carrying women, farmers, pilgrims and holy men.

"Market day," Carey observed. "Most of this lot will have set off at dawn to get here. They'll have walked miles." He pointed to a group trudging the last few steps to their destination, some pulling makeshift carts behind them, others carrying bags of produce.

Carey swung the jeep around, beeping the horn. Dracup drummed his fingers on the dash. As the jeep pulled up in front of the hotel Dracup was already swinging himself out, one hand on his bag.

"No, let me, boss! Nothing a problem, okay?"

Dracup turned to see a boy of around eleven grinning up at him.

"No problem. Mister let me take the bag."

Dracup patted his pockets and made an empty-handed gesture.

Carey dispensed a few words in the boy's direction; he shrugged dismissively in response, throwing back a few choice words of his own. He turned his back on Carey and made as if to leave them in peace, but couldn't resist a last-ditch attempt. Dracup smiled at his persistence.

"Come on, boss." He fixed Dracup with a persuasive grin. "I can help you out, man."

"*A bo teu weun!*" Carey aimed a kick. The boy yelped and ran off, shouting and waving his fist.

"I take it he's not wishing you a nice day." Dracup watched the boy until he disappeared from view.

"Give 'em an inch and they'll take a hundred miles," Carey warned. "Do anything if you cross their palm. Trouble is, once you say yes you never get rid of 'em."

Dracup's bedroom window overlooked Lalibela's rooftops and beyond these the distant mountains. The view was spectacular, the contoured peaks undulating like waves across the Ethiopian plains. The sheer immensity of the landscape reminded him of India. His boyhood seemed closer in this climate, the connecting years of adulthood pressed into a dim, grey background. Dracup retrieved his grandfather's tablet from the suitcase and scanned the markings.

Loc. Remaining part staff, trad. Ethiop.
Ityopp'is – Cush – sn of Ham- fnded Axum.
Match. crest. Lal., Ω 1921, TD,GRC. Left in situ.
Formed basis of expo. 1922 C of Tr.
K. zig. - 7 by 7

1921. Left in situ. Dracup clung to the phrase. Eleven churches to choose from. Or maybe what he was looking for lay hidden elsewhere, perhaps not even here in Lalibela. He drew out a photograph from his pocket. Natasha's face smiled back at him, small hands clasping her favourite teddy. He had spent a fruitless hour showing the image to the locals. Every approach had produced the same reaction. Dracup didn't understand the language but simply read the faces. *Pretty girl. Yes. Very pretty.* Then a sad shake of the head, a sympathetic smile. *No. Sorry. I haven't seen her.* He kissed the photograph and replaced it carefully in his breast pocket. Eleven churches. A lot of space to cover. Dracup set his mouth in a determined line. A one in eleven chance was as good as he was likely to get, and there was no time to lose. He needed answers and he needed them now.

Chapter 22

"Sara!" Natasha ran to her, leaving Ruth and Jassim behind. Sara hugged the child, dreading the next question. When it came she tried to smile confidently.

"Is Daddy here?"

She saw the warning look on Ruth's face. "Not yet, Natasha." She ignored the disappointed, questioning look and pressed on. "And how are you? What do you think of all this?" Sara lifted her arm and swept it in an expansive movement towards the worked stone roof.

"It's a bit spooky, but I like it mostly. I miss Mummy."

Sara looked at Ruth, then Jassim. Their faces were inscrutable. Had Jassim heard of their altercation?

They walked on towards the east passages where Ruth had her quarters. Sara decided to tackle the problem head-on. "Ruth, we must talk." One arm wrapped protectively around Natasha, she touched Ruth's shoulder. To her surprise, Ruth's face softened. She took Sara's offered hand and clasped it.

"Yes. We can go to my chamber. Jassim?"

"I will take the girl." Jassim turned to Natasha. "Come, little one. We shall do some exploring."

Natasha looked at Sara for affirmation. She pursed her lips and nodded. "It's all right. I'll see you later."

The sisters watched Jassim lead Natasha away along the passage. The girl looked back once and gave a small wave. Sara's heart went out to her. She took a deep breath and smiled at Ruth. "Come."

"I am sorry. I didn't mean to hurt you. It's been – so hard." Ruth sat, contrite, hands in her lap. Passive.

"I understand." Sara sipped her drink, a warm concoction of herbs and fruit. "Believe me, I do."

"Did you love him so much?" Ruth asked. "The girl's father?"

Sara stared into her cup, steam rising from the heady mixture. She felt uneasy, wondering at her sister's shift in mood. Ruth had always been constant in temper, pouring calm on her troubled waters. Sara wasn't sure if she knew this person any more. She nodded slowly. "Yes, yes I did – I do."

"But you came back."

"I had no choice. You know that."

Ruth came and sat next to Sara. "You came for the child, not him. Not for the *Korumak*. Kadesh knows that, but –" she smiled, a faraway look in her eye, "he will not hurt you." She took Sara's hand and squeezed it. "If you stay. He cares for you too much. But the girl, I don't know –"

"Surely he wouldn't harm her."

Ruth shook her head. "He has changed. He is obsessed with revenge. Since his father died he has taken the anger to himself. Remember it was a Dracup who stole our treasure all those years ago. And now *another* Dracup has killed his brother, Tarshish. In Kadesh's mind, an eye for an eye is the only retribution that will satisfy."

Sara swallowed hard. "She is a child. A little girl."

"He doesn't see it like that. He sees only the crime."

Sara held her head in her hands. "Can't you persuade him? You have looked after Natasha well –"

"He is playing with me. One minute he says he will spare her, the next –" Ruth raised her hands in a gesture of hopelessness.

"He should have left his bitterness behind," Sara whispered. "What is done is done. Why cause further pain? The girl will be our undoing – God will judge him for taking her."

"No. Kadesh wants what God himself wants." Ruth said the words slowly, as if their weight would make them true.

Sara changed tack. Natasha's fate seemed to strike a note of urgency in her sister. She had to exploit that while she could. "I have to get her out." Sara watched Ruth carefully. She remembered the wild-eyed Ruth, the stinging slap to the face.

"Yes, yes. I know." Ruth bowed her head. "I know. I can't keep her. Not when her life is at risk."

Sara hugged her sister. "I love you, Ruth. I'll help in any way I can. But we have to think. We may not have much time."

"He'll come after you."

"We have to give Natasha a chance."

"If he finds you he will kill you."

"He may kill me anyway. I failed, as Ibrahim failed."

"But you have returned as he commanded."

"The copies Simon made... it was my responsibility. Kadesh knew – and then poor Ibrahim. Oh Ruth, I'm so scared."

Ruth began to hum, a low, smooth sound like the wind soughing through the upper caves. She opened her arms. "Hold me."

Sara looked at her sister and saw the dark rings beneath her eyes, the lines of disappointment at the corners of her mouth. She frowned and touched Ruth's cheek. Ruth responded by running her fingers through Sara's hair, a gentle, soothing motion and then began to sing softly, a song their mother had taught them. She combed and brushed, combed and brushed, and for a moment they were children again; the burden of their future lay ahead, not behind them. Sara joined the chorus and as their voices blended she felt a hard pain in her throat, the prelude to tears. "We were happy once, weren't we?"

"Yes," Ruth said. "Yes, my sister." Her voice was soft and unhurried.

Sara turned and inhibited the comb's progress with a light pressure. "Come with me. We will leave together. We can go anywhere."

Ruth hung her head. The comb fell to the ground with a clatter. "Don't you think I've thought of that? Every day I think: today is the day I will leave him. Never to come back." She seemed to shrink, her body wilting into itself. "I want to be free, Sara. But I cannot. I have to be here."

"Close to him?" Sara nodded and caressed her sister's cheek. She understood. "I will pray for your heart's desire, sister. Tomorrow is not for us to know; only God knows the future. We both have to trust in Him." She squeezed Ruth's thin hand. They were sisters; they had to support each other. "Will you help me?"

Ruth tilted her pale face up to Sara's and gave a weak smile. "You know I will."

The women encountered few souls on their way to the stream. They had chosen this time of day for its stillness. Above the deep, the sun would be at its zenith. Sara linked her arm in Ruth's as they walked. They spoke in guarded whispers until they reached the waterfall, confident that its roar would drown their voices.

"They are dealing in weapons," Ruth told Sara. "Kadesh is meeting with the enemies of the United States."

"With insurgents?" Sara gasped. "What is this? We have no need to walk with such people."

"Protection. Money. Long term. These are the words they use," Ruth replied.

"Tell me Kadesh hasn't opened the caverns to men like this." Sara put her jar down and seized her sister's arm. She couldn't believe what she was hearing.

"They have a meeting place – far from here. Their vehicles return laden with guns."

"But what does Kadesh offer in return?"

Ruth smiled. "Safe passage. Guides, who travel the old routes and assist their comings and goings."

Sara swallowed. This was all wrong. It could only lead to disaster. "These men will take what they can then destroy us. Kadesh is jeopardising everything." She had a terrible vision of armed terrorists wandering the tunnels of her home, the staccato of submachine gun fire invading the tranquillity of millennia.

"He believes the American intelligence will find us. He is taking necessary steps. This is what he tells the elders."

"And this company of terrorists are going to help us? I don't think so."

"He believes he is safeguarding the *Korumak*."

Sara snorted. "He's mad. And Jassim?"

"He has not spoken against Kadesh. He is biding his time. Perhaps he will act, but I don't think he has been pushed far enough."

"Will he help us?"

Ruth shook her head. "I don't know. It's not worth the risk." She glanced round to be sure they were alone. "But all this to-ing and fro-ing may help you – and Natasha."

Sara nodded. "I'm listening."

"They have a regular rendezvous each month. But before this takes place there are vehicles – jeeps and lorries – made ready for the journey. They arrive from the city at sunset on the seventh day. They depart the following dawn. If you timed your departure you wouldn't be missed for hours."

"Where do they keep the vehicles?"

Ruth smiled. "I will show you."

Sara was shaking when she reached the solitude of her chamber. At any time she expected to be summoned. And if Kadesh had any inkling where she had been... She shivered and took a deep breath. Now she was committed. It could be done. No, it *had* to be done. But first, one further task had to be accomplished. Sara found her mobile and prayed that she could get a signal outside. She lifted her robe and tucked the phone under her suspender strap. Then she went to find Natasha.

Chapter 23

Dracup climbed above the town and looked over the ridge to the distant mountains. Carey had left earlier with a cheery wave and a promise to return in two days. Dracup wiped his brow and wondered if he would find what he was looking for in two years, let alone two days. He headed down to his first site – Bet Giorgis, the cruciform church. From there he intended to visit the remaining ten churches in the hope that he could pick up some sign, some nuance of meaning that would lead him to his goal. As he looked down on the scattered collection of huts and watched the inhabitants move about the honeycombed village in their unhurried, typically African amble he considered again the odds of stumbling across *Omega*, the sister headpiece of Noah's sceptre.

In the meantime there was a real chance that *Alpha*'s cuneiform would highlight some hitherto missing but significant detail – perhaps even the Lalibela connection. That being the case, he could expect CIA company any time – not an appealing prospect. Dracup wondered how Charles was progressing with his theories. What was it he had said at the airport? *I don't think Theodore's sceptre was originally Noah's at all.* Under normal circumstances his professional fascination would be vibrating like a tuning fork, but right now Dracup didn't care about the sceptre's provenance as long as it pointed him to Natasha. That was his cue to move. Dracup set his hat squarely on his head and went exploring.

The church of Bet Giorgis – the house of St George – was an astonishing building. It lay partially hidden in a deep gully cut out of the pinky-red tuff of the surrounding terrain. But it was the shape that had drawn Dracup to investigate this particular church before the others. The roof decoration was a relief of three equilateral Greek crosses inside one another, chiselled to fit within the shape of the building that was itself of cruciform design. Too obvious, maybe? He walked quickly around the perimeter, searching for a way in. Eventually he found a group of tourists and tagged along, finding himself in a trench leading into an enclosed tunnel. A jagged circle of daylight announced their arrival at the base of Giorgis, where he could take in the sheer wonder of the building.

The sides of the pit from which the church had been carved were studded with black openings; caves or tombs, he couldn't be sure, but now and then there was a flash of bright yellow or blue from within, indicating the presence of a priest or religious devotee of the church. Dracup gazed at the monolithic building. Seven steps led up to the main portal. *Seven.* He thought of Farrell, the Biblical encyclopaedia, and worried again that Potzner could arrive anytime to hinder or even curtail his own investigation.

Gathered in and around the church exterior were a motley assembly of priests and tourists, even a white-wimpled nun. One of the robed figures was chanting in a loud, alien lilt, watched admiringly by the camera-toting tourists. A group of young girls, pilgrims to the holy site, posed smiling for the clicking shutters, their white costumes a testament to inner purity. The atmosphere was charged, as if some hidden spiritual energy ran unseen beneath the foundations of the church.

He found himself ascending the steps. A priest bowed and extended an unspoken invitation to enter. Dracup passed into the interior, into a warm smell of stone and antiquity. A wall hanging depicted St George, the church's namesake, fighting the dragon – a strange echo from home in this faraway place. Long drapes of red and blue hung from the ceiling, the primary colours contrasting with the terracotta shades of the church walls. The priest beckoned. Dracup followed him to a far corner of the church. The priest smiled, whether in genuine friendliness or solely to display his extensively gold-capped teeth Dracup couldn't be sure, then chanted some unintelligible litany and disappeared behind a tapestry of symbols. Dracup peered at the runes of the ruffled curtain. Several represented a bright sun-like god, while others were obviously based on Biblical prophecy. There was the Lion of Judah, the crucifixion on Golgotha, and a nautical scene where the Ark of Noah balanced on the most precarious of waves. *Full circle.* Dracup exhaled in frustration. *Theodore... what am I looking for?*

The priest was back, gesticulating. Dracup followed him to a long wooden box. Widely threaded wooden screws ran into the container, which the priest firmly grasped and turned demonstratively, nodding and smiling all the while. It was obviously meant to signify something. He ran his fingers over the wood and the penny dropped.

"An Ark?" he asked. The priest's smile grew wider. There were many replica Arks in Ethiopia, as Carey had observed, modelled on the original Ark of the Covenant that was supposedly hidden away in Axum. These revered boxes contained holy books or relics of which the church was immensely proud. Could one of these boxes contain *Omega?*

"Does it open?" Dracup made an upward motion with his hands. The priest pointed to a large padlock and made a non-committal gesture before sidling away to attend to other tourists. Carey was right. They didn't give much away. He made a hurried reconnaissance of the interior. The floor was covered with a combination of rush matting and oriental carpeting. His feet produced no echo as he stepped around each cruciform nave of the church. He stole a glance at the door. Cameras were jostling for position. He returned to the wooden box. The floor was exposed here and Dracup noted the presence of a trapdoor cut into the stone. One large bolt was fixed in place, securing the building from unauthorised entry. He bent and took a closer look. Padlocked.

He examined a wall-mounted crucifix by a wooden lectern. On the lectern was a thick, leathery book. Dracup opened it and inspected the contents. His eyes lit upon a full-page illustration of a man, bearded and holding a wooden staff. Dracup read the title of the picture and the accompanying paragraph with a growing excitement.

> *The staff of Moses and Aaron, fashioned from the blessed Tree. The wood shall for ever live, indestructible in nature,*

miraculous in power. Blessed be the descendants of Adam touched by its perfection, tho' blackened by sin, yet shall they be raised to life everlasting.

He turned the page gently and caught his breath. A three-quarter-length illustration showed a scene of dark devastation. Stars fell from the sky and plummeted into a raging sea. A multitude was gathered on the shore, arms raised either in terror or supplication, Dracup couldn't say. At the head of the crowd, in a slightly elevated position, stood a man holding a sceptre high against the storm. It was the same staff as the previous page. Beneath the picture there was a line of indecipherable script. He pointed his camera and clicked.

The priest was at Dracup's shoulder. He reached over and firmly closed the book, shook his head and pointed to the exit. Dracup reluctantly retreated. Donning a pair of sunglasses, the priest joined him at the entrance to pose for photographs.

Grinding his teeth in frustration, Dracup walked twice round the building but saw no obvious external entry point. It was as if he were caught in the centre of some diabolical game where each puzzle, once solved, brought only further complexity and merely lengthened the distance between him and Natasha. He wiped sweat away from his eyes with an impatient gesture.

Perhaps somewhere in the complexity of tunnels and corridors there was a way back into the church via the trapdoor. He retraced his steps along the entry tunnel and trench, briefly inspecting every cavity, perspiring in the enclosed space despite being submerged in the shadow of the walkway. His thighs burned with the effort. To his horror he saw that some of the holes were occupied – a mummified pair of feet dangled from one, and slightly further up a skull lay separated from its skeleton in a dark recess, as if marking the way, watching each passing tourist with wide-eyed curiosity. Dracup stopped and beat the wall with his clenched fist in frustration. How was he supposed to negotiate this maze? Then he remembered Carey's comment about the boy who had offered to take his bags. *They'll do anything if you cross their palm...*

Cursing himself for an idiot he exited from the trench and walked swiftly back to the hotel. His next foray into the tunnels would be a guided one.

"Come on, boss." The boy waited for Dracup to catch up. He hadn't been hard to find, shying stones with a group of youngsters near the hotel, impatiently kicking his feet in the dust as others took their turn, hollering out his availability to any new arrivals wearing the *tourist* badge. "What's your name?" Dracup had asked.

"Bekele. Call me Bek, boss, everyone does."

"Well, Bek, we've got a lot of ground to cover, so let's get going."

The boy had grinned, obviously pleased with the prospect of a long-term contract. And so far, Dracup was getting his money's worth. Bek knew Lalibela and didn't hang about. He glanced up from under the brim of his hat. The boy's lithe figure was just in his line of vision, disappearing round the next corner.

"Hang on," Dracup shouted. He took the corner at speed, only to find Bek grinning, hands on hips, waiting.

"You have to be quicker, boss, okay?"

"Yes, but I need to be methodical. Where are you taking me?"

"Method-what, boss?" He grinned, showing dazzling white teeth. "You want to see a cross, I'll show you a cross."

Dracup nodded. He had shown Bek Theodore's sketch, filled in the gaps for the boy. He needn't have worried. Bek was bright. "Only half of it you've got there, boss, I tell you." And then he'd said something that had made Dracup's heart lurch. "Same as the Lalibela cross, you know what? Shape is just the same. Just like these here." He stabbed a dirty finger at the detailed, painstakingly drawn frieze.

"Are you sure?" Dracup asked. He restrained the urge to seize the boy and hug him.

"Sure? Of course." Bek seemed affronted at Dracup's ignorance. He widened his eyes and made an exaggerated gesture. "The Lalibela cross – it's the biggest deal above everything, boss.

We have a whole festival about it. It has power. People, they kiss it all the time – the priests rub it all over your body, your pains go away. You come. Follow."

Several minutes later they were outside another of the eleven carved churches. "What is this called?" Dracup asked Bek, disoriented.

"Bet Maryam, boss. Come – come along."

A number of white-robed monks were sitting on the steps of the church or talking in small groups of two or three. Their language was strange, even stranger than the Amharic Dracup had learned to recognise. Bek saw his puzzlement.

"Ge-ez, boss. Only spoken by the holy men of the church." As he spoke a bell began to ring. Dracup looked up and saw the iron instrument tilting on its timber frame, responding to a priest's enthusiastic tugging from below. The summons to worship concluded, he stood in the arched entrance and raised his arms. The small gathering began to move towards him, muttering prayers and making signs, Dracup assumed, of some ritualistic significance. Bek turned and whispered, "That one, boss, he has the cross here. He'll show you for sure."

"Can we ask to see it?"

"Yah – but not yet, they're starting their prayers."

"How long till they're finished?"

Bek shrugged. "A while. Until sundown, maybe."

"What? That's hours away."

"Sorry, boss. That's how it is."

Dracup moved forward. "I'm going in." He reached the archway and peered inside.

Bek scampered up behind. "You can try. They might not like it."

As his eyes grew accustomed to the reduced light Dracup's attention was drawn to the great central column, swathed in some sort of gilded cloth. The images were stereotypical – the manger, some knights on horseback. Angels with trumpets.

"Hey, boss?" Bek stage-whispered. "You know what they say is behind those pictures?"

Dracup shook his head.

"Only the past and future of the world." Bek grinned. "They say."

Dracup examined the cloth. He moved to one side to get a clearer view of the detail. The crucifixion. The garden of Eden. Dracup squinted. Again a nautical Ark, but land-bound this time, immersed not in water but in the process of construction. Ramps and pulleys strained and pushed the great timbers into position, workers tarred and pitched or toiled with hammers and saws alongside the huge bulk of the boat, the site overseen by a lone figure, standing at a distance, staff in hand. Dracup looked closer. The staff was surmounted by a great cross. Dracup caught his breath. He remembered the photograph he had taken earlier, the apocalyptic picture featuring the same sceptre.

"Bek, can you tell me what this says?" He thrust the camera under the boy's nose.

"Sure, boss, it's like I was saying. These are the last days, man. The end of the world and all that."

"Can you read it all to me, please?"

"Okay." Bek peered at the jpg. "It says '*Judgement falls – the sun grows dark and the stars fall to Earth. Omega.*' He cocked his head. "Like I said, boss: the future of the world. You take that photo in Giorgis? You're lucky they let you, boss."

Omega. Was it connected? Dracup knew the symbol was used extensively in Christian apocalyptic literature. Hardly surprising to find a reference in Lalibela, then. He grunted. "It's about time I had some luck, Bek. Wait – something's happening."

A strong smell of incense wafted across to where he and Bek waited like uninvited guests at a wedding. And then a priest moved out from behind the altar carrying an object that caused Dracup to gasp and lean on the wall for support. Bek nudged him.

"That's it, boss. The Lalibela cross." He looked oddly at Dracup. "You all right or what?"

Dracup inched forward. It was the right shape, but there was something missing. And then he realised. There were no inscriptions. The cross was smooth. Beautiful, exquisitely worked, yes, but *smooth*.

"I don't understand," he muttered. "Perhaps the other side –" But then the priest presented the staff to his assistant, who took it and rotated until he faced down the church towards them. Dracup had a 360-degree view. No inscriptions – even at this distance there was no doubt. And another thing – it was whole, complete.

"That's what you're after, huh?" Bek asked. "But no writing on it, that's the problem, yes?"

"Yes." Dracup was responding automatically to Bek's verbal spaghetti, like he'd always done when Natasha was little. He'd always had his mind on tomorrow's lectures, or some research paper. No time for a little girl's chatter. He pushed the thought aside. *No, wait. The boy knows something.*

"I'll tell you more if you want but, you know boss... I can't tell all of it unless..."

Dracup clicked his fingers. *It's not the real sceptre.*

"My mother, you know, she has five of us to feed."

The Lalibela cross is *a replica...* of the *original* sceptre.

"It's only money, boss, right?"

Dracup turned to Bek, his heart beating with excitement. "You know about this, don't you? You really do."

Bek drew him into the shadows of the church. In the background the priests had begun chanting. The building was fragrant with the smell of incense. "Look, boss. It's a big secret, right. I only found out by accident. If anyone finds out that I know – that I told –"

"I understand. I'll never breathe a word. Just tell me and you can disappear. Forget you ever saw me."

"Disappear what? You can't get to it easy, you know. You need Bek around for a bit at least."

"How much?" Dracup would have emptied his bank account for the information, but better not let the boy know that...

The deal was renegotiated, and they slipped out of the service into the sunlight. Dracup caught the boy's arm and held him still. "The cross in the church – it's a copy, isn't it?"

Bek nodded and gave an awkward grin.

"But how did you find that out, I wonder?"

"Bek knows stuff. I know Lalibela, okay?"

Dracup watched the boy carefully. There was something in his manner that concerned him. "Bek. What does your mother do to look after you? Does she work in the fields? Help the farmers?" He spoke gently, guessing at the pain lying below the effusive surface.

"Nothing much, boss. She manages good." He turned away.

"And your father?"

"We don't talk about him. He's long gone. And I don't care." Bek spat the words.

"It's pretty hard, isn't it?" Dracup looked into the boy's eyes.

Bek looked down, kicked a rock and watched it spinning away. "I need the money, boss. I look out for my mother, so she doesn't have to –" He broke off, stuffing his hands firmly into the ragged pockets of his shorts.

Bek's discomfort was painful to watch. Dracup put a hand on his shoulder. "Look, I'll make sure you're well rewarded for this. I promise. Now, just tell me where we have to go."

"No problem, boss. Stick to me and you'll be fine."

Dracup grinned at the boy's resilience. "Your call, then." Dracup held out his hand. "Pleasure doing business with you."

"Not like that, boss. Gimme five, okay? Look." He raised his arm threateningly. Dracup grimaced and received the slap.

"Now you. Come on, boss. You guys invented this."

"We most certainly did not." Dracup gingerly patted Bek's outstretched hand. "It was our friends across the ocean."

Bek laughed, then looked at him curiously. "You're a good guy, boss." He nodded emphatically. "You sure are."

Bek led Dracup up the plateau and away from the main town. His legs ached. He remembered Yvonne's words as he trudged along behind Bek. *What am I going to tell the police? That you're chasing off after some archaeological trinket like a British version of Indiana Jones?*

Bek turned and waved. "Almost there, boss."

"Almost where?"

"At the place. Seriously, boss, you'll be amazed when you see."

The vertical face of rock loomed over them, and Dracup could see the spots of darkness upon it that indicated the presence of openings in the mountainside. It was like the pit of Bet Giorgis but on a grander scale. Inanimate but inhabited none the less. Shadows moved within the shadows.

"Who are these people?" Dracup asked.

"Holy men, they live here all the time. Pretty crazy some of them, but they don't do any harm, boss. No worries there."

"How do they survive?" Dracup shook his head in wonder.

"Same as all of us, boss. We do it okay, somehow."

They passed a group of youngsters returning from the mountain. Dracup envied them their youth and tourist status. They were all smiles and "Hi theres" as they passed the boy and his toiling middle-aged charge on the uneven path.

They stopped for a rest. Dracup leaned on an emaciated tree and swigged from his flask. He offered some to Bek, who shook his head emphatically. Dracup hadn't seen the boy drink anything. He seemed indefatigable.

"The sun'll be going down soon, Bek – are we going to make it before nightfall?"

"It's right up this way now. Very close."

He followed Bek for a further ten minutes until the boy suddenly deviated from the path at a sharp bend in the track. He caught up in time to see Bek squeeze through a gap in two large rock formations into an open area studded with scrub and piles of boulders, haphazardly scattered about as if some giant had pulled pieces off the side of the mountain and dropped them carelessly on his way down. At the far corner of the clearing and set into the side of the rock face was a door, arched and surmounted by roughly hewn pillars. It looked almost natural but for the sculpted appearance of the supports – part of the mountain, yet, like the others, moulded by men into something remarkable.

Dracup wiped his brow and marvelled at the sight. "What on earth? This isn't one of the eleven –"

Bek was smiling oddly and shaking his head. "No, boss. I told you, didn't I? This is the twelfth, yah? The one nobody knows about. The *twelfth* rock church of Lalibela."

Chapter 24

"Diplomatically unwise? For the love of God, will you tell me what this guy is on?" Potzner threw the receiver at its base unit where it bounced with a dull, plastic crack onto the surface of the desk. "Tell me, Farrell, because I don't understand how diplomacy takes a higher priority than what we're trying to achieve here."

"I guess things are kind of sensitive right now. The President needs to keep the Brits sweet. The PM is a good guy for us – we don't want to piss him off by muscling in on their internal affairs."

"Muscling in? *Konska spierolina!* Unless we muscle in pretty damn quick this is going to slip away from us – possibly for good."

"It's a direct order, sir. We can't approach Moran."

"Then we'll be indirect. And as he's such a busy guy, we won't trouble the inspector. Yet."

Farrell settled back in his chair. Potzner was thinking on his feet. That was normal. The agitation wasn't. Neither was the Polack expletive – Potzner only resorted to his mother tongue *in extremis*. Farrell watched his boss pace the room and wondered how things would pan out. It wasn't looking good. Potzner's complexion was greyer than ever, the lines around his mouth more pronounced. They had a word for it in the Department. *Burnout*. Thing was, how close could he get to the fire without getting burned himself?

Potzner knocked on the polished front door. A second later he saw the shape of Dracup's wife peering at him through the translucent glass panel. Waiting. Hanging on every sound, every ring of the phone. When she opened the door he was struck by her composure. Attractive, petite. He knew why she and Dracup had split, but found himself wondering if he would have let it happen the same way.

"Yes?"

"James Potzner. I believe your husband may have mentioned me."

She looked him up and down. "He did. Come in."

Potzner followed Yvonne into her orderly domain. Fresh flowers were present in the hall and the lounge. The house felt prepared, expectant. *Ready for her baby to come home.*

"Have you come – I mean, is there any news of –"

Potzner shook his head. "No, ma'am. I'm sorry. I have to say at the outset that I haven't come to tell you any more about your daughter. I was rather hoping you could tell me something I need to know."

Yvonne nodded. "Sit down, please."

Potzner watched her carefully. Did she know? Had Dracup confided in her?

"How can I help?"

"I'll get straight to the point, Mrs Dracup –"

"Just Yvonne is fine."

"Okay – Yvonne." Potzner smiled. "I want to know where your husband is."

"My *ex*-husband. Well, so would I."

The reply had come back like a tennis backhand, straight down the line. She was ready for this. Potzner nodded. A tough cookie. "He didn't mention anything about your daughter – where he might have been looking for her?"

"No."

"I see." Potzner moistened his lips. "Tell me, Yvonne, do you live alone?"

"I don't see that that's any business of yours, Mr Potzner."

Potzner sighed. "Actually, Yvonne, it is. It's all *very* relevant." There was no one present in the house, he knew. Oh yes, there was a man often *in residence*, but he was busy with his networks on some client site in London. Potzner remembered Dracup's assessment of the IT specialist and his lip curled with amusement.

"Is there something funny, Mr Potzner?"

"Nope. Nothing funny." Potzner stood up and walked across the lounge carpet towards Yvonne. He felt in his pocket for the cold metal of the handcuffs. Now that he had decided on a course of action he felt a sense of detachment. What had to be done had to be done. Period. He watched Yvonne's face, how her expression had yet to show any sign of alarm. How frail she was. How frail *women* were, for all their bravado and self-assurance. "Now, Yvonne. It's just you and me. And I *really* need to know what your *ex*-husband has been saying to you."

Yvonne maintained her composure. Her mobile phone lay on the arm of the chair. "If you're threatening me, Mr Potzner, you'd better think again."

Potzner was taken aback by her confidence. Perhaps there was a reason she... his own mobile vibrated against his thigh with an insistent pulse. He gave Yvonne a curt nod. "Excuse me a moment."

Yvonne returned the nod and took the opportunity to escape from her chair. He heard her next door in the kitchen clattering cups. The running of a tap. Another noise – the kettle, zapping its current through ice cold water. But by then Potzner's world had slowed to a standstill. Because the voice on the phone was Al Busby, their neighbour on West Penn Street, Philly. Al was a good guy; Potzner had lost count of the baseball games they'd yelled through together, the bottles of Bud they'd shared on the patio of a summer's evening. He was the sort of guy you could rely on, and they *had* relied on him – and Evelyn, his fiery little wife of forty years. She was an ex-nurse – and boy, she knew her stuff. That had been reassuring, to know she was just a few metres away if they needed any help. Hospitals always listened up when one of their own made a report or request. Once, when Abi had needed something stronger for the pain, Evelyn had marched down to ER herself, taken no prisoners and organised a home assessment that same afternoon. Red tape cut to shreds. The Busbys. There when you needed them, invisible when you didn't and wanted a little space for yourselves. His extended UK stay had been made more bearable by their presence right next door to Abi.

And they never phoned. They never asked him about his job, never troubled him while he was on duty. *They never phoned.* Potzner walked into the hall and out through the front door. He opened his car with one hand on the button of the key fob and slid into the passenger seat. Yvonne's head poked curiously out of the space he had vacated at her front door, but his focus had moved on. Al was talking to him and he was trying to make sense of the words. He knew what they meant, but he couldn't assemble them into any coherent pattern that fitted his understanding. He heard his own voice interjecting, misinterpreting. "No, Al, wait. I don't – I can't –"

And Al's voice, that familiar East Coast drawl, was saying the same thing over and over. "I'm so sorry, Jim. It was very sudden. Evie took her down yesterday afternoon. You know she hadn't been that great – but she was a fighter, wasn't she? You should be proud of her. Jim – I'm so sorry. We both are. You know how we loved her. I – I didn't want to break it to you like this, but –"

Potzner listened to Al rambling on. He took in air, exhaled again. He couldn't prompt his vocal cords into life. Al was still talking, chatting like they were organising a party, or –

"Jim, you have to let us know what you want to do about – you know. They're asking already about the – arrangements. I said you were away, but Evie didn't pull any punches –" Al attempted a laugh here, "– well, you know what she's like. She said they'll just have to hang on until you –"

Potzner found his voice. To his surprise it sounded steady and authoritative. "Al, I have to ask you. Did she... say anything, I mean when –" he cleared his throat "– before she – slipped away, to pass onto me?"

Al stumbled on for a few sentences. He could hear the effort. There was nothing specific. It was sudden. And then the coma – he must understand. The deterioration was rapid. Twelve hours from chatting to Evie over the fence to the end. "Jeez, Jim. I don't know what to say – this is hard, you know, not face to face like it should be. We tried to get hold of you earlier. I – I know how you must feel."

Did he? Potzner doubted it. His light, his reason for living had been extinguished. In his absence. Without him even knowing. He stared at the plastic dash, counting the patterned lines, the fake leather indentations that seemed to him like wrinkles in an old world's face. Everything was different now. Everything had moved on. He hadn't even said goodbye.

"Jim? Are you still there?"

Perhaps it was a mistake. Perhaps Al had got it wrong. It happened. There had been cases where the patient had revived, stunning both doctors and family alike. Potzner nodded at the recollection. Why not? Thing was, he'd better get himself over to the US so he could be there when she woke up. But then his problem still remained. Dracup. And the research. It must continue at all costs. No, at *any* cost.

Al's voice was an electronic babble in the handset now. He put the noise back in his pocket and looked out of the car window. Moisture was scattered over the glass in small, bead-like tears. The front door was closed. Yvonne was standing at the picture window, arms folded. He'd read a book once, *The Naked Ape* – told you all about human gestures, what they meant. It was very informative because he now knew that when a guy raised his hand behind his head during conversation it meant he saw James Potzner as a threat. That was useful to know. There were lots of little responses and gestures that gave the game away. Arms folded. That meant *defence*. He heard the sirens in the distance, watched her face as she heard them too. Her shoulders relaxed fractionally. Potzner shifted across to the driver's seat and started the engine. The last thing he wanted was a confrontation with the policeman, Moran. Not yet. That would come later, on *his* terms.

As he steered the car out onto the trunk road he tried to remember: who had written *The Naked Ape?* And then it came to him: Desmond Morris, the renowned British anthropologist. Dracup was an anthropologist. When he saw Dracup again – and he surely would – he'd better be careful not to give too much away. No unguarded gestures. Potzner gripped the wheel and let his subconscious babble on inside him. He knew what was happening, rationally; his mind was trying to compensate for the earth-shattering news it had just received. He wanted to listen to his subconscious; it didn't hurt as much. But his training wouldn't allow it to continue. Despite his best efforts his rational mind resumed control. He let out a howl of anguish, a desperate, animal noise, battering his fist on the steering wheel. *He hadn't even said goodbye.*

Chapter 25

The chamber was in semi-darkness. The omnipresent glow, refracted light from innumerable solar ducts, lay over the living space like a luminous fog. Sara stole a last glance along the walkway before entering. Now she had trespassed. She'd better be quick.

Kadesh's quarters were basic: a table, a rack of clothing, shoes discarded in a corner. There was no concession to decor. Everything was functional. The laptop lay on the table, beside it a box of CDs, a pile of magazines. A pitcher of water. Kadesh allowed no other refreshment within the caverns. Her heart thumped. She could hear her brothers and sisters singing; their voices carried from the chamber of worship. It was habitually a comforting sound, evocative of her childhood, of times when this had been a safe place, the *only* place to be. *In God's will.*

Sara put one foot in front of the other, increasing the distance between her jittering body and the entrance. She was too far inside now to plead a social call. It was intrusion. *I can't believe I'm doing this.* As if in a dream she moved forward. The small of her back tingled as she reached the table and slid the computer's locking clasp open. She pressed the *On* button and watched the screen flicker into life, fumbled briefly under her robe and produced a 1Gb memory stick, sliding it into the USB slot with shaking fingers. Soft, floating hymnody filled the chamber. Sara prayed that Kadesh's roving eye would not spot her absence. If he did then she was as good as dead anyway. This was all or nothing. Double or quits.

The machine completed its start-up routine and Sara examined the desktop folders. *Military, Comms, BSc Hons, History.* She double-clicked, her eyes scanning the file list for significance. There. *CIA.* She clicked again. Ten, no more, all pdf documents.

There wasn't time to read them all now. Sara opened the remote drive and copied all the folders to her stick. She was in the process of stopping the device when her eye caught another 'My Documents' folder. *Sara.* She swallowed and double-clicked. Another folder. *Photographs.* Hundreds of them. She scrolled through the file list, randomly opening the jpgs. Herself and Simon outside the University. Simon and some friends, her house – an evening dinner party. Simon in his campus office. Another folder. *Childhood.* She opened it. Two folders. One, *Sara.* The other, *Dracup.* He's obsessed... She opened *Dracup.* Hundreds of files – all of Simon. Baby pictures, toddler shots, teen photographs. She bit her lip. *He knows everything about him, about us.* She was concentrating, unaware that the strains of worship had died away, leaving only stillness. And then with a start she realized her danger. She clicked the shutdown option on the main menu, pulled the stick from the USB slot. The laptop went into its closing routine. *Windows is shutting down.* Sara shuffled her feet in frustration. Come *on.*

She watched the blue screen flicker then fade to blackness, snapped the lid shut and walked quickly to the door. The passages were filling with her brothers and sisters, talking in small groups of two or three but in hushed whispers, low breathy exchanges, not with the laughter and confident chatter she was used to. She walked quickly away from Kadesh's quarters then stopped to compose herself, pressed her back against the wall and watched them go by. Sweat ran down her face and the back of her neck. She looked at the pinched, drawn faces passing by, felt their fear. A people who should be happy, ecstatic at the blessings of recent circumstance. But the truth was etched on her face as well, she knew. *We are no longer servants of God; we are servants of Kadesh.*

In her quarters Sara examined the CIA files. Her machine was illegal and she risked punishment if caught, but she had already crossed a more perilous line. And Simon needed this. She couldn't bear to consider the impossible goal of being reunited with him. And yet she couldn't prevent the thoughts creeping in: *He'll never take you back. You betrayed him.* She bit her lip hard. *I didn't. I tried to help.*

Sara forced her attention back to the files. They had been removed from CIA central archives over a period of time, cleverly, carefully and thoroughly. Whatever else Kadesh was, he was efficient. Sara shivered. It was all here: the links with the Smithsonian Institute who had sponsored the expeditions to Ararat, comprehensive logs detailing the exploration of the great boat and the discovery of the artefact that would eventually lead Theodore Dracup to the home of the *Korumak*. But for her purposes it was the record of US government intervention in the lives of the geologist and his expedition colleagues that was of paramount importance. They had been – what was the sanitised term? *Neutralised.* Their minds had been systematically shut down by an experimental drug – a drug that was destined in later generations to become the recreational preference of the hippy movement. Lysergic acid diethylamide. It had been an opportunity to trial the drug and to observe the effects of increased dosage. It was also a convenient way to exercise control. She read a brief excerpt, dated March 1927:

> *Re. Blackbird. Clearance has been given to proceed with Blackbird. Intentions and aspirations are to create an exploitable alteration of personality in selected individuals, specific targets include potential agents, defectors, refugees, POWs and others.*

Others. She couldn't forgive Theodore Dracup for his part in the rape of her heritage, but he had suffered enough at the hands of his masters. A picture of Reeves-Churchill shot into her head, bobbing and nodding in his wheelchair at the nursing home. Simon needed to know. He had already guessed that his grandfather's decline was caused not by some random biological failure but by a powerful and manipulative external influence. And the Americans had decreed that the discovery made by the second expedition was not for public consumption. *No*, Sara's mouth was a firm, angry line. *It was for furthering the knowledge of US Intelli-*

gence. She shuddered. The ultimate blasphemy. To think that they had actually begun to – the thought was overwhelming. She took a deep breath and calmed herself. *It's all right now. We can at least thank Kadesh for that.*

Sara closed her PDA with a soft click and glanced at her watch. It was almost time to leave. She was desperate to get the information to Dracup, but there was no available network for her to tap into. Kadesh monitored a private link and she couldn't access it even if she wanted to. So be it. She would just have to wait until they reached Baghdad. *If* they reached Baghdad.

At midnight she collected a sleepy Natasha from Ruth's chamber. Her sister was calm, almost her normal self. She had packed two bags with essentials, and hurried them on their way with a pinched face and dry eyes. Natasha was too befuddled with sleep to ask any awkward questions, and as Sara jostled her through the twilit corridors the girl seemed unaware of their newly acquired fugitive status. The air temperature slowly increased as they climbed to the surface until, like ants emerging from a nest, they found themselves under moonlight in the open air. It was a beautiful night, the stars airbrushed across the sky like a broken necklace. Natasha tilted her face upwards and smiled. "It's nice outside," she whispered.

The vehicles were lined up in the shelter of the mound, their angular geometries silhouetted against the horizon as Sara squinted, tried to pick out the one most appropriate for their needs. *Not too heavy. We're in a hurry.* A few minutes later she had settled on an open-topped four wheel drive with a robust set of fat, deep-treaded tyres.

"Okay. Hop in," she told Natasha. The girl sleepily obliged and immediately curled up on the passenger seat. The keys would be in the ignition, Ruth had assured her. *No car thieves around here.* Sara almost laughed aloud at the thought. The keys were not in the ignition. She opened her mouth to ask Natasha to look for a set on her side when they were bathed in a brilliant, blinding light. The voice that told them to step out of the jeep and stand with their hands above their heads belonged to the one man she feared more than God himself.

Kadesh stepped into the searchlight's exposing beam. His face showed a curious mixture of anger and disappointment. Sara put her arm around Natasha and waited for their fate to be decreed.

Chapter 26

Dracup stood just inside the threshold and shook his head in wonder. He removed his hat and allowed the cool, scented air to dry the sweat from his forehead. The place was enormous. It reminded him of an English cathedral, but without the clean lines favoured by mediaeval architecture. He angled his head to examine the distant roof, then returned his attention to the carved columns of reddish volcanic rock that served as gigantic, asymmetrical supports. The building was almost organic in structure, as if it had come into being not by premeditated plan or design but through some accidental quirk of geology – albeit enhanced by considerable skill. Dracup was speechless. It was as if he had stepped into Tolkien's Mines of Moria, into a space that seemed timeless and set apart from the world.

"So what do you think, eh, boss?" Bek prompted.

Dracup frowned and stroked his beard. Something wasn't right. "Think? I don't know what to think, Bek." He turned and looked at the boy. "How did you find it? It's well hidden – there'd be no reason to deviate from the path –"

"I told you. Bek knows stuff."

Dracup smiled. "Yes, I'm coming round to that idea. So – what else can you tell me?"

"Come further in, boss, I know what you want." Bek ran forward into the building and gesticulated impatiently.

Dracup glanced behind him. The entrance was a reassuring rectangle of light, but his intuition would not be placated. The church possessed an ambience, a stillness that bordered on expectancy. Dracup murmured quietly to himself, his attention concentrated on the young guide. *This feels different. Bek seems very keen...*

And then came the sound, a grinding, rolling noise of heavy weights coming together. The light diminished abruptly. Dracup, half prepared for the unexpected, didn't bother to turn. The entrance had been sealed. Bek was standing to one side, inanimate, as if his sideshow had come to a premature but premeditated conclusion and there was nothing more for him to do. In the darkness, a torch flared. Dracup stood still. There was nothing to be gained by running. He was standing in the central space, the nave of the church. Further pinpricks of fire danced in the darkness until their collective light allowed Dracup to make out at least ten figures advancing towards him. He called over to Bek, alarmed by the boy's transformation from extrovert guide to forlorn – and clearly frightened – teenager.

"Anything you can tell me about this, Bek?" Dracup spoke kindly, hoping for a few final words of explanation. But Bek was curled into a knee-hugging ball, rocking backward and forward in the shadows. His shoulders heaved in syncopated jerks. Eventually Dracup was able to interpret the repetitive mantra: "I'm sorry, boss. *He made me do it.*"

Dracup turned his attention from the sobbing boy to the procession. It was led by a tall figure in black. The man's face was partially obscured by the traditional Ethiopian turban-like wrap, but his eyes were bright in the torchlight. As Dracup watched, the figure held up his hand and the procession came to an obedient halt. The man peeled his scarf away and opened his mouth in a wide, gleaming grin. Dracup wasn't surprised. The runner from the Thames promenade had finally caught up with him.

Dracup walked between two priests – he assumed they were priests – with the man in black leading the way. Towards the altar, Dracup thought. Not good. But as they reached the plain stone block the leader turned. He looked at Dracup for a moment, studying him with interest. His opening words were preceded by a smile of evident pleasure. "Professor Dracup, I shall show you what you have been looking for. It seems only fair. And I have a great sense of fairness, as do all you – *British* people." He spoke in measured, educated tones and although there was a faint trace of accent it was hard to place. The nose was pure Arabic, his height – *very* unusual. Dracup had studied African tribes where the least in stature measured six and a half feet, but he had seen nothing outside the Guinness Book of Records to compare with this. His size lent the man an alien quality; there was something otherworldly about him. The voice went on confidently, as did Dracup's linguistic analysis.

"But I am being rude. I was speaking of fairness whilst all the time retaining an unfair advantage. My name is Mukannishum." He bowed, his long body folding over at the waist like a hinged gantry. There was something in the vowel inflexion that rang a familiar bell. Where had he heard that same intonation? That odd flattening of vowels?

The torchbearers had formed a circle with Dracup and Mukannishum a few metres apart in the centre. The altar was directly in front of them, and Dracup noticed that raised up on its surface was a curtained container of some sort – a tabernacle perhaps, not domed in the Catholic or High Church tradition, but broader and bigger. Mukannishum issued an order and one of the priests raised his torch, casting a clear orange light onto the altar. The material covering the tabernacle was pure white and the pictorial detail was of a great tree, its branches spreading over the fabric like a protective roof. The embroidered foliage portrayed a density of leaves and fruit through which slanted rays of brilliant sunshine. It was virtuoso art, so lifelike that Dracup could almost smell the fruit and feel the wind against his cheek.

Mukannishum moved the curtain aside with a rapid, precise movement of his fingertips, destroying the illusion. Dracup blinked, suddenly disoriented. He heard a scurrying noise behind. Bek had shuffled up to watch. The boy's face was grimed with dust and long tear tracks stained his cheeks. Dracup attempted to catch his eye, but he looked away and began to scuff the floor awkwardly with his feet.

"Gaze upon it, Professor." Mukannishum held an object aloft, the torchlight reflecting along familiar contours.

Dracup felt a mixture of emotions. Here it was – the mirror image of his Scottish find: *Omega*. It was forged exactly like a half section of the Lalibela cross, but the metalwork was covered with indented script. Cuneiform script. In the top left hand corner was a single mark: Ω He moved his hands slowly to his side. If he could just get one frame. Mukannishum was concentrating on the object, his face radiating satisfaction. The priests watched impassively. Dracup's hand reached his trouser pocket. And it was empty. *Empty*. How could it be empty? He had checked the camera thirty minutes ago... before or after their last rest break? It must have slipped out. No camera. And little time. Dracup's brain raced. If he could set up some distraction –

"What is this place?" he asked Mukannishum.

Mukannishum slotted the sceptre into a recess on the altar where it gleamed, reflecting the artificial light.

"This place?" Mukannishum smiled. "It was built by one of the first men to come to Africa. His name was Ham."

Dracup felt a growing excitement in spite of his predicament. Noah's sons: Shem, *Ham* and Japheth.

Mukannishum went on. "And he brought with him a reminder of his roots, a signpost to ensure he would never forget where his kin had settled, so that they could be found – if need be – in times to come."

Dracup nodded. "The sceptre. Yes. *Alpha* and *Omega* – when brought together they complete the stanza that reveals the location of Ham's brethren. His *special* brethren." Dracup paused to gauge the reaction. "Ham, Shem and Japheth did what they were told, didn't they? They moved away from the Ark and spread across the earth. But there was an elite band, a remnant of Noah's family who were charged with the protection of something, sworn to the preservation of a treasure. And my grandfather found it – with the help of this 'signpost'."

"It is so." Mukannishum's eyes were black marbles in their deep, hooded sockets.

Dracup wondered how far he could push Mukannishum – too far and he could seal his fate immediately; not far enough and he might lose the only chance he had. He gestured towards the object on the altar. "Well, I have a question for you, then: if it's so sacred to your people, why have you abandoned it here for so long?"

Mukannishum moved towards him with a lithe, darting motion. Dracup stood his ground. The zealot's face was centimetres away, the whites of his eyes webbed with tiny rivulets of blood. A thread of spittle clung to the thin lips. "This is not something I would normally share with a godless Westerner, but as your life is at an end I will show you leniency and explain." Mukannishum took a step back, his long body again performing that strange unfolding motion as he drew himself up to his full height. "It is written that in the fullness of time, the sceptre shall be made whole again and reunited with the one to whom it was given at the beginning."

Dracup was listening. He was also looking for an escape route, but the encircling priests seemed to sense his intentions. They closed in, tightening the circle. He had to keep Mukannishum talking. "And that time is now?"

Mukannishum smiled, a cynical movement of his lips. "Yes. Our prophet has decreed it to be so."

Dracup's brain was racing. "And apart from my grandfather's diary this is the only means by which your people can be traced, correct?"

"Correct." Mukannishum opened his robe and slid out a small book. "And I have both the *Omega* and the diary in my possession."

Dracup could sense Mukannishum's patience slipping away. But if he was going to die he wanted to die with answers. "Why my daughter?"

Mukannishum straightened to his full height. "She is not my responsibility," he said dismissively. "The prophet will decide her fate."

"Then take me to him. At least I deserve a hearing."

Mukannishum threw back his head and laughed. "He is a thousand miles from you – in distance and in spirit." Watching Dracup carefully, he added, "The girl is useful to him," he added a final phrase that chilled Dracup's heart, "in his service."

Dracup grappled with his conflicting emotions. The words confirmed that she lived. But a thousand miles away? He felt despair seep through his body like a sedative and dug his fingernails into his palms, forcing himself to think. Keep talking, Dracup. Keep him talking. "The Americans have *Alpha*. They may still be able to trace you."

"I doubt that," Mukannishum leered. "I have already made provision to acquire your recently unearthed discovery. US *intelligence* has already proved itself less than competent. *Alpha* will be in my hands very soon. As is its sibling." Mukannishum turned to the altar and unfixed the half-cross from its plinth. Laying it down carefully he produced a soft cloth from his bag and began folding the material this way and that across the object as if to protect it in transit. The priests, silent up to this point, began to murmur amongst themselves. Dracup eyed them with caution. Was this unexpected? They appeared surprised at Mukannishum's actions. One stepped forward and grasped his arm, said something in the strange language Dracup had heard earlier that day. The gesture was unmistakable. *It is not permitted.*

Mukannishum whipped his arm from the point of contact. "Do not touch me," he hissed in English. "Kadesh himself has decreed that the sign be returned to the *Korumak*."

Two names. *Kadesh. Korumak.* Dracup stored the information and waited to see what would happen next. He realized that, to these priests, Mukannishum was as much an outsider as he was. An important one, maybe, but not one of them. They were suspicious and their suspicions had evidently been confirmed. Mukannishum glared at the men and resumed his task.

What happened next surprised Dracup as much as it surprised Mukannishum. One of the priests produced a long blade from beneath his garment and swept it across Mukannishum's legs, disabling him in one stroke. The giant fell to the floor with a look of amazed horror on his face. Blood leapt from the wounds and spattered the onlookers in a rush of gore. Dracup heard Bek give a shout of revulsion and stepped back involuntarily, expecting the priest to turn on him as well. But the man with the sword had his attention firmly fixed on Mukannishum, who was lying on his back attempting to sit up. A pool of blood was forming around the stricken man's body.

Dracup looked from the priest back to Mukannishum, profoundly shocked. Mukannishum was ranting at his assailant. The priest barked a reply and Mukannishum twisted his mouth into a snarl. A sliver of metal appeared in his hand and the wrist twisted to flick the knife at its target, but the priest was quicker: stepping forward he pinned Mukannishum's arm to the floor and kicked the knife away disdainfully. The other priests, silent up to this point, began chanting rhythmically, their voices echoing round the building like monks at plainsong. Dracup edged back another metre and found Bek squatting miserably behind him. "What are they saying, Bek? What's happened?"

Bek clung to Dracup's leg. "They fall out with the long man, boss. He want to take the cross away. They say no, it belongs here. They will not allow him to have it. Long man says they are wrong – he is faithful to the *Korumak Tanri*, to Kadesh. And so should they be. But boss –" Bek grasped Dracup's arm, "– they think you want the same – they –"

A priest appeared at Dracup's side and struck Bek across the face. The boy reeled away into the darkness. Dracup's hands were bound and he was pushed forward. Mukannishum groaned as he was lifted and carried to a low door recessed in the rock immediately behind the altar. Dracup was prompted to follow, and ducked to clear the rough ceiling of the passageway. Hands pushed at his back and shoulders so that he almost stumbled and fell several times as he attempted to negotiate the steep and uneven route chosen for them by the priests. *Priests? What sort of priests carry razor-sharp scimitars under their vestments?*

He wondered what had happened to Bek, but couldn't turn to look in case he did himself an injury on the ceiling or the irregular path. He could hear Mukannishum shouting somewhere up ahead – whether in fear or pain he couldn't say – and felt his breath hot in his chest as the pace increased. They evidently wanted him somewhere in a hurry. Presently he felt cooler air on his face and was able to straighten his back. He looked up. The passageway was open to the stars, and with the light given by these and a full moon Dracup was at least able to walk without fear of falling. The priests resumed their plaintive hymns as they walked, a spiritual, mournful refrain with a slow, deliberate tempo. The cadences of the melody boded ill for his future. Dracup looked around in desperation but there was nothing to see, just the shadow of the mountain, the silhouettes of his escort and Mukannishum's arachnid body writhing in protest somewhere up ahead.

The song finished abruptly and he was forced to a halt by a firm grip on his arm and the back of his neck. The escort fanned out in a semicircle; Mukannishum was unceremoniously dumped on the ground like so much unwanted baggage. He screamed as his mutilated legs made contact with the earth. Dracup winced and quashed the instinctive response to help. There was nothing he could do. Two priests grabbed hold of Mukannishum's legs, an action that drew an unearthly, high-pitched shriek from the prostrate man's lips, but the cry was cut short as his arms were held and he was swung like a pendulum, backwards and forwards, backwards and forwards. Perplexed, Dracup wondered what they were doing. Then he looked down and realized they were standing on the edge of a pit; he could see its sandy coloured floor clearly in the moonlight. A few scattered rocks broke the even surface, along with a smattering of dark, scrubby grass and a squat, grey tree trunk fixed in the centre.

Dracup watched impotently as Mukannishum was released into the air and fell helplessly, arms and legs cartwheeling in protest, into the void. He hit the ground with a muffled groan and lay still. Then the nearest priest turned to Dracup. He tensed his muscles but knew it was a hopeless resistance; quickly overpowered by lean, black arms he was cast after Mukannishum like a puppet. Dracup tried to relax and roll, but mistimed it and hit the ground hard. The impact drove the breath from his body in a lung-emptying whoosh of air. His head followed his body, and gravity did the rest. The world uncoiled through a reverse telescope and the final pinprick of light went out like a snuffed candle.

There was dirt in his mouth. Dracup coughed and spat. He moved his head gingerly. His neck worked – that was good. He pushed himself up on one arm and tried to sit up. He fell back at the stabbing pain in his lower chest. That hurt a lot, and so did his back, but he could move his legs and feet so it was probably just bruising – plus maybe a cracked rib or two. He tried again a minute or so later, and eventually heaved himself into a sitting position. Above him the moon shone in the empty sky, empty but for the millions of stars stretched across the void.

It was very quiet. He scanned from right to left around the perimeter of the pit. No inquisitive faces peered down at him. No sonorous chanting broke the stillness. The priests had left him for the time being. *They must be pretty confident I can't get out.* Dracup supported his ribcage carefully with one arm and attempted to get to his feet. He made it on the third try and shuffled across to the wall of the pit. It was sheer. And crumbling. There was a small, stepped projection just out of reach. He stretched for it and cried out in pain. Even if it held his weight he didn't have a hope of reaching it. He placed his back against the pit wall and eased himself slowly onto the sandy floor. He was very thirsty – another problem he didn't want to dwell on. *First, get out, then –*

A soft moan startled him. *Mukannishum.* He had completely forgotten him. Dracup was horrified that the man had just been left to bleed to death. He flexed his muscles to get up when another sound rolled across the walls of the pit. His blood froze and he flattened himself against the uneven tuff, all thoughts of movement abandoned. Moments later a large shadow detached itself from the base of the tree and moved languidly towards Mukannishum's prostrate form. Dracup watched in impotent horror. Now he understood the priests' careless departure. The shadow gained substance as it stopped to sniff the air for signs of danger. It was an enormous animal, bigger than the Indian lions he had known as a child. This was a Barbary lion – black-maned, rare. A protected species. Dracup's bladder tightened with an uncomfortable pressure. He wasn't sure if the animal had missed him or if its curiosity was aroused to a greater degree by the bleeding form of Mukannishum. Dracup bit his lip. He watched the lion nuzzle Mukannishum half-heartedly and then move away to the other side of the pit where it began a ritual cleaning of paws and mane. Dracup let out his breath slowly. *It's not hungry – yet*. Dracup turned his attention back to the pit wall. He looked for a tool he could use to chisel out a foothold, but the pit floor was bare except for a scattering of dead branches and the odd fragment of tuff.

Mukannishum was moaning again, trying to move. Dracup wanted to warn him to keep still, but any signal he made was as likely to attract the lion's attention. It had ceased grooming and was staring fixedly at Mukannishum. The animal's paw was raised in mid-air, its posture reminiscent of a domestic cat. Dracup willed the injured man into stillness. With a softer groan, Mukannishum's head sank back onto the sand. Dracup hoped he had fainted. The lion remained in its fixed position for a long thirty seconds, then resumed its ablutions, lapping its great tongue across tawny, powerful paws.

Dracup waited. A faint iridescence was creeping over the night sky and the stars were becoming less distinct. Soon, pale beams of orange light began to pick their way into Dracup's prison, deepening the colour of the pit walls from brownish-red to deep crimson. He worried less about the visual exposure daylight would bring and more about the problem of water – or the lack of it. The heat of the day would be fearsome in his exposed position. He had lost his hat somewhere along the way and had nothing to protect himself except the shirt he was wearing. About the lion he worried the least. It would have attacked by now if hunger had been a priority, and he guessed it would sleep for most of the day until the cool of the evening and an empty stomach prompted it into action.

The increased visibility had revealed more about the nature of the pit. It was a man-made affair, he was sure of that. The circumference was too regular in shape to be natural. The tree had been provided for shade and claw sharpening. However, it was not the only source of shade. Beyond Mukannishum's body a shadowy opening broke the even tint of the pit wall. It looked like a tunnel entrance. On the other hand, maybe it was just a cool enclave provided for the lion's comfort with no connection to upper levels. Dracup made saliva and moistened his lips sparingly. If the lion chose to settle by the tree he might get the chance to find out. The sun's reddish-yellow disk appeared above the artificial horizon of the pit's perimeter and he felt its warm promise on his face. The seriousness of his position clarified his thinking and he made a quick decision. Before Mukannishum died, as he surely would, he had to capitalize on his unexpected opportunity to interrogate someone with a direct link to Natasha. Movement had its risks, but then so did continued ignorance. Keeping a close eye on the lion, Dracup began to inch his way around the pit, ignoring the aches and stabs of protest from his body.

Dracup estimated that around an hour had passed by the time he had reached the closest possible point to the prostrate man. He leaned against the wall and took stock. His biggest fear was that Mukannishum was already dead. The lion had spread itself into what Dracup hoped would be a long term posture – front legs at full stretch, rear legs tucked, the great head bowed over its paws. He spent a few moments in reflection. *If I die, God, then so be it. But let my little one live. Let her come home to her mother and strengthen her to face the future. Give her a fond memory of me. Let her understand, when she is old enough, that we both love her, whatever happened between us.*

The lion stirred and made a low noise in its throat. The tail flicked once and was still. Dracup held his breath. *Amen.* He lay forward in the dirt and began to inch his way towards Mukannishum. He rested on his good side to ease the pressure, then continued a metre at a time. He tried to make his movements economical, but the temperature was rising and soon bubbles of perspiration began to collect on his forehead and trickle down the bridge of his nose. Dracup stopped for a breather. Just a couple of metres and he would be there. Mukannishum twitched and the lion's tail moved minutely in response, but the animal was lethargic, indifferent to the prospect of another meal at this early hour. Dracup pulled himself forward and flopped down parallel to Mukannishum's fevered head.

He was in a bad way. Dracup could see the deep gashes in both legs, the torn fabric of his trousers woven into the fleshy lacerations. Flies busied themselves around the congealing blood. Dracup swatted them away but they were persistent and he soon gave up, allowing the insects to settle on his face wherever they chose; too much flapping around would only attract the lion. Dracup prayed that Mukannishum was too weak to make a loud, attention-attracting response, and pulled gently on the man's shoulder.

"Listen to me," he told him. "I can get you out of this, but you have to do exactly what I tell you." Mukannishum moaned and opened his eyes. Dracup put his face close to his. "We are in a pit. There is a lion, but it is sleeping. Do you understand?"

Mukannishum moved his head fractionally. His eyes showed that he had registered the danger.

"There may be an exit tunnel. I'm going to check it out later. Keep still and stay as quiet as possible."

Mukannishum tried to shift position and his face creased in pain. The man's injuries were significant: both legs fractured and one arm splayed uselessly. Dracup ripped off a strip of his shirttail and fashioned a tourniquet. First aid was not his forte, but he had to try to stop Mukannishum bleeding to death. He wrapped the material around Mukannishum's thigh and tightened it into a knot, speaking quickly as he worked to keep Mukannishum's attention.

"Before I check it," Dracup told him, "we're going to have a little chat. Let's start with an easy one. Who is 'Kadesh' and where can I find him?" He waited for a reaction. Mukannishum's skin was a yellowish colour and his breathing was becoming laboured. He shook the man's arm firmly. "If you want to have any chance of getting out of here you'd better start talking."

Mukannishum turned his head fractionally. The eyes slid open. "Kadesh is the prophet, leader and encourager, blessed be his name."

"The leader of the *Korumak?*"

But Mukannishum only grimaced and his head fell back. The flies buzzed around them with renewed vigour. Dracup kept one eye on the lion as he waited for a response. The animal was sound asleep, its chest rising and falling in an even rhythm. There was time; there had to be time. Dracup reached into Mukannishum's robe and found the diary in a zipped pocket. He slipped it beneath his waistband. That was one problem dealt with.

"Where are the *Korumak?*" he repeated, giving Mukannishum's cheek a firm slap.

Mukannishum opened his mouth and groaned. "Water."

"There isn't any. Not until we get out of here."

Mukannishum closed his eyes. Dracup was about to rouse him again when he began to speak softly, in English and in another, unfamiliar tongue. Dracup recognized the onset of delirium. He repeated his question. "The *Korumak*. Your people. Where are they?"

"*Korumak Tanri* – God's chosen. Blessed keepers of His law. Blessed protectors of His truth. Blessed children of Noah."

"Yes," Dracup cajoled. "Pure descendants of his line –"

Mukannishum muttered and writhed, slipping in and out of consciousness. Dracup shook him hard. "But *where?* Where is the girl?"

Mukannishum shouted in pain and Dracup froze. He clapped a hand over Mukannishum's mouth. A tense moment passed as the lion grunted and yawned but remained in its chosen location by the tree.

Mukannishum was fully awake now. His lip curled in distaste. "You killed him. And he has taken her in exchange."

"Killed who?" Dracup leaned in close, but the answer had already come to him in a moment of sick revelation. The man in the Aberdeen hotel. The assassin.

"His *brother*," Mukannishum hissed. "The blessed one's brother. Your forefather betrayed the son of God, and you murdered Kadesh's brother." Mukannishum coughed and spat a dry ball of vomit. The flies circled it gleefully. "The blessed one has pronounced your family to be cursed. For all generations." He gasped with the effort of speech and allowed his head to sink back to the ground.

Dracup remembered the smell of cordite, the hole in the pillow. The fractured glass of his hotel window. Now he knew why he was the victim of such pure, unadulterated hatred. But there was another reference he needed to explore.

"Son of God?" Dracup probed. "What do you mean by that?"

Mukannishum coughed again and a trickle of blood escaped from the corner of his mouth. He levered himself into a half-sitting position and opened his mouth to speak, but Dracup saw the look in his eye and knew what it meant. He was no longer looking at Dracup, but past him. Dracup turned slowly. The lion was padding purposefully towards them, its great head raised. When the roar came it was deafening, but more terrifying was the low growl it made as it closed the distance between them.

Chapter 27

Kadesh had dismissed the others. Natasha had been returned to Ruth's care. The searchlights had been extinguished and the only remaining illumination was provided by a silvery slice of moon. Sara sat in the passenger seat of the jeep, Kadesh beside her playing with the bunch of keys, passing them from hand to hand. Her heart was beating in a sick, slow pulse.

"I brought you back out of kindness," Kadesh said eventually. "I believed you to be a true worshipper."

Sara stared fixedly ahead. She knew she was talking for her life. "And I am. You know that. But your abduction of the girl is an injustice."

Kadesh looked at her disdainfully. "Don't speak to me of injustice."

"Tarshish was killed by a man acting in self-defense. Can't you see that?" Sara pressed on, ignoring the tremor in her voice. "I loved him too. You know I did."

"Tarshish was killed unjustly. He was my *brother*. Killed by an *outsider*. The price must be paid. It is the law." Kadesh spat the words.

Sara knew that argument was futile. His mind was made up. Her only chance was to stall the execution of his decision. Kadesh, ruler of the *Korumak*, master-planner and – to his people – successful in the most audacious of all enterprises, would not be moved to another course of action by a mere woman. Or would he? In this she sensed a slender opportunity. She knew of his passion, the passion that had sidelined Ruth and transformed her sister into a desperate, bitter woman. Sara smiled at the irony of it. Ruth, the girl most likely to be married the moment her first blood made its appearance, pursued by more young men than Sara could remember, had rejected all in favour of this cold, calculating saviour. But his eyes had not been on Ruth; they had been on her younger sister, the dowdy Sara. It was a situation that had prompted Sara's voluntary exit from her home into the strangeness of the West.

Her education had had a profound effect on her, the culture even more so. Could she not remain faithful to the *Korumak* and live out her dreams as well? But Kadesh's eyes were never far from her. Contact had been maintained; at first just a comforting sense of protection, but then demands had been made. The culmination of half a century of investigation, infiltration, checking and double-checking was upon her people. The moment was nigh. And the plan had succeeded. The American government had been caught half asleep as the wisdom of God and one man's brilliance removed their prized acquisition from under their noses. And then she had been sent to Dracup. The failsafe. Nothing had escaped Kadesh's attention, not even the death of an old lady in Aberdeen and the tiny time bomb that lay in a locked drawer waiting for Dracup to open it; the only means by which the *Korumak* could be traced.

"Come to me." Kadesh reached out and touched her hair. "Be with me in these times of fulfilled prophecy. Be with me at the end of the age."

She recoiled involuntarily. She found him repellant, although she could never say exactly why. He was handsome – perhaps striking – to look at, and his body, although slender, was strong and muscular. But his heart; it was cold like the stone of the caverns.

And he's not Simon Dracup.

Sara checked herself and forced a smile. "I'm sorry. I didn't mean to –"

"Why pretend?" Kadesh said, letting his arm drop. "Love is something that cannot be forced."

Sara's thoughts tumbled over themselves. What could she say to capitalize on Kadesh's reflective mood? "You have the love of your people. And in that sense, mine as well."

"You think so?" Kadesh shook his head slowly. "They fear me. It is not the same."

"But –"

Kadesh held up his hand. "No. You feel it too. The fear." He turned to her and his eyes were cold in the moonlight, like a cat's. "Let me tell you, beautiful Sara, I have not taken this course of action lightly. We have succeeded only through care, diligence and commitment. My father was wrong when he based his leadership on loyalty. Had he taken my advice our legacy would have been returned to us years ago. He was weak. I am strong. And strength, when combined with zero tolerance of failure, engenders fear; and fear is a greater incentive than loyalty." He leaned over and stroked Sara's hand. "Fear is an asset, a weapon. When used correctly it can produce startling results."

"Let the girl go, Kadesh." Sara let her hand remain under his. "I do not fear you, as you suppose. I appeal to you as my – as my brother."

Kadesh leaned back in his seat and laughed. "To do what? Deliver her back to Dracup? Perhaps I should free you as well – now, that would be generous." He squeezed her hand, applying pressure. "But your place is here. You are a part of us, not of them. Our God has set your path. He governs your destiny, not your selfish whims and weak emotion."

Sara held herself in check. The pain in her fingers was intense but she wouldn't give him the pleasure of succumbing.

Kadesh released the pressure and smiled. "So. Our destinies, it would seem, are misaligned and likely to remain so." He pondered in silence for a few moments. "God is telling me I must make a decision." Kadesh watched Sara intently, waiting for a reaction. "But maybe there is an alternative: let's see if Professor Dracup is as bright as you think. And we can make the whole *affair* more interesting by setting a deadline." Kadesh made a mock gesture of alarm. "Forgive me. A poor choice of phrase, but accurate nonetheless."

Sara went cold.

Kadesh held out his hand. "The PDA, if you please."

Sara took out the device and handed it to Kadesh. She watched as he accessed the electronic information. "Aha. *Urgent.zip.*" Kadesh scrutinized the files. He found Natasha's photograph, the one she had taken by the falls. "Very pretty. We'll send this, shall we? With a little note, perhaps. But the other attachments... maybe not." Kadesh looked up at Sara. "I went to a great deal of trouble to secure this information. American intelligence take their IT security very seriously. It would be careless of me to let it go so easily, don't you agree? Now, what can we say to your friend?" He drew out the stylus and began to write. When he had finished he held it up for Sara's inspection:

> *'Professor Dracup – I hadn't intended to contact you but as you are displaying such remarkable tenacity I am willing to offer a small incentive. You have 48 hrs. At dawn on the 28th day, the death sentence will be carried out. The girl and your lover will die – unless I have the sceptre in my possession by the time the sun rises. Up to now you have shown creditable resourcefulness. Please don't disappoint me.*

Sara swallowed. "But Mukannishum –"

"May fail." Kadesh slipped the PDA under his robe. "And the irony of a Dracup doing my bidding is too perfect an opportunity to miss."

"Don't underestimate him," Sara began, then gasped as Kadesh caught her arm in a pincer grip. She fought back, spitting the words out. "He will be your undoing – he –" She felt a crushing blow to the back of her neck, and then she was falling and all was darkness.

Chapter 28

The lion paused, sizing up the two men. Dracup kept very, very still and returned the lion's stare. He thought of his childhood friend, Sunil. Dracup's father used to call him the jungle boy, such was his expertise with animals. *What would Sunil do?* He heard his friend's voice across the years: *Don't look away. Don't turn your back. Make yourself as big as possible.* Dracup was vaguely aware of Mukannishum fumbling around with something – or was he just altering position to ease the pressure on his broken legs? Whatever, the lion was concentrating on Mukannishum now, pawing the ground deliberately. Its body tensed, the shoulders went down a fraction. *It's going to pounce.*

Dracup tensed with it. He prepared to fling himself to one side, and risked a glance at Mukannishum. The man wore a strange grin and his breathing was heavy. *Wait. His hand. There's something in his hand.* Dracup caught sight of a fat, cylindrical object. Mukannishum clutched it to his chest, as if holding a token of love. By then Dracup had realized what it was. He brought his foot down hard on Mukannishum's forearm and the fist sprang open as Mukannishum howled in pain. The object rolled off his ribcage onto the ground and came to rest against Dracup's boot. Dracup aimed a kick as the lion launched itself into the air, saw the grenade spin off the end of his foot and spiral away towards the pit wall. At the same time he was knocked to one side by the lion's body as it landed squarely on top of Mukannishum. Dracup was dimly aware of a high-pitched scream, but then felt himself lifted on a warm blast of air as the grenade exploded with a muffled *crack* against the volcanic rock of the pit wall.

Dracup sat up, dazed. He felt blood trickle down his face and wiped it away with an impatient gesture. Where was the lion? As the dust settled he saw the animal's bulky shape beside Mukannishum. It was immobile, perhaps stunned by the blast. *Or dead?* Dracup hawked and spat dust from his mouth. He was desperately thirsty; the afternoon sun was slowly sucking the remaining moisture from his body. He could make no saliva. For the first time he began to doubt his survival. A strange lassitude came over him. And then, as the settling dust gradually revealed the far wall, his heart leapt with excitement. The grenade had blown open a fissure, depositing a pile of rocks and boulders around its base. It looked feasible for a climb – if he could flank the lion. He prepared to crawl.

At that moment, Mukannishum writhed and shouted. The lion lashed out with a paw and followed with a lunge to the neck. Mukannishum's cries ceased abruptly. Dracup held his breath. The animal bared its teeth and let out an eardrum-perforating roar. Dracup began to crawl slowly, hugging the wall, in a direction that would bring him round to the fissure behind the animal's back. He hoped that it would be too busy with Mukannishum to concern itself with him. But Dracup had another worry: the noise of the explosion would surely bring the priests back to check on their captives. He crawled on. The heat was unbearable, his tongue a dry stick of flesh against the roof of his mouth. He drifted in and out of consciousness, startling himself awake as the lion's face filled his dreams. Once he awoke with a cry and froze in horror at the sound he had made. But the lion was busy; he heard chewing and the occasional crack of bone.

Dracup opened his eyes. The sun had set and a cool wind fanned his face. He had covered three quarters of the distance between his original position and his destination: the fissure in the wall. But now he saw that his way was guarded. The lion was crouched beside the larger rockfall, blocking his route. Beside the tree lay a pile of rags from which protruded the odd glint of white. Ragged strips of flesh hung from the mess like some careless butcher's offcuts. Dracup felt his gorge rise. The lion was licking its paws with slow, deliberate movements of its head. Where were the priests? He was curious at their indifference. But then, the pit wall could have muffled the noise of the explosion. Dracup tried to swallow and failed. Despair clutched at him again. No one would pass this way; he was miles from the town. He thought of his hotel room with its solitary suitcase. Another missing traveller. He thought of Natasha, and then of Yvonne, sitting in the darkness of her living room, counting the hours until daybreak. He began to crawl again.

For the first few minutes the lion ignored him, but then it shook itself abruptly, stretched, yawned and began to walk across the pit towards him. Dracup tried to get up but found his legs so weak that he faltered and fell into a kneeling position as the lion approached. *Like a man about to be executed.* He was surprised at how little fear he felt, just a sense of the inevitable. An image of Sunil came into his mind. *Never turn your back.*

Dracup watched the lion as it sidled up to him. The closeness of the animal made him hold his breath. He sensed the power under the yellowish, tanned hide. He admired the poise of the beast, its black mane, the huge, regal head. The lion paraded up and down restlessly, closing the distance with each pass. *Talk to me, Sunil, talk to me.* He raised his right arm and motioned gently to the lion; speaking softly but firmly, he made a soothing noise in his throat, then a long, sideways motion with his hand. The animal lowered its head and growled; its paws raked the pit floor. It seemed unfazed by Dracup's entreaties. He counted to ten and began again. Sweat ran down his face. He could hear Sunil as clearly as if he were back in the Secunderabad of the Sixties. The boy's turban was white, contrasting with his dusky skin. He was smiling and wagging his finger. *Confidence, Simon. You have to show them who's boss, you know? You can't show any weakness...* Dracup gestured again, smoothly, both palms down. He flexed his thigh muscles and straightened up. *Nice and slow, Dracup, nice and slow.* For the first time the lion seemed unsure. And then very suddenly it spread itself full length before him, resting its head on its paws.

"Strewth. I don't reckon you learned that at Reading Uni..."

Dracup looked up with a start. Halfway down the rockfall, regarding him with a bemused expression on his sunburnt face, was Dan Carey.

"Well don't just stand there, mate. If you've finished practising on old Simba," he waved a hand vaguely in the lion's direction, "then may I suggest we make a dignified exit?"

Dracup could have laughed and cried at the same time. He backed away from the lion and seized Carey's outstretched arm. His legs were an old man's, his hands trembling like a drunk's. Dracup leaned on the Kiwi and began to climb the rockfall towards the lip of the pit. The temporary platform created by the blast was treacherous and Dracup felt it slide precariously under his feet, but Carey picked his way expertly up the last few metres, digging his fingertips into the tuff to gain a handhold. Presently his head appeared over the lip of the crater and he stretched a muscular arm down to Dracup. Dracup felt himself hauled over the edge and soon lay splayed out on the shale and dust of the pit edge. Carey produced a water bottle and supported his head. "Slowly, mate. There's plenty here."

Dracup drank deeply, his fingers drumming a palsied tattoo on the flask.

Carey watched him with concern. "It's okay. You're all right now. You did well." He steadied Dracup's hands. "Let's get you out of here."

Dracup wobbled to his feet and, allowing the Kiwi to support him, stumbled down a slope of scree and loose rock towards Carey's jeep. Dracup stole a backward glance before collapsing into the passenger seat, half expecting to see the lion emerging from the pit. Carey revved the engine and dust obscured his view. Dracup took a deep breath, murmured a prayer of thanks and passed out.

In his hotel room Dracup poured himself and Carey a beer. He'd had a few hours sleep and felt calmer. His ribcage was painful but intact; his greatest discomfort was a throbbing headache and sunburn, the worst affected area being his face and shoulders which were raw and blistered. A small thing to endure, he reflected, considering how things might have ended.

It was late afternoon. A crowd of new arrivals had stormed the hotel and woken him from his listless dozing. He'd heard them – a bunch of American kids, clumping around as they vied for tenancy of the best available rooms. Now they'd dumped their gear and gone for a look around the place was quieter. Dracup looked over at Carey, relaxed and sitting astride a chair with his brown forearms resting lightly on the slatted backrest. "So. How did you find me?"

Carey studied his beer and wiped a finger round the rim to settle the foam. "Well, to start off I had a bit of trouble with the jalopy. Seems like the tank did take a little knock during the Battle of Britain yesterday." Carey took a swig of beer and shrugged. "I had to patch her up as best I could. By the time I'd got it sorted it was too late to get going. So, I decided to look you up. I figured you'd probably be heading back to the hotel by that stage. But there was no sign."

Dracup nodded and eased himself into a chair.

"So," Carey continued, "I asked around. One of the kids came with me as far as the path you were seen headed towards. After I parked up he was off, so I had to improvise a bit. Anyhow, I walked on a bit, then I got lucky. I found this." The New Zealander reached into his pack and produced Dracup's battered hat.

"Ah."

"Jammed in a narrow cleft in the hillside. I thought – now what does he want to go poking around in there for? You couldn't squeeze a cat through the space. But I had a go anyway, seeing as how you'd obviously done it – I've got *some* national pride, y'know. Had a gander about, gave you a shout, then clammed up quick when I saw the opening in the rocks."

"You were *there?* In the church?"

"Yep. Quite a place, by my reckoning."

"You saw what happened?"

"Pretty much." Carey nodded and cracked his beer can, sending it into the waste bin with a deft flick. "I got myself inside just as the flamin' door rumbled shut – nearly took my hand off. Then I saw you and the boy – and the others, so I kept myself hidden at the back to see what was going down."

Dracup listened with fascination. He wiped sweat away from his forehead and flinched at the contact with his sunburnt skin. "Go on."

"Anyways, when it all got a bit heavy I tuckered down pretty low. I figured there wasn't much I could do while you were still inside. I waited till they moved you out through the tunnel and sidled up to the altar. I figured I could do you a favour with the old metalwork."

Dracup leaned forward, heart racing. It was too good to be true... but maybe...

Carey was shaking his head. "No, sorry mate. I know what you're thinking. This is where it gets a bit hazy for me. I'd just reached the step by the altar when something whacked me on the bonce and I was on the deck."

"And then –?"

"Not a lot. When I woke up I could see daylight through the tunnel, so I took a stroll along there until I heard you shouting."

"Shouting?" Dracup frowned.

"Yeah. At the lion."

Dracup shook his head. "I don't remember –"

"Don't worry about it – sunstroke does things to you. Anyhow, you seemed to have Simba all sorted out. Guess he thought you were just too weird to eat, right?"

Dracup tried to laugh through the pain of his headache and failed. Then he remembered the sceptre. "Wait – in the church. *Omega –*"

"No chance." Carey pursed his lips and scratched his chin through several days' growth of reddish stubble. "Whoever clocked me one made off with the goods."

Despair grabbed at Dracup's guts. He had rescued the diary but without the sceptre – he *had* to find it. "Who was it? Did you get a look?"

"Nope. Only thing I can tell you is it wasn't one of them priests."

"How can you be sure?"

"He was wearing trousers. With turn-ups. I got a look just before the lights went out."

A thought occurred to Dracup. "The priests. That's why they didn't come back to check on me. They were –"

"Distracted. Yeah." Carey smiled. "There was a bit of a rumpus going on when we drove through the town earlier. I'll bet that's what it was about."

"But if it wasn't the priests who clobbered you, then who the – ?"

"Good question." Carey arched his eyebrows. "But there were two people in that light aircraft. It was the passenger who gave us a lead hosing."

"Mukannishum." Dracup shuddered as he remembered the zealot's demise.

"Sounds like it. But that leaves the pilot." Carey rattled his knuckles on the chair.

"But the pilot was probably a hired flier." Dracup frowned.

Carey shrugged. "Maybe he was. Maybe not." He finished the dregs of his beer and looked wistfully at the empty glass. "Question is, what now?"

Dracup poured himself a fresh drink. "That's a no-brainer. I go back to the church."

Carey spun round. "Are you totally crazy?" He looked at Dracup in amazement. "You've just avoided ending your days as a lion's dinner and you want to go back? You know what you *should* do? You should get the police in from Addis."

Dracup studied his fingernails. They were chipped and ragged. "No police." He shook his head emphatically. "I have no choice, Dan. I need to find the sceptre."

"Ah, but do you?" Carey smiled. He went to the door, opened it a fraction and whistled. Enjoying Dracup's bemusement he stood to one side and watched his reaction. Footsteps rattled on the threshold and Bek walked into the room.

"Boss, I didn't know. I really didn't. I'm very sorry. Bek will make it all right." The boy was obviously frightened. He was clutching a tattered canvas bag to his chest as if his life depended on protecting it.

Dracup felt a mixture of emotions. Overriding the more negative of these was a strong sympathy for Bek's situation. "Let me guess. The long man got to you before I did. Made you an offer you couldn't turn down?"

Bek's eyes were downcast. "I never thought anything bad would happen, boss. No way."

"You don't know the half of it, lad," Dracup said. He pondered in silence for a few moments, then extended his hand. "Tell you what. Let's start again."

Bek grinned as if an enormous weight had been lifted from his thin shoulders. He flashed Dracup a wide smile.

Carey watched approvingly. "And I think you have something to show Professor Dracup, young man. Am I right?"

Bek nodded eagerly. His hand went into the bag like a cobra striking at its prey. When the hand came out it was holding Dracup's camera.

Dracup's mouth dropped open. "I'll be damned."

"Wait till you see some of the holiday snaps," Carey advised.

A small beam of hope began to percolate in Dracup's head. Bek handed him the camera with a barely concealed look of pride. Dracup took it and flicked the selector switch to 'display'. The images appeared obediently, lined up in their digital grid. Each shot was crystal clear, the cuneiform clearly visible. Dracup's fingers were trembling as he hit the zoom button. He looked at Bek as if the boy had just presented him with a cheque for a million pounds. Carey's face was creased into a lopsided perma-grin.

"Are they okay, boss? I got all the writing for you, like you wanted."

"How –?" Dracup couldn't find the words.

"They weren't looking at me, boss – when the long man got the real deal out of the box."

"You stole my camera," Dracup said at last. He went up to Bek and embraced him, ruffling the wiry hair vigorously. "You marvellous child." He laughed in sheer amazement. "You stole my wretched camera!"

Red Earth

Chapter 29

The cool air hit Dracup's cheeks like a balm. The sky was a horizon-hugging grey, and as he descended the airliner steps to board the courtesy bus it began to rain. He hailed a taxi and was soon crawling through the evening rush hour exodus from London towards Junction 10 of the M4. He was debating whether to go straight to Charles' house or phone ahead when the minicab driver turned around and said, "Sorry to bother you, sir, but I thought you'd like to know we're being followed."

"Are you sure? This *is* a motorway." Dracup turned and peered through the back window.

"Quite sure, sir. He pulled out just as we left the airport. Nearly shunted another car, he was so keen to get on our tail."

Dracup wasn't surprised. He'd been expecting trouble. Another no-brainer. One of three possibilities: Moran, Potzner, or Kadesh. Of these, Dracup favoured Moran. Potzner would have been more direct, and representatives of the *Korumak* more subtle.

"Okay. Just keep going." Dracup had no intention of leading Moran to Charles, although a nagging intuition told him that the DCI would probably have paid his friend a visit already. The campus was a small place and his circle of friends even smaller. They would have to lose the tail.

The traffic began to thin and soon they were speeding along the A329M towards Reading town centre. "He's still with us, sir."

Dracup sat back and closed his eyes. "Well, then. Time to earn your money."

"Right you are, sir," the driver said, and floored the accelerator.

A few minutes later Dracup asked: "Any sign?"

"No sir. I've lost him for now."

They were close to Dracup's road. He didn't want to waste any time at his flat, but a change of clothes was a necessity. "Okay – next left and stop just under the first street lamp."

"Right you are, sir."

Dracup fumbled for his house keys. "Just up here on the –" Dracup's words dried up. His front door was a heavy replacement blank, the stained glass a missing image on his retina. The building was in total darkness. As they drew up he saw the signs. *Dangerous structure. Keep out.*

"Don't stop," Dracup told the driver. "You know the University?"

"Course I do," the driver chirped brightly.

Dracup sighed. "Let's go." He grabbed the seat belt as the car accelerated. "Take it steady." He twisted and looked out of the back window. A green BMW was doing its best to replicate their Le Mans-style departure. Dracup rapped on the seat in front of him. "Our friend is back."

"Just hold tight, sir."

The car careered around the next corner. Better let Charles know that trouble was on the way. He fished out his mobile and keyed the 'on' button. The car lurched into another turn and he nearly dropped the phone as the LED lit up with the familiar network logo. Dracup thumbed 'contacts' but was interrupted by a beep. *You have a new message.* The car straightened and hurtled on down the inner distribution road.

"Hey – be careful! You'll have the entire Thames Valley force on our tail," Dracup yelled at the driver.

"Don't worry, sir. I'll lose 'em all."

Dracup turned his attention back to the mobile. He pressed 'view media message' and fell back in shock. It was Natasha. She was standing by a river, or pool. There was a waterfall and... sirens began wailing somewhere behind; blue lights were flicking against the cream upholstery of the taxi. They were heading up to the University, negotiating the narrow roads circling the campus. Natasha's face looked out at him from the mobile. She was alive. She looked all right. His heart was thudding in his ribcage as he

232

opened the accompanying text message. And then it almost stopped altogether. He read and reread the text, with its final, mocking statement.

> *Up to now you have shown creditable resourcefulness. Please don't disappoint me*

He thumbed at the phone's buttons and found one of Bek's images he'd backed up from the camera. His fingers moved urgently over the keypad. *Create message.* He wrote: *I'll be with you shortly. Directions helpful.* He pressed the 'send' key with as much vehemence as he could muster. *Forty-eight hours?* But when had the text been sent? Presumably at dawn on the twenty-sixth. Today *was* the twenty-sixth. Less than thirty-six hours, then. Dracup pocketed the phone and leaned forward.

"Next corner – it's a tight one. Pull into the side and let me out. Then keep going." He pressed a twenty-pound note into the driver's raised hand. "Don't get caught."

"No problem, sir. Thank you kindly."

The cab screeched to a halt. Dracup grabbed his bag and flung himself out. With a melodramatic whirl of rubber the minicab disappeared around the bend. Dracup sank into the shadows. Thirty seconds later the BMW hurtled into view, this time accompanied by a squad car, siren blaring like a demented operatic. Dracup hopped over the campus perimeter fence. It was dusk and the grounds were quiet. He leaned against the fence and wondered what to do. Images of Sara came back to him, the night they had fled from the assassin. The dead man lying by the bridge, pale-faced in the moonlight. Dracup took a deep breath and strode on. The gatehouse was only a minute or so away. He fretted that Moran would appear before they had a chance to examine Bek's photos. He skirted the lake and crunched up the few metres of gravel before Charles' gatehouse came into view. It, too was in darkness. Dracup was unperturbed. His friend could be anywhere on campus – it was not unusual for Charles to be seen pottering around the various faculty buildings well into the evening. Dracup resolved to wait.

He approached the door and stopped, shocked into indecision. The porch was protected by a blue-chequered *'Police – keep out'* tape, and standing nonchalantly a few metres away by the road was a young, bored-looking constable. Dracup retreated into the bushes. *Oh no, not Charles.* He thought rapidly. *Check the back, Dracup, you idiot.* Risky with the police presence, but he had to see for himself. He cautiously circled the gatehouse and, when he was satisfied the rear was unguarded, walked quickly to the back entrance and tried the door handle. Locked. He moved stealthily along to the casement window. The small window at the top was open. He inserted a hand and slid the brass handle upwards. He paused and listened. A car rumbled past. He heard a faint whistling. The policeman, bored out of his mind. *Quietly, Dracup, quietly...* He inserted the tips of his fingers and pulled slowly. The window opened. He went in.

The house felt cold. Dracup picked his way through the bedroom and into the hall. Charles' study door lay before him. He peered through the hall window and checked the policeman's position. He was sitting on the wall with a notebook balanced on his lap, writing or doodling; it was hard to say. Dracup tiptoed into the study. He waited until his eyes had become accustomed to the gloom. He ran a finger along the desk. It came away covered in a powdery substance, like talcum powder. Forensics. *Oh Charles, Charles. What happened to you? What happened here?*

He slid his hands across the bare desk. Nothing. All of Charles' chaotic correspondence had gone. Probably in a polythene bag in Moran's office. Dracup staggered out of the office and back to the window he had left ajar. The cool air helped, but it was several minutes before he was able to climb out and retrieve his bag. He walked along the familiar path and found a bench. He heard Charles' voice in his head, as clear as a bell: *I'll pop something in the old electro-post if I think it's worthwhile.* Dracup got to his feet and strode resolutely towards the main University buildings.

His office was another world, one he had left behind. There was his inkstand. There was the pile of unmarked essays, the old jacket draped across his chair. And his PC – an ancient machine he'd constantly berated IT resources to replace. He sat heavily in the chair and switched it on. He emptied his pockets onto the desk as the PC booted. Mobile, airline ticket, passport. *Camera.* Dracup slid the memory card out and placed it carefully in his top pocket. The PC presented his desktop and he logged into hotmail. Dracup groaned. *You have 507 new messages.* He scrolled impatiently through the junk mail, deleting offers of Viagra and hot dates in his area with resolute clicks of the mouse. And then he found it. *Sturrock, Charles. Received: 4 Oct. Subject: As discussed.* Dracup hesitated, fingers hovering over the keys. Was that a noise in the corridor? He went to the door and looked out. There was no one. He sat down and opened the email.

My dear Simon

I hardly know where to start this communication. I would recommend you make yourself comfortable, pour a stiff drink and prepare for my unusual, but I have to say logical, conclusions.

Dracup shook his head. Charles was Charles, even via email; abbreviation would never have occurred to him. His smile faded as he remembered the dark gatehouse, the emptiness. *He could be just visiting friends.* Dracup ran a trembling hand through his hair. He caught himself in the mirror and groaned at the sight. Sunburned, haggard. He took a deep breath and read on.

I took the liberty of examining British Museum manuscripts from several ancient sources. The first of these is a manuscript I mentioned to you before we parted – my dear

> Simon – how remiss of me. I quite forgot to ask how you were, and if your adventure in Africa is parting the clouds of confusion for you. No doubt you will furnish me with all your news on your return.
>
> Now, this manuscript, the 'Cave of Treasures', is a compendium of early Biblical history although it also strays into New Testament territory. It is an embellished book, in that it was written to promote a sense of wonder and awe concerning the early dealings of God with man. It is also, I should say, considered apocryphal. I'm quite sure I don't have to explain the term, but for the sake of clarity I shall remind you. The scriptures considered to be the very word of God – i.e. recorded by man under divine inspiration – and known to us as the canonical scriptures were approved to be such by common agreement at around the time of the council of Nicaea, although some argument and debate continued for several years after the council over theological issues such as the nature of Christ's divinity and his human nature. The canonical scriptures were deemed authoritative because they had been <u>considered</u> authoritative from the times of the original apostles who had walked with Jesus. That, I trust, will serve as a brief reminder. The point I am making is that one has to take great care when dealing with the apocrypha and not get too carried away by some of the more fanciful illustrations.

Come on, Charles. Get to the point. Dracup scanned down the email.

> Now, bearing all this in mind, Simon, please indulge me by reading the following extracts from the 'Cave Of Treasures':

> *'But command thy sons, and order them to embalm thy body after thy death with myrrh, cassia and stakty' [God speaking to Adam]*
>
> *'And when Adam was dead his son Seth embalmed him, according to Adam's command, and they took Adam's body and buried it in the Cave of Treasures'*
>
> *'And God said unto Noah, Take thy wife, and thy sons, and the wives of thy sons, and get down from this holy mountain. And take with thee the body of your father Adam and set his body in the centre of the Ark, and lay these offerings upon him. He is to be revered unto all generations and I will set apart a people for his care and preservation until the end times.'*

Dracup frowned. Adam? Care and preservation...?

> *My dear Simon, I can only imagine how you are feeling having read these small excerpts. Let me first tell you, should you be inclined to write them off as speculative, that other ancient writings lend support to the 'Cave Of Treasures' text. 'The book of Adam', for example, states that Noah was entombed beneath a mountain, that the Ark was closed during these latter days of Noah but that Noah went into it each night to light the lamp he had made, and which burned before the body of Adam. He carried in his hand a staff of unparalleled workmanship, fashioned from Eden's Tree of Life and surmounted by a beautiful interlocking crest, the two halves of which form the recognisable Christian symbol of – a cross.*

Dracup was shaking like a leaf. He realised he was saying, over and over again, "It can't be. It can't be." He read on.

I would put it to you, Simon, that your sceptre is none other than the legendary staff of Moses, handed down directly from its first owner, Adam, through Noah's line to the patriarch Moses himself.

Also note that the Cave of Treasures itself appears to be a physical location, a subterranean mausoleum of the patriarchs, perhaps. And I have no doubt that, when properly translated, the remarkable crest of Noah – or should I say Adam – will pinpoint that location.

This may seem a fanciful observation, Simon, but I recall that the grandfather clock in your aunt's house was set to seven minutes past seven. This was the indicator that led you to the sundial and so to the artefact buried in your grandfather's garden. You will know that the number seven is deeply significant in ancient literature. And I believe your grandfather intended to show you more than just the location of the artefact when he set the timepiece so. The ancients divided the human frame into seven parts; the head, the chest, the stomach, two hands and two feet; and man's life was divided into seven periods. Consider: a baby begins teething in the seventh month; a child begins to sit after fourteen months (2 x 7); begins to walk after twenty-one months (3 x 7); to speak after twenty-eight months (4 x 7); ceases sucking after thirty-five (5 x 7); at fourteen years (2 x 7) he begins to finally form himself; at twenty-one (3 x 7) he ceases growing. The number seven points to the human span itself, and what better example of a perfect creation (seven being the perfect number) than the first man, Adam?

A final, it seems to me, defining observation is that the name Adam [Adamah] in the Hebrew means 'earth', the <u>red</u> earth of the Euphrates from which, according to the Bible, Adam was formed. This, I believe was also the name *your American friend gave as the codeword for his little operation?*

Dracup was gawping at the screen. He recalled Potzner's lugubrious face referring to his remit for recovery of the stolen material: Operation *Red Earth*.

I must press on – there is much more to discover, I am sure. I trust this will suffice for the time being. My thoughts are with you and my prayers also – I know that young Natasha will be reunited with you in due course. Press on, Simon, and God speed.

Yours,

Charles.

PS – I can see your expression, Simon – have a look at Luke 3:23; it may help. Do note that the last line of the genealogy 'son of God' is lower case – i.e. it doesn't refer to Jesus – otherwise it would be u/case. Jesus, of course, in the New Testament is referred to as the <u>second</u> Adam, the one sent to reverse the curse of Eden. Now dammit, there's someone at the door. No rest for the wicked, eh? Must go –
C.

Dracup's mind was paralyzed, almost numb. Charles' assertions rang in his head like a detuned bell. It wasn't Noah's body Potzner was after. *Noah's* body had been a mental stretch for Dracup to accommodate, but *Adam's?* Adam and Eve? The Garden of Eden? Dracup's anthropological professionalism fought against Charles' conclusions for all it was worth. The Genesis story was a fable, a helpful story of origins for an ancient and unscientific people. Adam's body? No, no, no. The Ark, maybe. But Eden? No. Never. He closed the email and with both elbows on the desk cradled his head in his hands. *Luke 3:23.* All right,

Charles. Just for you. Dracup pulled a Bible from his shelf and flicked through the pages to the New Testament. He began to read:

Now Jesus himself was about thirty years old when he began his ministry. He was the son, so it was thought, of Joseph, the son of Heli, the son of Matthat, the son of Levi, the son of Melki, the son of Jannai, the son of Joseph,

Dracup scanned down the list.

the son of Kenan, the son of Enosh, the son of Seth, the son of Adam,

the son of God.

Dracup recalled Charles' argument during a heated and lengthy discussion about the Bible and its place in ancient literature: *The Jews were scrupulous record keepers, Simon.* And then, with a bitter taste of shock, he remembered Mukannishum's strange words in the lion pit: *Your forefather betrayed the son of God.* He was shaking his head. It's not possible. It simply can't be. When four sharp knocks on the door interrupted him he was almost pleased to see the thin figure of DCI Moran standing impatiently on the threshold. There was something reassuringly routine about the crumpled raincoat and the cynical expression on the policeman's face.

"Welcome back, Professor Dracup. Phelps?"

Moran's assistant stepped forward. "Simon Dracup: I am arresting you on the suspicion of conspiracy to murder Charles Anthony Sturrock. You do not have to say anything, but it may harm your defense –"

"You don't have to arrest me." Dracup sat heavily in his chair. "I'll tell you what I know."

Phelps glanced at Moran. The DCI shrugged, produced a pocket tape machine and clicked it on. "Let's fill in some gaps. I asked you not to leave the country. It wasn't a joke." He walked to the corner of Dracup's study and sat in an old armchair, crossing his legs.

"I had to. To find out where my daughter is being held."

Moran looked at him analytically. "And did you?"

"Yes. In a way."

"Meaning?"

Dracup sighed. "You've probably read my emails. You work it out."

Moran got up and strolled to the window. He lurked behind Dracup. "As far as we know, you're the last person to see Charles Sturrock alive. He dies. You disappear."

Dracup shook his head. "It was the other way round. Charles was fine when I left him in Toulouse."

"Go on."

"He flew me to Toulouse. The last I saw of him, he was picking his way round the duty-free shop."

"So you're saying you know nothing about his murder." Moran began pacing the room. He stood behind Dracup again, gripped the back of his chair.

Dracup thought of Mukannishum. It wasn't hard to piece it together. His flat. His home PC. Charles' email and address. And then what? An interruption – probably Potzner. And Mukannishum's solution – an evidence-shredding explosion. Then a tidying of loose ends before following in his footsteps to Africa. Charles wouldn't have had a chance.

Moran was almost breathing down his neck. "Mr Dracup. I'm waiting."

"Okay. I believe my daughter was abducted by a group of religious terrorists to exact a form of revenge on my family for something that happened more than eighty years ago. Charles was helping me and I suppose they got to him – to cover their tracks."

Moran reappeared and took the seat opposite Dracup's desk. The DCI steepled his hands and leaned his sharp chin on the temporary structure. He wasn't laughing. Dracup glanced at Phelps. Neither was he. *They know more than they're letting on.*

"I come from Southern Ireland, Mr Dracup. I'm no stranger to religious terrorism." Moran sighed. "Let's apply a little lubrication, Professor, mm? D'you have a coffee machine?"

"End of the corridor. Turn left."

"Good. Phelps?"

Phelps' expression implied a degree of reluctance, but he shrugged and left the room. Moran clicked the tape off. "Now listen, Mr Dracup. I know you were in France at the time Sturrock was murdered. We checked out the flight logs with local airfields. I also know the CIA is into this in a big way, but murders and abductions in the Royal County are my affair, not theirs. If you want me on your side you'd better start talking – and if I like what I hear I *might* be able to exclude you from our enquiries."

"Have you read Charles' last email to me? It's a pretty good summary."

"I have indeed. And there are many who would dismiss his conclusions as fanciful gobbledegook."

Dracup laughed, a harsh sound in the enclosed space. "Yes. And I'm one of them."

Moran sat back in his chair. "Are you?" He paused as if deciding whether or not to verbalize his train of thought. "I come from a country steeped in religion, Mr Dracup. I was expected to enter the priesthood after I left school. I even attended theological college."

"Oh? So what happened?"

"Life happened, Mr Dracup. You know how it is. You grow up; you have a head full of ideals. Then you slowly begin to realize what a chaotic world this really is. People die. You can't find any answers or make any sense out of it. Ambitions are frustrated. You get older. Eventually, God dies as well."

"You lost your faith."

"Faith is a hard thing to maintain when you've seen what I've seen back home; the ruined lives, the widowed mothers, the fatherless children. I've seen some pretty unpleasant things in my time as a policeman. It doesn't help."

Dracup detected some seed of hope in Moran's eyes. Almost a hunger.

The DCI was leaning forward now. "Tell me about the diary. And the inscriptions on this thing you found."

Dracup told him. There was little to gain by feigning ignorance, and something in the policeman's manner suggested a willingness to suspend disbelief in the improbable. Dracup was having trouble doing just that himself, but the evidence, he conceded, was pointing him inexorably in the same direction. He produced the flash card. They viewed the photographs in silence.

"Well, like I said, it's all gobbledegook to me," Moran said. "You say this is the key to your daughter's location?"

"I believe so, yes. If it's translated along with *Alpha*'s cuneiform. And that requires expertise."

"And no doubt the CIA have an expert to hand?"

"Yes. Potzner had the first part of the stanza translated pretty quickly." Dracup wondered if the Thames Valley had a cuneiform expert on permanent standby. It didn't seem likely.

Moran paced the room. "This Potzner character. You think he had anything to do with Sturrock's murder?"

Dracup shook his head. "It wouldn't benefit them. It has to be the *Korumak*, the same person who was after me. I only know him as Mukannishum."

"And he followed you to Ethiopia?" Moran listened in ill-concealed amazement as Dracup told him of the rock churches and Mukannishum's demise in the lion pit.

Moran was shaking his head. "I can't put any of this in the report." He leaned over the table. "If you're spinning me one, Dracup, I'm going to take you to the cleaners. You'll go down for a long time, trust me."

"Why would I make it up?" Dracup heard himself yelling. "I'm an anthropologist, not a Hollywood script writer. I just want my daughter back."

Moran held his hands up. "All right, all right. Calm." He sat down and folded his arms. "So. I'm chasing shadows. That's what you're telling me. The man who killed Sturrock is dead. And his organization, run by some character named Kadesh, are nowhere to be found."

"I was relying on Charles to pinpoint their location. In any case, it seems likely that we're talking somewhere abroad. In which case there's not a lot you can do anyway."

"Oh, don't you believe it, Mr Dracup," Moran said quietly. "I can be very persuasive when I've a mind to be that way."

The door opened and Phelps reappeared with three plastic cups and a chocolate bar. He was walking stiffly with an odd, preoccupied look about him.

"Thank you, Phelps." Moran pointed. "Just there will be fine."

Phelps placed the cups between Dracup and Moran. He turned with an apologetic expression and looked at the door.

"Problem, Phelps?" Moran stepped forward, his face registering the first inkling of concern, but the door was already swinging open. There was a collective exclamation from the occupants of the room, and Dracup found himself looking down the meticulously rifled barrel of an automatic pistol.

Chapter 30

Potzner closed the door. He pointed the automatic steadily at Moran. "Gentlemen." He smiled a greeting to each occupant of the room in turn. "I do apologize for this unorthodox approach. Professor – would you be kind enough to stand up and walk slowly over to me?"

Moran spoke quietly. "This isn't a good idea, Mr Potzner."

"We'll be out of your way shortly, Detective Chief Inspector. My men are covering the building, so please don't entertain any foolish notions of heroism."

Dracup studied Potzner's face. The eyes were glazed, the expression one of zealous conviction. *Something's happened. He's lost it.*

Moran was attempting to reason. "This will cause a serious diplomatic situation. Professor Dracup is helping the police with their enquiries. It's a criminal offence to remove him."

Potzner nodded. "Is that a fact? Well, Detective Chief Inspector, I have to warn you that if you attempt to stop me I will shoot you where you stand. Do I make myself clear?"

Dracup's hands were hidden by his PC. Keeping a close eye on Potzner he eased the flash card out of the card reader and slipped it underneath his cuff.

Phelps was staring open-mouthed. Moran's hands were clenching and unclenching, weighing his options. Dracup looked at Potzner and had no doubts. *He'll do it.* He stood up slowly and raised a warning hand to Moran. "I think we'd best do as he says."

Potzner led Dracup out of the room and closed the door behind him, locking it carefully with one hand. The other still held the automatic. Dracup looked down the corridor. Potzner's men stood along it, spaced evenly like a wedding line. He looked in vain for Farrell. Surely he wouldn't condone this madness?

"After you, Professor Dracup." Potzner gestured with the automatic.

A sleek, black saloon awaited them in the car park. A number of agents were strategically placed like a scattered party of Mormon elders waiting for a sign. The sign apparently came and they melted into the anonymity of the campus. The engine purred into life. Dracup was in the back and the car was moving towards the exit.

Potzner holstered his automatic with an apologetic shrug. "Sorry about that, Prof. I don't think you'll do anything stupid, will you?"

Dracup had recovered from his surprise. "I think you've cornered the market on 'stupid'. This is England. You can't just kidnap a police suspect."

"But you're not a suspect, are you, Mr Dracup? I think DCI Moran senses something out of the ordinary and believes you can supply him with the answers. You're no killer. Anyone can tell that. He's fishing." Potzner turned to Dracup with a strange smile on his lips. "And did he catch anything?"

Moran's not the only one waving a net around, Dracup thought. To counter Potzner's question he said, "I know what this is about."

"Oh yeah. I imagine you do." Potzner seemed pleased.

"But I can't believe it."

"Can't or won't?"

"The discovery of Noah's Ark is one thing. The preserved body of Adam is another."

"Nevertheless, both are true."

There was something disturbing about this dry confirmation. Dracup's head began to spin. "Creation is a myth. Darwin set the record straight over a hundred years ago." He shook his head. "It's impossible."

"No. Darwin took the world down the biggest blind alley it's *ever* been down. You never heard of the Laws of Thermodynamics, Prof? I'll be surprised if you haven't."

Dracup's head was throbbing. "Of course I have."

"In any given system, neither matter nor energy can be self-created or destroyed. That's law numero uno." Potzner ticked it off with his forefinger. "Two. Over time, any closed system becomes less ordered and more random. The mechanics of evolution just don't work."

"Yes, but –"

"I told you, I'm no scientist, Prof. But it seems common sense to me. Evolution is just a flawed theory. A fairy tale. You going to argue with Einstein? Go right ahead. Anyhow, it's all academic. I've seen the proof."

The proof? Dracup thought of Charles' bizarre email. *Adam. Red Earth.* He couldn't get his mind around it. The car swung smoothly onto the M4. Dracup craned his neck to look out of the back window. So far there was no sign of pursuit. That was odd. "Where are we going?"

"To a US air base in Devon. I need you under US jurisdiction."

"And what makes you think I can tell you anything?" Dracup stalled. As he prevaricated he realized that Potzner was probably his only remaining hope. Who else could decipher the cuneiform?

"It's in your face, Professor. You found something in Africa, didn't you?"

Dracup patted his top pocket. The compact flash card was still there. "All right. I do have something – in jpg format. Your people can examine it."

Potzner looked as if he had simultaneously won the lottery and witnessed his team win the super league. His eyes were wide. "I knew you'd come up with something."

They drove on in silence for a while. Then Potzner said, "You ever have someone close to you die, Professor?"

"Apart from my parents, no. I –" Then with a sick jolt Dracup remembered Charles. "Not until recently."

"Right. I'm sorry about Sturrock."

"Thanks."

"You see, Professor, as I was telling you in London, we have the potential to accelerate human genome research exponentially."

"That won't bring back the dead."

Potzner shook his head. "No, no. You're right. But it *will* prevent unnecessary death by disease. And it will – in time – decelerate the ageing process."

"But there's more to all this than just research, Potzner. If it's true."

"Oh, it's true all right. I've seen it for myself."

Dracup fixed Potzner with a steady, probing look. "Are you telling me that you have seen, with your own eyes, the preserved body of the first created man?"

Potzner returned the eye contact. "Yes. Without a doubt."

"How can you be so sure? It could be anyone."

Potzner chuckled to himself. "No, no, no. Don't you get it? There was something pretty special about our first parents. Something that sets them apart from all their children."

"Namely?"

Potzner leaned in close. "They were created, not born. They have no umbilicus."

Dracup exhaled in disbelief. "A male body, with no belly-button?" This was insane. "And the female? Eve?"

Potzner shook his head. "Nope. Not a sign. It's possible she's buried in the location we all want to find. But, so far, there's no evidence that her body received the same treatment."

Dracup was thinking about the sceptre. Not Noah's sceptre. *Adam's*. "This is extraordinary. It means –"

"It means we have a chance at immortality," Potzner interrupted. "It means no more death."

Dracup shook his head. "No, no it doesn't." He struggled to articulate the outrageous thought. "It means – it means there *is* a creator. A designer. God."

"*God?*" Potzner guffawed. "If you want to call him that. But what do we know about him? I mean *really* know? What can we prove about the creator? For all you know, he could be half a million galaxies away from Earth by now. And do you think he – *it* – cares about – hell, even remembers – this speck of dust? So what if he set the ball rolling? It's rolling along pretty good without him, huh? No, what we have here is human potential. We can be masters of our own destinies. We will build indestructible bodies."

"Using Adam's blueprint?"

"Why not? His body is different, Dracup, *stronger*. His DNA is a work of art, according to our guys. What we have in here " Potzner thumped his chest for emphasis, "is some poor imitation, a flawed copy."

"But Adam died." Dracup frowned at Potzner's strange logic. "At some improbable age, granted, but he still *died*."

"Yeah, but think what you could *do* with a lifespan like that. Eight hundred, nine hundred years? C'mon, Dracup, where's your vision? Think of the knowledge you'd gain, the quality of life you'd enjoy with no disease to interrupt you. We can do it. All we have to do is keep the research going. We'll get there."

"I don't know. There's another dimension you need to take into account."

"Don't go all Bible-belt on me, Dracup. We're past all that."

"On the contrary. I think you're right in the middle of '*all that*'. Maybe this God isn't as disconnected as you think; maybe he still has an interest in what's going on here. And just maybe he won't take kindly to your 'research'." Dracup paused, surprised at his outburst. Where had that come from? He suddenly felt mind-numbingly weary and rested his head against the side window, the effort of conversation almost beyond him. "Anyway, don't you think the world should know the truth?"

"The truth? Are you crazy? What do you think would happen if we announced the 'truth' on the nine o'clock news? Do you think everyone would be going 'whoopee – there *is* a God'?"

Dracup rubbed his eyes. Potzner had a point. "I don't know. Probably not."

"Well, maybe the fundamentalists, the born-agains. But the whole thing is a minefield. Did you know that there is a widespread belief amongst the Islamics that the revelation of the Ark will be a sign that Mohammed is returning to purge the Earth of heretics in a holy war? And what if it became common knowledge that the Ark *had* been discovered and then looted by the West?

That unbelievers from the United States of America had tainted the sacred mountain? And we haven't even gotten on to the Islamic view of Adam and the Bible vs. the Koran yet. Release this news and you set up the biggest excuse for civil unrest since – hell – since I don't know when. You want Armageddon? Fine – give 'em the truth and that's what you'll get – the mother of all *Jihads*."

Small droplets of spittle were collecting around Potzner's mouth. Dracup pressed his face against the cold glass and watched the motorway slip by. His head was spinning. He tried to blank out Potzner's voice. He needed to think.

Given a choice of enforced custody, Moran would have been Dracup's preferred jailer. Potzner was like a gyroscope running out of energy; still turning but likely to fly off balance at any time. Dracup comforted himself with the thought that half the Thames Valley police force would be looking for them. But then where were the roadblocks and pursuing squad cars? And then he thought about Moran and the answer came to him: he's waiting for the flash card analysis. *He's cutting Potzner some slack.* And that meant the DCI would be expecting a progress report. Hope began to simmer again. With nothing visible from his window Dracup closed his eyes and ears to Potzner's warped evangelism. Vivid scenes of Ethiopia immediately invaded the blackness. In his mind's eye he saw Mukannishum in the church, elevating the Lalibelian sceptre like a Catholic priest raising a chalice. And then he remembered. Mukannishum's accent, the strange vowel intonation. He suddenly knew where he had heard it before; not in the bass register of a man's vocal cords, but a woman's. *Sara*.

Chapter 31

"You betrayed me." Sara flushed with disbelief. "My *sister*."

"I told you. The girl belongs to me. And *you* do not belong here anymore."

Sara's eyes searched beyond Ruth to where the chamber opening allowed a little of the cavern phosphorescence to colour the cell. Outside were two of Kadesh's elite, keeping watch. They wore desert combat fatigues and carried weapons procured from Kadesh's liaison with Al-Qaida. Sara's heart was full of fear, not for herself, but for the future of the *Korumak*.

"Ruth, please, be kind to the child."

"Of course. She is mine. She will enjoy a mother's love."

"But can't you see? There is great danger here. From the Americans and Al-Qaida. It's not safe any more. You have to get away."

"The blessed one is wise. Obedience to him is the whole of the law."

Sara studied Ruth's face. Her sister's words filled her with alarm. Was it too late? She approached Ruth with her arms wide. "Listen to me, Ruth. Kadesh is going to kill me. *And* the girl. He's lying to you. What else has he promised?"

"Not the girl." Ruth shook her head emphatically. Her oiled hair left a tang of perfume in the eddy of her movement.

Sara seized her sister's arm. "I saw what he wrote. He sent a message to Natasha's father. It was a promise to kill us both. Unless –"

"Unless your lover comes to save you." Ruth smiled strangely. "Yes. He must also die. Then it is over." She pulled herself free. "I have to go."

"Why did you come?" Sara shouted after her. To make sure I was still here? To make sure I was still *alive?*" Her voice degenerated with her anger. The door was locked into place and she was left alone in the twilight.

"Are you really going to be my mummy from now on?" Natasha asked.

"We'll have such fun," Ruth replied. "There is so much to see."

Natasha looked doubtful. "But I miss my house and my friends, and –"

Ruth bent low and gripped the girl's arms. "All that is past. This is your home now."

"You're hurting me." Natasha began to cry. "My daddy will be cross with you. He never hurts me. Neither does my mummy. You're not my mummy." She tore herself away and flung herself onto the bed. "I hate it here."

Ruth leaned over and touched the girl's head lightly. "I'm sorry, Natasha. I just want you to be happy."

She would make her happy.

Natasha's face was buried in the pillow. "I want my daddy. He'll come and get me soon."

Ruth sat next to the girl and folded her hands in her lap. She felt distracted, as if some vital instruction had passed her by. When Natasha's sobs had subsided she hugged her tightly. "Yes, child. He will come. He will come soon."

Chapter 32

"Okay, Mr Dracup. Journey's end. For now." Potzner held the door and Dracup stepped onto the tarmac. Around him he was aware of the bulky shapes of aircraft and the transient movements of US personnel tending to the myriad jobs of an operational base. Huge golf-ball-shaped radomes studded the airfield perimeter, bonding a veneer of science fiction to Dracup's embattled thought processes. Potzner ushered him quickly across the concrete apron to a squat perimeter building, within which nestled a warren of open-plan activity. He felt like an intruder, a feeling compounded by the curious stares he attracted as they made their way across the operations floor. A queue was forming around a white-aproned sandwich lady, through which Potzner shouldered his way without apology. Dracup closed his ears to the expletives and followed the American as he negotiated the maze with practiced ease, nodding briskly to a familiar face here and there until they entered a door simply marked 'Intelligence Officer'.

Sitting on a corner of the single desk was Farrell, who raised a hand in half-salute then let it drop back to his side with a curt nod to Dracup. *He looks worried.* Dracup caught the anxious glance that passed between Farrell and the man behind the desk, who had stood up to greet the newcomers.

"Colonel Gembala – this is Professor Dracup." Farrell performed the introductions. "He has the information we need."

Gembala extended his hand. "Nice to meet you, Professor. I've heard about your solo performance. You'll be taking a back seat from this point on."

"Has Fish arrived?" Potzner demanded. Farrell opened his mouth to reply but Potzner cut him off. "If not, why the hell not?"

Gembala walked round the desk and patted Potzner on the shoulder. "He'll be here in ten, Jim. Take it easy." The voice was firm but rang with a conciliatory note. Dracup watched with interest. *They're handling him with kid gloves.*

Potzner flicked his Zippo and lit a Marlboro. He blew smoke and held out his hand to Dracup. "May I?"

Dracup took the flash card from his pocket and placed it in the American's outstretched palm. Potzner jammed the cigarette in the corner of his mouth and held up the card between his thumb and forefinger. "You went through a lot for this, Professor." The sardonic smile was back in place. "The world will be grateful." Potzner addressed Gembala. "Is everything ready for us, Colonel?"

"Fuelled and waiting on your word," Gembala replied.

"Then we just need Fish." Potzner inhaled smoke and blew a thin stream towards Farrell, who waved a practiced hand in front of his face.

The desk phone rang. "That'll be him." Potzner stubbed the cigarette out on the corner of the waste paper basket. "Let's go."

They assembled in a larger room Dracup guessed was used for briefings. There was a projector and laptop set up for presentations as well as seating for around fifty bodies. A small, nervous-looking man entered the room from a side door and approached with an expression of pained excitement.

"Okay Fish, let's roll the slide show." Potzner handed him Dracup's flash card.

"Right. If you gentlemen will just give us a few minutes –" Fish indicated several other new arrivals who were engaged in animated conversation. One of them was fiddling with the laptop. A blank yellow square appeared on the screen, shrinking in size as the technician focused the lens. Familiar text appeared:

> *'From holy resting place to rest upon the water –*
> *But Noah, the faithful son –*
> *Once more in the earth you will find peace –*
> *From whence you came –*
> *Between the rivers –'*

Farrell nudged Dracup. The American handed him a styrofoam cup of coffee and a cellophane-wrapped sandwich. The label said *Dellow's Delicious Deli, Yeovil*. Dracup doubted the description but received the snack graciously. He unwrapped the sandwich and took an automatic mouthful.

"Fingers crossed, huh?" Farrell said.

"I need more than luck, Farrell. I need a miracle." Dracup gestured to the jostling group of boffins. "This guy is pretty good?"

"Fish? Oh yeah. If it's doable, he'll do it."

But in less than thirty-six hours? Dracup's mouth felt like sandpaper. He put his sandwich down.

A small cheer went up from the front. Farrell grinned. "There you go."

Dracup looked at the screen. It had been split into right and left sections, the original text on the left. On the right, some new text appeared:

> *'From holy resting place to rest upon the water – you have been brought, our father'*

Dracup's heart beat faster. Someone coughed. He looked round. Potzner was standing in a corner at the back of the room, enveloped in a cloud of smoke. His foot was tapping on the carpet tiles in a slow, constant rhythm. Farrell went over to Colonel Gembala and said something in a low voice. Gembala nodded and continued watching the screen. Dracup looked at the clock, a rectangular digital monstrosity that flapped over a plastic square for each new integer to display. It said 22:23.

There seemed to be some debate about the next translation. Dracup's jpg appeared again. One of the techies was making some phonetic point about an indistinct character on the Lalibelian sceptre. Dracup looked at the close-up of Mukannishum's long fingers and felt the sandwich turn to sawdust in his mouth.

22:45. The image disappeared and the text reappeared. With two new lines:

*'But Noah, the faithful son – shall lead you to cooler depths
Once more in the earth you will find peace – laid in the holy place'*

A rumble of excitement passed through the room. One of the techies clapped another on the back. Dracup heard an exclamation. "All *right!*" He realized he'd been holding his breath. And his bladder. He made for the door to find the toilets. Farrell was at his side. He shrugged. "Sorry."

When they returned to the briefing room the buzz of expectancy had grown. 22:52. Gembala was standing now, pacing up and down between two rows of plastic chairs. Potzner, a brooding figure, was keeping his distance. Fish and his colleagues were in a dense huddle. They broke apart. The screen flicked again.

*'From whence you came – to Kish the seat of kings
Between the rivers – beyond the gate of God'*

"That's it." Potzner was moving to the front. "That's it. *Kish*. Where the hell is Kish? Fish? Someone get me a map." One of the technicians laughed, a release of nervous tension. Potzner shot him a black look and the smile disappeared. Fish and his men scattered as Potzner approached.

Farrell turned to Dracup. "That's Iraq, isn't it, Prof?"

Dracup was taking it in. Natasha is in *Iraq?*

Gembala was talking urgently to two men who had entered the room just before the last verse was completed. They were in USAF pilot's uniform. Dracup caught one phrase: *Stand by.* They left on the double.

A map appeared. Potzner laid it out. "About eighty kilometres south of Baghdad." He stabbed a yellowed finger at the position. "Are our guys anywhere near?" He looked at Gembala.

"Well, yes and no. It's a protected area. We patrol but there's no permanent occupation. The government's pretty hot about the loss of archaeologically sensitive material. Since the museum in Baghdad was trashed at the beginning of the war –"

Potzner cut in. "Who knows anything about this place? Fish – get your ass over here."

Dracup hovered behind Fish and craned his head for a better look.

Fish adjusted his glasses and brought his face close to the map. "Well, ah, it's a ruined city. From what I remember the site would be around eight kilometres in total. It's been partially excavated. There are mounds – I believe a large constructed palace was unearthed."

"And?" Potzner probed.

"It was the first post-flood city," Fish blethered on, warming to his theme. "That's where it all started over. The royal seat was moved to Kish after the supposed flood. It's all documented in the Sumerian Kings list – er, that's an archaeological document they found in Mesopotamia," he added for the benefit of the surrounding blank stares.

Dracup felt numb. *Iraq is a war zone. They took my daughter into a **war** zone.*

"And something else –" Fish attempted to control his accelerating excitement. "The gate of God – p-probably refers to Babylon. The derivation is *B-Babil*."

"Appropriately so," Gembala muttered under his breath.

Fish looked to be in danger of hyperventilation. "Well, don't you see the metaphorical implication?" he stuttered.

The gathering waited patiently for enlightenment.

"*Beyond* the gate of God. *Outside God's gate*," Fish repeated slowly, as if teaching a class of very small children. "Adam was what? *Banished* from God's presence."

Potzner banged the map with his fist. "That's enough for me. Fish – I need detailed maps. Colonel Gembala – tell your fly guys we'll be joining them in ten. Dracup – you come with me."

Dracup was thinking hard. What would they do with him? A *back seat,* Gembala had said. Now that his hope had been rekindled he was terrified they might leave him behind. *Forty-eight hours,* the text message had read. Dracup did some swift calculations. Iraq was at least six hours by air. That was all right; there was still time. Somehow he had to contact Moran. He felt in his pockets for inspiration; his mobile had been confiscated, but he still had his fountain pen.

In the corridor they passed the sandwich lady on her way out. As he passed the trolley Dracup said, "A moment, please?" Potzner turned impatiently. Dracup held a five-pound note, which he pressed into the woman's hand. He quickly picked a cheese and tomato roll from the unsold items on her tray.

"Still hungry, Prof?" Farrell grinned. "I sure could do with a hot dinner. Reckon there'll be something on the transport, if it makes you feel any better."

They exited the building through a set of double doors and into a waiting jeep. It started to rain as they crossed the tarmac. Dracup heard the whine of jet engines before the winking red lights of the military transport plane appeared through the darkness. A door opened in the fuselage and a set of steps hydraulically extended to the tarmac.

"After you, Prof," Farrell invited Dracup with an outstretched arm.

Dracup followed Potzner up the steps into the aircraft. He turned and took a last look at the cool, English night. He took a deep breath, allowing the air to completely fill his lungs. Then he went inside.

Pam Dellow guided the *Dellow's Delicious Deli* van out of the airbase main gate. The sentry grinned and saluted. She gave him her usual cheery wave. Inside her heart was fluttering wildly. She glanced over to the seat beside her to make sure the piece of paper was still there. The man who had given it to her along with the five-pound note had also given her a long, lingering look. It was a long time since Pam had been the subject of such attention – especially from a good-looking bloke like that. A good-looking *clever* bloke – the American had called him 'Prof'. But as she bumped along the country lanes towards her home village she reluctantly conceded that it was probably a look of trust, rather than lust. She shrugged and gave a deep sigh. *Oh, well. It was a nice thought anyway, Pam.* He needed her to deliver the note. But what did it mean? She picked it up and risked another look as she waited to join the traffic on the main road. It didn't make much sense:

> *DCI Moran, Thames Valley Police*
> *Baghdad*
> *Dracup*

Pam shook her head in puzzlement. The van's clock told her it was just past midnight. An expression her teenage daughter used came into her head: *Whatever.* She would call DCI Moran when she got home. The police, like her, were used to working all hours.

Chapter 33

Yvonne Dracup carefully unpacked her shopping and made a cup of coffee. She looked at the packet of cigarettes she had bought but couldn't bring herself to open. *Cigarettes?* She was changing. Something was happening to her. She took a sip and scalded her tongue, pushed the kitchen chair back angrily and began to put the washing up away. First the glasses, then the plates, then the cutlery. Forks to the left, knives to the right. She picked up a large Royal Doulton bowl and flung it to the tiled floor. It exploded with a terrifying noise. A shard of pottery nicked her bare foot and drew blood. She stood in the wreckage, hands at her sides, and sobbed. She heard her voice rising in a loud howl: "*Why?*"

The house was silent around her, unresponsive. Her breath was coming in uneven gulps. *I can't do this anymore. No human being should have to bear this.* She looked at the knife block with its gleaming array of serrated steel. Her skin was so pale, so fragile. She selected a short filleting knife and pressed the blade experimentally against her wrist. It wouldn't hurt much; just a little sting, then a long, long sleep. She increased the pressure, fascinated by the way the blood fled from the indentation as if anticipating an unnatural exit from her flesh.

She dropped the knife in fright. The blade rang against the tiles with a metallic clatter until it came to rest, spinning in slow revolutions, underneath the breakfast table. Yvonne fled the kitchen and went upstairs. She stood for a moment on the threshold of Natasha's room before entering her own bedroom and throwing herself full length onto the bed. A long time later she slept.

When she awoke it was late afternoon. She felt better; her earlier despair had dissipated. *It's because you're on your own. It'll be okay when Malcolm gets back.* And he was due back tonight. She resolved to cook a special meal and turn the optimism back on. There was no news, and everyone knew that no news was good news. She went through into the study and switched on the computer. Her email was a lifeline of sorts; her friend Anna was in regular touch from Scotland and hardly missed a day without keying a few lines to make her smile.

While she waited for the machine to boot up she planned the evening menu. Malcolm would be tired when he got home. He travelled such a lot – it was unfortunate but it couldn't be helped. She didn't mind the odd day, but lately it had been weeks at a time. *And at a time like this.* Maybe he didn't realise how weak she felt, how every day was a journey of hope tempered with stubborn self-control conjured from who knew where. She wondered at her own tenacity and when she might reach her limit, the point at which she couldn't take any more; every day she had to dig deeper into her own psyche just to exist, just to get to the point when she could lapse legitimately into unconsciousness. But then the dreams would come...

She took a deep breath. Her lunchtime loss of control had frightened her. She had never thought like that before, never considered the possibility of... *Stop right there, my girl.* This was no good. Only one thought had the power to sustain her: *Maybe today is the day we hear something.* She opened her email and clicked send/receive. Nothing. Not even junk. She bit her lip and logged out. Should she phone Moran? As she moved to switch the machine off a message box popped up. *Security Alert.* She tried to close it by clicking on the 'x'. The message box remained frustratingly in the centre of the screen. *Go away. I don't need this.*

Yvonne clicked again, then dropped the mouse in surprise as the cursor began to move by itself. She watched it track across the desktop and open the Start menu. It moved to 'Run'. A dialogue box opened and text appeared as if an invisible set of digits was typing. Her hand went to her mouth as she dithered, wondering what to do. *I'm going mad.* Then she remembered Malcolm talking about rogue programs that could pass control of your PC to an external operator. *Hackers.* She watched in fascination as a new screen appeared and began to display data, scrolling automatically from top to bottom. It was all meaningless jumble to her. A new message appeared: *Decryption complete.* There was a copyright message at the foot of the message box. It flicked on and off in a second, but she was sure it had said: *Central Intelligence Agency, US.* Then the cursor began to pause at certain words. They didn't mean anything either: *'Blackbird'. 'Red Earth'...*

Yvonne backed away from the PC. *Why would the CIA want to hack into our – Malcolm's – computer?* She remembered James Potzner, how strange he'd been during his brief visit. She hadn't felt safe with him. Something about the way he'd looked at her – no, looked *into* her. She'd felt dirty afterwards, as if some invasion of privacy had occurred without her knowledge or consent. And now one of his people was crawling around inside their computer.

The text disappeared and a diagram took its place. It was – what? A circuit diagram? A plan of some sort? And then another – a type of pyramid? It looked like a picture her younger brother used to spend hours over, a cross section of a naval submarine, with all its compartments and passages exposed like an ant colony in a glass bottle. Yvonne bent over and flicked the printer on. She hit the print key, fished out the A4 sheet and examined it. There was something familiar about the design, but her memory couldn't place it. She heard a key turn the front door lock. *He's back.* Her heart leapt with excitement. A quick glance in the mirror – she didn't have any make-up on. Never mind.

She took the stairs two at a time and threw herself into the arms of the man at the threshold. Malcolm was pinned to the door-frame, key in one hand, overcoat in the other. She wrapped her arms around him and squeezed hard. "Hi. I've missed you."

"Steady." Malcolm placed his laptop case carefully onto the hall carpet. "Give me a chance to get in the door."

Yvonne looked at him and smiled. Everything would be fine now. Solid, dependable Malcolm would look after her. She felt a pang of guilt. "I haven't sorted dinner out yet – I was going to make –"

He placed a finger on her lips. "Don't worry. I was going to take you out anyway."

This was just what she needed. But he looked tired. Perhaps it wasn't fair to drag him out again when he'd only just got in. She opened her mouth to voice the thought, then suddenly remembered the computer. "Come quickly." She pulled him to the stairs.

"Hang on. I'm not quite ready for *that*."

"No, it's the computer. Quickly."

She dragged him into the study and pointed at the scrolling screen. "There. Look."

A change came over Malcolm's face. He darted to the computer and flicked off the power. Then he turned to Yvonne. "What are you doing on this PC?"

"I'm sorry – I thought it was all right to –"

"I told you to only use the laptop in the lounge. All your mail is accessible from there." His face had darkened with anger. She had never seen him so furious.

"But it was a – a hacker, wasn't it? I – I thought you should know."

"What did you see?" He took a step towards her.

"Nothing. There was a lot of rubbish on the screen, that's all. Then some weird diagrams."

He grabbed her arm. "I said, what did you *see?*"

"Malcolm. You're hurting me." Yvonne felt a flutter of panic. This was not like Malcolm. He was looking at the printout she had made.

"What is this?" He picked up the sheet.

"I – I haven't a clue. Something that was on the screen – I thought I'd print it so you could see –"

He struck her hard across the face. She spun backwards and fell across the small computer station, the one she had chosen with him in IKEA. She was so shocked that no words would come.

"What – ?" But he was coming for her again. She backed away and tried to duck under him to get to the door. Her mind was reeling. *This can't be happening.* He caught the back of her blouse and she wriggled free, feeling the material tear under his grip. She threw herself down the stairs, but he was surprisingly quick. He caught her in the hall and she felt his arm around her neck.

"Why couldn't you just leave it alone?" he hissed in her ear.

"I don't understand. Oh God, don't hurt me –" She was crying and fighting for breath at the same time as he increased the pressure. She felt a fogginess descending. *So this is what it's like*, she thought. *I'm going to find out after all.* And then there was a distant, heavy noise, like somebody striking a pillow with a hammer. As she drifted into unconsciousness she felt the arm relax its grip. And then she was kneeling on the floor, retching. A hand was on her shoulder, but it had a gentle, concerned touch.

"Mrs Dracup? Are you all right?" She turned and looked into the pinched, greyhound-like face of DCI Moran. Then she was violently sick on the parquet.

Yvonne sipped her tea. It was too sweet, but she didn't care. Moran was looking at her with an expression of sympathy and repressed curiosity. Malcolm had been taken away a quarter of an hour ago by a pair of very young-looking policemen. Moran assured her he would be charged with assault and remanded in custody. Somehow it didn't make her feel any safer.

"So," Moran said. "Do you know what this is?" He held up the print of the sectioned pyramid.

She shook her head. "I haven't a clue. Obviously something significant."

Moran was nodding. He looked like a hound that had caught the scent after a long search. "It's a ziggurat."

"A what?"

"A ziggurat. A kind of temple the ancients made to worship their gods. Or God." Moran's long face lit up with a strange smile. "It has seven levels."

Yvonne warmed her hands on the hot mug. Her brain was sluggish. She could still feel the arm around her neck, the squeezing. "I'm sorry, Inspector. I haven't a clue what you're talking about."

"Malcolm was a cog – an important cog – in this business from the start. He's an IT specialist, right? Do you know his area of specialism?"

Yvonne sighed. "I don't really understand it. Codes? Algorithms or something?"

"Security. Network installation and security. He could break into anything – and my guess is he was contracted to break into a *very* secure network. But now they've finally traced him."

"The CIA?" Yvonne's mouth was open in shock.

"Spot on. And whoever hired him had some other work for him to do. Something closer to home. Their home."

Yvonne paled. "Natasha's abductors? Malcolm *knew?*"

"I'm afraid he not only knew, Mrs Dracup. He's been actively working for them for the past few months – if not longer."

"I can't believe it." Yvonne felt paralysed, unable to take it in. "Their *home?*" she repeated, staring at the print.

Moran nodded. "A strange home, I'll grant you, but a home nevertheless. And a very old one at that."

"The *ziggurat?*" Yvonne was incredulous.

"The ziggurat."

Chapter 34

The interior of the aircraft had more in common with an executive lounge than a flying machine: comfortable seats, individual mahogany tables, what appeared to be a cocktail bar, two widescreen television monitors and subtle lighting. Dracup thought of his stomach-churning Channel crossing in Charles' two-seater and shook his head at the contrast. This was straight out of a Harrison Ford movie.

"Something the matter, Prof?" Farrell asked him. "Get yourself strapped in. We're clearing for take-off."

Dracup saw Farrell place a box carefully on the floor beside him. He didn't have to open it to know what was in it: *Alpha*. His heart beat slowly in his chest. He now knew Natasha's whereabouts and would shortly close the distance between them. That made all the difference to his exhausted mind. He had a chance. A small one, maybe, but a chance at least. Dracup felt a frisson of fear override his exhaustion. He buckled his seat belt and tried to concentrate.

Potzner appeared, his whole body vibrant with nervous energy. Farrell pointed to the seat belt signs and to his own secured strap. The engine note increased in pitch and Dracup felt an invisible pressure push him firmly back in his seat.

Farrell grinned and shouted over, "A lot more thrust than a conventional airliner, huh? It'll settle once we reach altitude."

When the scream of the turbines had quietened the seat belt signs flicked off and Potzner was immediately at the bar. He poured two shots of malt and sat next to Dracup. "Here's to a successful mission, Prof. Glad you could come along."

"I don't recall accepting an invitation."

"Sure you do. You want your little girl back, don't you?"

Dracup studied Potzner's face. He had lost weight and there were deep bags under his eyes. "Of course I do. But that's not why you want me on this trip, is it?"

Potzner looked at him with an amused expression. "Are you sussing me out?" He looked down at his hands. "Not giving anything away, right? No readable signals – isn't that what you guys call it?"

"I'm sorry?"

"You're an anthropologist. You study behavioural patterns, check out body signals, right?"

"You mean interpret gestures? Yes, it's an unconscious habit. But there's a little more to anthropology than that. Broadly speaking it encompasses the origin and behaviour of the human race plus physical, social, and cultural development."

Potzner leaned in close, the whisky on his breath a sour waft. "I'll bet you're having to do a little reconstructed thinking around that area now, huh?"

Dracup conceded the point with an irritated shrug. "So why do you really want me here?"

Potzner settled back in his seat with a sigh. "Because I'm willing to bet that whatever else you found up in Scotland is going to come good for you again. For *us*."

Dracup maintained a blank expression. Of course Potzner knew. The wax tablet was too bulky – and too fragile – to carry around indefinitely, and so Dracup had painstakingly copied Theodore's abbreviations to a thin piece of card and concealed it under his watchstrap. The truth was that he had despaired of making any sense of the final letters of the tablet.

Until Fish had come up with the translation. And then the cryptic *K. zig* of Theodore's tablet took on a whole new meaning. Dracup had, by necessity, a working familiarity with the ancient world, but even if this had not been the case he had heard of Kish. And he had heard of the Tower of Babel – and of other Mesopotamian constructions that had been built for the same purpose: *places of worship.* A place where men could reach up to God... Most of these buildings were ruins, of course, their composition of baked mud unable to withstand the harsh conditions imposed by the relentless passage of time. But it seemed that one had survived – fashioned perhaps from more enduring material because of its special nature. It was buried now, Dracup theorized, under the sand and dust of the Iraqi alluvial plain, but was very much a going concern. They had an unusual name, these stepped pyramidal structures, a name that had made Dracup's heart dance when he remembered. They were known to historians and archaeologists as *ziggurats*.

To Potzner he simply smiled and said, "I'm as much in the dark as you are."

"Oh yeah," Potzner said. "I'll bet."

In a corner of the cabin a fax machine hummed into life. Farrell wandered over and gathered the transmitted papers together. He scanned the documents and looked up with a frown.

"Fish is checking out the lie of the land. He's done a satellite scan – nothing new so far, just the known archaeology. 'Important remains still standing at Kish – *yada yada yada* – include the city's red-bricked ziggurat built perhaps by Nebuchadnezzar – *yada yada* – on a rectangular base. Also the grand palace and two other ziggurats –'"

"Give me that." Potzner snatched the documents and read them briskly. "This is crap. We're looking for something else – something subtle. Get Fish on the phone."

Fish was on within seconds. "You've got nine square miles to check out, Fish." Potzner bent and peered out of the jet window as he listened to the response. Dracup caught a glimpse of the sun, a red disk on the horizon, the clouds a scattering of grey and white cotton.

Potzner was pacing the small space now, glass in hand. "They've only excavated three out of forty mounds? So the other thirty-seven should keep you busy for a coupla hours." Potzner sat down heavily, his face contorted with frustration. "Uh huh." His voice took on an exaggerated emphasis, as if he was talking to the most challenging pupil in a remedial class. "*Anything* unusual.

That's right, Fish. No, I don't have any clues either. Just *get on with it*."

Dracup watched the sun reflecting on the surface of the cloud. He was so tired he had forgotten how it felt to be rested, or what it was like to wake up with nothing more than the mundane activities of a University lecturer to inform his mind for the day. He found himself thinking about the number seven. *Seven*. What was it Sara had said? Seven sevens – the square root of your age is seven. Seven sevens are forty-nine. *Forty-nine*. He closed his eyes as the figures jumbled and swirled with the clouds, like a white alphabet soup, but with tumbling numbers that refused to add up or make any kind of sense.

Dracup woke to the jolt of the undercarriage on tarmac. He groaned and rubbed his eyes. Farrell was looking at him with a thoughtful expression.

"Welcome to Baghdad International Airport, Prof. You'd better prepare yourself for a few surprises."

Dracup squinted out of the window and saw a vehicle moving alongside, shadowing their arrival. He felt rather than saw the glint of gunmetal from the vehicle's cabin. A helmeted US soldier, chewing vigorously on a stick of gum, kept his shaded eyes on the plane as it came to a standstill. The door hissed open and heat invaded the interior. Dracup was wearing a heavy jacket and thick shirt in keeping with a British autumn.

Wincing in the strong sunlight he descended the steps like a sleepwalker and allowed himself to be escorted to the military jeep that had jauntily roared up to the rear of the stationary plane. The driver was wearing light camouflage fatigues and sunglasses in an attitude of style only achievable by Americans away from home in a hot climate; they all looked cool. Dracup self-consciously took off his jacket and slung it across his shoulder. *So this is Baghdad.* He could feel oppression in the air, the nerve-tingling sense that he had arrived in a city where literally anything could happen at any time.

Farrell saw his reaction. "MANPAD attacks on incoming military *and* civilian aircraft are pretty common. They're having a day off today, but small arms are a backup contender. We don't want to stay out here too long."

"MANPAD?"

Farrell grinned. "Man-portable Air Defence missiles."

Dracup nodded dumbly. *Great.*

The jeep took them to the terminal where he was fleeced by a trio of wisecracking GIs and given a good-humoured OK to proceed. One of them called after him, "Toodle pip!" in a wildly exaggerated English accent. Dracup acknowledged it with a poorly executed salute followed by a thumbs up. Potzner was already striding proprietorially across the terminal floor. He followed in the slipstream of Potzner's cigarette smoke and found himself in a glass-fronted office that looked out onto the airport runways. The room was full of equipment – flickering monitors and damp-armpitted operators. There was a wide screen suspended from the mezzanine roof, a window into some remote centre of operations. A moment later Dracup recognized it as the UK air force base from which he had recently departed. Before he had recovered from his surprise the plasma display was filled with Fish's earnest yet harassed face. Potzner's reaction was immediate.

"Talk to me Fish," he yelled uninhibitedly at the screen. "We're all waiting."

"Okay, okay, I – I think I've got something." Fish combed a strand of hair carefully back into place. "It's remarkable actually, I'm not sure if –"

"Detail." Potzner sat with folded arms on the corner of a desk and crossed one leg over the other. He blew out a long stream of smoke and tapped his ring finger on the wood.

"Well, we, uh, we've taken some soundings of the area and, strange as it may seem, there appears to be a layer of volcanic rock strata under a large part of the ruins to the west of the site. It goes pretty deep. And even stranger, there's also a clear reading from the hydroscope."

"The what?"

"It, uh, it detects the presence of water. And there's a lot of it. We think it's an underground river."

"Are you sure?" Potzner scratched his head and frowned. "I don't know much about geology, Fish, but it's not what I'd expect to find under this kind of landscape."

Fish removed his glasses and waved them at the screen. He was clearly excited. "Precisely my initial thoughts. Funny thing is, this sort of anomaly has been seen before. In the Sahara – they found an underground river right there under the desert. It supplied water for fifty thousand townspeople in the area."

Dracup was listening intently. It sounded plausible.

"The soundings also indicate the presence of cavities – tunnels or caves – under the strata. And here's the best bit: right up there near the surface is Tell A23."

"*Gówno prawda*, Fish, will you speak English?" Potzner roared.

"Right. Sorry. Archaeologists refer to the mounds of Kish – and other Mesopotamian mounds – as *Tells*. This one is a biggie – fifty metres. And a solid construction."

"Solid?" Dracup forgot himself and addressed Fish directly. He had walked up to stand beneath the monitor.

The giant Fish peered down at him. He seemed mildly surprised to be entering into a dialogue with Dracup, but his excitement propelled him on. "It's not a ruin as such. It's solid. Intact."

"But buried?"

"Yeah. Buried. Right there above the volcanic strata."

Potzner stood very still in the centre of the room. "That's it," he said quietly. "That's it."

Dracup nodded. It seemed to fit.

"Get me the co-ordinates, Fish," Potzner yelled. He turned to one of the soldiers standing with his hands on his hips, automatic slung over his shoulder. "Is the Chinook ready, Major?"

The soldier nodded. He waved vaguely out of the window. "Sure thing, sir. Here it is now. Refuelling will only take a few minutes."

Dracup followed his gesture and saw a long, twin-rotored helicopter descending in a cloud of dust and diesel.

"Do you want me to deploy the troops, sir?" the soldier enquired.

"Just make sure the pilots get those co-ordinates," Potzner said. "Keep the troops on standby." He looked at his watch. "Take-off in thirty-five." He made as if to leave the room. Dracup grabbed his arm. "Wait."

Potzner turned with an irritated expletive. "Not now, Dracup."

"I want you to guarantee my daughter's safety." Dracup retained his grip on Potzner's arm.

"You know I can't do that." Potzner tore himself away and headed for the door.

"I'm coming with you, Potzner," Dracup shouted after his retreating figure. "This is my daughter we're talking about." The room had reverted to its earlier industrious commotion. No one was paying any attention to the Englishman standing in their midst. Dracup raised his arms and let them fall. He felt tears of frustration welling in his eyes and shook his head angrily.

Farrell was watching him from the nearest desk. He had placed the box containing *Alpha* on its plastic surface and was sitting, hands in pockets, beside it. He shrugged and waved a finger from side to side as if reinforcing Potzner's embargo. No help there. Dracup turned his attention to the activity on the airport tarmac.

The Chinook had manoeuvred itself so that the refuelling vehicle could attend to its needs. The pilots were standing next to their machine sharing a joke with the airfield personnel. One of them made a gesture with his arm that caused the group to fall about with laughter. *All routine stuff for them*, Dracup thought. *Just another day in Iraq.*

Potzner had reached the door and his hand was out to grip the handle. Before he reached it the door opened and two people entered the room. Potzner stepped back in surprise. Dracup's mouth fell open.

"Hello again, Mr Potzner." DCI Moran smiled broadly and gestured to the woman beside him. "This is Chief Constable Françoise Duraison from Interpol headquarters. We'd like a word in private, if that's all right with you?" He nodded genially at the American and waved briefly in Dracup's direction. "Be with you in a moment, Professor Dracup."

Potzner squared up to the duo. "We're running a military operation here. You're out of your depth, Moran. I'll give you thirty seconds to leave before I have the Military Police escort you out of here."

The woman spoke up, a trim brunette of around forty-three, Dracup estimated. She had a sharp, intelligent face complemented by the typical dark, Gallic pigmentation that enhanced many a French model's natural good looks and was doing a pretty good job with her own. "Mr Potzner: I have reason to suspect that international law has been violated by virtue of the fact that you removed – by force – a man helping the British police with their enquiries concerning a kidnapping *and* a related murder. DCI Moran and I have been working on an operation to trace the kidnappers. This is police business and you have no authority to detain Professor Dracup. I have a warrant for his repatriation." Duraison's accent was discernable but her manner was businesslike and confident. She held out the paperwork with a superior flourish.

For a moment Potzner seemed uncertain. The Major he had spoken to had unshouldered his weapon and was holding it loosely, his tanned arms cradling the stock. Around a quarter of the personnel in the operations room – those nearest the exit – were watching the scene while the remainder continued with their tasks, apparently unconcerned by the new arrivals. Dracup watched a small trickle of sweat run down Duraison's temple and disappear beneath her collar. From the corner of his eye he saw the refuelling tanker move slowly away from the Chinook, and the helicopter's engines roared into life. The sound penetrated the operations room and heads turned automatically to look. The rotors began to turn, slowly at first, then gathering speed until they became a spinning blur.

Potzner turned back to address Duraison. "You smug bitch. This is my territory." He pointed a stained finger at her chest. "I'll tell you what's going to hap—"

At that moment there came a whooshing sound, like a high wind, then the room lit up with a blast of incandescent orange. He heard someone shout out – was it Farrell? – *"Rockets! Get down!"* The window imploded with a splintering crack that sent shards of glass spinning into the room like jagged spears. The soldier next to Dracup dropped silently to the floor, his neck a torn gash of red. Dracup was lying flat, arms pinned beneath him by some dead weight. He struggled to free himself from the body that was crushing the breath out of him. He saw blood on his hand.

Duraison was lying beside him, her mouth moving in silent agony. Dracup saw the protrusion of shrapnel in her bicep. He crawled towards her, dimly aware of the lacerations on his exposed forearms. *Should have kept your jacket on, Dracup my boy.* His knees crunched painfully against the minutiae of mangled debris cluttering the room. For what seemed a long time there was a stunned silence, then, as the room began to fill with acrid smoke from the burning tanker, he heard the low, persistent moaning of the injured.

The Chinook's engine noise intensified as the pilot opened the throttle. *They weren't hit?* He blinked and tried to see through the smog. There! The spinning blades of the chopper cutting through the pall of white and black smoke. Dracup's hand brushed against the fallen soldier's machine pistol. A lunatic thought came to him. With one hand over his mouth, he picked it up and ran towards the space where the window had been. He stumbled over something – a body? – fell, picked himself up and crashed against the desk where Farrell had been sitting. He scooped up the box in his free hand. It was heavy and he almost dropped it. The chopper was a roaring shape in front of him. He ducked his head instinctively and made for the pilot's hatch. He was up on the step – the machine was moving, beginning to lift. He pulled the handle. It flew open and he hauled himself into the cockpit.

Jamming the pistol in the shocked pilot's face he fell into the cabin and yelled "Keep going! Take it up!" The clattering noise of the engine was overwhelming. He couldn't hear his own voice, but the pilot got the message. The Chinook was snatched into the sky and the airport fell away beneath him.

Chapter 35

"It's late. The child is ready to sleep." Ruth was tired, but the unexpected nature of the visit was compensation enough. "Please. Have a seat." She indicated a carved, wooden bench with a soft quilted cushion. It was a family heirloom, made by her mother in the early days of her childhood. She sometimes imagined she could smell her mother's scent on its fading fabric.

Kadesh gave an agreeable smile and settled himself at one end of the bench. His long forefinger played with the soft skin of his recently shaved chin as he watched Ruth gather her thoughts and emotions.

"Can I offer you anything?"

"I think not."

"Oh. Well, then." She sat on a small stool opposite the leader of the *Korumak* and wondered what he wanted. Despite the barren years of disappointment her heart was pounding with expectation. He had never come to her at such an hour.

Natasha was watching suspiciously from her bed. She held her dolly close to her chest, the blanket pulled up to her shoulders. Ruth put a finger to her lips. "Shhh. You must sleep now. We will talk quietly."

"I think it may be inappropriate to have the girl present," Kadesh said. His tone was reasonable. "I have arranged an alternative activity for her. Ah –"

Jassim appeared at the entrance. His expression was curiously flat, unreadable. He managed a curt bow but failed to make eye contact. Two of Kadesh's personal escort hovered by the door, just out of sight.

Ruth felt the first twinges of disquiet. "Jassim? What are you doing here?" Her disquiet turned to fear when she noticed that her brother was wearing his ceremonial scimitar. It dangled loosely at his side, glinting in the low light.

Kadesh spoke quietly but firmly. "Natasha will be comfortable. Please –" He indicated the stool which she had, in her anxiety and confusion, overbalanced.

Jassim beckoned Natasha, who cast a questioning look at Ruth. *They wouldn't kill a child. They wouldn't kill a child.* She took a breath. *He is our leader. He is wise. He is kind.* Ruth righted the stool and nodded. "It's okay. Go with Jassim." She injected her voice with as much persuasiveness as she was able. Natasha obediently allowed Jassim to take her hand. Ruth watched as Jassim led the girl away.

Now she was alone with Kadesh. She swallowed and composed herself with a huge effort of will. Kadesh seemed in no hurry. He looked around the chamber, allowing his eyes to wander across the dull, ochre blend of rock and clay that formed the walls and roof of the scalloped recess Ruth had made her home. The ancients of Kish had capitalized fully on the opportunities afforded by the departure of the Tigris and Euphrates from their antediluvian course, working the natural volcanic passages into numerous storerooms, living areas and meeting places. She was happy here, under the temple of her forefathers. It was all she knew and all she wanted. *Almost.*

Ruth sat very still, afraid to make an inappropriate gesture or give voice to her whirling thoughts. Was her dream about to be realized? Perhaps her diagnosis had been correct. He had finally responded to her patience with an acknowledgment of his own needs. Sara would not be his. He had accepted it at last.

"He is coming – as are the Americans." Kadesh played with the lid of a glass jar, gently tapping the rim and listening to the high note it produced. "But I am ready for them."

"How do you know –?"

"I know." Kadesh replaced the lid and turned to face her. His arms were folded. "I know. They are in Baghdad. Mukannishum failed."

Ruth was unsure how to respond. She had never warmed to Mukannishum, Kadesh's right-hand man from the time they were at Harvard together. There was a coldness about him, a ruthlessness she found repellant. His influence on Kadesh had been considerable, none of it positive. When Kadesh had returned to Kish, education completed, to lead the *Korumak*, he had returned a changed man. Gone was the warmth she had known in her childhood; gone were the dancing lights in his eyes. Instead there was a hardening of will and soul. As she looked at him now, she mourned the person she had once known. And yet, here he was, perhaps not entirely immune to her reasoning, or, she hoped, her feminine charms.

"I am sorry for your friend." She looked at the floor, unable to meet his eyes. "But they cannot succeed." She shrugged. The gesture felt inadequate, but the conversation was taking an undesirable detour and she was anxious to steer it back before it was too late. "They are no match for you."

She moved towards him. He needed comforting, reassuring. That was her role. She placed her hands on his shoulders, and then moved forward, encircling him in her arms. To her amazement he responded. Her heart beat wildly as he returned her embrace. His body was firm and strong, honed by the disciplined training she knew was part of his daily routine. His clothing smelt of musk and oil, some residue of incense that clung to the fabric. Perhaps his love was like that; maybe there was some essence of his old personality that could be redeemed.

She felt his hand gently stroking her hair. He was murmuring quietly, making soothing noises in his throat. And then he tipped her chin up to look him in the face. She had hoped to see the lights again, but in his eyes now she saw a new darkness, something deep and malevolent. She pulled away but he was too strong; he was crushing her in his arms. He spoke just once as the life was choked out of her: "It is time." She felt a sharp pain in her abdomen, then a numbing paralysis spreading over the lower part of her body. He let her go, and the floor came rushing up to meet her.

She felt no impact. As her body came to rest her soul had already stepped out into the endless tunnels of eternity.

Sara looked up in alarm as the door was unlocked. "Jassim?" His face was a mask of urgency.

"Come. Quickly." He took her hand. There was no one outside her temporary prison. Sara followed Jassim as they half walked, half ran through the dimly lit corridors. When they had reached a place Jassim considered safe, a little-used sacristy on the second level, he turned to her and whispered slowly.

"Listen carefully. I am sorry I cannot break this gently. He has killed Ruth –"

Sara's hand was at her mouth; she felt as if something was choking her. Jassim's fingers were on her lips. "No. Now is not the time for mourning. You must think of yourself – and the girl. She must come with you."

"Where?" Sara was stunned, her mouth dry with shock.

"To the place of your childhood. You have told me about it many times. But it is still a secret place, is it not?"

Sara nodded mutely.

Jassim looked at her with sympathy. "The Americans are coming. And I think your Dracup is with them."

Sara's heart leapt. He was not coming for her, but she would protect Natasha nevertheless. It was the least she could do. She took Jassim's hand.

"Jassim. Why are you helping me? He will kill you if he finds out."

"Kill me? No." Jassim smiled sadly. "I have waited and I have watched. Kadesh imagines that his success gives him license to act as he pleases. It is not so. There are others who share my views. Rest assured, I will be safe. His attention will now turn to you and the girl. Come – we have little time."

Sara hurried to the waterfall with Natasha's hand in hers. They waded across the shallow stream and she found the familiar groove that led to the funnel, her childhood haunt. Natasha was reluctant, but Sara's hands pressed her down into the darkness.

"Feel with your feet. It's fine. I've been down here hundreds of times." They reached the bottom and Natasha clung to her. "You'll get used to the dark. It's the safest place for us."

"Why? Where's Ruth? Is she coming here too?"

Sara swallowed hard and squeezed the girl's hand. "Hey. Just stop worrying, all right? Jassim will come and get us as soon as he can."

"Why did you give him your necklace?"

Sara hesitated, unsure how much she should divulge. "So that... so that a friend of mine might recognize it and trust Jassim when he meets him."

"Who?" the girl pressed. "It's my daddy, isn't it?" The tone of hope in her voice was agonising.

Sara nodded. "Yes. Bright girl." She smoothed an errant wisp of hair away from Natasha's forehead. "It's your daddy."

The little girl smiled. "Sara?"

"Yes?"

"You can call me 'Tash if you like."

Chapter 36

The machine pistol felt clumsy in Dracup's inexpert grip. The pilot was steadfastly ignoring his unexpected passenger, concentrating instead on steering the Chinook out of the black pall of smoke that hung over Baghdad International Airport. He shouted and pointed. Dracup looked at him blankly, then he understood. He picked up the headset with his free hand and clamped it over his ears. The pilot's voice spoke clearly in the space between them.

"What the devil do you think you're doing? Put that down before you kill us both. Strap in and hold tight." The accent was unmistakably English, southern counties. Dracup felt strangely comforted. Then the helicopter lurched violently upwards, making him clutch at the belt as he fumbled with the unfamiliar fittings. The pilot flicked a switch on the complex array of dials and buttons spread out across the cockpit interior. Dracup felt the machine yaw violently to the right and from the corner of his eye saw a bright yellow and red streak soar away from them, falling to earth in a long irregular arc.

"What was *that?*" he shouted into the microphone.

"ALQ – anti-missile flares. Sit tight and keep praying."

The Chinook climbed and banked as the pilot took evasive action. A dense white stream of smoke hurtled underneath them, chasing the flare like a greyhound running a rat to ground. Somewhere below there was a muffled explosion followed by another cloud of grey, sooty smoke. With clenched jaw the pilot bullied the machine into a rapid climb that left Dracup's stomach on the other side of the cargo hold.

At last the helicopter levelled off and Dracup breathed again. The pilot pushed back in his seat and blew his cheeks out in relief. Then he turned his attention to Dracup. "You don't look like a terrorist," he said tersely, "so stop acting like one or I'll have to shoot you myself."

"You're British," Dracup said. He slid the pistol self-consciously down onto the cockpit floor.

"Yes. We're part of the peacekeeping force here. You might have seen us on the news." He gave Dracup a witheringly sarcastic look. "Make sure the safety's on." He glanced down at the pistol.

"Yes. Right." Despite the clarity of the headset transmission Dracup had to resist the compulsion to shout above the vibration of the Chinook's thundering engines. "I was expecting an American."

"This isn't a New York taxi. Perhaps you'd care to explain what on earth you're playing at."

Dracup risked a quick glance earthwards. The landscape was skittering past at an alarming speed. "We're going down?"

"Yes. Best to be fast and low, unless you want to be fried by another rocket. It's harder to get an accurate shot in. Ground fire is a possibility, but your seat is armoured so nothing to worry about. Just ignore it."

"Thanks. That makes me feel a lot better."

"Well? Give me one good reason why I shouldn't chuck you out."

"My name is Professor Simon Dracup," Dracup yelled into the mike. "I flew into Baghdad this morning with James Potzner." Dracup wondered how thorough the pilot's briefing had been; he would be surprised if any more than map co-ordinates had been disclosed. "I believe you received instructions from his office for this drop."

"Mike Bishop." The gloved handshake was brief but firm. "US Intelligence, eh?" He appeared to consider for a moment. "Look, I'm going to take you to our flight airstrip and hand you over to my CO. He can decide what to do with you."

Dracup thought frantically. He was so close. Potzner would not be far behind, rocket attacks or otherwise.

"I'd take you straight back to BIA if I could," Bishop was saying, "but the security boys will have the place sewn up as tight as a duck's bottom by now. It'll be hours before they'll let any air traffic back in."

"Have you any idea why I'm here?"

Bishop was continually searching sky and ground with a repetitive, sweeping movement of his head. "I don't know and I don't care," he said. "Makes no odds to me one way or the other."

"I'm here to find my daughter."

Bishop said nothing for a minute or so. He appeared to be concentrating on the minutiae of flight, first busying himself amongst the plethora of cockpit switches and buttons and then holding a terse, coded radio conversation with someone called Delta Five, presumably some anonymous airstrip controller.

Bishop finished his transmission with an unintelligible coded signoff and turned back to Dracup. "Your daughter?"

"Yes. She's been kidnapped by terrorists." It wasn't far off the mark. He hoped his bluntness would get through.

"Really? I'm sorry, mate." Bishop gave Dracup a longer look up and down. "And you're working with the CIA to get her back?" Bishop searched the sky again and wiped the perspiration from his chin with the back of his hand. "I've heard about this Potzner guy. It's not all good."

"I'm watching my back."

Bishop laughed dryly. "Yeah. You'd better." There was another short exchange via the headset with Delta Five. Then Bishop said, "I have two boys. Eight and ten. It's pretty tough leaving them behind."

Dracup nodded. "It must be. But I imagine they like the idea of their dad being a pilot." He hesitated, then plunged in. "Listen, if you drop me at the co-ordinates you've been given, you're only doing your job. I'll take the responsibility."

Bishop said nothing for a minute or so then shook his head. "There's nothing there, mate. It's in the middle of nowhere." He looked at Dracup's clothing. "You have no provisions, you're not dressed for the weather – night or day. It'd be irresponsible of me to drop you anywhere except safely back at the airport."

"Which you can't do. Security and all that."

"Right. But that doesn't mean I can dump you wherever it takes my fancy." Bishop shook his head again.

Dracup pressed on. "Listen, if I get to her first there's a chance I can save her. If not –" He paused, wondering how much to say. "Anything could happen." It sounded weak but it was the best he could come up with.

Bishop made no reply. The Chinook flew on. Dracup prayed. His eyes lit on the machine pistol. He glanced at the pilot.

Bishop flicked on the radio. "This is Five Five Alpha calling Delta Five. Advising detour to drop zone co-ordinates zebra one, tango delta fifteen. One visitor to drop, repeat one visitor to drop. Confirm."

The headset static buzzed in Dracup's ear. Then: *Five Five Alpha, Delta Five, confirm. Repeat, Delta Five confirm.*

Dracup looked at Bishop. His mouth was dry. "Thanks." It seemed hardly adequate.

"I must be out of my mind," Bishop muttered. "If you get yourself killed, don't blame me."

Chapter 37

As the sound of the Chinook's engines receded Dracup took stock of his surroundings. It was late afternoon and the heat from the sun was intense. Bishop had given him a canister of water and two bars of chocolate. As far as the eye could see there was not a soul in sight, and he could see a *long* way across the flat alluvial plain, with its tussocks of rain-deprived grass and scattering of distant woodland. Above the treetops a shifting pattern of birds wheeled and circled in the still, blue air, their alien cries reinforcing his sense of solitude. Around him lay the remains of ancient Kish, although the only tangible signs were some distance away: a rough rectangular block, doubtless the foundations of some once significant building, and here and there, protruding from the arid soil, the exposed remains that marked the sites of previous excavations.

The landscape for perhaps two or three kilometres was broken by a number of hill-like swellings, each straining skyward as if the earth itself was bursting to reveal the secrets of the past. These were the 'Tells', the mounds that concealed the buried buildings of a once thriving city. The closest of these seemed innocuous enough, rising gently to a height of thirty or so metres and surrounded by the detritus of its own destruction. Dracup set the box down and picked up a fragment of reddish stone. It was well crafted, the mason's art still visible in the turned corners and gentle lines. Perhaps it had been the corner piece of some decorative window, leaned upon by generations of adults and children alike before time and disaster had caught up with it.

He replaced the broken shard amongst the debris and, tucking the box under his arm, began to walk slowly around the Tell. Was it his imagination, or did he feel a faint vibration? He set Farrell's box down and opened it, ran his hand across *Alpha's* markings. He withdrew his finger sharply. The metal was hot, hotter than it should have been even in the high temperature of the plain. Dracup resealed the lid and frowned. The answer to this new puzzle would have to wait.

He wondered if Fish's analysis was accurate, that beneath this area lay concealed a subterranean anomaly, a leftover from the upheaval caused by the great flood. He paused to take a sip of water, resisting the temptation to pour the clear liquid over his perspiring head. Far off by the distant line of trees some animal was moving sluggishly with lowered head and defeated posture under the ineffectual shade. Dracup squinted to identify it. Perhaps a wolf, or a jackal? He wiped dry lips with the back of his hand and watched until it disappeared. He shook the canister. He'd have to take it easy; he wouldn't last long out here without water.

But then he didn't expect to be alone for long. The explosion at the airport would represent only a minor setback to Potzner's obsessive mission. Dracup was sure he'd read Potzner correctly; the man was living on a razor edge, his entire focus narrowed to a single objective by some tragedy of circumstance. As Dracup resumed his exploration of the Tell, he considered Moran's unexpected appearance and the effect it had had on Potzner. The Irish policeman's tenacity was impressive, but Dracup felt sure that, had the rocket not interrupted the proceedings, Potzner would have responded to Moran's intrusion equally effectively. Nevertheless Dracup felt confident that Moran would find his way to Kish. Somehow. He didn't know why he felt this way about Moran's involvement. He just had a growing certainty that the DCI had a part to play, even if the nature of that part was still unclear.

With that reassuring thought, he came upon an area of rock and rubble packed loosely up against the main body of the Tell. The blocks were large, hewn monoliths, roughened by age but part of a once mighty building, piled high to a distance of perhaps twenty or thirty metres. Were they the remains of some external stairway? Dracup skirted the site with a rising feeling of awe. Whoever had built this knew a thing or two about construction. He rested on a boulder and thought of Lalibela. There was some similarity between these reddish layers of worked stone and the strange, sunken architecture he had witnessed in the Ethiopian highlands. *The cradle of civilization*, he thought. *I'm standing in the place where life began again after the flood.* He shielded his eyes and squinted at the colossus rising above him. *And perhaps in a place that predates even that.*

With a shock he realized the import of his words. His thinking was, as Potzner had observed, undergoing reconstruction. The eerie silence unsettled him and he forced himself to his feet for a closer inspection of the scattered ruins. There were some gaps through which it was just possible to squeeze, but they led him only into a wilderness of tangled masonry. He lingered for a while in the comparative coolness, undoing his shirt to let the dense, hot air circulate around his body. He resisted another mouthful of water and instead felt his way back out into the harsh sunlight. *Maybe Fish was way off beam. Maybe this is just what it appears to be: derelict.*

As he emerged from the gloom he shielded his eyes from the glare, bending underneath an overturned arch that incongruously called to mind the standing stones of far-off Salisbury Plain. He straightened up and cried out in surprise. A man was watching him from a distance of perhaps ten metres, on a slightly elevated section of the Tell. He was bearded, wearing a long garment of patterned yellows and greens. He stood perfectly still in an attitude of disciplined concentration, as if wanting to be certain of Dracup's identity before revealing his intentions.

Dracup stole a glance behind him, suddenly fearful that he had been caught in a trap. The man moved slowly down to his level, picking his way elegantly through the fallen masonry with the ease of long familiarity. Dracup stood his ground and waited.

"Professor Dracup. I have been told on good authority that you are a man of ability and determination. Now I see that I was correctly informed."

There it was again, that accent he had first heard in Sara's whispered words of love, and from the lips of the doomed Mukannishum in Lalibela. "On what authority?" he called out. His voice sounded puny and flat in the shadow of the great Tell.

The stranger smiled. "On the *best* authority."

"I can't trust someone I don't know. Who are you?"

"Please do not question me further. Simply follow."

Dracup hesitated. He remembered Bek's similar words of encouragement as he was led into the unknown twelfth church. He pushed the memory aside. *You have no other contacts, Dracup old son. No choice.*

"Come. Please." The man turned and began to ascend the Tell. Dracup followed cautiously, regretting his decision to leave the machine pistol in the Chinook. By the time they reached the halfway point his shirt was soaked with sweat and he began to grunt with exertion as his guide pressed on with confident tread to the Tell's summit. Dracup laboured up the final few metres and, on reaching the level plateau, bent double, hands on hips, sucking in the dry air.

"Twelve kilometres to the west is Babylon, the city of Nebuchadnezzar." The man pointed with his staff. "His palace was considered the greatest building achievement in the world. But, like all dictators, his time passed. Babylon crumbled to dust. Last century's dictator, Saddam, constructed car parks and concrete palaces on its ruins." He laughed softly and nodded. "You will know this, Professor Dracup, as a man who has studied the peculiar struggles of mankind through the ages, yes? But Nebuchadnezzar's grand enterprises of engineering were not confined to Babylon, with its hanging gardens, its fifty-three temples and great tower. Not at all." He leaned on the staff and looked at Dracup. "The king's greatest achievement was here, at Kish."

Dracup was nodding. "Yes. A greater construction than even the great ziggurat of Babylon took place here. It lies beneath our feet."

The smile was genuine. It lit up the man's face with haunting familiarity. "You are wondering where it can be. And how it has remained undetected for so many centuries." He wagged a long forefinger at Dracup.

It was puzzling. And yet, had Dracup not witnessed Fish's assertions regarding the subterranean structure of this area, he would have been entirely ignorant of what lay beneath the Tell. Another thought occurred to him. "Saddam must have known of your existence."

The laugh was disdainful, mocking. "Of course. But even he was afraid. And you may be surprised to know that political adeptness is not confined to the secular world."

Dracup thought of the CIA infiltration, the ease with which the body of Adam had been taken from the Americans. He shook his head. "No. No, I am not surprised. The *Korumak Tanri* are a people of far-reaching influence."

"You have learned a great deal." The brown eyes glinted with admiration. "And for that you have earned my respect."

Dracup remained unsure whether this conversation was a sinister prelude to violence or an oblique offer of assistance. His fists were clenched at his sides. "Then you will give me your name." Dracup held out his hand. "And tell me where you have taken my daughter."

"My name is Jassim." Again the long vowel inflexion. "And it was not my will that brought your daughter here, but the desire of our leader."

The sudden confirmation of Natasha's presence was an electric jolt through Dracup's body. He remembered Mukannishum's whispered confession: the name of Kadesh. "*Kadesh?* You must take me to him." He felt the tension in Jassim's bearing. He was beginning to suspect that the man's appearance on the surface was a solo initiative, but wondered whether he was acting merely out of curiosity or driven by some greater sense of urgency.

Jassim shook his head. "That would be unwise." He reached into the folds of his garment. Dracup tensed. The brown hand reappeared. As it opened, Dracup gasped; in Jassim's palm lay Sara's moon and star necklace. "Your daughter is with my sister."

"Your sis–?" Dracup was lost for words. And then he acknowledged the similarity in facial structure, the high cheekbones, the curve of the perfectly white teeth. "Sara?"

Jassim nodded. "They are both in great danger. You must do exactly as I say."

Dracup swallowed. His throat was parched. "I have many questions."

"But the answers may not serve your immediate need." Jassim lifted his staff again and pointed at the reddening sun. "We wait until it has set. Then I will lead you down."

The early evening brought with it a refreshing coolness and a spectacular sunset. Dracup watched as the sky was filled with a blaze of orange and red, sweeping colour across the clouds with the abandonment of some celestial surrealist painter. Jassim had quietly withdrawn to a nearby scattering of boulders and sat, staff in hand, apparently deep in thought.

Dracup puzzled over the non-appearance of Potzner. He wondered if the American might have sustained injuries in the airport attack. He thought of the Interpol woman and felt a pang of guilt that he hadn't gone to her assistance. He reasoned that help had been at hand, but also acknowledged – with some discomfort – that he had acted out of sheer, blind instinct. He found one of Bishop's chocolate bars and broke off a piece. It was partially melted, sticking to the foil. As the sweet taste filled his mouth his ears strained at the sound of approaching engines. Jassim seemed unperturbed, gazing out onto the plain, moving his staff languidly back and forth between his hands. A minute or so passed and the sound faded; whatever machine was responsible for the distant drone was clearly on some other flight path. Dracup, however, was under no illusions; sooner or later Potzner et al. would be paying Tell A23 a visit. He bit his lip. He had to trust Jassim's judgement.

The heavenly light show gradually faded and the shadows of the Tells fell darkly across the parched soil. Jassim walked over to join him. He seemed preoccupied and tense, in a hurry to begin the descent. "It is time. Let us face our futures, and may God be our judge."

Dracup followed Jassim to the base of the Tell and along its rubble-strewn length. At the northernmost point a natural formation of rock was buttressed up against the body of the mound, and as they drew nearer Dracup could see a number of elongated fissures in its composition; these scars ran vertically upwards until they eventually disappeared into the clumps of sparse vegetation adhering to the Tell's summit. They were unlikely portals to the hidden world underground, and yet Dracup was unsurprised to see Jassim squeeze his tall body through the second of these fault lines and disappear from sight.

He followed suit, and discovered that the gap widened significantly as he progressed, to the extent that he soon found himself standing in a circular clearing, overarched high above by an odd fusion of natural geology and derelict architecture. In front of him, set into the ground like a series of puckered mouths, was a triad of sink holes, openings into the body of the Tell. Jassim waited by the central hole, signalling impatiently with his staff. Dracup joined him and peered into the depths. A waft of warm, perfumed air emanated from the deep. It recalled, oddly, the sensation of standing at the top of the high escalator at Holborn tube station; there was the smell and feel of humanity somewhere in the depths, the sensation of unseen activity. Dracup's heart hammered against his ribs. Jassim was talking, his voice an urgent whisper.

"I can descend with you only part of the way. Then our paths must diverge."

"Diverge? How do you expect me to –?"

"I expect nothing, Professor Dracup. I must attend to my responsibilities. The hour of trial is almost upon us. I must play my part." Jassim's face was grim. "Take the steps where they will lead you. The passages will be clear at this time; our people are gathered in one place."

"How will I find my way? I have no torch –"

"There will be adequate light. When I leave you, follow the stairway to its end. Then listen for the sound of water. When you find it, turn to your right and follow the flow. Seek the hidden places. If you are seen, then your life is in your own hands – it is forbidden for an outsider to enter the sanctuary of the *Korumak Tanri*, but these are unusual times. Be warned: there are others, unlike myself, who will not hesitate to kill you the moment they see you."

Dracup grabbed his arm. "I have to know more."

"And you will," Jassim replied, "but I can share little else with you at this time, Professor, except perhaps –" Jassim pointed to the box nestled in Dracup's arms, "to advise you to take great care of your luggage. Now, please –"

Dracup took a deep breath and entered the hole. He felt his way down for the first twenty or so steps, then realized that a faint phosphorescence was filling the stairwell with an gentle blue light. He turned to Jassim, an unformed question on his lips. Jassim shook his head. Dracup turned and continued his descent into the home of the *Korumak Tanri*.

James Potzner nursed his bruised forearm and rolled another Marlboro between his lips. The Humvee vibrated as it negotiated the rough terrain. Too risky for choppers? No problem. The marines didn't care if they flew or rode – it was all the same to them. *James Potzner is in control*. Moran's presence was an irritant, but he could deal with the Irishman later; at least Interpol was out of the picture.

Potzner watched the fresh-faced marines joking and bantering in the troop carrier alongside. They were only kids, most of them. He hoped they were prepared for what lay ahead, because he was not prepared to return empty-handed. He had the location nailed; he had the ability. The only fly in Potzner's ointment was Dracup. The damned idiot could blow the whole thing apart on account of one kid. What was one life when the world was at stake? He clicked on the comms channel. "You there, Farrell?"

For a moment there was only the roar of the Humvee's diesel engine, then Farrell's familiar drawl in his ear. "Sure am."

"You have the map? Good. Now listen: go for the west entry point, and I'll take the east. I'm betting that the action is at the top of the central stairways, the converging tiers of the ziggurat. They all meet at the top – that's the focal point of the whole shebang. He'll be in there for sure."

A pause, then, "Right. Who's going in with me?"

"You take Moran – I want him out of my hair. His interest is Dracup and the kid. When we hit the site I'll give you thirty minutes head start. Check it out and call me when you're comfortable. Like I said, we'll come in from the east side and meet you at the top."

"What do I do when I find the Prof?"

"You help him find the kid."

"And then?"

"You know what to do, Farrell. None of this can leak. You *know* that."

A slight pause. "Right. And Moran?"

"At your discretion."

"Okay. You got it."

Potzner glanced at his watch. nineteen hundred hours. ETA: forty-five minutes. He chewed on the Marlboro's filter and thought of his dear, dead wife. It was too late for her, but there would be others – thousands, millions perhaps – who would benefit from the research. And fate had decreed that it was down to James Potzner to make it happen.

Chapter 38

The stairway seemed endless. Dracup stopped frequently and listened. The only sounds were his heartbeat and a low, bass vibration that seemed to emanate from within the walls. After a while he discerned an accompanying harmony, strangely discordant yet complementary to the sub-bass drone that had first caught his attention. He paused again, captivated by the effect. It was like some experimental choral composition, but surely no modern composer could create such a sound? As the notes rose and fell in weird, structured, codas Dracup sensed in its metre something old and profound; he realized he was listening to a music preserved from the dawn of time, a chorus of worship that was both ancient and inspired. From grey and enforced Sunday morning attendances he remembered a snatch of scripture: *Adam walked with God*. He felt a shiver run through his body, a sensation unrelated to the cooler underground temperatures. The unsettling soundscape followed him deeper into the bowels of the earth. *This is music from Eden*, he marvelled. *This is a conversation with the creator*.

The stairwell stopped abruptly. In front of him lay a T-junction. Right or left? Listen for the sound of water, Jassim had said. He tried to filter out the hypnotic refrains drifting along the passage. Was there a more elemental reverberation this way? He thought so. He hadn't travelled a hundred metres before he was sure he heard the rush of moving water. He stepped up the pace. His hands brushed the walls as he paused for breath; they came away covered in a white substance. *Salt*. The catacombs appeared to be constructed from a strange blend of sandstone, salt and some other material that defied his hurried analysis.

He crept on. Eventually the roof of the passage lifted away and he found himself in an open cavern. Dracup caught his breath. Now he could see the water source: a sparkling cascade ran from a hidden opening high in the cavern ceiling. He felt an inward exultation. *This is it.* He took out his mobile and selected the media messages menu. In the photo Natasha was standing just at that point over ... *there.* The waterfall fell directly into a pool, hewn out by years of erosion, bouncing on the mossy rocks and bubbling over into a narrow stream. Where now? The stream ran from one side of the cavern to the other, disappearing into a narrow channel on one side and a vertical shaft on the other. Dracup scoured the area. *Hidden places? What hidden places?*

He examined the waterfall. Wait. There was something. Through the spray, the shadows darkened at one point near its base. Dracup waded into the stream, drawing his breath sharply as the freezing water numbed his legs. He scrambled up the lichen-covered rocks, slipping back twice as his fingers failed to grip the surface. He was soaked through by the time he hauled himself onto the other side and sat, gasping for breath, by a black space in the waterfall bed. He peered into its depths. Surely not? But there were protrusions that would serve as footholds – for the careful climber. *This is crazy. She could be anywhere.*

As he hesitated he heard the sound of footsteps. Running. A shouted command. *Potzner?* Panic and freezing hands made him clumsy; he missed his footing and fell awkwardly, throwing his hands out to save himself. Through the screen of moving water he heard a cry and knew he had been spotted. He heard a popping noise, like multiple corks being sprung from a bottle, then a blow to his arm sent him spinning backwards, sprawling over the wet rocks. He sat up, shocked, and saw with horror a spreading red stain creeping through his jacket sleeve. Oddly, he felt little pain. A shadow fell across the waterfall, then another.

Dracup lay panting, clutching his arm. A face appeared; dark, bearded, unkempt hair tamed by a purple bandana. A bandolier was slung casually over the man's shoulders and his hands expertly clicked a new magazine into place. A contemptuous grin played about his lips. He raised the automatic and Dracup closed his eyes. He heard a muffled crack. A heavy weight crashed onto his legs and he opened them again. Someone was wading across the stream.

"Professor Dracup? Are you okay?"

He let out his breath in relief. *Farrell*.

The American stepped around the waterfall and crouched at his feet. "Should have got to you a little earlier – sorry about that. Let me take a look at that arm."

Dracup winced and peeled off his jacket. He was only mildly surprised to see Moran join Farrell at his side. Shadows hovered in the background. US marines, supporting. The DCI holstered his pistol, nodded curtly and prodded the dead man with his toe. "Al-Qaida. It's all happening here, isn't it, Professor?"

Farrell finished applying a field dressing to Dracup's arm. "Just clipped you, Prof. You okay to walk?"

"It's my arm, Farrell, not my leg – thanks, I'll be fine."

"I see you have my parcel." Farrell pointed his gun at the box, lying askew at Dracup's feet.

"Don't try to take it from me, Farrell." Dracup clenched his fists. "I'll kill you before I let you do that."

Farrell raised both hands. "Cool it, Prof. We're on your side."

"Are you?"

"You weren't thinking about going down there without a map, were you?" Moran pointed to the uninviting gash in the rock.

"Without a –?"

Moran reached into his trouser pocket and flourished a folded piece of paper. "This," he smiled, "is going to come in handy."

Farrell grabbed it out of the Irishman's hand. "Where did you get this?"

Moran's eyes almost twinkled. "Well, that would be telling." He gave Dracup an odd look. "I borrowed it from a little bird back home."

Chapter 39

A shower of pebbles alerted Sara to the presence of intruders in the funnel. *Jassim?* She nudged Natasha awake and pulled the girl into the shadows. Natasha looked up, fear etched across her face. The girl was pale and thinner, but she had a resilient streak that reminded Sara of her father.

Natasha was pulling on her cardigan. "Are they coming to kill us?"

"No. Of course not." She smoothed a hand over the girl's forehead. "Just stay here and I'll go check it out, okay?"

The girl chewed her lip. Her cheek was streaked with grime and her hair was badly in need of a wash. "Ruth's dead, isn't she?" Her large eyes watched Sara intently, daring a lie.

Sara hesitated, her throat constricted. "Yes, Natasha. I'm sorry." She gave the girl a brief hug, aware of the inadequacy of the gesture. "I have to go see what's happening, all right? *Don't move.*"

Sara found a loose rock and hefted it. She crept, cat-like, to where the funnel entrance spread out like a ram's horn into the gallery. *How many?* She craned her neck to look up into the blackness. Now she heard voices, the scrabbling of feet. She weighed her options. Stay put, or risk the unknown? She turned and looked down the gallery to where the ceiling dipped and turned. Somewhere beyond the temple perimeter lay the remains of something ancient, a barren, haunted place, blighted by God's curse. And here, hiding as a child in the gallery, she had felt the weight of its mournful presence.

She took a deep breath. *Okay. Stay put – flesh and blood I can deal with.* A pair of feet landed hard on the sloping floor of the funnel. Sara stepped forward and swung the rock, missing her target's head but scoring a direct hit between the shoulder blades. As the rock connected she let out her breath in a cry of frustrated anger. The man dropped to the ground with a grunt.

Then two things happened very quickly: something heavy dropped down from the funnel's twisted tube and wrestled her to the ground. She fought with all her strength, redoubling her efforts as she saw her hands stained with blood and heard the man gasp in pain. She felt a surge of adrenaline. *He's hurt. I can do this...* And then, twisting around in a final effort to free herself she saw who it was. *Simon?*

He froze in her grip, his mouth slack with astonishment. "Sara?" Then, "Where's Natasha?"

Sara stared at Dracup open-mouthed.

He looks awful.

She bit her lip as Farrell struggled to his feet, reaching behind his neck with a grimace to assess the damage. "Farrell. I'm sorry – I –"

"No problem." He flashed a smile, then turned to give assistance to the third climber whose legs were dangling, testing the rough steps before committing his weight. A lightly built man dropped down and landed easily on his feet. Farrell jerked his head in Moran's direction. "DCI Moran, from the UK," he told Sara.

Dracup was shaking her arm. "Where *is* she, Sara?"

"She's waiting over there." Sara pointed and called over. "'Tash? Come over. It's all right."

But the only response was the flat echo of her voice and the silence of the gallery. She ran to the spot where Natasha had been sitting, knees drawn up to her chin, dark eyes alert.

Sara looked at Dracup. It was impossible. She *had* to be there. "Simon, she *was* here. I told her to wait. She was scared –"

Dracup was at her side. "Where does this lead?" He swept his hand across the expanse before them.

"I don't know." Her head was pounding in a mixed reaction of confusion and anger at herself. "I've never – it's forbidden." Her heart was beating with fear. *Natasha. Why there? Why didn't you wait?* "We can't follow," she stammered. "It's impossible."

"What are you talking about?" Dracup turned to Moran. "What about your map? Does it show anything in this direction?"

Moran shook his head. "That's the funny thing. It ends right here. The gallery isn't marked at all."

Dracup led the way. He called her name repeatedly: *Natasha! 'Tash!* Moran walked alongside, observing, cautious. Sara was behind with Farrell, reluctant. *Scared.* And he could understand it. There was something about this place, something not right. The ceiling had crept lower and lower until for an uncomfortable five minutes they had been forced to bend almost double; then it rose sharply again, stretching out of sight and creating the illusion that they were no longer travelling underground, but under a remote, lofty sky. The ground became progressively featureless, the curious formations of rock they had passed at the outset being replaced by a plain, dry dust underfoot. The air was still, the temperature warmer than the area surrounding the waterfall and the funnel.

Dracup noted all this subconsciously. His arm throbbed with a dull beat. He concentrated on placing one foot in front of the other, all senses alert for a frightened child. His brain transmitted a repetitive mantra in time with his footsteps: *She can't have gone far.* He was relieved that their two-abreast formation had defaulted Moran as his travelling companion; he didn't trust himself to speak to Sara. He didn't know if he felt anger or disappointment at her betrayal. All the while she had known. She could have warned him. Said something. *Anything.* And yet, he conceded, she had tried to protect Natasha, or so it seemed.

The DCI broke into his thoughts. "Can you feel it?" Moran said.

"Say what?" Farrell's voice came from behind.

"A heaviness in the air? Yes, if that's what you mean," Dracup said. He noticed that he had slowed down, his legs somehow reluctant to take him any further. His breathing was laboured, yet they were on a flat trajectory. It was becoming more difficult to see the way ahead; the strange luminescence of the waterfall and its environs had faded to a thin, faint twilight.

Dracup paused. "Here." He bent and examined the ground. In the thickening dust were the clear imprints of a child's feet. Dracup straightened and cupped his hands around his mouth. "Natasha!" The sound was muted, as if an invisible fog had descended, trapping his voice and returning it void.

Moran pointed. "Do you see what I see?"

Sara took Dracup's arm. For the first time, Dracup hesitated. About a hundred metres ahead of them, two giant gates rose up from the cavern floor towards the distant roof. Dracup tilted his head but the apex was out of sight, lost in the enveloping darkness.

Farrell let out a low whistle. "That sure ain't part of the *Korumak* setup, huh?"

Dracup took a step forward. "No. No, I don't think it is. Sara?"

She shook her head. "I've never been here. I've heard rumours, but –"

"What sort of rumours?" Moran was beside her, his eyes glinting with excitement.

"Beyond the gate of God," Dracup muttered. "The body was laid to rest *outside* the gate." He turned to Moran. "Potzner's expert was *partly* correct – but the reference wasn't to Babylon." He felt a creeping sense of awe. There was no doubting the evidence before them. He was speaking very quietly now, almost to himself. "The reference was to *Eden*."

They approached the towering structure. Dracup stretched out a hand and placed it on one of the upright supports. It felt cool to the touch. His finger came away marked with a residue of carbon.

"Fire?" Moran was examining the metalwork.

"Sure," Farrell said slowly. He was looking up, soaking it all in. "This gate was guarded by fire."

All heads turned to the American. Sara was nodding, tight-lipped.

"When they were expelled from the garden, God placed an angel with a flaming sword to guard the gates of Eden." Farrell shrugged. "It's all there in the book of Genesis."

"But they're open now," Dracup muttered. "And look." He pointed to the continuing line of footprints. "She's in there somewhere." He began to follow the prints along the length of the gate until he came to the point of entry where the two great elevations separated. He beckoned. "Over here."

"I'm sorry." Sara backed away. "I can't. It's forbidden."

"Then stay put," Dracup told her. "There's no need for you to follow." He was conscious of a new sensation; a fragrance emanating from beyond the gate, a sweet, almost sickly smell. Its enticement was powerful.

"Can't you feel it?" Sara was trembling. "You mustn't go in."

"I'll stay with you, ma'am," Farrell offered. To Dracup he said, "Go right ahead, Prof. I'll watch out for her." He smiled awkwardly.

Dracup felt a momentary pang of disquiet. There was something in Farrell's demeanour –

Then Moran spoke. "There's no time for this. We go *in* fast and get *out* fast."

Dracup ran a hand absently through his hair. "Right then," he said, with more conviction than he felt. "We'll meet you back here as soon as." He retraced the footprints to the opening between the gates. His hand was on the cold material of the giant upright, Moran's feet crunching through the dead soil to join him.

And together they stepped into Eden.

Sara watched the receding figures. There was nothing more she could do here. Someone else needed her now. "Farrell. I have to find my brother. Will you help me?"

She looked at the American and realised with a shock exactly what it was that she had seen in his eyes. Confirming her thoughts, Farrell reached out and placed his hand gently on her cheek. "You don't have to ask. You know I will."

Chapter 40

The blighted subterranean landscape enveloped Dracup and Moran like a shroud. What little conversation had taken place between the two men had quickly been relegated to wordless glances and grunts of effort. The deepening layers of ash – and other remains Dracup didn't care to examine too thoroughly – impaired their progress. He grimaced each time the pressure of his weight produced a dull crack underfoot; bone or bough, it evoked the same feeling of horror and loathing. *A dead place.* And then there was the cloying, sickly smell inhibiting his breathing with every faltering step. It reminded Dracup of childhood summer days, when the summer sun had over-ripened what little fruit remained hanging from the trees or lay, wasp-ridden and wasted, on the water-starved grass of his parents' orchard.

Still the small footprints led them on. Dracup felt an invading weakness, a sapping of energy that made him want to stop, lie down, sleep forever. The box was getting heavier and he felt the heat of its contents against the bare skin of his arm. He shifted its weight and found himself struggling for breath.

"You have to fight it," Moran said through gritted teeth. "She got this far *and* further – so can we."

Dracup grunted a response, conserving his resources. He wanted to tell Moran that he was grateful for his company. To make this journey alone would be unthinkable. And yet, Natasha had done just that. He struggled to understand why. Was it fear? Or a response, perhaps, to some whispered summons? He mopped his brow and caught Moran's shoulder. "I have to put this down. I can't carry it any further."

Moran nodded. "No one else around. It'll still be here on the way back."

Dracup planted the box at his feet with a grunt. The box fell away, peeling back from the glowing metal inside. They watched the cardboard turn to ash.

"Come on," Moran prompted. "There'll be time for answers later." The policeman shifted his backpack with a grunt.

There was a strange look on Moran's face. Dracup wondered what was in the backpack. He opened his mouth to form the question, but Moran's expression silenced him. *Keep walking, Dracup. Just keep walking.*

They passed through a glade of petrified trees, the trunks huddled closely together as if for comfort. By an exposed root lay the skeleton of some old inhabitant, its skull resting upon yellowed forepaws, dark eye sockets observing their passing with ambivalent stare. Moran was muttering to himself. "My God, my God. This is awful." He had wrapped a handkerchief across his mouth, but Dracup could see the fear reflected in his eyes.

"Don't look at anything," he advised. "Just keep going." He passed Moran his water bottle and the DCI took a furtive swig.

"Thanks." Moran returned the bottle and mopped his brow. "It's getting warmer."

And it was. As the trees thinned, their breath became laboured. Dracup's lungs felt starved of oxygen, as if some unseen process was greedily drawing all the air to itself.

They emerged from the glade into a flat, empty space. Dracup raised his hand. "Wait." He pointed to the ground. Moran followed his finger and saw the problem. The footprints had disappeared. The plain ahead was covered, not with the now familiar layers of ash and bone, but with a fine, orange dust. As they stepped onto its surface their feet left only the faintest of marks.

Moran peered into the distance and caught Dracup by the arm. "Hold on." He pointed a thin forefinger. "Take a look over there, would you, and tell me I'm not seeing things."

Dracup looked. In the distance he could see a faint, green phosphorescence, quite different to the buried ziggurat's luminosity. It seemed localised; the light did not spread across the landscape but remained static, like a theatre spotlight picking out the leading actor in a play. He took a deep breath. Whatever it was, that's where they needed to be. Like a beacon, its magnetism was irresistible.

"She'll be there," Dracup said.

The smell grew ever stronger and Dracup was compelled to follow Moran's example, removing his jacket and partially covering his face with the material. He kept his eyes on the vision ahead, his fear for Natasha tempered with a powerful curiosity.

Moran broke the silence. "It's a tree."

Dracup squinted at the brightness and the object swam suddenly into focus. Moran was right. A magnificent tree, stretching its branches high into the fetid atmosphere. They were close now, perhaps a few hundred metres. The tree was standing in its own circle of light, the ground within alive with plants, flowers and shrubs of many different varieties. The scent was overpowering but Dracup had forgotten his discomfort. He held his jacket loosely by his side and gaped at the oasis of life surrounding the tree. He could hear birdsong, musical and delightful to the ear, the humming of bees, the gentle sigh of a warm midsummer breeze. But his attention was on something else: in the centre of this pool of fecundity, legs crossed, head tilted slightly to one side as if listening to a favourite story, was Natasha.

Sara led Farrell through the empty corridors. She felt very alone. Farrell touched her shoulder. "Wait." He stopped and cocked his head to one side, listening. Sara's shoulder tingled where his hand had rested. She clamped her teeth to her bottom lip angrily. What sort of a woman was she? How could her emotions be so wayward? In that moment she saw her future clearly. She murmured a prayer of thanks and gave Farrell a non-committal smile.

"It's all right. It's coming from the chamber of worship," she told him. "They'll be there until midnight."

"Who?"

"My brothers and sisters."

"Your family..."

"Yes. Farrell – we have to keep moving." Fearful of the Al-Qaida presence and Kadesh's security squads she held her breath, praying as she walked. *Be there. Be there.*

Hurrying around the next corner her prayer was answered. Jassim was striding towards them, staff tapping the ground as he went. Relief exploded through her. She ran to him and clasped his hand. "Jassim! Thanks be to God!"

"Who's this?" Farrell said. His hand strayed under his jacket.

Sara caught the movement. "No, Farrell! It's okay." Her eyes filled with tears. *Jassim, Jassim. You have done the right thing...*

Jassim held her tightly. "Praise Him that it is I who found you and not Kadesh, my sister." He turned to Farrell. "Mr Farrell," he said gently, "I am no threat. I have something to show you."

Dracup hesitated. Natasha seemed unaware of their presence.

"Careful," Moran said, resting a restraining hand on Dracup's shoulder. "Don't wake her suddenly."

Dracup's mouth was dry. He turned to the DCI. "Do you think she's all right?"

Moran rubbed his cheek thoughtfully. His skin looked grey, the colour of ash. "I'll take a look from the other side." He walked around the tree, taking care not to let his feet stray into the light. Dracup waited for his return.

"Well?"

The inspector shook his head. "She's awake. Eyes open. I don't think she saw me." He cleared his throat. "I don't think she *can* see me."

"I'm going in," Dracup said. He didn't care what happened as long as he could just hold Natasha, tell her everything was all right. *Daddy's here*, he mouthed silently. *I found you.*

"Go on, then." Moran gave him an encouraging smile.

Dracup moistened his lips. He reached a hand into the circle. It felt warm and pleasant. He turned to Moran. The policeman nodded. Dracup withdrew his hand, and walked slowly forward, bracing himself for – what? He realised he had closed his eyes. He felt the sun on his face, a soft wind against his forehead. He opened his eyes and his chin dropped in astonishment.

He looked round to give Moran a thumbs up, but Moran was indistinct, a mere shadow behind a curtain. Dracup looked at the tree, amazed at the size and shape of the leaves, the abundant fruit hanging in great fertile clumps from every branch, and the sheer girth of the trunk. It was alive in a way he could not find words to describe. *Alive.* And then it came to him: *The Tree of Life.* With the memory came a vague uneasiness. He placed his hand on the bark. It pulsed under his fingers. He pulled back in surprise, but felt immediately drawn to reconnect to the sudden burst of energy he had felt emanating from the wood. This time he let his hand remain. *This is – amazing.* He had never felt so alive; he could feel the blood travelling through his veins and arteries, the oxygen inflating his lungs, the small movements of a million cells and processes within. He was *alive*. He almost laughed aloud. *Alive!*

Dracup sank to the ground and listened to the sound of life. He was vaguely conscious of Natasha's presence, but the motive that had impelled him to enter the circle was now forgotten in the extraordinary sensations running through his body. Somewhere in the recesses of his subconscious he heard another voice. It was insistent, grating. He wanted it to stop. It was spoiling everything. And then he remembered, with a sudden sharp clarity: *Moran.* He turned his head. There was Natasha, his daughter. He reached out. "'Tash. It's me."

The girl looked at him. "Hello, Daddy." She smiled. "I like it here, don't you?" She frowned, a little furrow in her forehead. "You're thin. You need to eat."

Dracup's head was clouded. He couldn't think. "Yes, darling. I do. But –"

"Can we stay? Please?" Her eyes were appealing to him. "No one will hurt us here."

"I – I know, 'Tash. I'm not sure –"

Dracup!

The voice in his head was louder now. Perhaps he should listen. Talk to it. "What is it?" he shouted.

Hold onto the girl and I will help you... Feel for my hand.
What hand? Dracup looked. Nothing made sense.
"Don't shout, Daddy. You need to be quiet here."
Draaaacup!
"Here, Daddy." Natasha held out a fallen fruit. It was large and pear-shaped, but a deep, purple colour. The juice ran onto Natasha's fingers. She raised her hand to lick the juice.

"No!" Dracup leaned over and knocked her hand away from her mouth. The fruit fell, slowly turning, and smashed into a pulp on the soft, mossy ground.

"Daddy!"

Another voice in Dracup's head was speaking urgently and rapidly now.

... The man has now become like one of us, knowing good and evil. He must not be allowed to reach out his hand and take also from the Tree of Life and eat, and live forever...

With a huge effort of will Dracup grabbed Natasha's hand and turned away from the tree. There was Moran's hand, gesticulating urgently from the other side of the curtain that separated the tree from the wasteland of Eden. The policeman's shape was dim, but discernable.

"Daddy. Please. I don't want to..."

"We *must*," he hissed through gritted teeth, muscles trembling with the sheer effort of pulling away. "This isn't for us. Not now. Not in this life."

Moran's arm and shoulder appeared. Dracup prayed that the DCI would not succumb and join them in the circle. Natasha was resisting, digging her heels into the soft turf. "*No, Daddyyyyy –*"

Sweat sprang from his forehead. He reached out for Moran, felt his tendons straining as the steely fingers enclosed his wrist.

Sara knew where they were heading. Her feet could have found their own way, so often had she felt the cold stone of these steps beneath her bare feet. Here was the central stairwell that led to the chamber of Adam. How right it was that he should lie at the ziggurat's pinnacle, how fitting. But surely Jassim would not bring Farrell, an outsider, to *that* place, of all places? And then she remembered Jassim's duties, his role here amongst the *Korumak*. Jassim was the keeper of the flame, the high priest of the great chamber. And he kept his accoutrements appropriately close by, in a small storeroom accessed directly from the stairwell. She heard the jangling of his keys as he turned off the great staircase and down the narrow corridor that led to his domain. Farrell was expressing his unease by means of his usual tuneless hum. It jangled her nerves in sympathy with Jassim's keys. "Farrell – give it a rest."

Farrell stopped humming. "Okay. If you tell me where we're headed."

"You've agreed to come. Jassim has given his word that he won't harm you."

They were waiting outside a polished wooden door. It was set into the passage wall, surmounted by a low beam. Sara followed Jassim through the narrow space. Farrell was hesitating, toying with his automatic. "*He* won't harm *me?*"

"That's right, Farrell. Come on."

She watched with satisfaction as the tall American ducked his head and joined them inside. Jassim closed the door.

Sara inhaled slowly. The scent of the room evoked bittersweet childhood memories of visits to Jassim's predecessor, a wizened, hunched servant of the chamber named Mahalalel. Even with her small hand firmly clasped in her mother's it had seemed a forbidding place. Her young eyes had widened at the ointments, ceremonial robes, jars of musky oil and strange, illusory tapestries hanging from the walls of Mahalalel's sanctuary. Even now she felt the familiar foreboding settling on her. She gazed at the sacristan's paraphernalia and shivered, catching a similar reaction on Farrell's bemused face as he took it all in. Jassim brought her back to the present, his soft voice lulling childhood fears away.

"Mr Farrell. The weapon is unnecessary." Jassim made a slight, dismissive movement with his hand.

Sara watched Farrell. She could see the agent's fascination in the small, distracted movements of his head, the nervy moistening of his lips.

"What is this place?" Farrell holstered his handgun and let his arms drop. "There's a feeling, I can't –" He shook his head, bewildered.

"Mr Farrell. You know your scriptures, I am told." Fine lines appeared around Jassim's eyes, the faintest of smiles raising the corners of his mouth. "But as you say in the West, seeing is believing."

Sara caught her breath. Her brother had taken the greatest risk; now there was no going back for either of them. She felt a pang of guilt and caught Jassim's arm. "Jassim – I – I don't know... Kadesh is only doing –"

"– what he feels is right." Jassim nodded. "I know. And what about Ruth? Was that right?"

Sara took a deep breath. She watched Farrell moving around the room, touching, inspecting. Confusion raged inside her. She took her brother's hand and squeezed it.

"It just feels like a – a betrayal. He is one of us. He is our leader. Are you sure –"

Jassim's grip was firm. He looked into her eyes. "No, sister. This is not betrayal." Jassim held her by the shoulders, gently reinforcing his words. "This is *survival*."

"Where the hell is he?" Potzner slammed down his fist on the Humvee dash. He glanced at his watch. "Okay. That's it. We're going in." Damn Farrell. He'd have to look after himself.

He opened the door and stepped onto the baked earth. The marines silently disembarked, assembling in a disciplined phalanx around the vehicles. Conversation was limited to terse, monosyllabic checks and affirmations. Weapons clicked in the darkness as they were primed and loaded. A shadow approached.

"Mr Potzner?"

"Yes, Colonel?"

"Keep to the rear of the second squad. I've assigned two guys to you personally. They'll do whatever is necessary."

Potzner nodded with satisfaction as two marines materialized beside Colonel Osbourne. Nametags identified them as Cruickshank and Rutter. They were built like football players. Good. Things were going to get tough in there.

Potzner looked up at the great Tell, silhouetted against the skyline and blocking the stars with its bulk. He felt a rising excitement, a tingling in his loins. *At last.*

Chapter 41

The grip was firm, clasping Dracup's hand and drawing him towards the shimmering curtain. But Dracup's mind was in rebellion. He fought against the unrelenting vice that would sever him from Paradise. Natasha was screaming, pulling and kicking his legs. Dracup fought for control. *I can't leave.*

You must.

He felt a coldness seeping into his outstretched arm and with it came a reluctant clarity. He realised that he was half-in, half-out. He could see Moran, the tendons on the DCI's neck straining with the effort of dragging Dracup from the persuasive influence of the tree.

And then he was out. He felt a shock run through him, like a rapid electrical discharge. He was lying next to Natasha, his lungs struggling for breath. Moran was flat on his back, panting and cursing.

"Daddy?" Natasha shook him gently by the shoulder. "Can we go back now?" She pulled Dracup's hand. "I want to see Sara."

"Yes. We should go back." Dracup felt groggy, like an interrupted lotus-eater. He looked around at the stunted roots and grey, lifeless earth. Behind him, the tree pulsed with unremitting energy.

Moran was standing by the curtain, his hands caressing the translucent space in front of him. The air rippled and parted at his touch.

"Don't even think about it," Dracup said. "I haven't the strength to get you out."

"The Tree of Life." Moran's face was pressed against the solid air, trying to see. "This is the Tree of Life."

"I heard you speaking," Dracup told him. "I remembered the verses you quoted."

"I didn't quote anything," Moran snorted. "I was pulling like a dray horse."

"Thanks." Dracup smiled wryly. "But *someone* was talking to me –"

"Daddy, you *are* thin." Natasha assessed him with the uninhibited assurance of her years. "And your face is dirty."

Dracup fought back tears. He reached out his hand. "Come here. Just give me a hug." He cupped Natasha's face in his hands. She appeared unharmed, tranquil.

"By the way," Moran said, "have you noticed?"

"What?"

Moran pointed. "Your arm. Have you checked it recently?"

Dracup pulled up his shirtsleeve to reveal the rough bandage Farrell had applied. With a shock he realised he felt no pain. More than that – he had forgotten his injury. His fingers probed under the dressing. They reappeared dry. No blood. He unravelled the gauze. The skin was unbroken.

"Someone's on our side." Moran took a deep breath. "Come on. Let's get this over with."

Dracup took Natasha's hand and they walked away, retracing their steps. He wondered when the elation would kick in, but found that he was consumed by other, unbidden feelings; he dared not glance back. He could feel the tree's energy seducing him, as if he were straining against the insistent tug of some invisible, elastic connection. As he made one foot follow the other he thought about the voice. He hadn't imagined it. But if it wasn't Moran's...

Then whose was it?

Chapter 42

Potzner crouched low. He had heard *something*. Up ahead the leading marine hissed a warning. Behind him Cruickshank and Rutter's nervous banter had stopped, replaced by the sound of adrenaline-primed heavy breathing. The signal came to move on. The stairwell was firm under Potzner's feet, his steps confident. He felt unstoppable.

Suddenly there was nothing under his feet. The marines in front simply fell into the void, like stones dropped into a well. Potzner's arms shot out for purchase, catching the edge of the stairwell and finding some metal projection, part of the trap's machinery. He was a heavy man and the odds were against his being able to support his weight. He felt his back judder with the shock, a stinging pain in his bicep. For a moment he swung precariously above the blackness, then with gritted teeth he clawed at the crumbling stonework until he felt Cruickshank's farmhand grip on his wrist. It took all the marine's muscle to pull him up. Rutter added his energy to the final heave and then Potzner was lying across the staircase, the taste of blood in his mouth where his teeth had clamped against his tongue during the fall.

The sprung section had swung back into place by the time he had recovered sufficiently to get to his feet. He examined the stonework. They could pass if they clung to the side wall and moved slowly. He massaged his arm. Five men gone. Someone was going to pay.

By the waterfall Moran signalled caution. Behind the screen of water there was movement. And light. They exchanged looks. Moran shrugged and continued his appraisal of the area surrounding the falls. Every few seconds Dracup's hand wandered unconsciously to the spot where the bullet had passed across his skin.

What had happened at the tree? Who had spoken? He felt *Alpha*'s weight pulling at his belt and moved his hand down to ease the burden. The artefact had cooled by the time he had recovered it, but it was becoming harder to carry, as if its internal mass was somehow increasing without any visible change. And another problem gnawed at his mind: Farrell and Sara had disappeared.

Moran whistled softly. Dracup looked up. "If I'm not mistaken," Moran grinned, "those are US marines."

"Yes, but do we want US marines?" Dracup hissed in response.

"An armed escort? Sounds like a good idea to me."

Dracup weighed the options. Moran was right. They needed help. But could he trust Potzner? The troops had no doubt been briefed. But what *was* their brief?

Moran was gesticulating impatiently. He had to take the risk. Dracup gave the thumbs up and felt a cautious relief as Moran, hands extended upward, stepped into the marines' field of vision and stayed alive.

Moran signalled from the water's edge. Dracup broke cover, negotiating the slippery stones. They couldn't avoid a soaking from the spray, but Natasha seemed to enjoy it. She giggled and pushed her damp hair back from her forehead. The sound was a tonic to Dracup's ears.

"You'll be the Professor, I'd guess," said the first marine, a fresh-faced boy of around twenty.

Dracup nodded. The soldier was dressed in standard desert combats, the light from his assault rifle bathing the trio in an intense beam.

"I'm Jackson, and this is my buddy, Cannon." He cocked his head towards an untidy ginger-haired marine. "We have orders to see you clear of this place."

Dracup's fears resurfaced. He didn't want clear of this place. He wanted Kadesh. Face to face. Answers. Closure.

"We have to get going," Jackson told them. "The place is crawling with unfriendlies. If you would, please." He barrelled his light along Dracup's earlier route. The beam picked out the perfectly conjoined stonework that formed the passage's ceiling, the enduring handiwork of Nebuchadnezzar's master builders.

Cannon echoed the sentiment. "You heard the man. Let's move out, folks."

Dracup took Natasha's hand and they fell into step behind the probing glare of Jackson's light. How could he find Kadesh in this warren? Cannon's footsteps trudged behind them, his light casting their shadows onto the path ahead.

"This is the lowest level," Jackson called back. "We've got a way to go, so keep up."

"There are *seven* levels," Moran said, fumbling with his map.

Dracup moved in for a closer look. The map was a cutaway, exposing the innards of the ziggurat as if a giant knife had sheared through its centre. "Where did this come from?"

Moran shot him a strange smile. "What was it you said? 'Hasn't the imagination to be unstable'?"

Dracup was stunned. "*Malcolm?* What in the name –?"

He was interrupted by an impatient shout from Jackson. "C'mon now, let's pick it up. Everyone okay back there?"

"Okay," Cannon called. The passage began to rise under their feet. A faint susuration could now be heard; it filled the space with a primal, earthy urgency. Dracup heard Cannon muttering, "What in the hell is *that?*"

"It's just the singing, don't worry. We're near the chamber of worship on this level. I like it. Ruth taught me," Natasha said. An instant later Dracup caught his breath as Natasha's high treble joined in with the melody, adding her own harmony to the weird, ambient soundscape.

"Hold up," Jackson called back. Dracup pressed his hand to Natasha's shoulder and the girl fell silent. They had reached a junction and Dracup suddenly understood Jackson's warning: footsteps, moving fast – their way.

Jackson consulted his map and signalled right. They fled down the new passage, which stretched ahead in a slow, upward gradient. Dracup glanced to one side. Moran had drawn his pistol, checking the number of rounds as he ran. Jackson broke right, then doused his light. They were in a subsidiary corridor of some sort, narrower than the main thoroughfare but not, as Dracup had feared, a dead end.

Natasha spoke in his ear. "My room is right up at the end." She pulled at his sleeve. "Come and see. I know where we are."

"You do? Can we get out this way – further up?" he whispered to his daughter.

"Wait up," Jackson said. "I don't want to go in any deeper. This place is a warren. We stay here, then we get back on the exit route." He jerked a thumb towards the passage, a warning glint in his eyes. "Now *quiet*."

They waited. An escalating grumble coalesced into a conversation of raised voices. The slap of sandals on stone was close now, almost on top of them.

"Daddy?"

He put his finger to Natasha's lips and shook his head.

"I want to get something," she whispered. "Maybe Sara will be there," she added brightly.

Dracup frowned and pressed a finger urgently to his lips, flabbergasted at the carrot his daughter had used to entice him. *Good grief – and* s*he's only eight...*

A group of men passed the passage entrance, close enough to touch. Dracup pressed his back against the wall. The voices were harsh and argumentative, sparring in animated conversation. A tang of acrid cigarette smoke wrinkled his nostrils and was gone. The regular metallic clank of some loose piece of equipment receded with their unresolved discussion.

"Daddy, please."

"*Quiet,* 'Tash."

"We'll give it five," Jackson whispered hoarsely. "There may be more suckers on the way."

Moran blew out his cheeks. "*Jihadis*."

Dracup frowned. "How can you be sure?"

"They're not the guys who took a pop at you earlier. I'd guess they were some kind of internal security. These –" Moran waved vaguely in the direction of the departed group, "are definitely in a different league. Look at the clothing, for a start. *Isaaba*. Standard Al-Q action garb. Did you catch the hardware as well? That was a mortar."

Jackson chewed his gum and nodded silently. "Just keep it down. If they suss us out we're dead. Period."

Dracup squatted to take the weight off his feet. His mouth was furred and dry. He racked his brains to remember the last food that had passed his lips, and failed; he remembered 'Tash's first reaction on seeing him: *You're thin*. He smiled. Succinct, to the point. Just like Yvonne. The thought jarred. He wished he had some way to communicate Natasha's safety.

Moran was admiring the marines' armament. He listened as Cannon described the customisations he'd made to his weapon. Cannon flicked a switch; a red dot appeared on the ceiling, some way down the passage. "It's a laser sight," Cannon explained. "You can't miss with this baby."

Moran looked suitably impressed. "And this?" the DCI asked, pointing to another rocker switch situated above the magazine.

"Remote operation," Cannon told him. "I can even fire this sonofabitch from around a corner, provided I can get a clear view."

"How?" Moran was all ears.

Jackson showed his wrist. "With this," he said. "Radio controlled. Effective up to distances of two hundred metres. First button switches on the sights, second fires ten, twenty, thirty rounds. Depends on how you set it up."

"Daddy. Please can we go to my chamber?" Natasha repeated her request.

Dracup thought quickly. It might be his only chance to get away. "'Tash wants to collect something from the room they kept her in," Dracup said to Jackson. "It's close by – that okay with you?"

Jackson looked Dracup up and down. "No way."

Natasha appeared between them. She gave Jackson her best smile. "Please?"

"*Uno momento*, young lady," Jackson said, visibly weakening. He placed his hand gently under her chin and tilted her head up. "You've been here a while, ain't you? Okay, just hold on a little longer." They watched him creep to the junction and peer round the corner. He returned with a resigned expression.

"All clear," he shrugged. "Go with them, Cannon – pronto." Jackson waved them on. "And *hurry up*." He looked at his watch. "Two minutes max."

Cannon led them along the corridor. They passed two or three recessed doorways; other *Korumak* residences, Dracup assumed. He marvelled at the efficiency of this underground community. They had the basic commodities: light, heat, water. He was puzzling over the fourth, food, when Natasha gave a small noise of recognition. And then stopped in her tracks. "Here."

Cannon turned. Dracup looked over Natasha's shoulder. "What is it, 'Tash?" And then he saw.

A woman lay spread-eagled on the floor, her sightless eyes gazing at the ceiling. Natasha was staring at the body. "Ruth." She stretched out her arm and took a hesitant step forward.

Dracup grabbed her. "Don't look, 'Tash. Come away." He pulled Natasha back. She shook him off and pointed to an alcove, where a spread of furs and an intricately embroidered wrap lay partially concealed behind a fine, silken curtain. On the wrap lay a pile of carefully folded clothes. Dracup recognised Natasha's school uniform. There was also a dolly dressed in a bright blue pinafore.

Dracup stepped gingerly around the body, retrieved the uniform and dolly and ushered the girl out. His heart was thudding in his chest as they rejoined Moran and Jackson at the junction. Moran looked at Dracup and frowned, but the question died on his lips as a burst of machine gun fire broke the silence. Dracup instinctively ducked as it was followed by another staccato fusillade. A bullet hit the ceiling above the junction, raining down a small shower of loose shale.

Jackson cursed. "Sons of bitches have doubled back. How in hell did they know we were here?" He inspected his helmet; a burnt scar showed where a bullet had come close to finding its mark.

Dracup frowned. "'Tash. Give me the doll."

Natasha handed Dracup the toy. His probing fingers found a small, round disk beneath the dress. As he carefully extracted it, it gave a faint red pulse. He held it up for Jackson to see. "That's how."

"Woah," the marine whistled. "GPS tracking device."

Cannon took up a position at the bend. "You all right, Jacko?" He glared at Jackson with an accusing look, clearly rattled that his CO had nearly had his head blown off.

Jackson was reloading. "I'm cool."

"Where to?" Moran's face was grim.

"Sure ain't gonna be this way." Cannon clipped off a couple of rounds.

Dracup bent and held Natasha gently by the shoulders. "'Tash. *Is* there a way out past your room? Can you remember where this passage leads?"

Natasha pursed her lips. "If you follow it *all* the way it comes out at the big stairway. All the corridors in this level do. Then you can climb up right to the top – if you want. To *his* chamber."

The words sent a chill down Dracup's spine. "You mean to the top of the ziggurat – the pyramid?"

"There's a staircase. A big one."

Moran was poring over the map. "She's right – I think. Look." He traced out Natasha's suggested route.

Jackson nodded grimly, peering over Moran's shoulder. "We'll be out in the open a while –"

"We'll be full of freakin' holes if we stay here," Cannon called back over another burst of fire. "*Open* sounds good from where I'm standing. Get going. I'll cover you."

Jackson nodded tersely. "Okay – two minutes only," he told Cannon. "Then get the hell out of here."

Dracup took Natasha's arm and followed Jackson and Moran past the room where the woman – Ruth – lay stiffening in death. He wondered briefly what had happened to her. He also wondered at the absence of other *Korumak*. And then, remembering his encounter with Jassim, a thought occurred to him. *He's started to evacuate them. That's why the place is deserted.* But where would he take them?

The noise of gunfire faded as they raced along the passage, which instead of widening as he had supposed, grew more constricted as it turned sharply to the right towards what Moran had identified as the central stairwell. Dracup's side was aching, his lungs straining for breath. Without warning the passage abruptly ended. Dracup stopped with an exclamation.

"It's big, isn't it?" Natasha smiled. "I told you."

They were looking at a stairway, but a stairway of astonishing beauty. The steps glinted dully in the diffused light, gradually narrowing until they were lost to sight in the opaqueness of the roof.

"Up?" Moran cocked his head at Jackson.

"Looks like it," Jackson agreed.

"Not that way, Daddy." Natasha took Dracup's hand and led him to the left of the stairway. "You can't go up the wide stairs – that's only for special ceremonies. You have to go up here. There's no way in at the top of the big stairs."

Jackson and Moran looked at each other. The policeman shrugged.

Dracup let Natasha lead him into another passage, lower and smaller than the one they had just emerged from.

"Here." She stopped beside a heavy wooden door. It was ajar. Dracup pushed it open gingerly with his foot, revealing a stone staircase spiralling up to the distant apex of the ziggurat. He craned his neck.

I know what's up there.

"Daddy! Come *on*."

But I still don't believe it.

Gunfire again, but closer. He hesitated, turned to the others. "What about Cannon?"

"He'll be along soon," Jackson said. "He always is."

Dracup led them up.

Chapter 43

Dracup took a hesitant step onto the staircase. For the first time he felt like a trespasser. The stone was soft under his feet, warm. Machine gun fire echoed in the distance, a series of muffled rattles as Cannon returned the *jihadi* fire.

"*Daddy!* Hurry up."

Dracup battled the strange feelings working inside him. He felt – *unholy*.

Moran was waiting a few steps behind, his ferret face set in determination, but with the ghost of some deeper emotion simmering beneath the surface.

He feels it too.

They went up. And up.

Moran spoke. "We must be near." Dracup could hear the DCI's laboured breath.

Jackson had pushed past. His voice came from somewhere ahead, around the next spiral. "Well I'll be *darned!*"

The staircase ended at a blank wall. On the surface were imprinted a series of letters – cuneiform letters. Apart from these, nothing broke the smoothness of the stone.

Two short bursts of fire. Closer now. Cannon's voice raised in defiance, somewhere down the stairwell.

Jackson managed a tense grin. "He gets real riled when folk shoot at him."

"There *must* be a way in," Dracup was muttering, running his palm over the markings.

"Ain't no keyhole I can see," Jackson said, "leastways, not a *regular* keyhole."

"Exactly," Dracup said. "But there *is* one. Somewhere."

Moran was beside him. "They're on the stairs." There came another clattering burst of automatic fire confirming Moran's statement.

Dracup concentrated on the lettering. It was set out in a grid format:

𒁹 𒐏 𒈦 𒐐

𒐐 𒌋 𒌋

𒀹 𒐏

"Daddy. I'm scared."

Dracup put his arm round Natasha's shoulders and pulled her close.

It's not going to end like this. Think, Dracup.

He tried to remember the symbols from Fish's presentation. These markings looked nothing like the lettering the Americans had translated. But it was still recognisably cuneiform.

Jackson was backed against the wall, waiting. He turned his head sideways. Dracup saw the boy behind the soldier's uniform, a young lad far from home and probably more scared than he'd care to admit.

"Reckon they shoulda fitted a keypad entry system, huh?" Jackson said with a forced grin.

In Dracup's head the light bulb went on. "Jackson," he said, "go on thinking like that and you'll make General before the decade is out." His heart was racing now that he knew what was set before him. *Numbers. They're numbers, you idiot, not letters.*

Question was, what was the sequence? His fingers stroked the lines of script, willing them to reveal their secret. *Come on, Theodore. One more time, for your granddaughter's sake.*

From below came another burst, then a cry. The silence was more frightening than the gunfire.

Jackson moistened his lips. "Cannon's down." His voice held a note of disbelief. "He's *down*."

"*Daddy?*" A tremor now in Natasha's voice.

"We can hold them," Moran said. "There's only a narrow gap."

First symbol. One character. Right, let's follow old Occam again. Say that's <u>one</u>. Count the little golf tees.

Moran fired his pistol, a single sharp report against Jackson's *tak tak tak*.

"Stand in front of me, 'Tash." He shielded the little girl with his body.

One. Five. Two. Six.

Despair clutched at him. No pattern.

Three. Seven. Four.

He played with the numbers in his head.

Order them: One, two, three, four, five, six, seven.

Jackson reloading again. A scream: Natasha. A man had appeared at the stair's turn, ten metres below.

Bullets scudded around them. One buried itself in the wall. Dust flicked back into Dracup's eye. He swore and grimaced, ducking down, bending over Natasha. He squinted through his good eye. The *jihadi* was taking the stairs two at a time. Moran shot him through the chest. He fell back, tumbling.

Jackson was ashen-faced, bleeding from his leg. "Shit." Face twisted in pain, he levelled the rifle and helped the falling *jihadi* on his way with a quick burst.

"Be nice to get it open soon," Moran said to Dracup.

The last two symbols:

Four fish... four plus nine, or... forty-nine?

With a jolt Dracup remembered Theodore's inscribed wax tablet. Sliding the transcription from under his watchstrap he read: *K. zig. – 7 by 7*. Of course! Seven sevens. The ultimate expression of perfection. Adam was created a *perfect* being... according to scripture he didn't stay that way, but in the beginning...

What combination of seven sevens? He looked down at Jackson, on his haunches, rifle between his knees, covering Moran as he fumbled a new magazine into place. Another spray of bullets, ricocheting around the top of the stairwell. Natasha covering her ears. Above them, the wall stretched away. Nowhere to climb. He pressed the first seven symbols in sequence. Nothing. Then again, but repeated seven times. Nothing. He banged the wall in frustration.

Right. Last chance saloon. He pressed the four and the nine from the last group together, slowly and deliberately, seven times. On the last press the squares on which the symbols were engraved sank silently into the wall.

He felt a vibration under his fingertips, a rumbling of tumblers. And the pattern parted in the centre, the wall peeling back like an orange skin. He bent, hands under Jackson's armpits, Moran covering, slowly dragging the boy through the doorway.

Now what? How to close it?

Jackson groaned as Dracup propped him against the chamber wall. He turned to face the new room they had entered and felt his heart skip a beat. In the centre of the chamber was a long sarcophagus, black as onyx, raised up on a dais of solid gold. A clutch of bullets fizzed past his head. Moran was scrabbling at a lever inset into a small recess by the gaping doorway. Dracup shouted. It had to be the lock.

The door slid seamlessly together, like a closing mouth. Dracup had a fleeting impression of the *jihadis*, their faces contorted in hatred, racing towards them. And then they were sealed into the chamber with a final clunk of hidden weights and pulleys. Silence descended. Natasha was crying softly.

"It's all right." Dracup held her. "It's going to be okay."

Moran was tending to Jackson. The bullet had torn through his calf, leaving a ragged, flesh-tattered hole as it exited.

"I got some painkiller in my pocket," he told Moran. "Ow! *Jeez*, that hurts."

"It will," Moran said matter-of-factly. He finished packing the wound with his handkerchief and strapped the marine's leg tightly with his tie. "Keep it up. That's it, elevated."

Dracup approached the sarcophagus warily, felt the dry coolness of its lid. It was hard to see; there was some light, but –

Lights came on. Bright, *dazzling*. They tracked across the chamber and illuminated the sarcophagus. A harsh, electronic voice filled the room:

> *"Professor Dracup. And friends. You have entered the resting place of Adamah, or 'Adam' in your abbreviated vernacular. The chamber is sealed for a reason; namely, to aid the preservation process put into place millennia ago. This means, gentlemen – and young Natasha – that the oxygen is removed from the chamber when it is not in use. In the prophetic words of God himself, dust you are, and to dust you shall certainly return. Professor, your forty-eight hours are up."*

There was a soft click as the transmission was concluded. Already the chamber was warm, their breathing laboured in the confined space.

Moran wet his lips. Jackson's head fell forward as loss of blood and fatigue caught up with him. Dracup began scouring the chamber. There was only the sarcophagus. No other object broke the simple contours of what had now become a death trap. Dracup walked around the sarcophagus, placed his hands on the lid and tried to lift. It wouldn't budge.

Moran kicked the wall in frustration. "There's nothing." He laughed harshly. "Unless we open up the door again."

"Not a good plan," Dracup agreed. The *jihadis* wouldn't be far away. He conducted a full inspection of the walls, feeling for any bump or protrusion. There was only the sarcophagus.

"Is he going to die?" Natasha was looking down at the slumped figure of Jackson.

Dracup shook his head. "No one's going to die," he told her. He felt a rising desperation, hoped it didn't show in his face. From beyond the chamber, behind the door they had entered, came the sound of muffled thumping. They exchanged glances. The unspoken thought was the same: Would the *jihadis* crack the code? Death by gunshot wound or suffocation. It wasn't a choice Dracup wanted to dwell on.

Moran was at the other end, beyond the sarcophagus. "Reckon this is an exit too?" He looked in vain for a corresponding lever.

Dracup was thinking about the shape of the ziggurat. Surely multiple stairways ran up to the apex? "Yes, there's probably another stairwell through there. Maybe it's only accessible from outside."

"Great." Moran leaned against the wall and took a deep breath. The air was stale now, their breathing shallow. Dracup felt a series of sharp constrictions in his chest. For a moment he thought he was having a heart attack, then the pains left him and were replaced by a growing tightness in his lungs. Natasha was sitting cross-legged, her face expressionless as she fought to inhale the oxygen her body craved. She looked at Dracup and tried to smile. He too sank to the floor, and raised an arm weakly towards his daughter.

I won't let this happen.

Moran's eyes were closed. Dracup crawled to Natasha. By the time he reached her she was unconscious. He leaned over and pressed his mouth to hers, forcing in the last breath from his own lungs. His head swam.

Breathe, please breathe.

But breathing was becoming his own imperative. A cloud was descending, a smoky darkness, but a darkness interspersed with vivid colour. His mind began to replay scenes from the past, as if a giant spool had been placed on some eternal tape deck and the play button had clicked on of its own volition. There was his childhood. The Indian sunrise. His marriage, a warm July afternoon in Surrey. The hospital and a newborn baby. Yvonne's face, exhausted but radiant. Natasha's first stumbling steps. The tears in his eyes as she articulated her first word. His appointment at Reading; his first student address. The campus on a windy November morning, student bicycles competing for space on the narrow campus pathways. Sara's face in the lecture room, attentive, beautiful. Charles' empty study, the house wrapped in blue and white police tape. He was falling into space from a tiny silver aeroplane. His hand clutched at and missed every handhold. He heard Charles' voice clearly. Calling to him: "Hold on, Si. Just a while longer. Just a while –"

Dracup fought to remain conscious. He heard a faint scrabbling from Moran's end of the chamber. Dracup forced his eyes open. Moran was spread-eagled on the floor. The scrabbling persisted, as if a family of mice was scratching at the wall, trying to find a way in.

Then the world exploded. A crush of hot air ballooned into the chamber, followed by flying debris from the wall itself. Something struck Dracup on the side of his forehead, drawing blood. Smoke trailed into the chamber in a white, acrid afterstorm. But he could breath. Just about. Dracup rolled over and drew a lungful of air laced with swirling smoke and dust; he transferred it into Natasha's mouth. She coughed twice and was sick.

Dracup was elated. He turned his head and peered through the smoke. A powerful light shone into the chamber, silhouetting a lone figure standing in the debris where the wall had been. The attitude was unmistakable, as was the voice.

"Professor Dracup. If you'd like to step outside. Right this way, please." James Potzner spoke as though he had arrived to welcome candidates for an interview or conduct a tour of some city museum. Dracup blinked. Behind Potzner's tall shape he could see a supporting group of marines. They were positioned by the blown entrance, assault rifles raised, covering the interior of the chamber. He took stock of his surroundings. The force of the blast had rolled him alongside Jackson, who lay in the same position against the wall, rifle propped up on his raised knees. The boy was breathing, but in shallow, gasping intervals. Moran was struggling to his feet, coughing and cursing. Natasha was on all fours, hair covering her face as she tried to get up.

"Quick as you can, please." Potzner was standing by the sarcophagus. He swept a layer of dust and bits of rock from the lid with an impatient gesture.

Dracup helped Natasha to her feet. She had a small cut above her eyebrow from a rock splinter, but was otherwise unharmed. As his head began to clear he remembered the voice from the hidden speaker. Kadesh. He would surely be on his way.

As if in response to his thoughts the speaker crackled briefly, and Dracup froze in surprise at the unexpected voice. Farrell's southern drawl filled the chamber:

> *"Professor and all? Get yourselves out of there as soon as – bad company on its way – south side. We can't hold them – have to go – out."*

Dracup turned to Potzner, but before he could articulate his question he felt rather than heard the cuneiform door slide open behind him.

Potzner ducked behind the sarcophagus. Dracup spun around, reached for Natasha but grasped only the circulating dust. And then he became very still.

A tall, thin man stood in the doorway. His skin was dark, of Asian rather than African pigmentation. His bearing was aristocratic, an impression reinforced by the long nose and slim, refined hands. Hands that held a knife to Natasha's throat.

Behind him were a group of armed men, the *jihadis* who had waited outside the chamber. But Dracup had eyes only for the thin, brown fingers and the silver of the blade that played slowly up and down Natasha's exposed neck.

Kadesh's first words were for the crouching Potzner. "You appear to have mislaid part of your escort, Mr Potzner. The stairway can be treacherous."

"They were good men, you murdering son of a bitch." Potzner's voice was steady, but Dracup saw the smouldering hate in the American's eyes.

"That is a most unflattering and inappropriate term." Kadesh smiled benignly. "Although the terms 'murder' and 'United States' are familiar bedfellows. Now," he told Potzner, "down with your weapons if you please."

Potzner waved a signal to the waiting marines. The rifles clattered to the floor.

Dracup's legs were shaking. He lowered himself slowly to his haunches.

"Don't move again, please." Kadesh spared Dracup a single glance. "Mr Potzner. Do you still believe you have the right to take what does not belong to you?"

"Ownership isn't the issue here." Potzner held a snub-nosed pistol in his right hand. The grip was steady.

"But it is, Mr Potzner. And you have no such rights."

Dracup's eyes scanned from left to right. Moran was five, maybe eight metres away. The DCI's hands were empty, his gun holstered under his armpit.

Kadesh wore a disdainful expression. "In a way, this is better than I'd hoped." He turned his attention to Dracup. "To personally pay the debt to my father is an additional – a richer, one might say – blessing."

Dracup knew he had to play for time. "What debt?"

"Oh, please, Professor Dracup. By now, you know it all. My father died because of what happened in his generation. Because of what your family did."

"My family? A geologist, working – no – *coerced* into working for the US federal government? That's hardly culpable. Theodore Dracup was forced into a situation he would rather have left well alone. You know that." Dracup snatched a glance at Potzner, his heart in his mouth. The American's forefinger was stroking the pistol trigger, his eyes fixed, the pupils dilated.

"My father died a broken man, Professor Dracup. Your grandfather's interference brought ruin and desolation upon our people."

"Then I apologize on his behalf. What he did was wrong – even if he acted against his will."

Kadesh shook his head. "It is too late for apologies." He let the knife brush across Natasha's cheek. "You have failed to return the sceptre."

"You're wrong. I have *Alpha*." Dracup fumbled for his belt.

Kadesh's eyes flashed a warning. "Keep your hands in front of you." The knife moved to Natasha's throat.

"I also have the diary." Dracup tried to keep his voice even, reasonable. "It's yours if you want it."

Kadesh laughed softly. "Indeed? So, you overcame Mukannishum. Still, I regret that your efforts are sadly inadequate." He tightened his hold on Natasha. "Besides, did you really expect me to show you any mercy?"

One of the *jihadi* squad laughed, a foreign, heartless sound.

Beside him, Jackson stirred, groaning. The marine's arm fell loosely by his side, exposing the wrist. Kadesh drew a pistol and shot him through the head.

Dracup yelled, "No!" He stopped in his tracks as the pistol was levelled at him. His hands made fists then clasped his thighs in impotent fury. Kadesh was enjoying this. Dracup racked his brains. There must be something – think, Dracup, *think*. And then his pulse accelerated, a surge of adrenaline. What had Cannon said?

I can even fire this sonofabitch from around a corner, provided I can get a clear view. And the marine had shown Moran his wrist: *Radio controlled. Effective up to distances of two hundred metres.*

Dracup checked the angle of Jackson's rifle. It was pointing towards the roof, way off centre for an accurate shot. He had to entice Kadesh to move. "You can't kill an innocent girl." Sweat broke out on his brow. "Kill me instead. Let her go."

"Oh no, Dracup. I want you to see her suffer." Kadesh took one further step into the chamber. "I want you to look into her eyes as she bleeds."

"This is pointless. You have what you want. Let me hold her. Please." In Dracup's peripheral vision he saw a minute change in Potzner's posture, a fractional increase in tension.

I hope you're reading my body language now, Potzner...

And close behind came this thought:

But he doesn't care about Natasha. It's Kadesh he wants.

Dracup held out his arms to Natasha. Kadesh hesitated, moved a fraction closer. Behind Potzner, a muted muttering of protest; the marines, waiting for their chance. Dracup's right hand crawled to Jackson's wrist. He felt the buttons under his fingers. Which one? He murmured a prayer.

Natasha's eyes, saucers of terror. He chose the first button and pressed it softly. A red dot appeared on Kadesh's shoulder, just below the collarbone.

Thank God thank God thank God...

Potzner shuffled his feet, relaxed slightly.

He's seen it.

"Darling, don't be scared," Dracup babbled, willing Kadesh to move, just a pace. Just one. "Daddy's here. It's all right. I love you." He held out his free arm, palm upwards. Kadesh sneered, enjoying the moment, but Dracup's forward motion had caused him to take a small step back. The red dot tracked across Kadesh's dishdash and settled above his left eye like an angry wasp.

Dracup found himself hesitating.

I can't kill him in cold blood – can I?

Moran spoke up. Two words: "Do it."

"Enough." Kadesh said. The knife drew back and plunged towards Natasha's neck.

Dracup closed his eyes and stabbed the second button. The rifle exploded into life, emptying its programmed quota of rounds, filling the chamber with the stink of cordite. Dracup was on his feet, catching Natasha as she fell, stepping over Kadesh's body, grimacing at the bloody mess of bone and skin which was all that remained of the Korumak leader's head. A bizarre silence descended as both marines and *jihadis* tried to work out what had happened.

A voice in Dracup's head said *Move!* He leapt for the cover of the exposed hole in the west wall. Moran had the same idea. They collided, sprawling, half in, half out of the chamber. The *jihadi* automatics were chattering, raking the chamber with crossfire. Potzner, taking cover by the sarcophagus, barked out orders to the marines. "*Cover* me, you asshats!"

Dracup rolled, smothering Natasha's body. His shoulder blades twitched in anticipation of the ripping burst that would end his life. He inched forward, then shoved Natasha's bottom towards the gap. Moran grabbed her hand and pulled her out of the line of fire. Dracup stumbled after her, his head ringing with the explosive noise of the *jihadi* and marine automatic fire.

But they were outnumbered. The *jihadis* advanced through the chamber, bending low, using the sarcophagus as cover. Bullets pinged and whined off the lid. Potzner duck- walked backwards, yelling, "*Careful,* you morons – *not* the casket. Clear shots only."

Potzner made it to the hole. He came through and flattened his back against the outside of the wall. Dracup held Natasha tight. He could see, as he had supposed, a mirror image stairway beginning its long descent twenty metres from where they stood. Beside him, a squat, muscled marine winked at him.

"Nice shootin', man. This'll sort the suckers out." He showed Dracup a grenade grasped tightly in each fist. Potzner was reloading, fingers working methodically as he fed the magazine. The marine stepped forward, into the gap. Potzner glanced up, realised his intent too late. He held up his hand and screamed.

"No! *No grenades!*"

In slow motion, Dracup saw the marine turn, a quizzical look on his face. *Why not? We want to waste the creeps, don't we?* The grenades left his hands in two rolling, overarm pitches.

Potzner yelled again. "*No!*"

Dracup watched the American dive into the gap. He knew what was on Potzner's mind: the contents of the sarcophagus. Protect it. At all costs.

He's going for the grenades. He's crazy.

Dracup had to look. He pressed Natasha into Moran's arms and picked up a fallen marine's rifle. He edged his face round the wrecked wall into the chamber. Through the smoke he saw Potzner in a half dive, half lunge, stretching for the second grenade, the other already secure in his left hand.

He's out of time – it's going to blow.

A *jihadi* loomed over Potzner's prostrate body. Dracup aimed, pulled the trigger. The rifle breech wheezed and clicked. Empty. Potzner had fallen alongside the sarcophagus. Dracup watched him raise his arm to speed the grenade away towards the *jihadi* stairwell; parallel with Potzner's head it exploded in a flash of brilliant light. A microsecond later there came another sharp crack as the second grenade exploded. The chamber roof groaned, heaved and fell with a noise like a tearing thunderclap.

Dracup was pushed back by the combined force of the explosions and the sudden shifting of masonry. His head was ringing, but he moved forward again to enter the chamber. Perhaps Potzner could be saved. No more deaths. Enough was enough.

A hand was on his arm, pulling. "Get the hell out of there. *Fall back!*" Dracup turned, dazed. A marine roared in his face. "Move *out!*"

Dracup stumbled away a second before a sheet of flame burst from the chamber and flicked towards the stairwell. Moran was shouting, Natasha's face pale and shocked beside him. He made the stairway and lurched down, two, three, five steps at a time. Three marines ahead, one, maybe two behind him. Moran glanced back, nodded briefly in acknowledgement. He felt for Natasha's hand and grasped it firmly. Smoke billowed down the stairwell, overtaking them as they fled.

At the foot of the staircase they emerged into a wide hall delimited by a blue marbled portico. The hall was bare of ornamentation except for a solitary central fountain. The marines spread out and secured the area. Two guarded the stairwell.

Dracup sat on the bottom step and tried to make sense of what had happened. Natasha sat on his lap, head buried in his neck. He held her close, staring fixedly ahead. Moran was walking slowly up and down, brushing his thin hair back with stiff, repetitive motions of his hand. Dracup's throat ached; his ears were whining with a shrill, high-pitched whistle. He was thirsty, but the fountain was too far away. He watched the marines take their turn and held out his hand automatically as Moran pressed a bottle into it. He gave it to Natasha, who drank deeply. He took the remaining liquid into his mouth and swallowed with a reflexive, unconscious action.

In his mind, he replayed Jackson's death. If he had been quicker. If he had grabbed the rifle and used it straight away. If he had remembered the remote operation a minute earlier. Thirty seconds earlier. Ten seconds. He held his head in his hands, closed his eyes. And saw Potzner's last suicidal dive, the explosions that ended his dream. So close. All for nothing.

Moran sat next to him. "Nice shot," he said quietly, and placed a hand on Dracup's shoulder; he let it rest for a second and withdrew it with a shrug. "You did what you had to do."

"I could have saved Jackson. He was only a boy." Dracup felt his bottom lip vibrate. He looked at his hands; they were still shaking.

"Just take it easy." Moran produced a flask, shook it experimentally and headed towards the fountain. Dracup prised Natasha's face from his chest. "Hey. You all right?"

She nodded. "We're in Fountain Square," she whispered. "That's the Great Passage." She pointed to a yawning opening beyond the fountain; the main exit, he imagined, from the ziggurat's first level to the outside world. Natasha smiled weakly.

He gave her another hug. "We'll be out soon. I promise."

When he looked up one of the marines was staring at him. There was something awkward in his manner. Dracup frowned. "Problem?"

The marine chewed his gum and looked past Dracup, up towards the ziggurat's pinnacle. An ominous vibration shook the stairwell. Dracup read his name tag – *Cruickshank*.

Bad sign, Dracup thought. No eye contact.

"Thing is, Professor, we had orders, from, ah –"

"– Mr Potzner." A second soldier appeared at Cruickshank's side, finished his sentence. His tag said, *Rutter*.

"And?" Dracup looked directly into the second marine's eyes.

"Orders are – anything happens to Mr Potzner, we take charge of the girl."

"What?" Dracup was baffled.

"She has to come with us."

Now Dracup understood. The order could be summed up succinctly in two words.

No witnesses.

"I do mind, actually." Dracup weighed his chances. Not good. Moran was by the fountain, talking to another marine. Having the same conversation. He saw Moran fling the water container to the ground, take a step back. He shot Dracup a look that said clearly, *They wouldn't murder us. Would they?*

Dracup cursed himself for his stupidity. He'd been invited not because he might have contributed to *Red Earth*, but rather to ensure Potzner's operation remained as he had intended: top secret. If he *had* contributed, so much the better, but the end game was always going to have the same result.

Cruickshank tried to make his face impassive and did badly. "If you would, sir. Don't make this any harder. Believe me, we're only following –"

"Orders? Maybe. But you'll have to kill me first." He backed towards the stairwell, shielding Natasha.

Rutter was grinning. "I wouldn't, Professor." Rutter was different. He was *enjoying* this. He raised his rifle. "I can take you out where you stand, Prof – trust me on this, okay? Messy, though. You saw what your li'l shootin' episode did to that creep up there." He waved the snout of his rifle up towards the roof. "Well my baby's been customised to the nth degree." He stroked the assault rifle lovingly.

All eyes were now on the scene by the stairwell. Dracup sensed a change in atmosphere. He looked at the fountain, along the portico walkway. The marines, Cruickshank and Rutter's buddies, were standing, watching.

"Then shoot me, Rutter." Dracup turned his back and began to climb the spiral. He had little idea of what he would do if he made it any further. There was only fire at the top to meet him. And a gang of unhappy *jihadis*. He heard Rutter's sharp click *clack*, as he flicked off his safety.

And then someone said, "Drop it *now*, soldier."

Dracup let out his breath. Farrell was standing by the fountain, his automatic trained on Rutter's head. Rutter turned. "What –?"

Farrell stood his ground. "Who's your commanding officer, Rutter?"

"Major Mortimer. And he ain't here."

"Right. And who directed this operation on his behalf?"

Rutter sighed. "*Mr* freakin' Potzner. And he's dead."

"Right again. And I'm his number two. That means I'm in command."

Rutter looked at Cruickshank, then back to Farrell. "But you told us to –"

"I know what I told you. I'm countermanding that order."

Cruickshank chewed gum and shrugged.

Farrell's voice was hard, insistent. "Put it down, and walk away."

Rutter lowered his rifle, spat on the ground and strolled nonchalantly towards the fountain.

Dracup released his grip on Natasha's arm and sat heavily on the step, relief flooding through him. "Nice timing, Farrell," he said. "We missed you."

"Looks like you did just fine on your own." Farrell ruffled Natasha's hair. Then his face became serious. "You've met Jassim?" The agent pointed to the portico.

Dracup suddenly became aware that the portico was crowded with *Korumak* – quietly standing, observing. A figure detached itself and walked into the open: Jassim.

Dracup felt a hand on his arm. Moran was opening his rucksack. The DCI reached into the bag and to Dracup's astonishment eased out the Lalibelian sceptre, *Omega*. "I think you'll need this."

Dracup took it from him in wonder. "Where on earth… how did you –"

Moran gave a knowing smile. "From the same source as the map."

Dracup put the pieces together. "Malcolm... It was him. In Lalibela."

"Yes. He was employed by Kadesh. But my guess is he wanted a better deal, followed Mukannishum – and you – to Lalibela, bribed or bamboozled the priests and made off with the goods."

Dracup was stunned. "To blackmail Kadesh for the return of *Omega?*"

Moran nodded. "Exactly. A risky game, given what we know about Kadesh. But it fits. When you've been in this business as long as I have, you learn not to prejudge people. Especially those on the sidelines."

On the sidelines. Dracup thought of Malcolm's pudgy face, his white hand on Yvonne's shoulder. He felt sick. Another thought occurred to him. "You had *Omega* all the time – you could have let me know – in the chamber."

"And give Kadesh what he wanted?" Moran's eyebrows arched.

"It would have spared me a few grey hairs."

Moran grinned. "I knew you'd come up with something. Go on," the detective prompted. "He's waiting."

Dracup released Natasha's hand and approached Jassim.

"I'm pleased to see you again," Dracup said.

Jassim bowed. "Change has come upon us, Professor Dracup. But it is a manageable change. I apologise for the hardship you have endured. It is not the *Korumak* way."

"I understand that you played no part in this." He took the man's hand in his. "I'm sorry for your loss – after everything." He groped for words, failed to find anything adequate. "I didn't... I hadn't expected –" He gave up.

Jassim's eyes wrinkled. "Our loss is –" He swept his arm around the expanse, pointing with his staff. "Only this. There are alternatives, where we shall continue, as God has ordained."

Dracup thought of the chamber, the sarcophagus enveloped in flames. He frowned. "But I –"

"Do not understand? No." Jassim smiled. "You must come. Quickly. There is little time. Very little time, according to Mr Farrell."

"Come on 'Tash." Dracup took his daughter's hand and followed Jassim to the portico. The *Korumak*, those who had remained with Jassim, parted to let them through. He felt their warmth, hands on his arm as he passed, a squeeze of the hand for Natasha. *Her friends.*

A group were standing together, slightly apart from the others, at the far end of the portico. Beside them on the paved surface was an object Dracup immediately associated with something he had seen before in Ethiopia: an Ark – not a Noachian Ark, but a container, like the fabled Ark of the Covenant. Two poles ran along its length to facilitate transport. But the central box was not chest-shaped; it was longer and shallower. Dracup's heart began to hammer slowly and forcefully.

Surely not?

Jassim was watching him carefully, leaning on his staff. "Kadesh has done you a great injustice. It is only right that you *see.*" He said something to one of the attending *Korumak,* a striking young man with flawless brown skin, as tall as Jassim himself. His son or nephew, perhaps? The youngster stepped forward and carefully, reverently moved the covering aside. Four of his friends joined him at each corner of the box. At Jassim's signal they bent and gently opened the lid.

Dracup stepped back.

I'm not ready for this.

And then he realised, *–I'll never be ready for this.*

He took a deep breath. "You moved him. He wasn't in the ziggurat's chamber. Was he?"

Jassim's eyes reflected pinpricks of turquoise light. Dracup saw in their depths a wisdom that spanned the centuries. "You are correct. We transferred him to a safer location."

The lid had been placed on the floor. Natasha looked up at him. "Can I see? I've seen him before."

Dracup swallowed. "Of course, darling. Of course you can."

And then he looked into the open sarcophagus.

For a moment all he could see was a shifting translucence, an indistinct outline, as if he were peering into a frozen pond in the depths of winter. Presently, the shape of a man began to form, the features swimming in and out of focus like some cleverly contrived *trompe l'oeil*.

"You have to wait, Daddy." Natasha squeezed his hand. "Just keep looking."

The veil lifted. Dracup caught his breath. There, in the box, lay the body of a man. He was naked, muscular, extraordinarily *big*. Dracup estimated at least three metres. The face was shockingly young, the eyes closed as if in sleep, the mouth set in an expression of profound peace. His hair was shoulder length, jet black with no trace of grey.

"I like him, Daddy. He looks kind."

"Kind, yes." Dracup regarded the handsome features, tracking down from the noble head to the torso. He paused here, and smiled. The stomach was smooth, devoid of umbilical depression. The genitals were large and well proportioned, framed by strong thighs supporting the astonishingly long legs.

I'm looking at the start of it all. The seed of the human race...

Dracup thought of Potzner and his obsessive quest for immortality. He thought of his friend, Charles, lying cold in some indifferent pathology lab. He lifted his hand and placed it on the surface of the material enclosing the body. It had an unexpected warmth to it, a pliancy he had not expected. Under his fingertips it was the shifting colour of a river, blue and green, then grey and flecked with white. A substance unknown to science. Something created, like its contents, *ex nihilo*.

He realised he was holding *Omega* tightly, caressing its ancient contours. He wanted to understand the connection – that there *was* a connection, he had no doubt. He untucked *Alpha* from his belt and held out both artefacts to Jassim. "These belong to you."

"I am indebted," Jassim replied with a slight bow, "as are all our people. Your family's involvement in these matters has come full circle." He slotted *Alpha* and *Omega* together and raised the staff aloft. "Do you see, Professor? You have returned the two sections of the headpiece for this, the original staff."

"You mean –"

Jassim held the staff aloft. "It belonged to Adamah; he cut it from the tree before he was expelled from the garden. The headpiece was crafted by Adamah himself, in the early days of his kingship – a symbol of his dominion. But after he fell from grace he fashioned the staff and set the headpiece upon it. God became angry; He divided the sceptre and named the sundered pieces *Alpha* and *Omega*, the beginning and the end, to remind Adamah that he was now mortal, and only God himself was eternal. To Adamah's sons he gave the two segments. Eventually they were parted, one to Africa, the other remaining with Noah and his descendants. You may read of these events in our scriptures."

Jassim went on. "You entered the garden of beginnings. Not many have walked where you were permitted to walk. Again, it is in His providence that you followed in Adamah's footsteps." Jassim bent and placed his hand on Natasha's head. "It was for this little one, for her healing." He smiled down at the girl. "But the life conferred by the tree is a life forbidden to Adamah and his children in these days. In time it will be different, but that time has not yet come."

"In time. . . " Dracup felt light-headed. "Please – please, go on."

"Angels once guarded the portals of Eden, but I am permitted to allow entry to the garden in rare circumstances. Many have attempted to find it and failed. Were you to look for it now, it would remain hidden. It is 'off the map', in your colloquial English. Yet within its wastelands, as you have seen, there is life in an abundance the world cannot imagine. One day that life will be revealed in all its fullness. That which the human race lost millennia ago, it shall have again."

"And that is what Noah's children, the *Korumak,* wait for?"

Jassim's eyes twinkled. "That is what the world is waiting for, if only it would open its eyes. Do you see? Now that *Alpha* and *Omega* are reunited, the end is closer to the beginning. This accords with our prophecies, of which you, my friend, have become a part." He elevated the staff, and the headpiece cast its cruciform shadow on the ground at Dracup's feet. "The world will hear His voice again, even as you have heard it, Professor Dracup."

"But where will you go?" Dracup asked Jassim hoarsely. "Where will you take him – *Adamah?*"

"There are hidden places," Jassim said softly. "God has ordained that there will always be a home for the *Korumak Tanri.* Until the end."

Farrell was at his shoulder. "We have to move, gentlemen." He took Dracup aside. "Listen, Prof, I've handed this over to the mainstream peacekeeping force. They're moving in to clear the place out. They'll burn the *jihadis* out like an ants' nest. You don't want to be here when it happens."

Dracup could not tear himself away. He looked once more into the face of the first man, fixed the image on his retina as the lid was closed and sealed.

Led by Jassim, the *Korumak* began to file silently towards the Great Passage, melting away from the place of the fountain. Many were women, as evidenced by the face-concealing *hijab* they wore. Dracup felt a pang of longing. Where was Sara? And then he saw the gesture, a momentary hesitation as she looked back. Their eyes met for an instant in a fragile spark of valediction before she too faded from his sight.

He craned his neck as the Chinook lifted above the Tell and turned to the north, but of the *Korumak* there was no sign. Marines were scuttling away from the area, Humvees burning a line of departure in the sand like scattering beetles. The Tell receded but Dracup kept it in sight, wanting to see the end. A line of black dots zeroed in, a swarm of destruction. Orange flames blossomed into the sky, followed by a pall of smoke that eventually obscured the Tell from view. He whispered to Natasha, asleep in his arms: "We're going home now, darling. Everything's all right. We're going home."

Towards the east a scattering of clouds was gathering. Dracup watched the formation coalesce as a zigzag of white lightning cut the horizon in two. He rested his head against the padded seat and closed his eyes. The Chinook flew on, into the eye of the coming storm.